GUILTY *of* HONOUR

GUILTY *of* HONOUR

TONY MEAD

authorHOUSE®

AuthorHouse™
1663 Liberty Drive
Bloomington, IN 47403
www.authorhouse.com
Phone: 1-800-839-8640

Published by AuthorHouse   10/29/2012

ISBN: 978-1-4772-3932-2 (sc)
ISBN: 978-1-4772-3931-5 (hc)
ISBN: 978-1-4772-3933-9 (e)

Any people depicted in stock imagery provided by Thinkstock are models, and such images are being used for illustrative purposes only.
Certain stock imagery © Thinkstock.

This book is printed on acid-free paper.

Because of the dynamic nature of the Internet, any web addresses or links contained in this book may have changed since publication and may no longer be valid. The views expressed in this work are solely those of the author and do not necessarily reflect the views of the publisher, and the publisher hereby disclaims any responsibility for them.

To Linda, thank you for your patience and support. Veronica, thank you for your help.

CHAPTER ONE

———•❀•———

It was the wildest of nights, on the bleakest of moors. Ben Stone ran for his life; he was soaked to the skin and the bitter cold wind cut deep to the bone. With each thud of his heart and every staggering step, he grew wearier. It was the insistent, terrifying baying of the chasing hounds that forced him on.

The rain was driving so hard into his face that he could hardly see, and most of the time he was just running blindly on. At times, he staggered forward on the uneven dirt track; the loose stones twisted his ankles.

Suddenly, his hands slapped against the stonework of a bridge. It was cold, and wet, the surface hard and abrasive; yet it was familiar to Ben. He knew it well, in fact only a month before he had picnicked here with his family. He remembered how he had enjoyed summers here playing amongst the rocks of the glen. On a hot summer's day, the stream's clear, refreshing water was a good place to cool toes, and the huge, flat black rocks made a perfect place to lie upon and eat a picnic.

Catching his breath a moment, he used the old, weathered stonework for support as he desperately tried to clear his head. The panic subsided a little and a flash of inspiration gave him hope. Brushing his dark hair from his eyes and taking a deep breath he slithered down the banking into the water, and then ran a figure of eight around, over, and under the bridge. From the stream bed, the banking looked as high as a mountain, but undaunted he clambered out the far side. His soft leather boots lost their grip; his ankles buckled under the strain, a burning pain shot up through his legs. There was desperation in his actions as he grabbed at the coarse stalks of heather; they cut into his frozen flesh as he slithered back into the water.

The sudden and unexpected immersion revived him a little. He sat a moment, steadied his breathing slightly, and from somewhere deep inside found the strength to lift himself again. A silly thought went through his mind, and he could not suppress a smile as he thought of how his Aunt Dot, if she was here now would be telling him off for getting into such a mess.

On the hillside opposite, a bolt of lightning struck and split a nearby tree sending a spray of sparks and flames into the air. It reminded him of the consequences of being caught. Taking a couple of deep breaths he readied himself to carry on.

He waded along the stream, hoping that it might further confuse the dogs. The stream's course suddenly grew almost vertical into the stormy sky. Looking up, black jagged rocks seemed to growl at him through the cascading waters. There was nothing for it but to grit his teeth and climb. Inch by inch, pounded by the ice cold water, he felt for toe and finger holds. He worked his way to the top of the waterfall and into the biting cold wind. It buffeted him so hard, that it threatened to knock him back over the edge again. Muttering a small prayer of thanks for the extra strength he had found he staggered to seek firmer ground. The rain was being blown so hard that it cut across the moors horizontally. He could see nothing through it, but between gusts, he caught the frightening sound of the dogs echoing along the valley.

Soft, heavy, sticky mud replaced the loose pebbles and rocks. It clung to his feet and legs. Sinking onto all fours he could feel the last of his strength drain away. There was no strength in his arms and as he tried to push himself up he collapsed face down. With his head resting on the crook of his arm, he struggled to catch his breath, and then slipped through a grey swirling mist into unconsciousness.

The handlers were as confused as the dogs that dragged them from the stream onto opposite banks, then around the bridge and back into the water. The dogs barked and howled their frustration, and began to fight and the handlers argued as their leather leads entangled as they met again mid-stream. Sir Geoffrey Hutton-Beaumont sat on his big bay hunter in the middle of the bridge, like a huge stone statue. He watched the scene with growing dismay. He was soaked to the skin, and his fine leather boots felt to have completely filled with water. He stood in the saddle and with an impatient backhand wiped away the streaming water from his face.

"Stop that infernal racket! Damn you! You useless fools, take those stupid flea-ridden mutts home. We'll catch him when it's light."

The authority of his voice silenced the chaos, despite most of his words being lost on the wind. In a great flurry, he spun his mount, scattering the dogs and handlers, then spurred it along the old drover's road, leaving in his wake a swirling mist. The handlers glared at each other for a moment, the cold rain coursing over their faces; with a shrug, they trailed after the squire, glad to be getting out of the weather.

Cold weary and very afraid, Ben lay staring at the clouds as they crossed the moors. Running away was not his usual style but on this occasion, he felt he was running for his life.

He began to worry about what was happening back at his home. It brought happier thoughts and he longed for the warm little bedroom, where, as a child, on cold winter's nights he had crept into bed with his Aunt and Uncle. She would cuddle him to her ample bosom, and the rest of the world seemed far away from that safe, soft haven.

He had lived most of his life, with his Aunt Dot and Uncle John, his father's brother at their inn in the bustling town of Bingley on the river Aire. They had adopted him as a baby, after his parents had died in a cholera epidemic that had swept with devastating consequences through their hometown of Halifax. Uncle John had told Ben the story of what had happened to his parents and how they had brought him home several times.

After receiving an urgent letter from Edward, Ben's father, John and Dot had made all haste to try to help rescue what was left of the family. It had been a heartbreaking sight to see the plight of his brother and his wife, in their squalid little factory house. Ben's mother, lay pale and feeble, unable to rise from her bed. Edward had the look of death about him, his skin was grey, and his dull unblinking eyes peered from deep black craters of flesh.

"Ah know tha'll look after't bairn John," Edward said. "It's 'is only hope, there's now't but death in these streets these days. God protect us all." The tears spilt freely across his ravaged features. The voice tapered away to no more than a hoarse whisper.

"Come with us brother, we have room for you all," John said.

"She cannot travel, and I fear neither of us will survive the week out. Go, take the lad, we've buried the other two bairns already."

Reluctantly, John agreed, "may God be merciful Edward, so that we can that all be together once more."

There was no more to be said. The brothers embraced both knowing that this would probably be the last time they would meet. Edward went and quietly sat by his wife on the edge of her bed comforting her as John and Dot left with the Ben.

Outside was a macabre scene with the stench of rotting corpses filling the squalid streets, it seemed that everywhere there were dead and dying bodies. Dot embraced the child as if trying to protect him from the horrific scenes around them. Pulling a woollen shawl tightly around her and the bundle in her arms she wept, "why didn't they come to live with us sooner when we offered?"

A small half-naked child ran out almost into the path of their horse; it stared with great dinner-plate eyes up at Dot. She was tempted to reach out and pull it to her bosom. John steadied her, placing a loving, reassuring hand on her shoulder.

"We can't take 'em all lass," he said.

His voice, was gentle, it hid his true emotions. He glanced back to his brother's house, remembering his youth and the fun and games he and Edward, had had with their five other brothers and two sisters, it made a shiver run through his whole body. Pulling his knitted scarf more tightly around his face, he flicked the whip to make the horse pick up its step a little. He could only guess at their fate, but he never heard again from his brother.

Fifteen years had passed since that day, Ben, had grown into a strong, healthy and very handsome young man. He was popular with all the locals at the inn, and a favourite with their daughters. It was this very fact that led him into his present predicament.

It was not just any girl however, Ruth Hutton-Beaumont, a stunningly beautiful young woman who was the same age as Ben, but from a very different background. She was tall and graceful with the best education money could buy; she spoke several languages, played the piano and violin, and could ride a spirited horse as well as anyone. However, she had a rebellious spirit, and at times her mother despaired with her, and her antics.

Her mother was Lady Jane Hutton-Beaumont who belonged to one of Yorkshire's wealthiest families; they owned two of the largest textile mills in the county; as well as several farms, a vast estate in Scotland (a legacy of their Stewart ancestors), property in London, and a huge sprawling villa in southern France overlooking the Mediterranean. Sir Geoffrey also happened to be the regional magistrate.

Sir Geoffrey, despite his wealth and position, was a very down to earth type of character, who would think nothing of putting his shoulder to the back of a bogged down cart. His only weakness was his two children, whom he spoiled unashamedly. They in turn exploited him, abusing their privileges terribly at times.

The snug of Ben's Uncle John's inn held the local assizes each quarter, and so Sir Geoffrey was a regular visitor there. This was how Ben and Ruth had initially met. She had accompanied her father and to keep her out of his way, while he dealt with that session's business, he had put her under Dot's care for the day. Ruth and Ben were both seven when they first met and from the very first moment, Ben was under her spell and she in turn was infatuated with him. After their first meeting, Ruth came every time she could with her father and immediately sought out Ben. Sir Geoffrey, who had a soft spot for the Stones, never discouraged the friendship. As long as his daughter was happy, that was all that mattered.

However, Ben was never encouraged to visit Bramble Grange. Ruth's mother had a very different opinion on her daughter associating herself with such people.

CHAPTER TWO

---•◦✿◦•---

Ben climbed to his feet as dawn was breaking. The clouds had cleared to the east the morning glow was warming the air. He listened for the sound of the dogs, but only the sound of a distant curlew with its distinctive call broke the silence.

Why had he run? The question bounced around his mind but it was too late now, he had to keep on. "Amos!" he exclaimed out loud, "that's where I'll be safe for a while."

It had started to rain again. Ben followed a drover's track, running hunched over, trying to keep from sight. His friend's old cottage was nestled in a deep almost sheer sided valley, invisible from the moors.

Amos was a strange character; ever since anyone could remember, he was referred to as *'Owd Amos'*. He was a thickset man with long grey hair, which he kept in a tight knot on the top of his head; his pointy beard had two plaits that hung like fangs from the side of his mouth. He lived with a vast array of animals that had the total freedom of his home. It was rumoured that he once took himself a young wife, but she ran away with a travelling preacher who had sheltered with them for the night.

However, he was never short of visitors, despite people thinking him strange. He had a gift of healing, and because of his great in-depth understanding of the use of herbs, people came from far and wide for love potions, treatments for boils and warts, even potions against nagging wives, all of which he would concoct in the dim depths of his little cottage.

Ben had been friends with him for as long as he could remember, he loved to visit his mysterious and somewhat controversial friend. It was very rare that the old man went into town, but whenever he did, he would call at the King's Head to see Ben and his family.

Slithering down a grassy banking, Ben bounced amongst the trees trying to catch at branches to steady him. When he reached the valley bottom he followed the path and let out a sigh of relief as he saw that there was a thin wisp of smoke drifting from the cottage chimney.

It triggered a memory of the time not so long ago when he brought Ruth to meet Amos. She had laughed at the old man and been so cruel about the man's looks. Angry with her, he left her on the moors and returned home alone. Always if they fell out, which like most children they had a tendency to do, Ruth was able to wheedle her way back into his affections. This time however, he had resisted her for some while. Even her 'little girl lost' look which she managed to use to such good effect on the whole male population had failed.

At first she had made out that she did not care, but she was not the sort to let something that she felt she owned get away from her that easily. He was working in the stables behind the inn, one day when Ruth came to try and re-enlist her most faithful follower. Aunt Dot innocently told her where she would find him. She crept into the barn. For a moment, she watched from the shadows, fascinated; he worked stripped to the waist. She could see the sweat running like strings of pearls down his back and she was transfixed, her breathing quickened, and for a moment she thought she might faint. They were now both fifteen, and she was very aware of her physical development. Like a cat watching a mouse, her eyes never left the well defined, rippling muscles of his arms, back, and chest. Almost involuntarily, she moved towards him, stalking her prey tiptoeing through the straw. Without a word, she reached out her cool fingers until they touched his sweating flesh. It was as if an electric shock had hit them both, he spun on the spot.

"What?"

"Sh . . ." she cooed.

They stared into each other's eyes, he made as if to speak, but she silenced him again. They were so close he could feel her breath. She felt for his hand and walking backwards towing him after her into the shadows. They knelt in the straw and her trembling fingers traced the features of his face and then pushed them into the waves of his hair. Pulling him forward they kissed briefly, but she pulled away and held him back by his hair. She smiled, as she licked her lips, her tongue quivering, teasing him.

He could only watch, as she loosened her own hair and traced her hands down across her breasts, and then popped the buttons of her blouse open. Her inquisitive fingers reached out for him again, exploring every part of him. She gently pulled him to her as she lay back in the straw. As she held him to her, she guided his trembling hand onto the swell of her breast. His every murmur she silenced gently brushing her soft lips against his. Their bodies intertwined limbs coiling together with raw passion. His fingers began their own explorations tracing over the soft curves. The fragrance of her body aroused his passion, making every inch of his hungry skin tremble.

They lay together naked in the warm straw, exploring and experimenting with their bodies and emotions; no words could express their joy, nor sonnet express their wonder and in that brief moment, their hearts beat as one, their souls kissed and their bodies floated on a wave of contentment.

Later, as trembling fingers hurriedly tried to fasten buttons they stood back to back both feeling suddenly shy, and awkward, deep in thought, and unsure of what they had experienced, but there was no guilt for their transgression.

Ben remembered being a little confused, he was certain that he had hated her after the way she treated his friend, but at that moment, he was not sure of anything. He had turned to watch her, caught in a beam of golden sunlight he thought she looked like an angel. He stood but she was already dressed and ready to leave. She gave him a wicked smile and picked a piece of straw from his forehead.

"Are you still cross with me?"

"Yes!"

"I didn't mean to be unkind. Please say we're still friends, I'll be so miserable if you don't," she pouted.

"Very well, but you will have to come to say sorry again soon," he said with a wicked smile.

"This means you'll belong to me for ever," she said.

Her words had an ominous, almost sinister ring to them. She picked up her bonnet; a fleeting satisfied smile crossed her face as she plucked a few stray blades of straw from her clothes, and then she left with a single contented glance.

Ben reached the cottage and took a moment to catch his breath. He tapped gently at the door, immediately Patch, Amos' old dog gave a couple of short barks. There was a sound of shuffling from within, and then the door opened just a fraction.

"Amos it's me Ben."

"Lord preserve us, come in lad and be quick"

Ben hurriedly stepped through the gap into the dim room. Amos pushed a chair up to the fire and stirred the ashes to bring them back to life.

"Tha's wet through," he gave him a blanket. "Take yer jacket off, before ye catches yer death."

Ben thankfully wrapped himself in the blanket and gave the old man his coat and shirt.

"Squire's men 'ave been here seeking thee." There was genuine concern in his voice, "what's tha done?"

"Something so stupid," Ben said trying to think straight. "There was a fight in my Uncle's hay loft; Bart, Ruth's elder brother has for some time been following her about," Ben said.

"What! Hutton-Beaumont's evil offspring?"

Ben nodded he stared into the fire not daring to look into his friend's face. "We've had a couple of skirmishes before, he really dislikes me, anyway we were wrestling in the hay loft and Ruth charged him with a broom and knocked him over the edge."

"On purpose, like?"

"Good God no! It was an accident. Truly."

"Then why run?"

"We climbed down to him, he was in a pool of blood, and it was obvious he was dead." Ben looked shaken as he recalled the look on Bart's face. "We just panicked. Ruth said it was best if I escaped before anyone found out."

"Not a good idea lad."

"She just kept saying her Father would be sure to send me to the gibbet; what with him being the magistrate an' all."

"Tha's made a fine mess on it, and no dispute. Tha can stay here, but squire's men are bound to be back."

"Thank you, but I'd hate to get you in to trouble too. I'll just rest awhile, and I'll then be gone."

Amos fetched a plate and piled it high with porridge from a great iron cooking pot that hung above the fire. He poured some fresh goat's milk and sprinkled a few herbs from a stone pot into it. He gave it to Ben with a reassuring smile. The old man went and watched out of the window.

"Go north, as quick as you can. I have a friend who you can easily find any market day in Skipton."

Amos shuffled into the shadows and then returned. "Here give him this," he handed a small leather pouch to Ben. "Tell him I've sent you and ask if he will help. He may be able to give you a job or something. His name is Edward Clough."

Ben looked suspiciously at the pouch.

"It's a remedy he's wanted from me for some time."

"Thank you Amos, you are a true friend."

Amos shuffled away again and returned with a length of heavy woollen cloth with a head hole cut in it.

"Here wear this it will keep some of the weather out. There are a few coins here too, you will need food." Amos smiled reassuringly.

"I can't take money from you."

"Don't be daft lad o'course you can, I've put some bread in this knapsack and some oats to keep you going. There's scores of navvies, and such like wandering the countryside nobody will take any notice, but be on yer guard thar's a lot o'evil folk out there."

It felt peaceful in the gentle glow of the fire, for an instant Ben relaxed the previous night's events seeming far away. Some time later, Amos gently shook his shoulder.

"Rain's stopped again lad. Put some miles between y'sen and here as quickly as thee can." They shook hands at the doorway. Amos gave Ben an old hat.

"I hope we meet again."

"So do I lad. You're a good lad. There's many who'll not be sorry to see the end of yon fellow." They embraced briefly.

Without a backwards glance, Ben ran along the valley and into the woods. He took the old man's advice and headed north. He knew well the moors above Riddlesden and Keighley; following an ancient drover's road, he headed over the tops towards Silsden. Twice he spotted groups of men with dogs and had to dive for cover.

Ruth had been questioned repeatedly, but each time she changed her story, it was just an exciting adventure to her. She told how Ben and her brother had been involved in a terrible fight and how Ben had thrown him off the hayloft to his death. Then she said that Ben had killed her brother with a single punch. She never mentioned the fact that it was she who had actually knocked her brother over the edge, and she was sure that Ben would never tell.

Sir Geoffrey was trying not to show his feelings, but he was becoming increasingly angry at the almost flippant way his daughter was treating the whole incident. He had already taken a verbal battering from his wife for the foolish way he let the children mix with ruffians from the town.

Her Ladyship had taken to her bed with a sleeping draught prescribed by the doctor. The whole of Bingley was astir with the news and rumours spread fast.

John and Dot were beside themselves with fear as to what had happened to Ben. As the constable questioned them, Sir Geoffrey came in to their private room.

"Forgive the lad, your Lordship; I'm sure it must have been an accident," Dot cried. Her head was bowed, mopping her face with her apron.

Sir Geoffrey took the chair offered by John near the fire, and sat down staring wearily into the flames. He sat perfectly still, and it was obvious that his emotions and fatigue were beginning to get the better of him.

"I hope it was; nay I am sure that it was, just that . . ." There was a long pause, and he continued to stare into the fire. "But the lad should not have run. He must be brought to justice. You understand?" He looked up almost apologetically at them.

"Oh yes indeed Sir. But he has always been a good lad."

"Yes indeed Ma'am." He stood up again, looking tired and much older than his years. Sir Geoffrey had to bow his head under the low doorframe, he stopped a moment, as if he was going to add something further, but shook his head and left.

John embraced his wife, trying to comfort her. They sat together before the fire waiting all night for news.

In the private chapel set in picturesque grounds some way from the Grange, Ruth stood next to the body of her brother. She had been commanded by her father to go see her brother as he lay in his coffin. She stared at her brother's body for a moment; the only emotion she showed was one of anger.

"I'm glad you're dead, you fat pig. Why did you always have to spoil everything? God, how I hate you!" She almost spat the words at the corpse.

She thought of Ben for a moment, envying the adventure he must be having. She wondered if she would miss him, and finally decided that she would, perhaps more than she wanted to admit. She really did hate her brother, and knew that under no circumstances would she miss him.

She now regretted that after that first affair in the stable with Ben, she had foolishly boasted about it to her best friend, who in turn had told her brother, who just happened to be Bart's school friend. Armed with this secret he crept in on his sister one day as she was dressing.

"So little sister what have you been up to?" He twisted her arm until she screamed.

"Leave me alone or I'll tell father!"

"Tell him what? That you've been rolling in the hay with your little peasant boyfriend?"

"It's a lie!"

"No it's not sister." His other hand squeezed her breast through the thin material of her dress, "you had best be nice to me, or else."

"Never!" she said.

He twisted her arm even higher up her back and then tore the material away from her breasts. For a moment he ogled with evil intent.

"Come on sister, if you're so free with your favours."

"Let me go," she hissed. Her voice trembled slightly, and she could feel the tears building up.

"Is little sister going to cry?" he mocked. There was an underlying sinister tone.

Ruth stuck out her chin defiantly not wanting to give him the satisfaction of seeing her cry. She could feel the tension in him and suddenly she was afraid. She kept still and quiet, submitting to his groping, refusing to cry. She had been saved from his mauling by their father arriving home and calling them down for lunch; however, ever since her brother had held the secret like a knife against her throat. She had no doubt that he would tell if he so wished.

She stared at the prone body of her brother and whispered under her breath, "I hope you go to hell."

She spun on the spot and then stormed out of the ancient building. Angrily she untied her horse, with an agile and most unladylike leap, she landed on the big hunters back. Her spurs dug deeply into the animal's side and sent it racing, not towards the gate, but straight at the wall. The animal took the dry-stone wall with a single leap; it landed squarely without missing a step.

.

Chapter Three

---◦◦❀◦◦---

The weather had improved slightly. Fortunately the rain had stopped for a while, but it was still bitterly cold. Ben tried to pace himself, running in as relaxed a way as possible to conserve his energy.

After a long arduous climb he reached the watershed, and took a breather resting against a boulder beside the path. He ate the last of his food; fingering the few coins that Amos had given him he wondered how far they would take him. He looked across the open, rolling hillside that tumbled down from the moor top into the little town of Silsden. From his vantage point, he had a clear view both ways along the thin ribbon of a path that fluttered down the hillside. There was no sign of anyone following, so with a sigh of relief he wiped the sweat from his brow, drew a deep breath and then pushed on again.

Skirting the small hamlet he kept out of view behind the high hedgerows. Now he questioned the wisdom of risking coming this way in daylight. Fortunately he went unobserved as he skipped lightly over a low wall onto the canal towpath. A couple of narrow-boats, with thin wisps of smoke coiling into the air from their cooking fires, were moored further along the tow path. The smell of their food was a reminder of how hungry he was feeling.

The level tow path was far easier to run on than the uneven tracks of the moors and he soon put some distance between himself and the town. He reached a wooden stile that bridged a wall, and for a moment he let it take his weight and tried to gather his thoughts. He was feeling quite wretched as he rubbed at his aching legs; his trousers were sodden and the woollen blanket Amos had given him felt to weigh a ton.

With a determined effort he pushed on again when suddenly he heard voices. He scrambled up the embankment to find cover amongst the trees. One minute he was running, the next he was somersaulting through the air with the world spinning around his head. Completely winded he rolled to an untidy halt.

"Well, well what 'ave we 'ere? What's yer 'urry me boyo?" The voice was light, with an unusual accent. "Now why should a fine young fella like y'self be running for cover I asks mesen?"

Trying to sit up Ben felt the weight of a heavy boot force him back. As he struggled, the pressure increased, and he was forced to lie still.

"You in trouble boy? C'os if you is, and you bring the law down on me an' my little family 'ere, then I might be forced to get proper angry with you."

For the first time Ben noticed the tight knot of people hiding in the shadows. The foot lifted and strong wiry fingers gripped the front of his shirt, dragging him to his feet. Ben was looking straight into the man's eyes. The face had black protruding teeth that forced their way through thin, cracked lips, and cold, calculating eyes that cut like the blade of dagger, it was not a face to forget.

"You behave or else . . ." A gloved finger was stabbed up into Ben's throat, pressing hard into the soft flesh, and there was no need to finish the sentence.

"Tie 'is 'ands, we'll take him with us, young lads is fetching a good price in Liverpool."

Ben shrugged away giving the man a look of contempt. There was an immediate reaction. Suddenly the unshaven face moved within inches of Ben's. There was nervous laughter from the circle of faces that now closed in around them.

"Don't you ever, look at Mace like that again boy." The whiskey-heavy, stale breath almost overpowered Ben. A huge character with a great shining bald head moved forwards, grabbed hold of Ben's wrists and bound them tightly with a length of oily rope. After heaving on the rope to check that it was secure, he grinned at Mace and nodded everything was okay.

"This is my friend Bren. He comes from somewhere in Europe, we're not sure where. He can't speak, but he's not stupid, and more faithful than any hound. He's gonna watch over you and make sure you behave y'self." Mace pinched Ben's cheek then gave Bren a broad grin and a heavy slap on his gigantic square shoulder.

Ben tried to asses his position. There were fifteen in the gang, which included six older women, and two teenage girls. For the time being he realised there was little he could do about his predicament.

With hardly a word spoken they trooped through the dense undergrowth of the forest in single file dragging Ben at the rear. They made a strange sight all dressed in a mixed assortment of clothes; most had several layers to protect them from the weather. When they reached a rocky outcrop that gave them a clear view of the valley, the leader raised his hand.

"This'll do. Get y'selves set up," Mace shouted. Two of the women cut sods to make a place for the fire, whilst the men set up tents and bivouacs in a tight circle around them. In very little time they had set up their makeshift camp.

Bren lifted Ben as if he was a rag doll and carrying him under his arm he deposited him away from the camp with his back to a cluster of boulders. Using another length of rope he tied Ben's feet together. Giving Ben what could have been a friendly grin; he made a grunt from deep within his throat and then returned to the others.

As night descended, the naked trees offered little protection against the bitter, cold wind that brought fine snowflakes dancing through the forest. In a tight huddle around the fire the gang tried to keep warm, waiting and watching the black iron cooking pot that bubbled suspended above the flames.

Ben was cold, his whole body was shivering but he felt safer in the dark, although the smell of the food reminded him that he had hardly eaten since leaving Amos's cottage.

One of the girls suddenly appeared behind him, keeping in the shadow so as not to be seen from the fire.

"Hello, my name's Jenny," she whispered, her voice was light and soft, bubbling like a mountain stream. He tried to turn to see her, but she placed her hand on his shoulder to keep him still.

"Keep still. If Mace finds me here . . . I don't know what he might do."

"Who is this Mace?" he said.

"I don't know really," She said with a little embarrassed giggle. "He just looks after us all."

She held a bowl of food; with a rough wooden spoon she offered some to him. He ate thankfully, hardly chewing the thick, savoury mixture, just gulping it down until the bowl was empty. Over the brim of the bowl he studied the girl's pretty features, highlighted in the glow from the fire.

"It's not spoilt your appetite," she giggled.

Suddenly a figure loomed out of the darkness at them, casting its ghostly shadow over them, they looked up in terror.

"What's yer game?" Mace growled angrily at them.

"I . . . I didn't mean any harm . . . honest Mace." The girl whimpered, cowering against the rock.

Ben let out a cry of pain as Mace roughly checked his bonds.

"Please sir; I can hardly feel my hands; the ropes are too tight."

"Then they'll not be 'urtin; will they?" Mace grinned amused by his own comment. He lifted his hand, as if about to strike the girl, but pushed her over with his foot instead.

"Be gone lass; you asks me afore ye comes near 'im. Understood!" There was real venom in the words.

Jenny nodded, picked herself up, and then scampered back to the fire taking a wide detour to keep out of Mace's way. Mace gave Ben a terrifying glare that almost froze his blood.

"You're trouble." He rubbed the stubble of his chin, "I can smell it on you, and I should just leave you here. You cause me any problems lad and I'll slit your throat without a second thought."

He followed the girl, muttering as he stumbled back to the fire. The ring of bodies parted to allow him back into his place.

Despite the discomfort and pain the bonds were causing, somehow Ben managed to drift into sleep. The sun was not quite up, but the sky was lightening, when Bren shook Ben's shoulder to wake him. A cold grey mist hung across the valley clinging to the trees and frozen ground. Ben was stiff with cold; he showed the big man his purple hands, signalling for his bonds to be slackened.

Bren carefully looked around to see where Mace was, using his fingers he warned Ben that if he tried to run he would break his neck. Ben nodded that he clearly understood the mime. Bren nodded back and slackened the rope. As soon as the blood pumped back through his fingers Ben could not stifle a cry of agony. Bren clamped his huge paw-like hand over Ben's mouth to silence him. Rubbing vigorously at his swollen limbs trying to get his circulation going again Ben thanked Bren. He tried to stand, but his ankles gave way under his own weight.

Jenny appeared; she pulled at Bren's sleeve to attract his attention. The huge man beamed when he saw who it was. It was obvious that he was very fond of the young girl.

"May I feed him Bren," she asked with an impish smile.

Checking that all was clear still, he nodded his approval. She gave him a big smile and squeezed his arm affectionately. Suddenly there was a deafening roar as Mace flew between them; he struck Ben a heavy blow across his face, knocking the food from his mouth. Coughing and spluttering Ben bounced against the rocks, Jenny tried to hold him, to stop him from falling, but they ended up in a heap together. With another angry snarl, Mace pulled Ben by the shoulder, throwing him hard against the rock.

"What's this?" It was almost a scream.

Jenny cowered into a ball waiting for the blow that must surely fall. She held her breath, but nothing happened. Peeping out between her fingers, she saw Mace was poised with his hand above her, but Bren held his arm in a vice-like grip, immobilising it. For a moment Mace glared into Bren's eyes; slowly he relaxed.

"You're right my ox-like friend, it would be stupid to damage my best girl." He smiled, Bren let go. Mace went back towards the fire, venting his anger on anyone who crossed his path.

"Thank you Bren." She stood on her tip-toes, and kissed his cheek. "That was close."

"Has he ever hit you?" Ben rubbed his swollen cheek.

"Not often. Not as much as my father used to."

"Your father?"

"He sold me to Mace for three shillings, when I was eight, I think. It's funny, I don't even know where I lived," she gave another little giggle.

"I'm sorry you must miss your family."

"No. Why should I? This is my family now." She cocked her thumb towards the camp.

Soon there was no trace of where the camp had been. The turf was replaced, the firestones were buried, and the ashes scattered, and then covered with fallen leaves.

Throughout the day they kept to the wooded valley sides, carefully avoiding all signs of habitation, a cold mist aiding their secretive progress. As they went the women foraged for mushrooms and berries, anything that could be eaten.

For a short while Ben forgot his main problem concentrating on the new challenge that had snared him. Jenny walked with him and Bren to keep out of Mace's way.

"Why all the secrecy?" He said as they stopped to take a drink.

"We're going into Skipton., and there are people Mace would rather not bump into," she whispered, shielding her mouth with her hand.

They found shelter late in the afternoon in a disused barn just outside the little village of Carleton.

"We wait 'ere till dark. No noise and no fires. Billy, up on that roof with yer."

The boy climbed as agile as a cat up onto the roof timbers; finding shelter against the gable end he settled down.

"Let's be into town now Mace, there's bound to be some fine pickings; it's market day." The woman who spoke had a strong Irish accent.

"Stop yer cackle woman, I decide when we go into a place!" His face was black as thunder as he rounded on her. She immediately shrank to the far side of the building muttering under her breath. Inside the dimly lit barn, everyone found themselves a little corner to squat down. Jenny sat close to Ben gently rubbing his hands which were again starting to discolour.

"Why are we waiting here?" Ben asked, in a low whisper.

"Because Mace says so. When it's dark, we girls go into town, and entice gentlemen into dark alleys, where the others are waiting, they do the rest."

"Do they kill them?"

"No, not unless they have to, just rob 'em, sometimes give 'em a sore head," she giggled. "Be careful of Mace, he has a terrible temper." There was real concern in her voice. "I once saw him kill a man with his bare hands; funny, sometimes he can't remember anything about his anger afterwards."

"He's probably mad."

"He certainly would be if he heard you say that." They giggled together but their words froze in the air, as Mace came and towered over them.

"Well, well, ain't we cosy. If he escapes, you's dead girl." He put his face dangerously close to Jenny's, "hear me?"

"Yes Mace," she said meekly.

"And you boy, had best be able to run like the wind if you's tries anything."

Jenny slipped her fingers into Ben's, as Mace moved away.

"Why do you stay with them?"

"What else is there?"

"Watch yer tongue young 'un." a voice came from the shadows behind them.

"Molly! You frightened the livin' daylights out o'me." Jenny whispered to the woman.

"Mace'll kill you for sure if he ever hears you say anything like that. Be warned!"

"I meant no harm."

"Aye well, Jenny's better off with us than on't streets o'Liverpool wi'pox ridden sailors for company."

"Molly lived there." Jenny explained to Ben.

"Lived is not the right word. My mother had me on the streets at nine. I'd a kid at thirteen, poor little mite never stood a chance. Me mother wrapped it in a rag and threw it in't river," her voice trailed away.

"You mean it was dead?" Ben felt shocked at the woman's story.

"I don't know. There was eight of us in one room, there was no room for another. Anyway I'd not have been able to work the streets with a young 'un to look after."

"Having some sort of meeting are we?"

"We's only talking Mace," Molly said, the hard edge to her voice had quickly returned.

"Well get some sleep; we'll be busy tonight."

The light faded quickly, and by late afternoon it was pitch black in the barn. It was a freezing cold night, everyone huddled together to try keep warm. At last Mace gave the signal that they had all been waiting for, and in small groups they drifted into the town.

The streets were quiet now, only a small group of people huddled around a blazing brazier and hungry dogs fought over some scraps of food. Only hours before they had thronged with a bustling market; people, traders and animals right up the full length of the high street to the ancient castle gates. The traders and farmers had packed away their stalls and had either headed for home or were enjoying the comfort provided by the taverns and inns.

Mace led the way through the streets until they came to a bridge which crossed the stream running behind the castle. Ben was pushed down a dark flight of worn, stone steps.

"You move from 'ere, or make a sound, and it'll be your last." Mace whispered, only inches from Ben's face.

Mace and Bren disappeared back up the steps. Left alone Ben tried to keep out the bitter cold; restlessly he considered whether or not to make his escape. It was tempting but he was afraid of what Mace may do to Jenny. He heard footsteps and quickly hid in the shadows below the bridge.

In a nearby tavern, Jenny had already gone to work on a likely candidate. Sitting in a quiet corner with her victim, she laughed and giggling at his chatter and he was soon under the spell of her girlish charm. She sat close leaning against him on the little bench seat, making sure her leg rubbed against his at regular intervals. The farmer was well satisfied with his days trading. All the livestock he had brought to market had sold, and now the proceeds were burning a hole in his pocket.

"Have another drink lass; keep out the cold," he said, plying her with drink, his weathered face was flushed, and his eyes slightly bloodshot. He could feel the girl's body heat and was becoming aroused by her presence.

Jenny was beginning to feign being the worse for the drink, slurring her words slightly and giggling loudly. Despite the comfort and warmth of the inn, she was in a hurry to get back outside to complete the deed.

"I should be going sir. My mistress will wonder what's happened to me, and the drink's going to my head."

"Nay lass, party's only just started."

"You're a wicked man," she threw herself across him squeezing his leathery cheeks with her soft hands.

"I bet you've led many a girl a-stray. You could walk a little way with me; I have to go by way of a couple of unlit alleys, and I get so afraid." She gave him a melting little girl smile.

"You wicked girl," he smiled placing his rough hand on her thigh squeezing the soft, warm flesh. Nervously he worked his hand higher.

"I must be off," she placed her hand on his, stopping its advance, but not removing it. As soon as they were outside he threw his arm around her. She led him like a lamb to the slaughter. She giggled and laughed continuously keeping him off his guard. Mace and Bren had returned to where they had left Ben, joining him in the shadows below the bridge. Ben's teeth were chattering he was so cold.

"Be quiet." Mace hissed angrily at him.

One of the other women, who had been keeping her eye on Jenny, came down the steps.

"She's coming Mace!" The woman hid behind Bren.

As the couple reached the bridge, Jenny stopped and leant her head back for the man to kiss her.

"I know a short cut, and there'll be nobody about." She gave the man an enticing wicked smile. Leading the way down the steps, only she caught sight of a moving shadow to her right. Walking away from the bridge a few paces she turned, the farmer's attention was firmly on her as she lifted the hem of her dress. It was the last thing the man saw.

Bren hit him from behind, a stunning blow that would have felled an ox. Mace dived on the back of their victim, and triumphantly pulled out the cloth bag of coins.

"Hey!" A shout from the bridge made them all look up.

The town constable had been on his rounds; suddenly he appeared on the bridge. Without hesitation he bounded towards them. Bren, warned by Mace reacted fast; and before the constable was halfway down the steps, he was caught in a vice like grip. Bren lifted him into the air, took a couple of steps, spun on the spot, and then hurled the constable down the long drop into the dark water below.

"Come on!" Mace said grabbing the girl's arm. Bren took hold of Ben and dragged him back up the steps. Word was sent to the rest of the gang, they all met up half a mile outside the town, on the Settle road.

"We must get onto the moors before daybreak."

Their journey up the steep hillside was hindered by a freezing wind that blew into their faces. Two of the gang trailed behind as a rear-guard. Up on the moor-top, the weather was even worse; flurries of snow blew in great clouds across the wide open expanse. Ben found Jenny, and together they climbed hand in hand over the frozen rocks trying to find shelter from the wind. By morning the whole gang was exhausted, but Mace rounded them all up like a sheepdog refusing to let any of them fall behind, or stop. Everyone grumbled but kept moving. They reached a high hill top, where Mace at last said they could take a breather. He positioned himself so that he could watch back across the moors; with satisfaction he was certain that they had escaped and for the time being at least they were not being followed; the worsening weather would put off anyone thinking of giving chase.

It took two full days travel to reach the place Mace was heading for, and everyone was totally exhausted by the time they arrived. In other circumstances it was a picturesque place, a well hidden fosse, with a waterfall that fell thirty feet into a small deep pool surrounded by overhanging trees. Along one of the rock faces was a cave just big enough for the gang to squeeze into. They built a fire and huddled around it trying to warm their tired frozen bodies. Mace had used this place on several occasions, he knew the terrain well. Sentries were placed near the moorland road and at the top of the waterfall, high above the valley. Quickly the camp took shape; some built their own shelters away from the cave. Cooking pots bubbled and the gang settled down for a long rest.

"How long will we stay here?" Ben said.

"I've only been here once before. Mace say's it's safe so we stay, until Mace say's move."

The next day's weather was a complete contrast. It started with a beautiful clear morning, still very cold, but sheltered in the fosse away from the wind it felt much warmer. Ben and Jenny sat together at the top of the fall, watching the activity of the camp below. Mace had given them a long meaningful glance before he carried on with his work building a shelter.

It was to be the weather that determined their length of stay, as two days before Christmas it began to snow; great broad flakes that soon buried the whole landscape. Ben and Jenny had made themselves a little shelter near the cave, between two great grey outcrops of stone.

They dried moss by the fire to line their little nest, and made a roof from woven branches and dried ferns they found nearby. Each night they cuddled together covered by the woollen blanket Jenny always carried strapped to her back. It was their own secret little world hidden from Mace and the rest of the gang.

"What was your house like?" They lay together in the dark.

"I lived at an inn," Ben said.

"Sounds wonderful, did it belong to your parents?"

"No, they died when I was young; I lived with my Aunt and Uncle."

"Do you miss them?"

"Of course, I'd give anything to be back there now."

Jenny turned away from him. She rolled into a tight ball and gave a sad sigh.

"I don't mean I don't like being with you, but . . ."

He thought of home, worrying about the problems he had no doubt caused for his family; mostly he thought of Ruth. He liked Jenny but he could not help wishing it was Ruth who was next to him.

When he awoke the next morning she was gone. He hoped that he had not hurt her feelings. How could he make it up to her he wondered? There was a rustling outside the shelter, immediately Ben was on his guard. Jenny popped her head round the corner. She gave him a broad innocent smile, her bright blue eyes never leaving his. She came and knelt before him, holding out her hand to him.

"What's this?"

"It's a rabbit's foot." She had cleaned it, and stitched it onto a leather thong, "it brings you luck."

"Thank you but . . . ?"

"It's Christmas morning." She kissed his cheek, and placed the talisman around his neck.

"It's the best present I've ever had, thank you. I'll always wear it." The girl glowed with pride and satisfaction.

"I have another for you," she gave a little giggle, and opened her overcoat.

Ben's mouth fell open, all he could do was stare; she was totally naked. She smiled and then cuddled up to him.

It kept snowing until three days after Christmas, by which time it was almost impossible to get out of the fosse. By the following week the weather was even worse, and food was getting short. Mace sent out the men in small groups to search for something to eat, he and Bren left early one morning. Two days later they returned, but all they had were a few eggs and a rabbit. Two of the men brought in a couple of sheep, and although they were welcomed by the rest of the gang Mace was furious.

"What d'you want? Some shepherd to come stumbling in here! Never do this again!"

"Sheep always go missing in the snow; no one will ever be the wiser," one of the men said in his defence.

"Listen to me . . . if yer want to stay, yer do as I say or go."

"I'm hungry and so is everyone else, this will feed us!" The man moved forward menacingly. Bren closed the angle on the man slightly, but Mace waved him back.

"Don't be foolish Sean. It's going to be hard enough to come through this winter without trouble between us," Mace said.

The man was set on his action; he made a quick movement drawing a long blade from out of the folds of his coat. He stood poised, but suddenly he had doubts that delayed him just a fraction of a second. That delay cost him dearly. Mace struck like a cobra: in a single flowing movement he lifted a stone from the fire, sprung to his feet and hammered the stone into the man's face. There was a sickening crack as the stone smashed through his front teeth, at the same time breaking the bone of his nose and sending a gush of blood flying through the air.

The blade flashed in the firelight, but Mace caught the man's wrist, and twisted his arm until the knife fell from his grip. With lightning reactions, Mace caught it before it hit the floor. He spun round and sunk the blade deep into the man's chest. There was a look of confusion and fear in Sean's eyes as he sunk to the ground with blood bubbling from his lips.

"Get rid of him." Mace growled at two of the others who were sat close to the fire.

The sheep were butchered and roasted and the gang's spirits were lifted. After their meagre rations the mutton was welcomed by everyone including Mace.

Jenny and Ben sat together with their portion of the mutton, it tasted good and they realised just how hungry they had been.

"I think that's the best meal I've ever had in my life," Jenny said. She lay back in their little shelter sucking what remained of a rib bone. "We don't often get mutton, and I get fed up with rabbit and berries."

They cuddled up together to keep out the cold and Ben listened to Jenny's soft breathing as she fell asleep. He was tormented by the fear of what might have happened to his family after the incident in the barn. His emotions were in turmoil, because although he really regretted running and despite the fear of Mace and the hardships they were going through, he was enjoying the experience of being with Jenny. It was thoughts of Ruth that really haunted him, he did not want to doubt her, but he was afraid of what she had said about the incident. Was she in trouble, after all it was Ruth who had sent her brother flying over the edge? Had she admitted it? Or was she letting him carry the blame?

The following week two men deserted, slipping out of the camp in the dark. Mace warned the remainder of his gang that if he ever caught the deserters he would kill them. All who heard knew that the speech was no idle threat.

Fortunately by the end of January the weather eased, and a sudden quick thaw flooded the land. The stream gushed with terrific force over the waterfall and down through the fosse, flooding the valley bottom. Mace had imposed rationing, and had been very strict with the food; somehow they survived until the first week of February.

Mace gave orders to break up the camp and make ready to move on. There were moans and groans, but everyone set about their own tasks and within the hour there was no trace that they had been there.

Ben could now understand the loyalty of the gang, as none of them would have survived the winter without Mace. Despite himself he felt a certain amount of respect for the rather obnoxious leader, and he couldn't help wondering about the man, where he was from and why he did what he did.

Following the road to Settle they set off in the middle of the night. It was more hazardous for the gang to follow the road, but the moorland paths and drover's roads were still almost impossible to travel. They stopped about midday and sheltered in a derelict barn just off the road; it was only ever used for lambing and unlikely to be investigated by anyone.

CHAPTER FOUR

---·•❈•·---

Settle had the only bridge for miles, and with the river in full flood there was nowhere else to cross. It was early morning as they entered the outskirts of the town. Mace had worried about getting through the town without being seen, but there was no place to hide for the day, so against his better judgement he forced the gang on. When they reached the first of the houses the air was filled with the wonderful smell of baking bread.

"Move it! Come on move." Mace pushed and kicked to hurry them. Lights were already coming on, and bleary eyed traders would soon be out lifting the shutters of their shops.

Constable Farrar rubbed his tired eyes; he had been up all night after receiving a report of a gang moving towards the town. He was certain that they would not try coming through during the day, if they came at all. As usual he stopped for a pipe of tobacco with his friend Jack Hill the baker.

"I'm thinking them ruffians'll not be heading this way." He said spitting a small piece of tobacco from the end of his tongue.

"Some say it's same gang as killed Constable Davies in Skipton afore Christmas." Jack said.

"Nonsense, where could they have been wintering?" Despite his doubts, he fingered the ancient, rusty flintlock he carried. It was many years since the piece had been fired, and he doubted as to whether or not it would work; he primed it just in case.

"Well I'd best be off, finish my rounds and then it's bed for me." He stood up, stretched his long arms and let out a huge yawn. Jack wrapped up a couple of still hot loaves and stuffed them in the constable's pocket.

"It'll keep you going until you have time for t'missis's breakfast."

There was just a soft veil of morning mist drifting slowly along the road and between the houses of the sleepy town.

Mace dodged as silent as a shadow from one doorway to the next. He still doubted the wisdom of leaving it until this hour to try and get through the town. The gang made a comical sight as they bobbed in and out of doorways like a long ragged snake trying to blend into every contour of the stonework. Ben and Jenny were somewhere in the middle of the snake, like the others trying not to be seen. Ben realised that this could be his chance to escape, Bren was in front and kept disappearing down the side of buildings and as they worked into the town there were more and more opportunities to slip away. His worry was what they would do to Jenny, as they were bound to blame her should he get away. They were running hand in hand and as they slipped into a doorway they cuddled together. She smiled up at him and it was obvious that she was enjoying the excitement of the situation.

Mace rounded the corner into the cobbled market square and was on his guard; he immediately sensed trouble. With a sharp, single gesture of his arm he stopped the snake dead. For a moment they waited, frozen, inert, watching for the sign that would either scatter them or signal the advance. Nothing stirred. Slowly the arm fell, and with an inaudible sigh the snake uncoiled. Unseen by Mace the uniformed figure of Constable Farrar, Settle's ageing constable, had appeared out of a side alley less than twenty yards away from him.

Suddenly, a shout from across the square brought the snake to a shuddering halt again. A bright flare of light diffused by the mist flooded across the street. An old man dressed in a long smock and butcher's apron appeared, and he called to the constable from the middle of the light. As soon as he was certain that Farrar had seen him, he disappeared back into his shop. He left the door open allowing the warmth of the shop to escape into the cold morning air in a swirl of mist. With slow ponderous steps Farrar crossed the open square. He hoped Walt Banner was not going to complain again about the children playing along the alley behind his shop again. All he wanted at the moment after his long night was the comfort of his wife's ample bosom and his warm bed. He hated winter he decided as he braced himself for what was to come.

"Morning Walt. What's up this time?"

"You come in here, and see what them kids have done now."

Farrar entered the shop, ducking slightly under the low beam above the door.

"What's that for then?" The shopkeeper pointed to the rusty sporting piece Farrar carried.

"The Sergeant thought it a good idea, seems as if they're expecting them buggers that killed poor Alf Davies Skipton's constable to come this way; no chance says I. Where've they been all winter?"

Mace breathed a sigh of relief as the door closed behind the constable. With an urgent wave, he signalled the column forward again.

"Come on; come on," he hissed, pushing each member past him, he was already caught in two minds as to whether or not to beat a hasty retreat and leave it for another day. He knew that they were almost through and once they reached the bridge the mist would hide them completely. Moments later they were through the market square, where the street narrowed. Mace kept his eyes on the butcher's doorway. He signalled the others to cross the street so that they were out of sight of the shop window. Two giant steps took him across the street and into a doorway with a wooden porch; he hit against it rather harder than he had intended and to his surprise and horror it flew open inwards.

"What's your game then?" A voice behind him cried from the dimly lit room.

Like a hare before a fox without waiting to look or give an answer Mace began running.

"Hey there! Stop thief! Stop!" a portly man puffed his way out into the street waving a walking stick.

Like rabbits scattering across a meadow the gang fled along the street towards the bridge. In their panic they tripped and stumbled over each other, cursing and swearing at each other as they ran. Ben was not slow to see a chance to escape; he grabbed Jenny by the arm, "come on this way," he said heading back along the road toward the square.

Jenny hesitated; her instincts were to follow the others towards the bridge. She was afraid and confused as she wanted to go with Ben but the bond to her old friends was very strong. Mace saw them and guessing Ben's plan, against his better judgement he ran back after the couple. Emerging out of the mist like a demon, snarling and angry he landed a single slap across Ben's face that spun him to the ground. Jenny screamed but could not dodge the second back-handed slap that sent her staggering against the wall, splitting the tender flesh of her cheek wide open. Mace took Ben by the scruff of the neck, and dragged him along.

Heads bobbed through doorways and windows all along the street to see what the cause of the commotion was, but the mist created confusion and no one knew what was happening for sure.

"Get going" he snarled at Jenny, "I'll deal with you later."

"Halt! Stop or I'll fire." Farrar levelled the flintlock and peered along its sights, through the mist he tried to find a target.

The constable was more surprised than any of the spectators when the gun recoiled hard against his shoulder; a thunderous boom deafened him for a moment. Immediately there was the smell of burnt powder and a thick cloud of smoke obscured his vision even more.

Mace never saw the gun, but he caught the flash from the muzzle. Instinctively he raised his hand shielding himself with Ben. The heavy piece of shot slammed with a thud into Ben's body, he twitched and jerked as if taking a fit, then slumped like a rag to the floor. Feeling the warm blood ooze over his fingers, Mace dropped Ben, and then bolted into the safety of the mist towards the bridge dragging Jenny with him.

Constable Farrar was visibly shaken as he stared down at the result of his marksmanship; gingerly he knelt down and rolled the limp figure over, its handsome features were a deathly white.

There was soon a crowd gathered in a morbid circle around the body. Farrar stared at them and the blood stain on his own hand from the bullet-wound in Ben's back. From the back of the crowd, a tall figure with square features pushed his way through.

"Quickly man don't just stand there with your mouth open, get him into my house and fetch the Doctor!" The Reverend Baxter barked with a voice like a Sergeant Major. Everyone was suddenly released from their stupor. A make-shift stretcher appeared from somewhere. Three of the crowd lifted the limp figure and began a procession to the huge gates of the vicarage only about fifty feet or so from where Ben had fallen.

"What is it?" Reverend Linton called; he had heard the commotion and was already part way down the path, and he watched his friend lead the procession towards the vicarage.

"Call Mrs. Hill and ask her for hot water and towels quickly!"

Linton was used to his friend's brusque manner and dashed off to find the housekeeper.

"Lad looks proper poorly to me." Baxter said in a whisper, as he watched Mrs. Hill bathe Ben's wound.

The town's men had carried Ben upstairs into one of the guest rooms, where Mrs. Hill with great proficiency cut away the ragged shirt; she had managed to staunch the bleeding before the doctor arrived. When he did arrive he was able to begin probing for the shot straight away.

"Got it," he said with a satisfied grimace as he pulled the rough shot out of the badly bleeding wound with a set of surgical tweezers.

Doctor Thorn stood near the large open fireplace examining the shot; luckily he had managed to remove it in one piece.

"What are his chances Thorn?" Baxter asked.

"I've done all I can, fortunately the shot did not split, or penetrate too deeply, I think it hit his shoulder blade; it may have chipped the bone though." He looked up at Baxter, " He's lost a quantity of blood; perhaps you could use some of your medicine; his life's with the Maker now I'm afraid."

"It always was, and I would not be afraid of that." Linton was a little annoyed at the doctor's flippant remark.

"Yes well, I'll call again tomorrow shall I?"

"Thank you old chap." Baxter said escorting the doctor to the door.

Back upstairs, Linton was trying to peer over Mrs. Hill's shoulder. "What on earth possessed Farrar to shoot the lad?"

"He say's the lad was with a gang of cutthroats heading through the town."

"He hardly looks the cutthroat type to me." Linton said.

Baxter managed to suppress a smile at his friend's remark; no one ever looked a bad sort to Linton. They had been friends since their college days together more years ago than either of them cared to remember, and in that time he had never known Linton to condemn anyone.

They stayed a little longer in the guest room before they retired; Mrs. Hill slept that night in a chair at Ben's bedside.

"I'm sorry I must leave you this morning George; I've to be in Manchester for tomorrow evening." Linton said briefly staring into the hall mirror to square his hat.

"Don't worry my friend; I've Mrs. Hill to take care of me." Baxter replied with a mischievous smile. He hardly needed anyone to look after him, but Linton always worried about everyone.

"I'll call here on my way back to Cartmel."

"If you wish, but your good lady will be wondering where you've got to."

"I'm sure she will be used to my little ways by now." he said; a smile crossed his face as he thought of his beautiful young wife, Emily.

"That poor girl certainly has a cross to bear being married to you."

He escorted his friend out to catch the early morning post coach, then called in at a couple of main street shops to see if anyone had been a witness to the events of that morning.

There were other eyes watching that coach from the fells high above the town. Mace kept his eyes on the comings and goings of the town for the whole of the day.

He had no intention of losing Ben and intended to find out what had been his fate. Under cover of darkness that evening, he left all but Bren and Billy, his best house breaker up on the fell. Stealthily they crept back to the outskirts of the town and waited until the shops were closed, and only the house lights and lights from the public houses could be seen. Once all was quiet they made their way to a tavern that stood twenty yards from the bridge. In the smoke filled room, they bought drinks and retired to a quite secluded nook and sat in the shadows at a table in the corner of the room. As the evening wore on the barroom filled with locals, and of course the main topic of conversation was the events of the morning. No one paid much attention to the strangers sat in the corner. Mace followed every conversation in the smoke filled room with interest, and soon discovered what had happened to Ben.

They waited until almost everyone had left the bar, before slipping out into the night. Mace had a fairly good idea which direction the vicarage was, and as usual he led the way slipping with practised ease through the shadows of the night.

It was an impressive building, set in its own grounds, surrounded by a high ivy covered wall. An ornate iron gate opened onto a well kept gravel path, bordered by two parallel matching narrow lawns. There were just two lights showing, one in an upstairs room, and the other at the back of the house. Mace instinctively knew this was the place. Carefully, without a sound, they followed the wall until they were well away from the gate. Mace tugged at the long strands of overhanging vegetation, testing to see if they would support his weight. Finally he found a place where the strands had woven themselves into a thick rope. Bren held his hands together making a step for Mace to stand on, and then hoisted him up. Using the ivy, he hauled himself onto the top of the wall, and sat astride it to give the other two a helping hand up. An old oak tree at the other side, gave them an easy climb down into the garden. They crouched amongst its exposed roots. Only when they were satisfied that they had not been heard, did they move across the lawn, and into the shadow of the house. Suddenly a light appeared in the room nearest them, they froze, crouching down below the level of the windowsill. Mace crept to the window and peeped over the stone work, the curtains had not been drawn giving him a clear view of the room. He ducked down swiftly as Farrar entered the room behind Baxter. Mace kept perfectly still, waited a moment, and then crept back to his men.

Inside the house the men were talking about the morning's events too.

"I was aiming for the fellow that was dragging this one; I didn't mean to hit the lad. I'm sure the other was the leader. They're wanted in three counties for an assortment of crimes. There's talk that they may even be the gang that killed Constable Davies in Skipton, although I doubt if it's the same mob."

"Are you sure this one was part of the gang?"

"Certain, although he did seem to be fighting the other one. You can never tell with them sort. I'd keep your eyes on your valuables whilst he's here." Farrar said with a knowing wink.

"I don't suppose you have time for tea."

"Not really Sir, but if you insist." Farrar sat himself near the fire, holding the palms of his hands towards the flames.

"I'll ring Mrs. Hill to fetch us some."

"Where's Basil tonight? Usually he comes to say hello as soon as I arrive."

"If I know him, he'll be full length in front of Mrs. Hill's fire."

Basil was something of a celebrity around the town. Baxter had brought him back from a trip to Europe, and no one had ever seen the like before. Weighing in at a mere fifteen stone, the adolescent brown and white Saint Bernard had quickly become everyone's favourite. He was a gentle giant, the children loved him, he was also an excellent house dog, and had proved himself on a couple of occasions. However, he did create some problems, in as much as his main pleasure in life next to eating seemed to be antagonising Mrs. Hill, who in turn had a love-hate relationship with the brute.

She appeared in the study; Basil pushed past her, and greeted first Baxter, and then the constable. After sniffing around a moment, the giant dog settled in front of the fire with its huge head lightly resting on Baxter's feet.

"It's like the fires gone out when that great brute of yours gets his carcass in front of the flames." Mrs. Hill complained.

The dog lifted his great head, as if he knew she was talking about him. He yawned, and then settled down again.

"Mrs Hill, be so kind as to fetch the constable and myself a fresh brew of tea."

"Come on dog." She called as she left. All the way along the hall and down the steps to the kitchen, she mumbled to herself. Basil leapt after her, almost knocking her down the steps.

"If you were mine; I'd . . ." She threw the duster from her apron pocket after him. In the kitchen she tied him to a hook on the larder wall with a length of cord.

Sometime later, Constable Farrar left, unaware of the eyes that followed him down the path. He turned the collar of his cape up against the cold wind that was threatening to bring more rain.

When all the downstairs lights had been extinguished Mace gave Billy the nod and the lad pulled a long, flat bar of metal from beneath his coat. He forced one end into the window frame, and with practised ease worked the window open. The window had not been opened for some time, it creaked slightly, Mace held up his hand to stop Bren. Billy slipped in and then eased the window enough to allow Bren and Mace to follow him.

Downstairs Mrs. Hill had fallen asleep in front of the fire; she snored quietly, every now and again giving a deep sigh. Basil listened for a moment, then gnawed at the rope, determined to investigate the noises from upstairs.

They lit an oil lamp in the centre of the table, to investigate the room. Against one wall a glass fronted bureau containing a shining silver tea service, lovingly polished by Mrs. Hill, distracted them for a moment. Bren heaved on the ornate little door handle, but Mace pulled him away, signalling him to leave it. There was only one thing on his mind, finding the boy. Holding the oil lamp in front of him, Mace looked out into the hall. Every nerve in his body tingled as he strained to listen for any movement in the house. So far it had been easy, but he knew that it was not always a good sign. He did a quick survey, peering along the dark corridor; his agile mind worked summing up the situation. There were five doors that he could see, including the house front door; it sported three bolts, as well as two heavy locks. At the other end were the stairs, but no windows that could offer another exit in an emergency. There was also a short passage along the side of the stairs that he could not see down; that bothered him a little. He signalled the others to follow him and slowly he edged his way towards the stairs. They stopped at the old Grandfather clock whose steady heartbeat seemed to fill the whole house. Its enamelled face glowed in the lamp light, and the eyes of the ornate moon face above the minute-hand seemed to be watching them. There was a sixth door that Mace had not been able to see. A huge black nose pushed it open just enough to be able to sample the air. It twitched slightly as it caught the strange scent; each nostril flared in turn, and the eyes narrowed as the animal concentrated on the abundance of information it was receiving through the air. The faint squeak from the door hinge alerted Mace, he turned down the light; the others behind him stood poised ready for flight if need be. There was a short silence; even Mace was on edge as he strained his hearing.

Suddenly the hall was filled with deafening barks as a huge shape bounded out and along the hall towards them. The thunderous noise was more than the men's nerves could stand and they bolted back down the hall. The lamp fell from Mace's hand, leaving the hall in complete darkness. Tripping and stumbling over each other somehow they all made it back into the room. Bren slammed the room door shut just in the nick of time. With a heavy thud Basil collided with the woodwork. Angry and frustrated by the door, the dog began howling and barking so loud that he threatened to wake not just the household, but the whole town.

Mrs. Hill darted from her chair confused and startled by the sudden uproar. The cup of tea which was precariously balanced on her finger tip whilst she slept was sent crashing to the floor as she tried to gather her senses. She shouted at the top of her voice at the dog, but could not be heard over the din he was making. Reverend Baxter, dressed in long night-shirt, slippers and night-cap came to the head of the stairs, he carried a blunderbus. He had half suspected that the gang might come back for its lost member, so he had left the gun by his bedside when he retired. Shouting at Basil he raced headlong down the stairs.

Unaware of the oil spilling from the dropped lamp, which was slowly seeping across the polished floorboards, he charged onwards. As soon as he hit the slick, he lost all control of his movements. Confusion clouded his mind as he slithered across the floor. In the same instant his hand tightened its grip on the gun's trigger. His yell was drowned out by the deafening retort that echoing up and down the tight refines of the hallway. Plaster fell from the wounded roof in a great cloud, as the shot ricocheted around.

Mrs. Hill was half way up the steps when the shot rang out. She stopped, unsure which way to go. Bravely she swallowed her fear and raced forwards. Basil, surprised by the shot and concerned at seeing his master in a tangle on the floor, bounced from one end of the hall to the other, barking loudly. On his return journey Mrs. Hill stepped out in front of him. Too late he saw her, and although he tried to sidestep her, in the confines of the narrow passage and with the oil now covering the floor there was very little hope. She screamed as the dog's huge weight struck her in the middle of her back propelling her down the hall.

Baxter, slithering about in the oil, was trying to regain his feet just as housekeeper and dog reached him. The three of them rolled over in a heap there was an audible bump as they hit the outside door. For a brief moment all seemed quiet, just the constant tic-toc of the grandfather clock.

CHAPTER FIVE

———— ·•✻•· ————

Not since the Coronation of King George, had the little town been so excited. There seemed to be a constant buzz of conversation filling every street, never had there been so much to talk about. When Reverend Linton returned nine days later, the subject was still red hot.

Almost every resident of the town had been woken by the commotion; some had even dragged themselves away from the comfort of their warm beds and given chase with the constable. The post coach had carried the story as far as Manchester. Linton had heard about the break in and shooting at the vicarage almost by accident. Standing in a short queue waiting to book his return ticket for the following week, he had listened, only half interested at first, but the mention of Settle had grabbed his attention. Without hesitation he cancelled the rest of his business and returned on the next available coach.

"My dear Baxter, what on earth has been going on, the rumours said that there had been several people murdered, and a score of heinous crimes committed." Linton called through the coach window.

"The main crime is one of gossip. We had burglars that was all, there was no harm done, apart from a little damage to the woodwork of one window." Baxter said with a dismissive gesture, but loud enough for several townsfolk nearby to hear.

"Oh, and a little damage to the plaster work of the hallway roof." He added, slightly red-faced.

"Here let me help you." Baxter put out his arm to help Linton down from the coach. They strolled back to the vicarage, it was a fine day and the two old friends had spent many such hours, just walking.

"How's our young friend?" Linton finally asked he'd not wanted to seem too impatient.

"There has been a definite improvement."

"When was the last time the Doctor examined him?"

"This morning."

"Splendid; when he is quite fit enough to travel, with your permission, I'll take him back to Cartmel with me."

The Lintons owned a small farm, high on Cartmel Fell, just behind St. Anthony's Church, where he was vicar. The old farmhouse was a secret, private place, hidden from view amongst the undulating hills of the fell. In winter it was shielded from the cold winds by the surrounding hills, and in summer its south facing position meant it had sun the whole day long. There was not much farming done anymore, the place was more like an orphanage and over the years there had been a long procession of waifs and strays sheltering there. Elizabeth, the first Mrs. Linton, had started it by taking in a couple of children orphaned after their parents had died during a cholera epidemic. Soon their family grew, as children began arriving from various parts of the district. A barn was converted to provide sleeping accommodation for up to ten quite comfortably, but it was not unknown for there to be as many as twenty children sheltering there. Elizabeth Linton had been bitterly disappointed when it was obvious that she would not have children of her own, and so she dedicated her life to her ever-changing family. There were seven very happy years for the Lintons; however the seventh winter was the worst in living memory. Deep snow drifts cloaked the landscape, isolating the small scattered communities of the fells for several months.

As the snows began to fall, the Lintons had taken into their care a young girl aged about four years. She had a severe racking cough that shook her tiny body and drained her strength. Elizabeth was convinced that with a lot of love and affection she could get the child well again. Within a month, two more of the children were ill. They all suffered the same symptoms; high fevers, followed by severe shivering, and then the cough would begin.

It was soon obvious that care and love were not enough; Elizabeth wept rocking back and forth clutching in her arms the third child to die within a week. Sadly, she was the next victim. She tried to hide the symptoms, fighting with all the strength she could muster against it, then one day she fainted, crashing to the kitchen floor during dinner. The children screamed as dinner plates rolled and smashed. Linton tried to revive her, but it was no use. She lay as limp as a rag doll in his arms.

Leaving one of the older children in charge he made a valiant effort to get through to the doctor in Cartmel, but it was impossible. For three hours he fought neck deep through snowdrifts until he was finally exhausted. With tears burning down his frozen cheeks, he had to admit defeat. The mist of his breath in the cold night air hung like a shroud around his face as he raised it to heaven and asked for the strength to get home.

Elizabeth was dead by the time he managed to get back to the farm. There was no way that he could continue alone and although he was reluctant to end the work they had been doing, when spring came he found alternative homes for the children. Somehow without Elizabeth, he had no heart for his work. The farmhouse was silent, almost as if it mourned for the loss. The following summer he was back in his home town of Oxford.

Silently mourning, he threw all his energies back into the academic world. This had been his first love; and now he used it as a shield hiding from the world. But there was dark emptiness to everything he did. It was whilst he was lecturing at one of the new colleges for women, that he met a very talented and attractive young student by the name of Emily Harris. There was an immediate attraction between them despite the difference in age. It had been over two years since the death of Elizabeth, but the pain was still there like an open wound. He felt guilty about the sudden and unexpected appeal of his new acquaintance. He tried avoiding her, but somehow fate seemed to thrust them together. They began to spend hours together walking through the parks and gardens of the city, drinking tea in quiet cosy little teashops, or attending lectures and then concerts together.

It came as a great shock to him the day he finally admitted to himself that he had fallen in love with the girl. He spent hours soul searching, angry with his weakness, and yet he could find no sin in his love. He realised that it did not diminish the feelings he still felt for Elizabeth.

They married on a glorious spring morning. Baxter attended the wedding and invited them to spend a honeymoon of sorts in Settle with him. Emily knew all about Linton's first wife, and the farm on the fell. She persuaded Linton to show her it.

He felt a little apprehensive as they turned off the fell road into the once familiar gateway of the farm. Old wounds were torn open, and there was no way that he could hold back the tears as they entered the cosy little kitchen.

Dust sheets covered everything. She smiled placing a loving hand on his shoulder.

"It's more beautiful than I could ever imagine," she said, trailing her fingers over the huge rustic kitchen table. Her words seemed to exorcise the ghosts of the past.

Much to the little communities' joy the couple moved back to the farm. A few tongues wagged about the age difference, but she soon wooed the local women over to her side.

"Why don't we pick up where you and Elizabeth left off? There must still be an awful lot of children needing homes." She said.

They were sat with their feet to the warm glow of the kitchen fireplace.

"Is it really what you want?" He sat forward as he spoke staring deep into her eyes.

"Yes. This place needs children."

Once again the barn was made ready, local workers were drafted in to repair the leaking roof and generally tidy things up. Sadly, before it was finished children were already beginning to stream into the barn and too soon they were completely full.

Six years had elapsed since then, and Linton was certain that Emily would welcome the new boy He stayed overnight with Baxter.

"As soon as Dr. Thorn agrees, I want you to send me word, and I'll come back for the lad."

They shook hands as Linton climbed aboard the post coach; he always felt as if the bumpy ride north was some sort of endurance test. There was a sweetener to the journey however and that was the thought of Emily and home and of course the children, and his Parish.

"Now don't forget, as soon as he is fit let me know."

"Of course, I only hope that the lad appreciates what you are doing for him."

"That's not important, and you know it."

"Not to you. God speed my friend." The coach pulled away,

Linton leant out of the window, as it pulled out of the market square.

"Don't forget!"

Baxter smiled to himself as he wandered home, never in all his life had he known anyone with a heart as generous as his friend Linton.

"Quickly Mr. Baxter! Lad's opened his eyes." Mrs. Hill shouted from the top of the stairs as he entered the front door.

Doing as he was bid he went up the steps two at a time, and was quite pleased with himself that he could still find the energy for such a task.

The curtains were still partly drawn and a soft light filled the room. Baxter sat gently on the side of the bed.

"Well boy, how do you feel?"

"Not too well Sir, I've a dreadful headache."

"How's the back?"

"It's sore, but not as bad as my head. Thank you Sir." Ben's voice was still very croaky, his lips felt dry and sore. He had been afraid when he first opened his eyes, but Mrs. Hill had soon put his mind at ease.

It was another week before Dr. Thorn pronounced Ben fit enough to be allowed to get up and sit by the side of the bed for a few hours. Mrs. Hill had made sure the fire was blazing like a furnace before she allowed Baxter to help Ben out of bed and into a soft armchair

"There now, you sit still and I'll bring you some warm broth."

"You're honoured young man; Mrs. Hill has been with me for fifteen years and never spoilt me so."

They sat together a little while in silence, enjoying the warm orange glow of the fire. Ben felt at ease, but remained on his guard.

"Sounds as if she's on her way up now." There were the sounds of cutlery on a tray, then a sudden dull thud, followed by muffled muttering.

Suddenly the door was sent banging against the wall. Basil, who had managed once again to get out of the kitchen bounded into the room. Instinctively he headed for the fire, but stopped mid-flight as he suddenly realised that there was a stranger present. His great head was level with Ben's, cautiously he approached, nose twitching with each step.

"This is Basil."

Ben held out his hand and patted the front of the furry expanse. Basil responded with a great lick of his enormous pink tongue; boy and dog, it was somehow a natural relationship. Each day after that, they would seek each other out, confident of a friendly welcome.

One morning as he was dressing he caught sight of himself in the long mirror in his bedroom. He stood for a moment hardly recognising himself; 'no wonder they have taken pity on me' he thought as he stared. The long winter on the moors had taken its toll, still he had the broad shoulders and deep chest, but now every rib poked out, his arms were wasted, and his face was thin and gaunt. He dropped the loose trousers he had been given as pyjamas and stared at the bony hips and scrawny legs. He sat on the edge of the bed and stared at his hands, their long thin fingers like strangers to him.

He dressed in his new clothes provided by Mrs. Hill, and then went off in search of his new friend Basil, who he knew would be delighted to see him.

"Now then young man you keep this scarf wrapped around your neck, it's still not all that warm." Mrs. Hill tucked the scarf in as she spoke.

Ben was allowed out each day to take a short walk in the garden, accompanied of course by Basil. They had a favourite spot beneath a great elm that grew some distance from the house sheltered from the wind, where they basked in the warm, spring sunshine. Constable Farrar and Rev Baxter had both tried questioning him about who he was, and how he came to be with the gang. Although Ben had not refused to answer their questions, he had managed to avoid giving too many answers.

"What should I do old fellow?" He whispered into Basil's enormous hairy ear.

As he spoke he toyed with the lucky rabbit's foot Jenny had given him as a Christmas present, he wondered how she was. He missed her and wished she was there for him to confide in, they had grown close in their short time together and at that moment he needed a friend. Inevitably his thoughts returned to Ruth, he felt guilty about his feelings of affection towards Jenny but decided Ruth would understand him being unfaithful to her.

Basil listened, tilting his head from side to side as if studying the problem.

"If I tell them who I am; they'll probably send me back to be hanged by Sir Geoffrey. It was an accident; we didn't kill him on purpose honestly."

The dog gave a wag of his tail and Ben knew that his canine ally believed his every word.

"Come on you two, tea's ready." These magic words brought an immediate response and without further discussion they raced across the lawn and crashed back into the kitchen.

CHAPTER SIX

---◦•❈•◦---

"Well I'm sorry Reverend, but I think I should now take the lad into custody, until the magistrate arrives," Constable Farrar said.

"Nonsense man, I'll not here of it," Baxter was adamant, "the young man is obviously suffering from some form of amnesia, and he cannot remember his involvement with the gang. It would be most unfair to arrest him. You've spoken with him, does he seem like a cut-throat to you?"

Farrar knew when he was beaten; he left Ben in Baxter's custody, and with a nod of his head he made for the door. For just a moment he thought about saying something else, but the look on the other's face put him off.

Winter softly melted into spring and Ben was recovering well, with the help of Mrs. Hill's cooking he had put on some weight. The incident in the town was a blur, but some nights he would wake, sweating and trembling. The surreal world of dreams with its distorted images and jumbled facts creating one nightmare after another and it was giving him many unsettled nights.

He ate his meals with Mrs. Hill and his new friend Basil in the kitchen. They all got very well and Ben knew he would be sorry when the time came for him to leave. It was obvious that she had become quite fond of him too.

Ben liked helping around the kitchen and especially enjoyed helping Mrs. Hill with the baking. When the rich, thick cake mix was poured into the baking tins, there was always the bowl to lick out, a job he found to his taste.

Occasionally he would sit on an evening with Baxter in front of the fire in the upstairs living room.

"So young man has your memory returned at all, can you remember why you were with the gang?"

"Not really sir. Mace the gang leader was taking me to Liverpool I think, to sell me. I can't tell you very much else at all."

"Well never mind now, perhaps later it will all come back."

Ben was not pleased with himself and his supposed lost memory, he knew that it was easy to make a mistake, but also he liked Baxter and Mrs. Hill and felt guilty about lying to them.

When Reverend Linton returned to Baxter's he sent word asking the constable to call at the vicarage, as soon as possible. That same afternoon Linton took Ben and Basil out to the garden seat to tell him his plans.

"So how are you feeling now?" Linton said.

"I'm very much improved, thank you sir,"

"Is Mrs. Hill feeding you properly?" Linton smiled.

"Oh yes sir, very well," he patted his stomach.

"I wonder if you would like to come back to my home? I think my friend Baxter has been telling you all about it."

"It sounds very nice sir, but what would I do?"

"Well . . . first of all you could get yourself fully recovered, and although you are a little older than we normally take in, I'm sure there would be lots for you to do."

"You don't know anything about me sir. You don't know that I wasn't part of that gang, other than I told you I wasn't."

"Would you lie to me?"

"No Sir."

"Then I know you were not a member of that gang."

Ben was forced to smile, "what if I wanted to leave?"

"Well in that case, we would sit down by my fire and discuss what you did want to do," Linton smiled back.

He told Ben about the farm and the fells and quite soon Ben was keen to go with him back to Cartmel.

Once more alone with his canine companion Ben thought about his predicament he wondered if it would be better to tell Linton just why he had been with the gang and return to Bingley to face the music there. The farm sounded great fun and although he knew everyone at home would be worried about him, it seemed better to perhaps give it more time.

When the constable arrived Linton met him in the drawing room and told him of his plans too.

"I wish to take the young man home to Cartmel with me."

"That's not possible Sir."

"Why?"

"Well," the constable stopped, and thought a moment, "he was with them there cut-throats. He may be a wanted criminal."

"Nonsense, I will accept full responsibility for him. He is not fully recovered yet."

"Reverend Baxter thinks the lad has ambrosia." The constable said, deadly serious.

"Indeed, well then it would be impossible to take him to court. Surely you know the laws regarding that type of thing." Linton said somehow restraining a smile

"Of course I know the laws!"

"Well then?"

"Very well, but if anything does come to light about this lad, he must be returned here to face whatever is coming to him."

With that settled, the arrangements were made for Ben to travel north with Linton back to his home on the fells. As soon as the next coach arrived, Ben's few things were collected together and parcelled for the journey. It had felt safe at the vicarage, yet he knew that he was still too close to his real home to be out of danger. Mrs. Hill made a fuss over him, having to mop her face with her apron every few minutes, and repeatedly made him promise to come see them again as soon as he could. As the coach pulled out of the market square, Ben leant out of the window, waving frantically to Mrs. Hill and Rev Baxter.

The coach crossed the bridge out of the town with Ben still leaning out and waving, but soon his new friends were lost from sight. He remained a little while longer at the window almost afraid to sit back in the coach.

Even though his companion was almost a complete stranger to him, he knew nearly everything there was to know about him. Rev Baxter had talked constantly about the Lintons

"Sit down and rest, we have a long journey ahead of us." Linton said in a gentle coaxing way.

The coach bounced its way up the steep road over Bucker Brow, the driver could be heard shouting at his horses as they strained in their harnesses. It felt chilly and there was some early mist on the landscape: somewhere close to the roadside a curlew called its morning song. Once over the top, there was a long downhill stretch that was almost as much a strain on the animals as the climb had been.

"I hope we will become great friends Benjamin."

"Ben." Ben corrected. "Everyone's always called me Ben."

Linton laughed. "Yes very well. Very well, Ben it is."

"Have you any brothers or sisters?"

"I think I did have, but I think that they're all dead."

"Are your parents dead?"

Ben studied the man; he was not sure where the questions were leading. "Yes Sir."

"Well you're going to have some new brothers and sisters. How do you feel about that?"

"I don't know."

"You'll fit in nicely. We don't have anyone your age, but still I'm sure you'll soon make friends with my little family."

One of the horses began running lame, which put the coach behind schedule, and forced them to take a longer than usual break in Clapham. Whilst the limping member of the team was being replaced, Ben and Rev Linton took the opportunity to stretch their legs. They strolled aimlessly towards a small picturesque pond, very near the coach inn.

"I love to get away from the cities. One can really appreciate God's wonders out here," Linton said.

"I like the moors," Ben said "but you have to treat them with respect."

Linton felt as if he had made a slight break through. "Yes the moors are beautiful, especially when the strong autumn winds blow hard across them."

The coach driver called them and they slowly, almost reluctantly strolled back.

"What time d'you call this to be away. You've always some excuse." An elderly gentleman dressed in a heavy black cloth suit shouted up at the driver. "My good wife and I have important business in Carnforth."

"Can't help it if damn horse turns lame can I?" The driver saw Linton. "Beg yer pardon Reverend."

"That's all right. There are times when we all feel like using stronger expressions." He turned towards the gentleman, and in his usual diplomatic way said. "I'm sure they are doing their best. Perhaps if you took your seat we might not be delayed any longer than need be."

Grumbling under his breath the man helped his wife climb into the coach. They took the last remaining seats. The lady, who was very large, took the seat next to Ben, squashing him against the woodwork of the vehicle. He let out a groan. When the lady glared at him down her nose he managed a weak smile in return.

"Don't fidget young man." The woman snapped after they had travelled only a few miles.

"I wouldn't if you'd keep to your own seat ma'am."

"Well really." She said.

"Are you to let *this boy,* get away with such insolence?" The man barked angrily at Linton

"No one should be punished for speaking the truth." Linton replied.

"How dare you sir!"

"Perhaps if you will exchange seats with me and sit beside your wife, the whole matter will be resolved."

It sounded a simple manoeuvre, but in the bouncing swaying coach it proved almost fatal for the man. As he stood up, the coach hit a rut in the road and swayed violently to one side. He was thrown hard against the door. It popped open and he was almost thrown out onto the road. Fortunately Linton managed to catch a hold of the tail of the man's jacket and dragged him back in to safety. He wedged himself in against his wife looking quite pale. The couple grumbled all the way to Carnforth where the coach pulled to a halt outside a huge Jacobean building in the town centre. The woman squeezed her bulk out of the door, still grumbling.

"Good day to you Sir, Ma'am." Linton said touching the brim of his hat

"Indeed, and to you Sir a pleasant journey." The man replied begrudgingly.

As soon as they were safely out the driver, still trying to make up the time he had lost earlier in the day, whipped the horses to set off. The coach lurched forward its wheels spraying mud at the couple.

"Is it far yet Sir?" Ben asked.

"Another couple of hours, and we should be in Cartmel."

Rumbling through the night the coach headed north. It bounced along the road lit by a full moon that hung as bright as a new coin over the distant mountains. At Arnside they picked up a guide to take them across the sands of the estuary. Finally they reached Grange over Sands, where they dropped off mail and then carried on to Cartmel. Wrapped in blankets to keep out the evening chill, Ben slept for the last hour of the journey.

"Come on lad we've arrived!" Rev Linton shook Ben's shoulder.

The small town came alive as the sound of the horses and steel tyres on cobblestones filled the town square. There were a few oil lamps lit hanging from walls, but as people came out to greet the coach they brought more with them.

Still half asleep, Ben staggered a little as he climbed down the three steps out of the coach. With his feet securely on the ground he glanced around trying to get his bearings. He shivered a little as he waited for Linton to sort out their baggage.

They were approached by a stout man leading a horse pulling a gig.

"The coach is a little late Reverend." The man called.

"Yes we had a little problem with one of the horses." The Reverend put his arm around Ben's shoulder. "This is the young man I was telling you about." Linton pushed Ben forward.

"This is Finlay, Ben, he helps us out from time to time, and we would be completely lost without his help."

The man came forward and nodded awkwardly a little embarrassed by the remark they shook hands.

"It's my pleasure I'm sure Reverend." He had a slight Scottish twang to his voice.

There were only a couple of pieces of baggage to be loaded and Finlay strapped them onto the back board of the gig.

"We must get you some new clothes as soon as we can young man." Linton said as he squeezed in beside Ben.

Once beyond the cobbles of the village street, the wheels of the gig grumble and moaned as they crunched over the loose stones of the deep rutted track they were following. When they reached the steeper fell road, Finlay leapt to the ground, and walked alongside.

"Cracker's not as young as she was. She's been a good old lassie; but the fells are getting just a bit much for her, with a full load." He said patting the old horse's solid, thick neck.

An icy crosswind hit then as they reached the open moorland above the wooded slopes. Ben rubbed his shoulder; the wound still pained him, especially when it was cold. Linton pulled the blanket tighter around him, to try keep out the cold.

"Not long now my young friend and we'll enjoy the comfort of the fireside chairs." Linton said.

Linton was obviously well pleased to be home, his face glowing as he pointed out the cottage and its outbuildings as they rounded the last hill. The wide gate was open and welcoming, bidding them to enter the farmyard, which was a downhill journey of about two hundred yards from the road to the house.

Ben could see lights shining in several rooms. As the gig came into the yard a broad shaft of light from the doorway bathed them in its warm glow. Suddenly there seemed to be children everywhere, the quiet of the night shattered by their chatter. Linton stood up and raised his arms in the air.

"Quiet!" He shouted, trying to be heard above the din. "This is Ben and I want you all to make him feel welcome. We are both very tired, and deserve to be at least let into the house."

The noise and excitement had not abated even the slightest. Ben was caught up in it as the children surrounded him, and they fired questions at him from every angle. A slim figure glided through the press surrounded by a relaxed aura of peace and serenity. The soft light from the open doorway glowed halo-like around her as she stepped forward. Her long dark hair was tied back in a tight bun on the back of her head revealing an exquisite face. Her cheeks glowed like polished marble and her lips curled sensually into a knowing smile.

Ben suddenly realised that he was staring open mouthed at her, she was not what he had expected at all; she was the most beautiful woman he had ever seen. Even in what were obviously her working clothes, she looked more beautiful than the elegant ladies of title that he had sometimes seen visiting at the Grange. It took a couple of moments before he could compose himself.

"Hello Ben," she said in a quiet voice that fitted perfectly with the vision.

He was incapable of speech; he took the offered hand hardly daring to touch its softness. He gave her a quick embarrassed nod, and then stumbled out of the gig.

"You must both be frozen. Come on children out of the way," she said

"Now come on all of you; time for bed," Linton said.

There was a loud chorus of groans, but the children obeyed. One by one they presented themselves before the Reverend, pecked his cheek and wished him a goodnight.

"Straight to bed; I will be along later to tuck you all in," Emily said.

Ben took an offered chair near the fire; he rubbed at his legs, trying to restore some feeling in them. With some effort, he managed to keep his eyes away from the woman, almost afraid to look at her. She brought him a steaming bowl of stew, accompanied by a thick slice of brown bread. Carefully she placed it on the little table by the side of his chair.

"Now be very careful, it's very hot," she said.

She handed him a heavy spoon.

Warming one hand with the bowl, he gratefully attacked the food, hardly stopping to draw breath between the first few mouthfuls. He stared into the fire trying to concentrate on the meal, aware that both his hosts were watching his every move.

"My words! Has the Rev Baxter not been feeding you?"

"Oh! Yes ma'am." Ben said not lifting his head.

Linton took the seat opposite Ben, and then ate in silence, after dipping his head a moment in prayer.

"Would you like some more? There's plenty." She asked, staring in amazement at the empty bowl on Ben's knee.

"No thank you ma'am, I've had sufficient." He replied a little embarrassed.

"We've got to know each other a little on the way up. Haven't we?" Linton said.

"Yes sir."

"You didn't say where you were from." Linton said.

"Hush sir, can you not see the young man is far too tired to be answering questions? There will be plenty of chance for us to talk later," Emily said

Linton smiled, "of course, you are correct as usual my dear."

"Well young man I'll show you to your bed now."

"You rest my dear, I have the others to see to; I can show him." She gently kissed her husband's forehead.

"Can you carry the lantern please?" She said to Ben.

Outside the moon was high above them casting a hard silver light into the yard. The cottage was sheltered from the winds of the fells by a huge pillow of a hill behind, and in the yard all was still. They walked in silence; Ben sneaking a sidelong glance at Emily. The light of the lantern seemed to highlight her gentle features. As soon as they opened the door to the barn the dim of arguing children flooded out. Suddenly there was a deathly hush. The occupants had heard the sound of footsteps on the wooden stairs.

"I thought I said for you all to go to sleep."

"We are!" Came the indignant reply from beneath one of the heavy woollen blankets

"Oh well. I'm certainly glad to hear that. Thank you Timothy." She said to the bulge beneath the blankets.

They went up another flight of stairs. There were two beds along the wall, neither was occupied. Ben placed the lantern on the table. She lit a single candle from it.

"You may have whichever bed you choose." She said.

Ben sat on the first one nearest the door. Again he kept his eyes away from her, although he wanted desperately to look at her.

"We always put the older ones up here. It's lovely in summer, the old hay door still opens, and the sun fills the room."

She gently pushed Ben's hair off his forehead. "Try and get some sleep, we can talk in the morning."

Ben listened as she said, 'good night' to each of the children on the floor below. For a long while after she had gone he just sat staring at the floorboards. Her gentle fragrance still seemed to fill the room. He suddenly felt confused and angry. He lay back on the bed still fully dressed, slowly drifting into a troubled sleep, filled with leaping characters and made even more uncomfortable by a guilty conscience.

Next morning the chatter of the children below woke him, as they hurriedly dressed for breakfast. Two of the oldest and most daring quietly sneaked up the steps to take a peep at the new arrival.

"Hello. I'm Timothy. You can call me Tim, everyone else does. You're Ben. aren't you?" the boy said.

Soon all the children who were staying with the Lintons were surrounding Ben, they were bombarding him with questions.

"Where have you come from?" A very pretty girl called Polly asked.

"Oh . . . you wouldn't know it if I told you," Ben replied

"Bet I would," Tim said.

The sound of a bell ringing silenced them for a moment. It saved Ben from further questioning and from across the yard Emily Linton called them to breakfast. There was a mad scramble down the steps and across the yard. Ben followed them into the house, where he was given pride of place at the top of the table. Twice during the meal Emily had to silence the salvo of questions that were still being fired constantly by the children at him.

CHAPTER SEVEN

— ⬧ —

There was no doubt about it; life with the Lintons certainly was entertaining. Emily Linton knew just how to keep the children both busy and happy. Each day seemed to be one long game, and there was endless laughter and smiles. The children actually argued to do some of the jobs that needed doing around the cottage, just so that they were always part of what was going on.

To the south side of the cottage there was a kitchen garden and now as spring set in there were endless jobs to do. Vegetable plots had to be cleared and winter crops picked ready for the summer ones to replace them.

There was the livestock to look after too: the eggs had to be collected, the four cows milked, the goats also had to be milked, and then there were the other usual tasks of making cheese and butter. Although some of it was sold to make money for the cottage, most was eaten by the constantly hungry mouths living at the cottage.

It was all new for Ben, but he found that he enjoyed the physical side of farming and soon began to make a number of jobs his own. Emily was glad of the help and someone she could rely on to work unsupervised. Ben found looking after their two ponies his favourite work, he made it his job to clean out their stalls and bed them down on a night. Often he would just find solace in the barn away from the constant chatter of the children, it gave him chance to think, to remember, and try to solve his problems. Almost six months had flown past and he had regained his strength, but he was still sleeping fitfully and ran a constant battle with his conscience.

Two of the young girls followed Ben around like ducklings, Clara the eldest of the two who was probably only ten years old, declared her love for Ben at every opportunity. When Ben was helping with the schooling on an afternoon she would sit as close to him as was physically possible without actually being on top of him. Tim, a lad of about eleven also trailed dutifully after Ben, and constantly tried to shoo away the girls. Quite often he would search Ben out in the barn and volunteer his help.

With each passing day, Ben was beginning to feel more relaxed in the Linton's company. He joined in with a lot of the work but still gave nothing away about himself.

It was an easy routine of work and play. The Linton's ran daily classes on reading and writing, with a little mathematics thrown in. After evening meal, they would all troop to the little church to sing a few hymns and receive a little religious instruction. Emily would tell them all stories from the Bible and there was not a sound from the children as they sat in a circle around her.

Some evenings Linton would play the slightly out of tune piano in the main living room, the children would swarm around and sing hymns and some popular songs. Ben would then fetch in logs for the fire ready for the morning and help Emily clear up, until Linton declared it was time they all took some rest by the fire for a while. One by one the children were dispatched to bed until the kitchen gained an unusual calm.

In the warm glow of the kitchen fire, and surrounded by the smell of rising bread and baking loaves, Ben would sit and talk with the Lintons until late into the night. He liked their company, enjoying Linton's many anecdotes and observances of people and life in general; Emily was witty, well read and charming. They drank cider made from the cottage's own apples and ate oat cakes baked in the kitchen range.

"How do find life here with us?" Linton suddenly asked.

"I am enjoying it greatly Sir."

"Mrs. Linton tells me you are a very important member of our team here now and something of a favourite with the girls."

Ben blushed a little, "I enjoy the work Sir and try to earn my keep," he said rather more stiffly than he actually meant.

They had never pressed him on other issues, about his past or how he came to be in Settle. In private the Lintons had agreed that it was best to leave Ben to tell them of his own accord whenever he was ready, realising that after the traumatic events that had happened he might still find them too painful to recount.

Sometimes during these evening conversations he had been close to telling them the story but he felt guilty for running away, and confused as to what he should do.

"Do you know your age at all?" She asked without looking up from the dress she was mending.

"Do you mean me?" Linton laughed.

"No silly, you know who I mean."

This was typical of the light hearted banter that was often exchanged.

"My birthday's in July, I believe I am sixteen this next time." He said pondering slightly on the issue. Time had gone so fast, it seemed a lifetime since he had fled the comfort of his home.

"I think next time I'm in Ulverston I need to get you some more clothes, you've grown out of everything these last few months."

"It's your fine cooking that is to answer for that." Ben laughed trying to hitch his trousers up a little.

"Well said Ben, Mrs. Linton's fare can repair any ill." Linton chipped in.

At breakfast one morning Emily spoke to Ben. "The orchard fence and wall needs repairing. Could you do it?" she asked, "I can't even lift some of the stones."

"Yes of course, I'm feeling much stronger now."

"I'm pretty strong you know," Tim butted in.

"Yes of course you are, perhaps you can both do it."

"Good! Polly you start the washing up, I'll show the boys what needs doing." They all trooped out to the little orchard beside the cottage. "Polly! You and Clara are supposed to be washing up."

"Oh but . . . . !"

"Never mind, inside both of you." she shooed them back to the cottage.

Ben examined an old broken swing that hung between two of the larger trees.

"That's been broken for years. I suppose we might get around to mending it one day."

"I could do it after we've done the wall. If you'd like that is?" A piece of the rotten wood broke away in his hand; he tried to hide it slightly embarrassed.

"Yes it would be very nice. I always fancied sitting out here on a summers evening drinking lemonade in the sunshine." She waved him just to drop the wood, and smiled, "I think the whole thing will collapse one day."

"I like lemonade." Tim interrupted.

"Yes we know that, every time I make some it's gone before it's had time to settle in the jug."

Ben climbed up onto the top of what was left of the wall to survey what was needed to repair it. One section had completely fallen over, and the rest was not going to survive much longer. Stones were scattered everywhere, some were lost, covered in tangled dead bracken and weeds.

"Well what do you think?" she said." The goats and sheep are forever raiding the garden vegetables."

"Easy!" Tim said. "We'll have it done in no time, aye Ben."

Ben kicked at a couple of the stones, "we'll need some tools from the stable, and I've seen hammers and things in there."

"Very well I'll leave you two men to it."

She hummed to herself as she wandered back to the kitchen picking at the tall dried grass heads as she walked.

"What you think of her?" Tim asked. "I think she's alright and I can tell you like her."

"Come on, this is going to take some time," Ben said ignoring the question.

"Polly says that Emily is the most beautiful woman in the whole world, because she has seen a real Princess and she says that the Princess was only half as beautiful." Tim finally stopped to draw breath waiting for a response when there was none he continued anyway. "She says that the Reverend is old enough to be her father, and that they were caught up in a whirlwind romance and got married."

"I think we need to work more and talk less," Ben said handling one of the wall stones.

They sorted the stones into two piles, usable and rubble. Ben had helped a couple of farmers near his uncle's inn to rebuild their dry stonewalls, so he had some idea of what was needed. Tim handed the stones to Ben as he replaced them in the wall. It was heavy work, and despite the cold wind, they were both soon sweating. Ben took off his shirt.

"Cor! What's that on yer back?" Tim asked.

"I was shot."

Tim prodded the scar with his finger. "Blimey! Did it hurt?"

"I don't remember much about it. It certainly did afterwards."

Tim peeled his shirt off too and showed Ben his back, "I've some scars too, look."

There were several scars across his back; a couple of them looked as if the wound had been quite deep.

"My Dad used to hit me with his belt, just for fun I think."

Ben ran his finger along one of the welts, "that must have really hurt."

"He killed my Mum, beat her death, it was horrible, and he just kept on punching and kicking. I ran away." There was a long pause, "I really am sorry for running, I feel such a coward now. Do you think I was a coward?"

They had sat side by side on the wall, and for a moment neither of them spoke.

"You're not a coward Tim, sometimes problems are just too big for us to face alone. My uncle always said it was a wise man who knew when to run, and when to fight. Run away and fight another day, was his motto," Ben said with a wry smile.

They worked all morning, Tim kept losing interest, but Ben kept him busy. As soon as they had cleared away the weeds and fallen stones they began to rebuild the wall. Despite the slight age difference, a bond had formed between them. Above them in the tall trees, crows were calling and arguing; Tim amused himself and Ben shouting back at them, imitating their calls, until a call from the house brought them in for lunch.

"He's been shot!" Tim announced to everyone at the table. "He's got a great big scar on his back."

There were demands from the other children to see the scar.

"Don't be silly; Clara, sit down and eat your meal. Now stop it all of you. Behave yourselves," Emily said.

The girls cleared away the plates, and each time they took a diversion behind Ben's chair in the hope of catching a glimpse of the scar.

It took a few weeks but eventually the wall was finished and to celebrate they held a party in the orchard. It was still chilly, so they lit a small bonfire; the children had spent all afternoon in the woods finding dry sticks and branches to use. They brought out kitchen chairs and a makeshift table was made from an old door with wooden crates as legs. In a great mixing bowl they mixed barley flour and water into sticky dough which they wrapped around clean cut sticks to cook in the flames. Potatoes were cooked in the ashes, and then the whole thing was served with marrowfat peas that had bubbled in a huge iron cook pot. They danced around the fire, singing at the tops of their voices and just before bed Linton told them the story of David and Goliath by the light of the dying fire.

Ben realised that he was going to have to make a decision soon and face up to his problems. The decision was not an easy one; he was so enjoying life with the Lintons that he was able to almost forget his past. However, in the dead of night, frightening ghosts still haunted his dreams, images of Ruth, Mace, Batty falling from the loft and most of all being taken to the gallows to hang. After a particularly bad night, he finally decided that whatever the consequences he would have to tell the Lintons the truth.

As he entered the kitchen, he could hear Emily humming a little tune as she went about her work. All the children were playing in the little orchard, and so the house was unusually quiet, even Tim was out of sight.

"Oh! I'm sorry Ben, you startled me," she said.

"I'm sorry; I thought you'd seen me come in."

"What can I do for you?" she said drying her hands on the front of her apron.

"My auntie, the one that I grew up with, she used to do that when she'd been baking," he said. "I'd like a word with you, if you can spare a moment."

They sat opposite each other across the table, but before Ben could say a word Emily was on her feet again.

"I had better make sure the children are safe, and that they do not disturb us." Quickly she went into the orchard and charged Timothy with keeping them all in order.

"Sorry," she said resuming her seat across the table.

Ben was glad of the break, which had given him just a moment to compose himself.

"I have to tell you . . ." Ben told her the whole story, he told her much more than he had intended, talking about his Aunt and Uncle, and their inn. He had not meant to tell her everything about himself, but once he had started, the words just seemed to flood out. It was like putting down a heavy load, suddenly he felt as light as a feather, and as if he had not a care in the world.

Emily Linton knew well the art of listening; her strict upbringing and schooling in her hometown of Truro in Cornwall had taught her that. The whole time Ben had been speaking she had hardly moved. She had said nothing, and her eyes had hardly ever left his face so that he knew she was listening to his every word. When he had finished they sat in silence a moment. One of the children suddenly rushed in, as kindly as possible she hurried the child back outside.

"May I relate this story to Linton?" She asked.

"Oh yes. I feel very guilty for not telling him myself, after his many kindnesses to me."

"I'm sure he will understand, and be glad that you have at last taken us into your confidence."

When Linton returned later that evening, Emily went through the story; she was confident that her husband would know what the right course of action to take would be. He was quiet for a moment, deeply saddened by the story, but true to form, his concern was for Ben and his family, and the worry they must be experiencing over his disappearance. After the other children had gone to bed, he called Ben into his study.

"I'm truly glad that you have unburdened yourself my boy."

"I'm sorry Sir."

"Sorry! What for?"

"Well; not being honest with you, or Rev Baxter, after your kindness."

"It is not always easy to do the right thing." He studied Ben a moment.

"Enough of that; I will not force you to do anything that you do not wish, but what I ask, is that you allow me to contact your guardians; in confidence, and tell them that you are safe."

The question hung in the air for a moment, Ben knew that there would be no betrayal.

"Yes I'd like you to."

"Good man. Tomorrow I'll write them a letter."

"Thank you." There was a pause. "Will you still let me stay here?"

"Yes of course! You are welcome here for as long as you wish. Anyway the choice is yours."

There was another awkward silence.

"At some time you will have to return and face the consequences but, you say that you were only partly involved in the other young man's death, and that it was actually Ruth who pushed him over the edge. I think things will not be as bad as you fear."

"Yes, but I could never betray Ruth."

"Telling the truth would hardly be betraying her, and in any case perhaps she has already owned up to her part in the incident; in which case you could return home without any problems."

"I never thought of it that way. Perhaps I could write a letter to my Aunt and Uncle and ask them the situation."

"Fear not my son, God works in mysterious ways. I am sure that when the time is right you will make the right decision."

Winter melted into spring and the landscape threw off its grey cloak. The woodlands around the cottage seemed to yawn and stretch as they awoke from their hibernation. Suddenly a great explosion of life burst out and the bright colours of early spring flowers filled the hillsides, accompanied by the buzz of insects and joyful songs of the birds.

The little churchyard was a mass of daffodils and bluebells, so on fine evenings the children would sing their hearts out amongst the flowers. Sometimes other local families joined them and an impromptu open-air service would develop.

Ben was growing stronger and more confident almost daily. He took on more and more the responsibility of improving the cottage and dealing with its day-to-day repairs. With the ever-faithful Tim never too far away they worked tirelessly clearing new areas for the garden, and repairing derelict walls.

When July arrived the weather was overpowering; for almost a week searing heat had brought everyone to a standstill. At last the swing was repaired and they took turns on it to cool down. One afternoon they were all seated in the shade watching as black clouds slowly built until it went as dark as night.

There was a slight rumbling noise, then moments later a brilliant flash and an almighty bang that echoed around the fells. Some of the children screamed and ran to hide in Emily's lap she cuddled them to her. The rain arrived in huge heavy drops that at first just patted the dust-dry earth, but within minutes the downpour was torrential. Everyone ran for cover to the cottage. At least now there was a freshness to the air and they sat almost in silence just listening to rhythm of the rain. Just as quickly as it had started it ended and within ten minutes the sun burst through the clouds breaking the spell.

"What is the date?" Ben suddenly asked.

"July twelfth 1802." Reverend Linton said a little surprised.

"I'm sixteen today" Ben declared.

There was pandemonium as everyone tried to congratulate him.

"I think that this calls for a party," Emily said. "you're a young man now."

One evening, after all his jobs were finished Ben sat on an old tree stump on the fell-top. He liked to sit on his own, and look down the hillside towards the cottage; he had grown to really love this place and felt more at home here than he had ever done anywhere before. In his hand he held the letter that had just reached him from his Uncle John. It was not good news; Ruth had not cleared his name and there was still a warrant out for his arrest. His uncle had filled the letter with other news and gossip and warned Ben not to come home yet.

"There you are Ben." Linton puffed as he climbed the last few yards up the hill. Linton sat down beside Ben, and for a short while, they both stared out over the scene in silence. A fresh breeze carried the sounds of the moorland birds and from somewhere to the south of them came the soulful sound of cattle waiting to be milked.

"May I ask about the letter?" Linton said.

"Ruth has not said anything to help my case. I fear she will be afraid of her father, not that he is wicked or anything but . . . oh I don't know."

"I'm awfully sorry. You know you can stay here as long as it takes. At least we have good news from Baxter; the constable in Settle has accepted my explanation that you were a prisoner of the gang. I did not tell him your name of course in case he knew of the other thing."

Ben looked a little surprised at Linton.

"The Lord allows us to make some judgements ourselves you know," Linton smiled. "How would you like to learn to drive the gig tomorrow?"

"Very much Sir," Ben said.

"Finlay's very busy these days with his farming. I don't like always to be asking him. The man's so kind hearted that he'll give you his time even when he can ill afford to."

"I know how to look after the tack already. I'd love to drive you Sir."

"Good then first thing in the morning we'll be off."

Sure enough over the next few days Ben learned to master driving the gig. Linton was always buzzing about the Parish on all kinds of business, which meant that he and Ben were together more and more. As they spent more time together, a deep, strong bond of friendship was forged between them. On all their journeys, they would spend their time talking; it never ceased to amaze Ben how much of the world Linton knew. No matter how far a distance they had to travel, there never seemed to be enough time for them to finish their conversations. One day they headed towards Barrow for Linton to attend a meeting of the parish council.

"Well here we are lad," Linton said as they arrived outside Barrow Town hall. "I should only be a couple of hours. Keep away from the waterfront; it's not safe down there any longer."

Ben kicked his heels for a while, and then decided to take a walk. He left the gig, he knew his way around the town and despite the warning, he found himself heading towards the busy docks. The protracted war with France and Europe was putting a tremendous strain on the countries resources of both men and ships. Old and captured vessels were being refitted and put back into service to try and maintain the navy's strength.

The needs of the Royal Navy to find a safe port away from the French coast had completely transformed this one-time sleepy port. The dockland area had become a warren of narrow streets and alleyways. The streets around the wharfs and warehouses were filled with milling people and everywhere seemed chaotic. Desperately the council was trying to stem the flood of violence and crime that swirled like a whirlwind through the streets. Cut-throats and thieves were drawn like vultures to a carcass. Now the onetime friendly town was festering like an open wound, infected by vice and poverty.

Wandering through the mayhem along the waterfront was an irresistible adventure. For just a moment, Ben leant against a stone wall and observed the goings on. Barrow-boys, ran along the streets pushing squeaky wheeled barrows with precarious loads that were piled so high, that they seemed to defy the laws of gravity. Street merchants worked from stalls selling all manner of goods, Ben felt exhilarated by the atmosphere. There was a heady smell; a mixture of fresh sawn wood, ship's tar, the sea, and tobacco smoke. All of this was accompanied by a cacophony of noise from every direction. Along one of the wharfs, a ship was unloading its cargo, and he watched fascinated as the derricks swung great nets filled with wooden crates ashore, where they were loaded to waiting wagons, which stood in line ready for the loads to be transferred.

He timed his return just right, and met Linton as he left the building, unaware that he been followed. Cold eyes watched from the cover of the opposite buildings.

"T'is 'im, sure enough. Well done Bren." Mace licked his lips as he watched.

"Seems as if our young friend's fallen in with some good company. I think 'e'd probably want to share 'is good luck wi'is old mates," Mace said.

Mace took Bren and another gang member, nicknamed Fang because of his irregular and rather large front teeth, with him as they followed the little gig, keeping well out of sight. Fortunately, when they were on the open road, their quarry was so busy talking that neither of them looked back.

"Was it a difficult meeting?" asked Ben

"Terrible. Nobody knows what the answer is. There are just too many conflicting interests to reach a satisfactory solution. The constant war with France is going to ruin this country forever." They were silent for a moment. "The whole world is going mad." Linton said with a sad shake of his head. They say the Jacobins are trying to gain support in the industrial towns of the midlands, and the textile towns of the north. They'll not be happy until England rebels against the Crown. Where will it all end?"

"Do you think there'll be a revolution here?"

"Who can tell? Word is that the King has gone completely mad. We must be ready for anything. I've seen towns like Manchester boil before, but never like this."

It was dark by the time they reached the fells, but Toby their old pony knew his way home and needed very little driving. He picked up his pace as they neared the gate no doubt thinking about his stall and the bag of meal waiting for him.

There was a general sigh of relief as they stopped in the farmyard. Ben and Linton exchanged smiles as the smell of cooking and fresh bread greeted them.

"I'll see to Toby Sir, I'm certainly ready for dinner."

Ben unharnessed the pony, and then let him into his stall.

"What's the matter boy?" Ben said. He could feel the animal's unease. Suddenly it seemed nervous, flaring its nostrils and scraping the ground with its front hoof. "What is it, a fox?" Ben fetched a bucket of water from the pump.

"Here, now settle down." He slapped the pony's solid neck. Out in the yard he stopped and listened to the sounds of the night, 'probably just a fox' he thought; everything seemed normal.

CHAPTER EIGHT

Mace had almost missed the entrance to the farm cottage, but Bren had pulled at his sleeve, showing him the gateway. Keeping close to the wall, they followed the track, quickly diving for cover as they rounded the corner and saw the cottage lights. Skirting in a wide arc around the brightly lit yard they reached the orchard.

From amongst the trees they had a perfect view of the cottage. A shaft of light cut across the yard as the stable door opened. A harsh sneer came to Mace's lips as he recognised the figure leaving the barn. From his belt he pulled a long, crude, vicious-looking blade and rubbed his thumb along its edge, enjoying its sharpness.

"I'll teach you a lesson." The words were no more than a hiss.

Following the wall they worked their way to the stonework of the cottage and then ducked down below the level of the windows and crawled round to the door.

Mace checked that everyone was ready and then with Bren to one side of the door, they burst in with a terrifying yell.

Emily had just put out a late supper on the table, the children were all in bed; she let out a scream and dropped the iron pan she was carrying, so that steaming hot potatoes bounced and rolled across the floor.

"Mace!" Ben yelled instantly recognising the leading figure.

He rolled from his chair, and instinctively searched for something to defend himself with. His fingers closed round the handle of the dropped pan. There was no time for thought. In a blur of speed, Mace made a grab for Ben, but Ben's fast reaction took him out of his grasp. The scrawny fingers pawed frantically at thin air accompanied by a frustrated menacing growl. Ben let fly with a backhanded swing, landing the pan square into Mace's face. Ben felt well satisfied with the blow: they say 'revenge is sweet' and at that moment all the fear and pain of the last few months flushed away. There was a loud clang as metal hit bone. Mace staggered backwards blood oozing from cuts above both eyes, and with a moan he slumped dazed against the kitchen sink.

The gang had temporarily halted, until Fang swept the things off the table with his arm and leapt across it at Ben. His long fingers locked round Ben's throat and the two of them rolled into the big open fireplace. As if crashing into the gates of hell, a great shower of sparks and red-hot embers flew into the air as they hit the fire grate. Both yelped as they felt the flames on their flesh. The hair on the back of Ben's head was smouldering as he rolled free.

Anger mixed with pain and a newfound confidence brought out the fight in him. Fang's clothes smouldered and smoked as he tried to stand; one side of his thin gaunt face was blistered and red.

Bren, who had stood confused by the sudden activity, crossed the room. Linton had to intention of letting the brute get to his family, the brave man, undaunted by Bren's size, he threw himself forward. His effort was wasted; he just bounced off the huge body. Bren stared down angrily at Linton and then knocked him out with one vicious punch, that shattered the nose bone.

Bren however was in for another surprise; Emily's maternal instinct overcame her fear, she picked up a heavy length of firewood, and smashed in down on the back of the huge bald head; the big man fell forward, a deep cut in the back of his scalp.

Mace had recovered a little and could see Ben through a bloody haze. He punched out with one hand and grabbed a chair with the other to steady himself. The punch landed squarely on Ben's cheek; it made his head spin and sent him crashing to the floor. However, he was still conscious enough to realise how vulnerable he was and tried to crawl for cover. Mace staggered forward and kicked Ben in the face. The blow whipped his head back, and Ben was sure his neck had broken. Desperately Ben rolled sideways under the solid protection of the kitchen table, the sweet taste of his own blood filled his mouth.

Fang, still in agony from the fire, leapt at Emily. She screamed as she felt the bony fingers sink deep into the soft flesh of her shoulder. Blindly she struck out with the log, hitting the man's wrist, knocking his hand away. In fear and panic she struck out wildly again. He held up his arm to defend himself from the torrent of blows, but she managed to land two telling strikes to the side of his face, that sent him staggering backwards.

Mace was throwing furniture left and right, trying to dig his way through to Ben who had managed to crawl completely under the table. When Ben heard Emily scream, he scrambled out determined to protect her. With a swinging punch, that landed on Fang's temple he knocked her attacker to the floor.

Ben was now at the opposite side of the table to Mace, and still suffering from the kick to the head. His vision was blurred but he tried to make his way to Emily and Linton.

Suddenly a chair hit him, thrown from across the table by Mace. It had not enough force to knock him over, but one of the legs caught his already painful face. Ignoring the pain, and in a fit of temper; Ben swung the chair like a club, and crashed it down onto the table, breaking a leg free.

Mace took a couple of backward steps, and then with an ear splitting yell launched himself across the room. He skimmed off the table top and without stretched arms managed to lock his fingers into Ben's hair dragging the two of them together. Ben could almost feel his brain bounce inside his skull as Mace head butted him twice.

Mace suddenly found the exertion too much; the initial blow to his face with the pan had finally taken its toll. He sank slowly to the floor still holding Ben who had now lost consciousness.

Fang did not intend to stay any longer as soon as he saw Mace fall, he began his retreat. On all fours, he crawled back outside. The cool air revived him a little, and he managed to stagger back to his feet, and then stumble his way across the yard towards the churchyard. A small stream ran along the side of the wall, he fell face down in the water, and washed his face. Gently he tapped water onto the tender scorched flesh of his cheek; it felt wonderfully cool. He looked back at the cottage, and was tempted to go back, but decided he was best out of it.

Back in the kitchen Mace slithered across the floor to where his blade had landed. As if drunk he lurched to his feet and closed in on Ben.

"Ben!" Emily cried from where she had slumped in the corner of the room. She held a log in front of her pointing at Mace, as if daring him to attack.

Through a muffled haze Ben heard her scream, it brought him to his senses again. He felt her hand on his arm and he managed to fight back to his feet. Emily's gaze was fixed on the cold eyes across the table that stared like the yellow eyes of a hungry wolf. Slowly Mace edged towards them making short stabbing actions with the blade. They managed to move together keeping the table between themselves and Mace. He herded them round the table.

"Get out of the way missis it's 'im I wants." Mace had to keep mopping at his brow to clear the blood from his eyes. Slowly they circled the table, Mace skilfully pushing them like a sheep dog with a couple of scared ewes. He reached his objective.

"Bren! Shake yer useless carcass." He pulled, and shook at the big man. "Come on!" He growled through clenched teeth. For a split second he took his eyes from Ben as he tried to lift Bren. Ben took a single great step and was within range to use the chair leg. Committing all his strength to the blow, Ben threw his arm in a great sweeping arc.

Some sixth sense must have warned Mace, and he ducked in the nick of time. Ben felt the agony of disappointment as his blow bounced off his enemy's shoulder. The momentum of the swing carried Ben closer to Mace. He saw the flash of the blade, but there was nothing he could do to get out of its way. The blade slashed across his chest, its tip scything through the thin material of his shirt, opening the flesh beneath in a straight six inch cut. The pain was instant. Ben clutched the wound that wept a crimson shower soaking the front of his shirt.

Emily struck once, twice, three times, against Mace's arm and the blade went spiralling into the air. She was relentless with her attack like a tigress defending her cub. She diverted her attention from Mace only long enough to strike Bren, as he slowly lifted himself to one knee.

The blade landed at the side of Ben; he closed his fingers around its handle. Hardly able to move, he rolled over onto his back. Mace was still ducking and weaving; trying to get beneath the attack from Emily, with one lunge, he took hold of her throat viciously trying to crush the windpipe. His back was towards Ben who despite the pain forced himself onto his knees, and at the same time he stabbed straight-armed with the blade, driving it into the man's thigh. Mace's arm dropped as a look of surprise and confusion crossed his face, and then a flurry of blows struck him. Almost on all fours he scrambled towards the open door. Escape now was his only thought. Ben staggered to the door after him, but there was no way he could give chase.

The entire parish was horrified and thrown into a total panic by the attack. The fells and towns were scoured for the gang. By the time the alarm had been raised, and the constable fetched from Grange, there was no trace of any of them. Bren had been the only one caught as he lay unconscious on the kitchen floor.

A few days later, after a second visit from the doctor, Ben and Reverend Linton sat in front of the fire in the kitchen, looking like a couple of battered war veterans. Ben, his chest and head bandaged, sat stiffly in a chair. Any sideways movement still caused him a great deal of pain.

"What'll happen to Bren?" Ben asked.

"Prison, they'll probably hang him, I'm afraid," Linton replied.

"I'm sorry to have brought this on you," Ben said.

He felt sickened and guilty; his eyes never left the flickering flames as he spoke. Deep inside, he wished that one day he could take his revenge on Mace.

"Don't be so down hearted, you're not at all responsible for what has happened."

Ben looked up at his friend, "you would find good in the devil himself I suspect."

However, Linton was a greatly changed man; since the attack he had lived on soup because chewing was far too painful a task. Most days he just sat by the fire in silence. He still sported a heavy bandage across his face to try and hold his nose straight until the break healed. Although he was brave about his injuries and would not admit that he was in pain, Emily knew that he was suffering.

"You have a visitor," Emily announced suddenly one morning as she appeared in the doorway. She opened the door and two of the town council, John Wiggins the treasurer, and Arthur Clayton the chairman entered. They stood a moment looking stiff and awkward, obviously taken aback by what they saw.

"Nice to see you two up and about," Clayton said. "You had us all worried for a little while."

Emily brought them a chair and offered tea.

"No thank you Mrs. Linton, most gracious of you to ask, but unfortunately we can only stay a moment." He turned towards Linton.

"How are you? We are all so worried about you." He said in a hushed tone full of sympathy.

"Oh . . . not too bad. I still keep getting a bit of headache, and the nose feels enormous." He spoke quietly, hoping that his wife would not hear.

"And what about you young man, how are you?"

"I'll mend I think, thank you Sir,"

"You will be pleased to know that some good has come from your unfortunate adventure," said the chairman. "We've had permission to increase the constable force in Barrow, and we've been able to force a great many of the ruffians out." A smug smile crossed his face.

"Out! Out where?" Linton sat forward in an unfamiliar aggressive manner.

"Well, out of the town of course." Clayton answered looking slightly confused.

"Surely they'll just congregate somewhere else. Just pushing them out doesn't solve a thing."

"Well, let someone else worry about them. The whole council is behind me on this issue, we must do something to preserve the town." Clayton indignantly puffed out his chest.

Linton sat back in his chair and tried to calm himself down a little before he replied. He glanced across the room towards Emily; she was staring at him, unused to seeing him red faced and angry.

"I am sorry gentlemen, but I am feeling a little weary," Linton said "Perhaps we could discuss this another time."

"Yes of course. Come on Wiggins," Clayton said. "Anyway I am glad that you are feeling better, and I hope we shall see you in town before long." He bowed politely to Emily, obviously relieved to be leaving.

CHAPTER NINE

---•◦❀◦•---

It was almost two months before either of them was fit enough to travel into Barrow again. Linton's nose had mended, but with a sharp kink just between his eyes; the headaches were not improving, and some days they were so bad that he was forced to stay in bed.

The council was scheduled to meet, and harsher measures of controlling the town's population were on the agenda. There had been four hangings and the jail was bursting at the seams. Almost daily there seemed to be some sort of disturbance, the constables were ever-present on the streets, and things were getting very much out of hand. Linton was determined to be present to try and cool things down. He leant on Ben as he climbed the steps of the council building.

"I have a friend on King Street by the name of Burrows, he owns the chandlers shop and yard. Go there and I will make my own way to his house after the meeting. Be very careful Ben."

King Street was in the old part of the town, a busy thoroughfare that ran from the main street to the naval dockyards; along its entire length were merchant's yards and shops. Ben wandered along, occasionally glancing down the alleys or peering into the windows of various shops as he looked for the one belonging to Linton's friend.

'NAUTICAL INSTRUMENTS & SHIPS CHANDLER'
'PROPRIETOR MR.P.A.BURROWS RN.'

The sign hung proudly outside the shop like a battle ensign, and was repeated on a small brass plate at the side of the little doorway. Ben cleaned a small circle in the centre of one of the tiny window panes, so that he could see inside. The shop looked deserted, but it was filled with a host of intriguing looking objects that hung along the walls and dangled from the dark ceiling beams.

A little bell above his head jingled tunefully as he pushed open the door. Inside there was an aromatic mix, a blend of soap, ropes, and tobacco. Stepping towards a high counter that bisected the room he felt a surge of excitement and anticipation. Just as he was about to call out, there was a shuffling sound from behind the counter and a muffled voice called out from somewhere out of sight "Just a minute."

Suddenly a head popped up, it beamed a broad smile at Ben. The face was round, and weathered, and was topped by a bright red woollen hat. Wisps of grey hair escaped from beneath the headgear, like steam from a leaking radiator.

"Now then young sir, to what do I owe this honour?" the man said. He adjusted the front of his jacket, pulling at the collar with both hands.

"Mr. Burrows?"

"Indeed yes. At your service young Sir" he clicked to attention.

"Reverend Linton sent me to see you sir."

"Indeed, then you must be Benjamin."

"Yes sir, but everyone calls me Ben." There was an awkward silence for a moment. Mr. Burrows put the heavy looking object he was holding carefully down on the counter top.

"I'm just mending it. It's a sextant you know." He lovingly caressed the polished brass instrument.

"What does it do?" Ben moved nearer the counter to take a better look.

"Do! Do! Dear me. Bless my soul." The old man cleared his throat as if about to give a speech. He paused at first as if thinking better of it, but then went into a long involved description of the full function of the instrument. Despite the slightly baffled look on the face of his audience he waded on through a deep mire of technical information.

"Now then m'lad. What about these?" With great pride, he withdrew a roll of parchment from a wooden trellis rather like a wine-rack. "These are my sea charts." Carefully he unrolled the parchment. "What do you think to that?"

The parchment had discoloured slightly, but the decorative images around the edges were bright and vibrant. With care, he placed a couple of heavy lead weights at the corners to stop the chart rolling itself back up.

"Marvellous Sir."

Burrows glowed with pride, "you are right young Sir, and they are indeed marvellous." He straightened out a crease across one corner.

The edges were beautifully decorated with a variety of sea creatures, all drawn and coloured with great care, and the map's legend was written out in a flowing italic hand as glorious as any religious manuscript.

"Did you visit all these places?"

"Indeed yes. All these charts are my work."

"You are indeed a fine artist sir."

"I like you young sir," Burrows said with a broad grin, "but I think you are a flatterer."

They unrolled several other charts. Ben felt a pang of envy and excitement as Burrows chattered on about his adventures at sea.

When Linton arrived, Ben could hardly believe that the time had passed so quickly.

"May I call to see you again sir?" Ben asked as he was about to leave.

"I would be honoured if you could find the time young sir."

They left and headed back towards the fells chatting the whole way, with Ben doing all the talking for once.

"What did you think of Mr. Burrows?" Linton finally managed to get a word in.

"He's an interesting man."

"I've spent many a happy hour in the back of his shop, listening to his tales of the sea." Linton said with a smile.

"Would you mind if I did go to see him again?"

"You may go anytime you wish, and if I know Burrows, he'll be only too glad to see you."

Ben's dreams that night were of sea battles and pirates, exotic places and sailing the high seas. He told Tim all about his visit, as they sat on the ends of their beds that night.

The visit began a friendship that was to have a remarkable effect on Ben's life. Despite the age gap, they were soon good friends.

"Will you teach me to use these instruments and draw like you do?" Ben said one day to his new friend.

"Yes of course m'lad, I'd be delighted. Now, I've something very special to show you."

Burrows appeared with a parcel wrapped in oilskin. With great ceremony, he placed it on the counter.

"What is it?"

"Wait and see."

Slowly he unwrapped the covering, to reveal a polished wooden box twenty inches long and eighteen inches wide. The lid of the box was inlaid with exquisite marquettery depicting a sea battle. Ornate brass hinges matched a neat lock that protected the contents from unauthorised eyes.

"What is it?" Ben said with boyish enthusiasm.

"Be patient young friend."

Burrows produced a small key from a chain around his neck; teasing Ben he stopped to polish the lid before he inserted the key. Slowly he turned it, and then he lifted the lid and removed a thin silk cover. Ben breathed a low whistle as two perfectly matched pistols snuggled in a nest of vivid red velvet were revealed. The light of the lamp glinted along their long, slender, blue steel barrels. Each of the polished wooden handles was inlaid with a rampant lion crest made from mother of pearl.

"Hawkes himself gave me these after the battle of Quiberon Bay, back in fifty-nine. I was only a young lad myself then." He said with a wistful look in his eyes.

"What a battle that was. We were aboard the Royal George, a fine ship o'the line. We'd been stationed off Brest for I don't know how long. The weather had been bad for weeks, and there was no sign of it letting up. One night a westerly gale hit us; it was so fierce that it forced us off our station, and we had to set course back to Torbay to find shelter. De Conflans, the French Admiral, took his chance and put to sea with twenty-one ships of the line, including the Frenchies most famous flagship the Soleil Royal." He wiped a little speck of dust from the barrel of one of the guns, but Ben urged him on with the story.

"Where was I? Ah . . . yes. The weather was still bad. Word reached us that their fleet had moved. We went in hot pursuit; De Conflans was forced to take refuge in Quiberon Bay. He hoped that the devilish tides and shoals around the bay would protect him. But Hawkes was not a man to be put off, and England sorely needed a victory. 'Burrows!' He said to me. 'I want you to take us in.' it was my proudest moment: stood by Hawk's side, I navigated us safely through the shoals. It was hard nerve-racking work, the wind trying to push us onto the shore the whole time. We caught their rearguard completely off guard. The French seventy-four gunner 'Formidable' flagship of Rear-Admiral Verger and the 'Heros' were so badly damaged that they were forced to strike their colours within the first few hours of the battle. That night we anchored across the bay as tight as a cork in a bottle, there was no escape for the French, and they knew it.

We had not had it all our own way, and that first day we had suffered some losses, in particular the 'Essex' and 'Resolution' both were sunk. There was no thought of turning back; Hawkes was determined to have a conclusive victory. We'd kept them bottled up before, which meant we were as tied as them, but this time Hawkes wanted more. By the end of the second day, eleven of the Frenchman had been captured, or sunk, and when the dawn finally broke on the third, we could see the 'Soleil', almost totally dismasted. But before we could attack, they grounded her. The remainder of their fleet took refuge up the River Vilaine, where they were forced to remain for the next two years. They say the French had plans to invade England, and that Hawkes's victory prevented it." He sat back, a glow of pride across his ruddy face.

"And the pistols?" Ben asked excitedly.

"The admiral said if it had not been for my navigation, we should have run aground ourselves. The pistols belonged to old Conflans, and were taken as part of the prize. Hawkes gave them to me we sailed out of the Bay. He was a cool customer, and every man-jack aboard respected him, and knew that there were very few other men could have taken us in and out of that battle so skilfully."

Ben touched the stock of one of the pistols. Burrows lifted it out, and let him feel the weight and balance of the weapon.

"They're beautiful."

"They're deadly accurate too. Made by one of France's best known gunsmiths."

Ben turned it over in his hand and for the first time saw the ornate firing hammer, covered with interlocking scrolls. Carefully he replaced the pistol in its nest. His fingers traced the decorative artwork and the beautifully worked compartments along the bottom edge of the box, containing shot and cleaning implements. There was a small powder horn, made from silver with an ivory neck that sat in its own cut-out, and a tool for casting shot for the pieces.

Burrows gave both pistols a wipe with a piece of soft cloth, then rewrapped the box and returned it to its place beneath the counter.

"Were you in many battles?"

"Enough to fill a book lad." He nodded his head sagely, and then sat on a three legged stool. He made himself comfortable. "The best bit of sailing I ever did was when I was transferred to serve with Captain James Cook on the Endeavour. A rum Yorkshireman he was," he laughed loudly. "Been captain of a collier out of Whitby, but what he didn't know about navigation wasn't worth knowing. We sailed to Canada and mapped Newfoundland and along the coast. We got back to Portsmouth in seventy-one, and I was forced to retire, a couple of old wounds were giving me trouble. That's when I came up here; my Aunt, God rest her soul, owned this place then. It was just a chandlers, I added all the other stock. I need an assistant, you could come and stay here through the week and go back to the fells for Sundays."

Ben was a little taken aback by the offer, but it had his mind racing. "Do you mean it?"

"Yes of course, we can work on the charts and go out in my boat. Maybe catch something for tea, and I could teach you to navigate by the stars and the sun.

When Ben returned to the cottage, he waited until he was alone with Linton.

"Sir I would like to take a job working for Mr. Burrows." He somehow felt a little guilty about asking.

"Indeed, and what does that gentleman have to say about it."

"It was in fact his suggestion Sir. I thought I might stay there through the week and return here to help with the work at the weekends. If that's alright with you?"

"Indeed it is. A young man needs a trade, and Burrows is just the man to give you one."

"Thank you sir."

"I hope that you will come here to see us regularly; we should all miss you if you didn't."

"Don't worry about that Sir." Ben's spirits soared with the words.

Tim cried when Ben told him, but Ben offered some comfort by saying that he would relate all Mr. Burrows stories to him whenever he came back to the cottage.

Emily gave him a big hug and kiss before he left, which almost had him staying, but he was thankful to be away.

So that settled it, and Ben moved into the little shop. Burrows cleared out what had been his Aunt's room and Ben made himself at home. From its window, Ben could just see the docks between the gable ends of the other houses. Each night he would sit on the windowsill and watch the lights of the town. Most times, he would imagine himself in the exotic places his friend spoke of. True to his word, every Saturday he went back to stay with the Lintons, and catch up on some of his jobs there. Most of the time, was spent telling them all about what had gone on at the shop that week. Early Monday morning he would ride back into town on a little pony Mr. Burrows had lent him.

The shop stocked a huge range of hardware, and ironmongery, as well as ships requirements which kept it busy the whole time. Ben fitted in very well, and soon got to know the regulars; mostly ladies buying soap and household goods. He liked the life of being a shopkeeper, it was not glamorous, but he felt safe and secure within its structure. Whenever naval officers came in Ben would try to be the one to serve them. It allowed him to show off his newly acquired knowledge.

As the weeks went by Burrows left more and more of the work to Ben, enjoying the freedom of being able to work on his beloved charts. Each day he would lay them out and begin colouring and filling in details from hundreds of margin notes he'd made. For hours they worked silently. Ben began reading and drawing charts, copying out some of the old ones that had become a little tatty. Burrows with his red cap pulled tightly over his ears made an odd sight, looking like a strange porcupine because of the number of brushes and pens woven into the cap so as to be handy when he needed them.

"You're doing mighty well now my boy," Burrows said admiring Ben's latest effort. "Your young eyes can see the detail better than my old ones these days."

On days when the shop was quiet, they would hardly exchange a word, just sitting bowed over their charts, absorbed in the detail. Other times Burrows would give Ben lessons in navigation, how to use the charts and various instruments involved. Occasionally he would look up, rub his eyes and stare at the old clock ticking away on the mantle-shelf. "I think we've had enough for today," he would say and wander away to make a pot of fresh tea for himself and Ben. But there was always time for another tale.

Burrows had a small ketch-rigged sailing boat he left moored in the docks, and on fine days they would sail along the coast. Occasionally they would venture out into open water to give Ben experience of navigation. They were enjoyable days out, and they had plenty of time to fish and chat. Quite often they would sail round the headland into Morecambe Bay to the little church on the beach at Aldingham. There was always plenty of driftwood and fallen branches for them to make a fire and cook some fish. With the boat beached safely they had plenty of time before the next tide to enjoy their picnic.

"Did you never want to be a captain?" Ben asked.

"No, not really, anyway to be a captain you need a sponsor, patrons they call 'em. Someone with plenty of money who can help with your career."

"You were a ship's Master though."

"Ah yes, but you took an exam for that, not like the Lieutenant's exam, I had to go to Trinity House in London to do that."

"I think you would have made a fine Captain." Ben said.

"Aye well, look lively there and pull in that sail or I'll have you keel-hauled."

CHAPTER TEN

———— ❀ ————

Winter's arrival came as a severe shock after such a mild autumn; blizzards suddenly turned the fells into a featureless wilderness. Despite the weather, Ben still trudged back to the cottage on a weekend. On bitterly cold nights, to pass the time he sang sea shanties Burrows had taught him, but failing to remember the words he had to be content with humming and la la la-ing the song.

One particular night a shiver suddenly shook right through him, gripping him with a sense of urgency, and digging in his heels he urged the pony forwards. As he climbed the fells the snow thickened and he was forced to dismount and lead the pony.

Ben reached the track that led to the cottage and was delighted to see the welcoming mellow glow from the cottage kitchen window greet him. He suddenly felt much warmer.

"Oh Ben! Thank goodness you've arrived." Emily had dashed out into the night as soon as she spotted him coming down the track.

"What is it?"

"It's Linton; he's been gone most of the day, he should have been back hours ago."

"Where did he go?"

"The Frampton's, they've a small holding down near Alithwaite."

"How on earth did he travel, surely the gig couldn't get out on the roads as they are?"

"You know how strong willed he is; he rode the old mare."

"What about Finlay?"

"We've not seen him since the weather closed in; his farm is so isolated it'll be spring before we see him again. I can't leave the children." There was desperation in her voice.

"What on earth possessed him?" Ben declared.

"The Frampton's are so very poor, I saw them a month ago in Cartmel, and the children looked half starved then. He just took a few provisions for them."

"I'll go to Alithwaite, I'm sure I know where their cottage is."

"Be careful Ben," she said taking hold of his hand. "Take a drop of brandy first to warm you, and here, I've some fresh bread to take to them too."

Ben stood a moment to get warm by the familiar fire, he tried to remember the directions to the Frampton's cottage and work out his route. Emily handed him a silver hip flask and a bulky package in a waterproof cloth, then in a motherly fashion, rearranged his woollen scarf around his neck. It suddenly dawned on her how he was changing; no longer a boy but a man, the stubbly facial shadow, and the obvious strength of his jaw line; embarrassed, she withdrew her hand.

The urgency of the situation, and his own anxiety were a terrific defence against the cold.

"I'll be as quick as I can, but try not to worry it may be better to shelter the night with the Frampton's." Ben said.

Emily watched him leave, the knuckle of her thumb gripped firmly between her front teeth. She knew she would not sleep that night and tried to make herself comfortable by the fire.

The descending journey down the fell road was very difficult; the pony skidded and hopped through the ever-increasing snowdrifts that were built up by a strengthening wind. Sometimes the snow reached the pony's shoulders, forcing the creature to advance in a series of unsteady hops and stumbles. Ben was forced to dismount and lead the pony again. They both walked head down to keep their faces out of the bitter wind, Ben prayed that Linton had had the good sense not to try and venture home.

Occasional dense, blinding flurries of snow began complicating the journey, and with hardly any landmarks and the poor visibility, Ben realised he was in danger of losing his way. Arriving at where he thought the Frampton's cottage should be, he was confused slightly because at first glance there was nothing there, apart from a huge drift. Then a weak flickering light showed through a half buried window to give away its location beneath a curved snowdrift that completely covered the cottage. Digging with his hands in the cold snow, he managed to find the doorway, and then hammered with his fist on the woodwork. A sallow face with deep sunken eyes peeped around the door at him.

"Is Reverend Linton here?"

"Yes sir," the man answered.

Knocking off as much snow as he could before entering he followed into the cottage. The sight inside which greeted him stopped him cold; five children wrapped in sacking blankets were huddled together with their mother beside a few dying embers in the fire grate. Linton, wrapped in a blanket, was laid on a wooden cot alongside the fire. Ben approached carefully almost afraid to make a sound. It was almost as cold inside as it was out. He was pleased to see Linton's eyelids flutter slightly, and then partially open.

"It's you my boy. I'm sorry to be a nuisance," he croaked.

"Here take a sip of this." Lifting Linton's head slightly he placed the flask to his friend's lips who gratefully took a sip, then immediately began to cough. Once the coughing fit had abated, he nodded to Ben for another drink.

"Thank you my boy."

"We didn't know what to do with him." Frampton said.

The man trembled slightly, slowly sinking back to his chair as if the effort of speech was too great.

"Do you not have any firewood?"

"My husband's been too ill to chop it. We have plenty of logs by the barn, but they're too heavy for us to move. I've tried to cut them, but I can hardly lift the axe." With thin fingers, the woman pulled her ragged shawl tighter over her arm as she spoke.

"Show me!" Ben demanded, and then remembered the bread. "Here, for you and the children." He gave the flask to Frampton, "take a drink sir it will help."

There was delight on everyone's face as four golden loaves tumbled out of the package, immediately Mrs. Frampton began cutting one of them up.

"You're a lifesaver Sir," she said bowing and kissing Ben's hand.

Feeling more than a little embarrassed Ben wrapped his coat against the weather, and went out to the small lean-to barn. First he took in his pony out of the weather, found where Linton's old mare was, and gave them both water and hay, then digging both axe and logs from beneath the snow he dragged them into the barn doorway. Spitting in both palms he picked up the axe and began to chop the wood like a man possessed. He was soon into a steady rhythm with his swings, sending wood chippings flying in all directions. Two of the biggest children had come to watch and help him, and as the chippings flew towards them, they giggled and made a game of trying to dodge them.

Ben conscripted them into taking in the first manageable pieces, and then resumed his cutting. He carried in the next load, which was gratefully received and then stacked them near the fire. Satisfied that the fire was picking up, he returned to his work out in the barn. He was warm enough now.

After working non-stop for two hours his back felt as though it would never straighten again. He wrapped a bandage of sacking around the blisters that were bulging like white slugs across his hands. Leaning against the axe shaft for a moment, he studied with satisfaction the result of his labours.

A huddled figure wrapped in a sackcloth cloak ran from the cottage.

"Here drink this, it'll keep out the cold."

"Thank you, "Ben looked a little suspiciously at the steaming brew.

"It's dandelion tea. It's very good."

"Thank you ma'am. I'm afraid I can't do any more tonight," he showed her his palms.

"Come in, I'll fix them for you."

The fire burned brightly, filling the room with light and warmth and Ben felt that his labours had been well worth it. He sat at a rustic table as the children, who had all regained a little colour, gathered around him to look at the wounds.

"Out of the way you lot," Mrs. Frampton said.

"How's the tea?"

"Very nice thank you," he said. He smiled and took another sip of the slightly bitter infusion.

"Give me your hand," she said.

Ben winced slightly as she smeared a thick oily cream into his palms; she was obviously used to administering to cut hands and such minor wounds. Immediately it took the sting out of the blisters.

"Mrs. Frampton is quite famous here about for her remedies and teas." Mr. Frampton boasted.

"Oh hush your flattery Bill Frampton."

"Well it's certainly done the trick." Ben said rubbing his palms together to rub in the cream.

Later Ben sat on the floor beside the Reverend, as the children slept in a heap across the hearth from him. He tried to sleep, but his mind was too active to let him rest. The light from the fire was now the only light in the room and he watched the ghostly shadows it sent dancing along the walls. Occasionally a log would settle and fall in the hearth, sending up a flight of tiny red-hot sparks that flew like fireflies up the chimney. He wished there was some way to get a message to Emily, to tell her that they were alright; he knew she would wait up for them, all night if needs be. He pictured her sat waiting at the kitchen table, her fine features highlighted by the soft glow of the table oil lamp.

He drifted into a light sleep, his dreams taking him back to one beautifully fine day many years before. It was early autumn, and he and Ruth had gone to the moors to gather wild blackberries along the hedgerows. She had been skipping and hopping, making up silly songs as she danced in the heather like a fairy. Wearing only a thin cotton skirt and blouse that seemed to hide nothing of her slender figure, he was besotted by her. Ruth caught him staring at her; she smiled a secretive smile, which was hardly a movement of her lip, just enough to snare her prey. Slowly she had approached him; when they stood within inches of each other, she traced a sprig of heather over his handsome features. There was a kiss waiting on her lips but as Ben moved to capture it she skipped away, laughing brightly, teasing him with a little dance, making sure the full length of her developing legs were on show.

The weather forced them to stay another two days with the Frampton's as the snow had drifted so high that travel was completely out of the question. When finally the weather eased a little, Ben wanted to go back to the fell cottage on his own, fearing that Linton was still not strong enough to travel, but Linton would have none of it and insisted that he go back with him, arguing that he was too much of a burden on the Frampton's to stay any longer.

"I do apologise for us being such an extra burden upon you." Linton said as they were finally about to leave.

"Not so Reverend, Ben has more than earned what meagre fare we offer." He looked towards the huge pile of cut logs beside the cottage door.

They made slow progress back up the fell road, having to plough forwards through the drifts. Linton had wrapped a thick blanket around his shoulders, to try fight off the bitterly cold weather. Most of the way they travelled in silence except for the sound of them breaking the frozen crust that topped the snow.

"I'm sorry my boy for being such a fool. But I feel so useless these days; if I can't tend my flock when they're in need, what use am I?"

Ben wanted to say something to ease his friend's discomfort, but he could not find the right words; he placed a comforting hand on Linton's arm.

Emily threw her arms around her husband the instant he appeared in the yard outside the cottage. She held his head between her hands, and gently kissed it. "I was so worried!"

"I'm sorry my dear. The snow was too bad to get home again."

She put her arms around Ben's neck and catching him slightly off guard she kissed his cheek. "Are you too old to be hugged?" she teased with a gentle smile.

They exchanged smiles, "I must get back to Barrow. Mr. Burrows will wonder if I'm safe."

It was a real effort for Ben to leave the fells, only now did he realise just how strong his feelings for the Lintons had become, and although they were not his real family his feelings for them could not have been greater if they had been.

The going was tough and he had to walk his pony all the way off the fells, but thankfully the coast road was almost clear, which made the journey a little easier.

Five weeks passed before the weather finally eased. Ben had been busy working for Mr. Burrows with more of the charts, but he was unable to return to the fells on a weekend as usual, and he was worried just what was happening and how everyone was.

The answer to that came very abruptly. Emily sent an urgent message to Ben with one of the parishioners asking him to return to the cottage as quickly as possible.

Mr. Burrows said he was to go at once and not to rush back this time if the Lintons needed him.

"I came as soon as I could" he said, as he entered the familiar kitchen doorway.

"It's bad news Ben." Emily leant heavily against the side of the open fireplace as she spoke. Her voice was quiet, soft, but sad and Ben placed an arm around her shoulders, trying to comfort her. She had always seemed so strong, so independent; he had never seen her look like this.

"He'd just finished the sermon and as he stepped out of the pulpit, he just fell to the floor." She stopped a minute to catch her breath. "It was the first service for weeks. Finlay and a couple of others carried him over here. Fortunately Dr. Morris was in the congregation, and was in immediate attendance."

Ben guided her to a seat by the fire. He wanted to ask a whole string of questions, but did not like to interrupt.

"He is so ill, and he did so want to see you. It has not been the same since you left." A huge sob shook her whole body, made worse by the fact that she tried to suppress it.

"Can I see him?"

"He was asleep when I left him a few moments ago, but I'm certain he would be overjoyed to know you were here."

As quietly as he could, he climbed the narrow staircase. When he reached the door, he gently pushed it open, just far enough for him to take a look. He gasped at what he saw. Linton looked to have aged twenty years, his breathing was rapid and with each breath there was a slight chest noise, followed by a groan. Standing by the side of the bed hardly daring to breathe Ben watched in silence. Suddenly the eyes flickered open; they lit up when they saw him.

"Oh Ben! You should not have troubled." He tried to sit up.

"It was no trouble, and anyway the fells are too beautiful to miss at this time of year." He said trying to make light of his effort.

"How are you?"

"Not too bad now." Linton lied.

"I'm going to stay on a few days, or until you're better. Mr. Burrows can manage, he sends his kindest regards."

Ben was the tonic Linton needed. Two days after his arrival, he was up again; his face was still a ghostly grey and deeply furrowed, but his eyes had managed to climb from the depths of the deep, black pits they had sunk into.

Each day saw some improvement. The snow finally cleared, until only in sheltered places beside dry stone walls or under hedgerows was there any trace remaining; once again Spring, with its bright rush of yellow daffodils reached the fells. Each day sitting together on an old wooden bench overlooking the churchyard, they enjoyed the warm spring sunshine. With a blanket over their shoulders to keep out the chill of the wind, it seemed like old times again; sometimes they would talk non-stop, and other times just sit and watch the world go by. It was a time of very simple, peaceful enjoyment that Ben would often recall later in his life.

One evening after the children and Linton had been put to bed, Ben and Emily were walking through the orchard. The air was heavy with the scents from the great clouds of blossom that hung heavily from the branches. They sat on the swing and just for a moment they enjoyed the peace.

"I have decided that we must get other homes for the children." In the dim light, she could not see any expression on Ben's face. Ben made no immediate response; he fidgeted with the rope of the swing, almost trying to avoid an answer.

"You know how ill he is, I just don't have the time to look after him and the children."

"Have you discussed it with . . ." he always had the urge to call Linton his father, but had never dared. Not remembering his natural father, Ben had always thought that if he had been able to choose one, Linton would be the one he would have gone for.

"No, not yet," her voice was sad, almost inaudible. "I feel to be letting him down so, but I'm not strong enough to do everything." She hung her head, and let out a single sob into her hands.

"Please don't upset yourself, you've given all you possibly could," he said.

His arm slipped around her shoulder and they sat together motionless for a while, until the sudden call of a fox in the nearby trees broke the spell.

Linton was understandably upset, but he realised how difficult it had been for Emily to cope with everything. He wept unashamedly as the last of the children left to go to their new homes. All the children faced the new prospects differently, some refused at first to leave, but their new guardians promised them that they could come see the Lintons whenever they wanted. Timothy tried to act the little tough, as ever, but the thin veneer shattered when the time for him to leave arrived. Ben helped all he could; he gave the Lintons the strength they were both suddenly short of. He ferried the children to their new homes in the gig, making sure they were settled before he left them.

"I feel so terribly guilty." She said to Ben after the last of the children had gone. "It's so quiet, any moment I expect one of them to rush in. Did I do wrong?"

"No not you. I did! I came and destroyed your world; if there is guilt here then it's mine alone," Ben said solemnly.

"Don't blame yourself, neither of us would change anything. You brought him, both of us so much happiness. Perhaps this is a punishment. Perhaps no one has the right to be as happy as we all were." There was no bitterness in her voice, but there was an edge to it that had never been there before.

There were some bright days, when the pain was not too bad, and then Linton would seem to be his old self again. The extraordinary weather of the summer seemed to help, the long days of July and August were hot, without a cloud to be seen anywhere. The bench swing in the orchard was in full use every day, and gallons of cool fruit drinks were consumed amongst the welcome shade of the trees. Without the children to worry about, Emily was on top of everything again.

Ben was torn between the Lintons and his friend Burrows, whom he had only managed to call and see three or four times since the spring.

"Would you mind if I went into Barrow for a few days?"

"Not at all." Linton said, trying to keep cool by wafting himself with his straw hat.

CHAPTER ELEVEN

---·•✸•·---

"I'll be back for the weekend."

Reading the sign pinned to the door; 'back at four o'clock.' Ben was very disappointed that after his long journey Burrows was obviously out somewhere, perhaps on an errand. He considered his options for a moment; it was most unusual for Burrows to leave the shop during business hours, but he decided there was nothing he could do for the time being but wait. Perhaps his friend had gone down to his boat.

The excitement of the quay side beckoned him, and rather than just sit on the doorstep he decided to walk down to the docks and find his friend. Ben found the whole atmosphere of the docks thrilling; the dockside was in its usual state of confusion, two large barges were in and busy unloading their cargoes, bales of wool stacked high waited to be loaded onto the barges, along with cut timber, hides and a number of large barrels. Heavy horses attached to solid wooden wagons waited patiently in the summer heat with their heads bowed as if dozing; once their wagon was filled they clomped forwards and away to their next destination.

There was a great deal of activity. H.M.S. Seagull, a third rate seventy-four gunner that had been badly crippled during the mid-Atlantic sea battle known as 'The Glorious First of June' had been under repairs in the docks for nearly four years and was about to sail back into service. He decided to take a look at her before she departed.

She was a wonderful sight, and Ben stared in awe. Fighting fit again, her masts tall and newly varnished, her sailcloth neatly furled, she sat proudly like a newly fledged eagle waiting for the wind to carry her across the water. Her ship's boats buzzed around her like bees with their queen, fetching and carrying supplies and men, servicing her every need. Her new officers and Captain had arrived, but as usual, she was short of hands, and so the press-gang was sent into town to look for any likely volunteers. The navy called on a number of local thugs to help round up likely victims in exchange for immunity from having to serve themselves, which meant that the handling of prospective candidates was not too kind. Ben cut down a narrow alley that led onto the quay side. Suddenly both ends filled with men. Alarm bells rang in his head as he realised that he was trapped. Standing his ground, he waited for the men to close in, realising that escape was impossible. There was little else to do.

"Well what have we here?" One of the sailors advanced on him, a tough looking character with tattooed arms and a shaggy beard. "We're looking for volunteers to serve his Majesty King George. It seems to me, that you might like to volunteer."

"No! I can't!" he kept his voice steady.

"No! Did you hear that? This 'ere one's said, no! Thing is mi'lad I have a warrant 'ere signed by the king 'imself that says for this bright shiny shilling you'll be only too pleased to 'elp out." He held aloft the coin.

There was a movement behind Ben and he turned quickly, but too late. Hands grabbed him from all directions; he fell to the floor beneath the free-for-all scrum. He fought and struggled like a man possessed, but in vain and he never saw the cosh as it swung down onto the back of his head.

Dropping through a swirling grey void, he lost consciousness; pain engulfed him, and then melted away, only to return with sharper fangs than before. Through the whistling and clanging of his dazed mind, he could hear a sound; somehow, he recognised it, and yet it seemed very alien to him. He tried to listen, but concentration made his headache even worse.

It was the evening of the following day before his mind began to function again. His mouth was dry, his eyes refused to open. Slowly his senses returned and he realised that he was laid face down in a thick litter of not too clean straw; there was an unusual tremble to the floorboards and the whole thing was definitely moving from side to side. He quickly worked out that he was on board a ship and that it had obviously set sail.

Shaking himself, he sat upright, but there was very little light for him to get his bearings. Something near him stirred, he held his breath a moment.

"OOOH! "The untidy heap beside him let out an eerie moan.

The dark, dusty air in the hold was split by a couple of shafts of weak light that found their way in through cracks in the woodwork. With his head still ringing, Ben tried to crawl away from the sound.

"OOOH! I'm dead! I'm dead, and I've landed in 'ell. Holy Mother." The bundle wriggled and moving like a caterpillar.

"I don't think you are." Ben said trying to sound reassuring.

"T'is the sound of the devil himself." The voice wailed with a strong Irish accent.

"No sir."

"I'm not dead you say." Suddenly the heap came upright. "What right have you to go frightening a poor soul to death?"

"I could hardly have frightened you to death, if you believed yourself to be dead already."

"My name's Fletcher, my friends call me Fletch." He held out his hand and the two shook. "Lord preserve us. Are we aboard a navy ship?"

"Yes—I think so."

"Then we'll both think that I was right about being in 'ell; it'll be better than what's in store for us."

"What do you mean?" Ben said.

Suddenly the hinge on the hatch above them creaked as it opened, a voice boomed in at them.

"Come on you miserable swine, get up here!" Ben staggered to his feet, but a sudden rush of bodies heading for the steps knocked him flying. He had not realised that there were others around him. There was a shock waiting for them all, because the docks and dry land had vanished. They were already well out to sea. Like lost children, they stood in a ragged cluster on the deck in the blazing sunlight.

"Is this the best you could do Boson."

"Aye 'fraid so Capt'n."

"I'll go back, if we're not suitable for you sir." Fletch offered.

There was a loud crack as a knotted piece of rope landed hard across his back. He sank to his knees.

"Anyone else got a comment." The boson shouted.

Captain William Mitchell looked the men over. He liked to think of himself as an excellent judge of character. He stopped at Ben who returned his stare with a slightly defiant look.

"Name?"

Ben, hesitated he was reluctant to use his own name of Stone, afraid that somehow the Captain might know it in connection with the death of Master Hutton-Beaumont.

"Burrows. Benjamin Burrows." A sharp thump in the middle of his back knocked the wind from him.

"Sir! You say Sir when addressing the Capt'n." The boson barked in his ear.

"Burrows Sir." Ben corrected, his eyes wandering to the knotted rope that the boson snapped across his open palm.

They were kept on deck for some time as the Captain discussed with his officers something of pressing urgency on the poop deck. Finally, the mate led them to their quarters; each man was issued with a rough cloth hammock, a pewter plate and mug.

"Look after these fine wares mi lads, or the King'll charge you for 'em if they're lost." The boson shouted with a loud laugh, " an' take good care o'yer hammock or we'll not be able to bury you in style."

The weather was very kind to the new hands and Seagull had a chance to stretch her new canvass without excessive strain. She cut the water holding her line perfectly in balance. The shipwrights had done their work well.

That day a small cutter was spotted approaching, obviously chasing them. Seagull slowed allowing the other ship to come alongside.

"Ahoy there, a message for Captain Mitchell."

A young rating clambered on board Seagull with a leather satchel slung around his shoulders.

Barraclough took the satchel and went below to the Captain's cabin.

"It seems we are to meet up with a small flotilla off the Irish coast. It seems a little bit strange; our last orders were to head for the Med."

"Do they need a reply Captain?" asked Barraclough.

"No; send the lad back with my thanks to his Skipper."

The Captain called his officers to a meeting and explained the very brief message to them, "it appears we will get further orders from the ships that will act as our escort, so for the time being we will change course and rendezvous with them off the southern tip of Ireland."

It was obvious to the crew that they were now under new orders as the ship veered onto its new heading. As usual, speculation was rife as to where the destination would be and what was going on.

Sat eating his evening meal, which was a thick broth of uncertain origins and biscuits, Ben was quite philosophical about his predicament. He thought that at least now he could not bring any more problems to the Lintons and that he could have been much worse off with Mace, or if he had been caught by the constable and sent to prison or worse. At least now, with his new identity, he was safe from discovery for a while.

The following day Ben clung desperately to the ropes as he climbed higher up the swaying, lurching main mast. He could hear the voice far below shouting orders, but the breeze carried the words away, and anyway he had only one thing on his mind and that was not falling off. When he finally reached the relative security of the platform half way up he blew a sigh of relief. Following the more experienced hands, he inched his way along the yardarm; gripping the broad timber with his arms he slid his feet gingerly along the thick rope slung below the yardarm.

"Don't look down! "Fletch advised.

"My knees are shaking so bad I can hardly move," Ben yelled.

He tried to rest against the timber, but he felt the bile rise in his guts. The mast swayed wildly and he vomited out over the grey waves. The yardarm jolted and kicked when the wind caught the sail, spinning Ben around on the timber; he hung upside down somehow managing to cling on with his ankles locked together. For a moment, he stared at the upside down world, until the realisation of the danger he was in hit him. Fletch grinned down at Ben. "Now don't you be showing off just 'cause the Captain's on the poop," he said laughing heartily.

With agile ease, he swung down, caught the back of Ben's shirt, and hoisted him up to safety.

"You've done that before I think," said Ben

"Aye a couple of times."

"Thank you, I owe you my life."

"You'll not be so quick to thank me after a few weeks in this hell hole." Fletch said with a broad grin.

Day after day as Seagull cut through the waves, the men ran up and down the great web of rigging, until each one knew exactly his task. Ben was beginning to feel a little more at ease aloft, but he was always pleased when they were back on deck. He and the Irishman Fletch were becoming good friends and Ben was always ready to listen to his advice on how best to survive life in the navy.

The day was spent in the ordinary duties of navy life, and on an evening when their watch was over the crew would divide into eight-man messes to eat and entertain themselves in telling stories of things most rare and wonderful. The genuine old tars were as adept at spinning yarns as sailing the ship. Some of them, in respect of variety and length of story, were as good as any of the giants of literature. To this yarn-spinning was added the most humorous singing, sometimes dashed with a streak of the pathetic, which was most touching; especially one very plaintive melody, with a chorus beginning with, "Now if our ship should be cast away, it would be our lot to see old England no more."

"Have you sailed with this captain before?" Ben asked Jonathan Mould, an old salt who was in his mess.

"Indeed I have lad and a mighty fine man he is too," Mould replied. "Stick with him my lad and your future's secure. Our Capt'n's one of the most successful captains when it comes to capturing rather than sinking his foes. All us old hands has already a nice nest egg waiting; they reckon Mitchell has already banked 80,000 guineas in prize money for himself."

"Do we all get prize money?" Ben asked with interest.

"Indeed lad; the prize money is split right down to the powder boys with proportions sent to the widows of men killed in service, so it's in everyone's interest to make a capture."

Ben had made another friend in their mess whose name was Brendan Joyce, a mountain of an Irishman from Galway Bay. His nickname was The Bear and with the first glance at him, the reason was obvious. He was a fierce looking character six foot six tall and almost as broad, with a great fuzzy beard down to his chest, and if that was not enough, one time whilst sailing in the South Seas he had had his face tattooed Maori style. Despite all that, he had the temperament of a dove. He was legendary for two things: first his laugh, which began as a deep rumble and slowly built into an infectious bellow that had everyone in hysterics around him, and secondly, without doubt he was the wrestling champion of the ship and ship's strongman. They held competitions in the mess to see who could stand longest, arms outstretched with a twelve-pound cannon ball in each hand, and long after his rivals had conceded Brendan would still be standing arms locked, outstretched, like a huge oak tree. Hodges, another member of the mess snored loudly; he had downed both his rum and beer ration and fallen asleep on the end of the makeshift table head in arms. The others laughed and turned in, clambering into their swinging hammocks until their next watch.

Life on board was divided by the watches; the crew were split into three separate watches who all took it in turns to man the ship at sea. The ship's day officially began at noon when her speed and position would be checked by the Master, his mate and the midshipmen, who would also check the sun's position. Each watch stood four hours, and then had four hours off except for after supper at 4 pm when they stood what were referred to as 'dog watches' of just two hours duration. Between 8 and 9 pm the hammocks were put down and those not on watches retired.

There was very little idle time, but occasionally there was time to think about things. Ben realised with surprise that he was enjoying the life. He still had reservations about climbing the rigging but sometimes he would sit high in the crow's nest and enjoy the wind in his face and the feeling of freedom. He thought of the Lintons quite a lot and of Ruth even more; he wondered how she was and what she was doing and if she ever remembered him. He occasionally thought of little Jenny and hoped that she was safe somewhere, but his thoughts always went back to Ruth.

If he had time he would go sit in the little chart room and chat with the Ship's Master about navigation and chart making. He showed off some of the skills he had learnt from Burrows and was allowed to work on some of the charts.

Captain Mitchell stood hands behind his back watching the men work. He was handsome character, in his mid thirties, with dark hair, deep brown eyes and a sophisticated air about him that had the ladies swooning at times. He had been in the service from nine years old, and had been fortunate to learn his profession under a number of good officers who had spotted his potential at an early age. This was his third commission as Captain, and he was looking forward to the challenge of running a seventy-four gun ship. He shook his head as a series of thoughts went through it, then with a final nod to himself he reached a decision.

"Mr. Barraclough, I think it is time we had a little gunnery practice. We should meet up with our escort tomorrow, and after that there may not be much time for any."

Barraclough was a tall thickset officer also in his early mid thirties, who had served alongside Captain Mitchell for nearly ten years, so he knew his moods and expectations completely. He moved quickly to the guardrail and passed the information onto the other lieutenants, who in turn bellowed orders at the crew. Like frantic ants, they scurried across the decks to their positions. There were a number of new men in each of the crews, and it was some time before all the gun officers could announce that they were ready.

"I'm thankful there are no Frenchmen watching this display Mr. Barraclough. We would now be at the bottom of the ocean."

To begin with, they went through the drill of running out the guns. This was followed by loading and firing procedures which they did several times without actually firing. Satisfied that everyone knew their job, the order to load was given. Young boys known as powder monkeys seemed to be everywhere carrying their deadly loads of black powder from the ship's magazine.

Ben was out of breath as he and the rest of his gun crew waited, nerves on edge, for the next order. Their gun was a 24 pdr which weighed almost three tons, and although it ran on wooden wheels, it took a great deal of effort on a rolling deck to move it into place.

"Fire!" the gun officers shouted, and a frightening, deafening roar built up, the guns thundering, their muzzles belching great clouds of acrid smoke out across the waves.

"Reload! Come on get the lead out." The bosons harangued the crews.

From the poop, the senior officers watched with dismay the confused scene on the decks.

"Watch out Fletch!" Ben called.

But it was too late. With a flash, the hammer fell and the gun leaped backwards with a roar; the ramrod that Fletch had failed to remove from the gun barrel went whizzing like a harpoon out across the waves.

"Who the 'ell do you think you are, Robin Hood?" The Boson advanced on Fletch, who shrunk under the heat of the glare.

The Captain groaned as he saw it spiralling out towards the untidy plumes of water lifted by the other gunshots. He went below shaking his head.

For the rest of the day, the decks resounded to the rumbling of gun wheels. The crews practiced over and over again, running out and loading their heavy weapons.

"Cease Fire!" The echoes of the last shots faded across the open sea, and the exhausted men collapsed beside their ungrateful mistresses.

Ben threw himself down, his head dropped back against the woodwork. He could feel his heart thumping as if it would burst, and his ears whistled. His soot-covered body ran with sweat, but he was too tired to make any effort at all.

"Get y'selves washed down and fed." The boson shouted at the crews. He leant against number four gun, knotted rope held like a rosary. "Not you lot." He said pointing at Fletch, "this 'ere deck's to clean. You and yer merry men can fetch the buckets."

There were whistles and catcalls from the other crew-men as they relaxed and watched as Ben and the rest of the gun crew hauled buckets of water over the ship's side to swill down the deck.

"I'll kill you one day Fletch." Hodges, said under his breath.

"Me, you'll kill me! What for?"

"T'is your fault Hodges." Ben chipped in, "you pulled the lanyard too soon."

"You watch yer step as well Burrows." Hodges turned threateningly towards Ben.

"It's a shame yer brains not as big as yer mouth." Fletch said in a light singsong way. Suddenly one of the buckets went over and Hodges lashed out with his mop at Fletch. The little Irishman ducked out of the way skipping lightly across the deck.

Hodges followed, but Ben stuck out his foot and the man toppled heavily to the deck. "You . . ." Hodges leapt to his feet.

"Stop that, you three!" The boson glared at Hodges daring him to make a wrong move. There was a moment of hesitation; Hodges fighting hard to control his anger made a slight move towards Ben.

"Don't be a fool man. I've not had to use the cat so far this trip."

"What's to do Mr. Harris?" Barraclough the first Lieutenant shouted down from the quarterdeck to the Boson. "Just getting these lads shipshape Mr. Barraclough."

"Very well . . . Carry on." The boson gave them all a warning glance, Hodges wiped across his face with the back of his hand and went back to his mopping. By the time Ben's crew hit their hammocks they were far too tired to continue the argument.

CHAPTER TWELVE

───────●❋●───────

As Seagull pushed her way through the waves, high above the decks in the fore and main mastheads lookouts constantly watched the surrounding horizons making sure that the captain knew just what they were approaching at any time.

"Sail ho!" Came the cry just before midday

Barraclough rushed to the rails exclaiming, "mast-head there!"

"Aye Mr. Barraclough."

"Where away is the sail?"

"Two points to starboard: three ships."

From the deck they were still not visible, but all eyes were scanning the horizon. Mitchell appeared on deck he nodded at his officers on watch. "What news Mr. Barraclough?" he said.

"Three ships captain," he pointed over the starboard bow.

It seemed as though the sails were never going to show to the impatient crew scanning the horizon. As they eventually came into view the captain became a little agitated; he had his telescope to one eye.

"It's the Neptune, with a frigate and a sloop," Barraclough said.

"At last; our orders, let us hope that we shall soon be joining Admiral Nelson's fleet." Mitchell snapped his telescope closed.

Sailing with a strong wind behind them the flotilla soon caught up with Seagull. Neptune, which was the same class as Seagull, but a slightly newer ship, came alongside. Her Captain waved to Mitchell who acknowledged, with a stiff nod of his head. He recognised Captain Atkins immediately. "Oh Lord, it's Atkins," He said. He spoke out of the side of his mouth without changing his smile towards Atkins. Barraclough who as usual stood close by his side replied, "Yes captain I remember him."

"The man's a complete fool. If it was not for his patron being an Admiral he'd not be let aboard any blasted ship."

Mitchell was the senior of the two captains and therefore had to act as host to Atkins. He signalled for the other to come aboard Seagull.

Captain Atkins saluted smartly, and then doffed his cap as he came aboard; despite the heat he seemed quite cool and wore his full captain's uniform as if attending the admiralty. He straightened his cap, and then marched smartly towards Mitchell.

"Admiral Jarvis sends his complements," Atkins said.

He handed a pouch containing sealed orders to Mitchell.

"Shall we go to my cabin?" he said to Atkins. "Take over Mr. Barraclough."

"Aye aye Capt'n."

"Please be seated Captain."

Mitchell pointed to the chair opposite his in the compact cabin. Using the point of an ornate dagger which he kept on his desk as an opener, he carefully prised open the seal. He opened the document and laid it flat on the top of his desk. A scowl crossed his face as he read the script. After a moment, he sat back with a very dissatisfied grunt, and said "What do you know of this?"

"Only that the Admiral received news less than a week ago. But the fleet is so hard pushed in the Med that he had very few ships he could spare for the task." Atkins looked slightly embarrassed at knowing the contents of the order.

There was rather a long, embarrassing pause as Mitchell considered what he had just read. "Thank you Captain Atkins, excuse my abruptness I had expected to be joining the main fleet. Will you take a drink?"

"Very kind of you Mitchell. How is the old Seagull performing?"

They chatted for some time until Mitchell was satisfied that he had been a reasonable host and then he dismissed the other back to his ship.

"We shall sail at point if you will be so kind as to take up station on the lee," Mitchell said, as Atkins reached the door.

Barraclough came in as Atkins was leaving; immediately he sensed the tension in the air. He stood silently before his Captain knowing better than to interrupt the other's thoughts.

"Damn them!" Mitchell said angrily, "we're to sail to the Indies." He glanced at Barraclough. "Two companies of infantry and goodness knows how many civilians are trapped on Martinique. They may not be able to hold out long, in fact, there is the possibility that they may have already fallen to the French. We are to support the garrison, get them off if all else fails or try to rout the attacking forces."

"I thought we were to meet up with Nelson's fleet?"

"So did I; I'll wager Jarvis did not dare trust Atkins on his own."

"We're not provisioned for such a voyage," Barraclough said.

"The sloop Hero is carrying for us. Set course and tell the Master and the Purser I want a word with them."

News soon reached the fo'c'sle that they were bound for the Indies, and rumours about their exact destination were rife. Ben sat with Fletcher and a Scotsman by the name of Bruce.

"T'is most beautiful place on earth to look at, but it's the nearest I've ever been to hell in all my life," Bruce said. His weathered face creased with a deep scowl. "There's more diseases, than you can ever imagine, but the island girls . . ." he let out a slow meaningful whistle "they make up for it." He laughed a loud booming laugh that echoed around the deck. "Them native girls will eat a lad like you alive; no trouble," he laughed again punching Ben's arm.

Five days out, they were hit by a storm that threatened to separate the small fleet, but it was short lived, and the ships were soon all back in line astern. Seagull led, like a swan with her cygnets.

The weather remained unsettled and life aloft was hard and dangerous. Seagull shuddered, as each huge wave battered into her bows. Each time she laboured forwards, a wide fan of spray would burst over her flooded decks, and there was a danger that anything not fastened down would be washed away.

Ben clung on as the ship rolled beneath him; at times the sideways motion was so severe that the yardarms were close to the wave-tops and it seemed as if he would be plunged into the cold grey water. Then the ship would swing back the other way, rolling until it almost touched the wave-tops again. At least now, Ben seemed to be over the seasickness.

Ben and Fletcher had been working together high up the mainmast; their hands were so cold they could hardly feel them.

"We can go down now," Fletch shouted over the din of the storm.

Clinging to the rigging Fletch made his way off the spar and onto the shrouds, leaving Ben still out in the middle of the yard.

Suddenly, there was a loud crack as the yardarm supporting the 'main royal sail' broke free directly above Ben. He looked up in time to see it hurtling down, but there was nothing he could do to get out of its way. It hit him, knocking him off his perch and all he could do, was grab at the falling spar and fall with it towards the deck. He yelled as he watched the deck get closer, and was within feet of it when the ship lurched over to one side swinging him out over the sea. By a small miracle instead of hitting the woodwork that would have surely killed him, he hit the top of a wave. The ice-cold water knocked the breath out of him, it dragging at his sodden clothes, but just as he thought that he was about to drown, he was flung high in the air again gasping for breath. Spinning like a top, he locked his fingers and ankles around the rope and held on for dear life. For a moment as he spun he seemed just to hang there in midair. The ship bobbed like a cork and then rolled the opposite direction flinging him back across its deck. He hit the foremast with such force that he lost grip of the rope and then slithered down it to the relative safety of the deck. He lay a moment winded, staring up the length of the mast at the tangled ropes above him.

"They say the devil looks after his own," Second Lieutenant Myers said as he dragged Ben to his feet. "You all right lad?"

"I think so," Ben croaked. He was definitely shaken and feeling much the worse for his dunking. Through stinging eyes, he could just make out the blurred outline of the officer's face. He tried to stand, but sank back to his knees like a rag doll.

"You two, take him below." The boson snapped at Fletcher and Bruce, who were laughing loudly and applauding the acrobatic display.

As soon as the weather gave them a chance, the ship's carpenters were out making repairs to the damage. The weather had split up the little fleet and it was two days before they were reunited, and could sail on together again at full speed.

The ship's commanders, Captain Atkins of the Neptune, Lieutenant Small of the Hero, and Commander Benn of the Pegasus, sat around Captain Mitchell's table as he explained the battle plan.

"It seems to me, gentlemen, that we have very little choice in the matter. Here on this side of the bay, which is approximately six miles across, is the garrison fort. The last news we have is that the French have batteries along these ridges behind the fort, and are bombarding it. We have very little intelligence about how big those guns are, or how many of them there are. They have a number of small ships, or at least they had." Mitchell waited for any comments before he carried on "Lieutenant Small, you will take Hero in first, and try pick up as many of the garrison as possible; we will stand off, and try keep the guns on those hills busy."

Everyone stood, Mitchell finished by saying, "there is just one other thing; we have intelligence that there could be one or more of Bonaparte's ships in the area, and so we need to keep a good look out whilst we are engaged in this task. The last thing we want is to be caught in that bay."

"What of the Leeward squadron?" Atkins said, "Will they join us?"

"I'm afraid they are caught up with other duties at the moment, so it is just up to us." Mitchell smiled.

The officers were dismissed with orders to have all hands on deck at first light. The crew fed well that night and they were issued extra rum, and beer rations to help give them all courage for the following day. There was an unusual quiet below decks, as each man considered what was to come. Some wrote letters, or played cards, those on watch went about their duties, the rest just waited.

Next morning, the weather was good, with a steady breeze and hardly a cloud in the sky. The crew had breakfast and there was a sense of anticipation in the air, as the decks were cleared for action.

Ben had recovered after his ordeal and stood with the rest of the crew ready at his battle station. Someone played a jolly tune on a fiddle, raising spirits and calming nerves.

"You'll be alright lad," Bruce said to Ben. "Just keep your head down and work like the devil's after you."

Mould gave him a reassuring wink, "your head will buzz so loud you'll not hear the guns. It's only afterwards you'll feel washed out."

Slightly before noon they sighted the island. Ben was keen to get a good view, he asked the midshipman who was there gun captain if he could borrow his telescope.

"Fletch take a look at this . . . it's a volcano!" Ben said excitedly.

Fletch just nodded, he was not in a mood for sightseeing. Ben gave back the glass. "Have you ever seen one erupt?"

"You're gonna see more than a mountain erupt soon." Mould said. His voice was calm and quiet.

Each of the ships now busied itself making last minute preparations. There was a constant exchange of messages between the ships as they began to take up their various stations. It took another three hours before they had reached the edge of the bay. It was a jagged coastline with several small bays, behind was a dense forest that covered the sides of a low range of mountains. Away on the far side, they could see the fort and town, where an ominous cloud of black smoke was billowing up into the sky.

A whisper ran amongst the crew, they were getting agitated.

"Beat to quarters, Mr. Barraclough if you please."

The drum and fife beat to quarters; bulk-heads were knocked away; the guns were released from their confinement; the whole dreaded paraphernalia of battle was produced. After the lapse of a few minutes of hurry and confusion, every man and boy was at his post, ready to do his best service for his country, except the band, who, claiming exemption from the affray, safely stowed themselves away in the cable tier. There was only one sick man on the list, and he, at the cry of battle, hurried from his cot, feeble as he was, to take his post of danger. A few of the junior midshipmen were stationed below, on the berth deck, with orders, given for all to hear, to shoot any man who attempted to run from his quarters.

The sounds of the battle echoed across the bay to them, the deeper booms of artillery fire punctuating the steady crackle of small arms fire.

They crossed the bay in a perfect straight line, and not until they were within two miles of the fort did little Hero break towards the coast. Half a mile in front of her, two great plumes of water spurted into the air. The sound of the shots reached Mitchell on Seagull. He and Barraclough scanned the rocky cliffs with telescopes searching for the battery. It was not hard to find after those first shots, as twin clouds of white smoke drifted into the air from amongst the trees.

"Run in closer Mr. Barraclough, I want to silence those guns before they do us any damage."

Even though the carronades of the upper deck packed a hard punch they were not very accurate over such a long distance, but the 24 and 32 pounders on Seagull's decks were deadly accurate; their crews were ready, waiting for the signal to fire. Seagull heeled over to her larboard side giving her guns better elevation. Barraclough waited until the exact moment when he knew the ship was at her steadiest, and then gave the command to fire. The massive pressure of the broadside forced Seagull down hard into the water, shaking her beams as if the devil himself had burst from the guns. The shot screamed through the air making a terrifying sound. The steady breeze took away the swirling cloud in time for the gun-crews to see their shots crash in amongst the trees. Neptune and Pegasus joined in the deadly chorus, their guns barking loudly at the enemy. As Seagull's first shots were landing, her crews worked at top speed, and then fired another salvo. The practice sessions had paid off, and now each gun crew worked like a well-oiled machine even if their speed was not yet what was expected.

Ben blew hard, his gun-crew had worked well, and now their gun was reloaded and ready once more. There was time to exchange a nod and reassuring smile with the rest of his mates.

"I can't see a blind thing," Ben yelled as he tried to sight his gun.

"Just fire the bugger!" Bruce bellowed.

Ben did just that and it kicked and recoiled with a deafening noise, and immediately the sweating crew reloaded and pushed it back into position to fire again.

All along the wharf, small boats were beginning to put to sea. A thirty-two foot ketch was leading the flotilla out but it was making hard work of the journey towards Hero. It was overloaded, crammed with soldiers and civilians all hampering the oarsmen and with its gunnels barely above the water, each wave threatened to sink it.

High on the cliffs above them, the French battery began firing. There were far more guns than Mitchell had at first thought, and suddenly the sea around the small boats began to boil and foam as the deadly shots threw great fountains of water into the air. The skipper of the ketch must have known that he was a prime target, and he tried to take evasive action, but his overloaded ship was slow to respond.

The English ships kept up their fire against the cliffs, but now due to the thick clouds of smoke they were all having to fire blindly into the dense forest.

Several of the small boats had disappeared, hit by the relentless bombardment from above. There was a loud explosion, and Mitchell swung his glass towards the ketch. Her main mast was broken in half as the timber was shattered by a shot. As the heavy mast tumbled, its sail folded and tangled in the rigging. The ship lurched, spilling some of the people from its deck into the sea. Two further direct hits rocked her; the decks were covered in debris, but still the valiant little ship kept going. Her crew hacked and chopped at the tangled ropes, and finally they freed the trailing mast. The crews of the warships cheered as the ketch finally struggled out of range of the French guns. Almost as soon as the battered little boat pulled alongside Hero, what remained of her compliment was swarming up the side of the warship.

Commander Benn of the Pegasus scanned the far horizon with the powerful telescope mounted on the aft of his ship. His lookout high in the fore-topgallant had called a warning to the deck. "Mr. Carter!" he boomed at the first lieutenant. "Frenchmen! Captain Mitchell should be informed immediately."

Ben and Fletch watched the sudden exchange of signals with some interest; thanks to Mr. Burrow's tuition, Ben knew just what was being said. "I think we are going to be a little bit busy very soon," he said. He watched as a new set of signal flags ran up the mast. "I think Commander Benn is a bit nervous."

He took a welcome minute breather, and managed to grab a drink of not too clean water from a bucket beside him. He had stripped off his shirt, and the well defined muscles of his upper body were smudged with a mixture of sweat and the black soot of battle.

The rearguard in the fortress was having difficulty breaking off the fight. The French, realising that most of the garrison had left, fired several salvos into the fortifications and then their troops stormed the fort. They breached the walls, and entered the town, slowly forcing the rearguard to give ground until finally they were driven out onto the cluttered jetty and had to take refuge behind crates and boxes that were stacked there.

With one eye on the approaching enemy ships and one on the battle, Mitchell made a snap decision. "Mr. Barraclough, have your best gunners put their next shots into the town. Let's hope that we can get the rest of them off the wharf."

The British soldiers ducked and cursed as the shots from Seagull screamed close over their heads, the waterfront buildings disintegrated, sending splinters and planking spinning into the air. Volley after volley tore up the buildings and within minutes the town was almost levelled. The ploy worked and what was left of the

French troops, torn apart by the holocaust, retreated in confusion.

He swung his telescope over the larboard bow, watching for a short moment the approaching sails of the French warships. He had made it clear to his officers that he did not intend to leave until they had picked up as many as possible of the garrison. Even so, he knew that they must move soon or be caught at a terrible disadvantage by the approaching enemy. Their ship's boats and barges scurried to and fro picking up as many from the sea as they could, marines on board fired their muskets to try and provide even more cover for those still stranded.

The English ships had come about, and were now heading almost into the breeze which slowed them considerably. They tacked again to get the most speed from their ships as was possible.

Once again, the French guns high above the town began firing. Several small boats had run the gauntlet again and returned to the wharf, where the troops gratefully jumped aboard. The warships now began a colossal bombardment of the forest batteries, columns of grey and black smoke showed their effect, and the battery was silenced.

As the first of the boats reached Hero, she was already turning into the wind, aware of her vulnerability so close inshore. She had sailed closer to the shore to speed up the pickup, and in doing so had received a couple of hits from the coastal guns; nothing serious, but her sails had been holed in several places.

"Do you recognise any of them?" Mitchell asked Barraclough.

"Aye captain, unfortunately I do. The ship at point is the Formidable. Ninety-six gunner, and behind her is the Pluton a seventy-four. The other two I'm not sure of."

"Thank you Mr. Barraclough. Signal the others to close up the line, we need to get clear of this bay, there are shallows to the south of here."

The French ships were sailing in perfect line astern it was a daunting sight to the watching crews on the

English ships. Away from the shelter of the island they were catching more of the wind and were making good use of it.

Confidently aware that they outgunned the British, their ships seemed to swagger arrogantly towards the British. With their battle ensigns fluttering they were obviously ready for the fight.

"Their Lords at the Admiralty would be interested to know that the French had such firepower in these waters," Mitchell said. His gaze never left the approaching enemy, his skilled eyes assessed them searching for a chink in their armour. He had been in this position several times, he thought himself first-rate at battle tactics, and he was confident that he could beat his enemy. With his decision made he said in a calm voice, "come to larboard, I want to cross their bows."

The French held their course, trying to draw the English ships into a parallel course so that they could use their advantage of firepower. They wrongly presumed that Mitchell was taking a wide course so that he could take the wind as he sailed into battle. In fact, Mitchell did not intend to run alongside the French; instead he made a sharp course change that turned his ships at right angles to the French line.

It was a risky strategy, because it meant that the French could fire at will, without the English guns being able to reply at first. However, should they survive this course it then meant that the French ships could be savaged mercilessly by the English guns.

Seagull headed between the stern of Pluton and the bow of the seventy-four gunner behind her. Mitchell would have preferred to get behind the Formidable first, because it was potentially the enemy's most dangerous ship, but they were not able to get into position in time. As she came into range of the French guns, Seagull was to be the first to be scourged by their first shots that tore into her sails and rigging.

The French held steady. The English ships as yet could not bring any of their main guns to bear. Seagull had a couple of carronades on her fo'c'sle that could be fired forwards, and she used them to good effect firing barshot into the enemy rigging. It was not much of a reply, but anything was better than getting pounded without fighting back.

The crew steeled themselves as the French shot screamed over the waves towards them. The French used a different tactic to the English in naval warfare; as a general rule the French felt that the best way to disable an enemy ship was to destroy their means of manoeuvring. They therefore concentrated their fire on the masts and rigging, launching their broadsides on the upward roll of their ships. This fire policy often crippled the English ships, preventing them from pressing home their attack, and was less deadly to the crew.

The British tactic was firing on the down roll into the enemy hulls. This created a storm of flying splinters that killed and maimed the enemy crew. These tactics were accentuated by the fact that the English tended to choose the weather gauge and the French the lee, so the tendency was for the French guns to be pointing high and the English low as their ships heeled in the wind.

Men had stripped off their jackets and most, except the officers were down to their bare skin as they waited. The powder boys waited, they chattered and shouted at each other, hidden behind a heavy woollen screen made up of bales of raw wool and a thick blanket of wool, which was erected around the magazine entrance to try to prevent an accident and Seagull being blown up by a stray spark. The first mate ordered them quiet, and to make ready to serve their guns.

Down below the ship's surgeon prepared his small team for their battle. Tables were wiped down and a thick layer of sawdust covered the deck. There was no anaesthetic, but there was plenty of rum and beer. They had the unenviable task, of trying to patch the wounded back up enough to get them back into action as quickly as possible.

Ben and his gun crew huddled behind their cannon, but even so as the first shots struck their ship, flying debris showered them. Ben looked up attracted by a strange noise, such as he had never heard before. It sounded like the tearing of sails, just over their heads, and he soon realised it to be the wind of the enemy's shot. The whole scene grew indescribably confused; it was like some awful thunderstorm, whose deafening roar is attended by incessant streaks of lightning, carrying death in every flash and strewing the decks with the victims of its wrath. Only in this case, the scene was rendered more horrible than that by the presence of rivulets of blood, which began to run across the decks and soak into the thick layer of sawdust scattered for that very purpose.

Their nerve held; each minute seemed like an hour, every shot seemed to be heading directly at them. The gun officers, in their calmest voices offered encouragement. "Be patient lads, we'll get our chance to blast these bastards to hell."

Seagull was taking the full force of both broadsides. Debris littered her decks, as iron shot split and shattered oak. Deadly splinters whizzed and buzzed through the air like mad hornets. Above the decks, her sails were ripped and torn, tons of canvas flapped from broken spars. Mitchell watched from the poop, he silently prayed that her sails would be able to carry them on to complete their task. Surrounded by his senior officers he could not show any emotion; it was a deadly game of chance, and not only did his reputation, but his life and that of his crew depend on the outcome.

The ships following Seagull could see the battering she was taking. Atkins may have not been the brightest star of the British Navy, but he was no coward. He could hear the battle; the screams, the explosions, the tearing of sailcloth, but despite the feeling that he was about to be sick he too stood motionless.

On Seagull the injured men were being carried to the cockpit, those more lucky who had been killed outright were thrown overboard. There was very little conversation going on apart from the barking of orders to the sail-trimmers working hard in the rigging to keep the ship on the captain's course.

Suddenly there was a lull, they were almost between the two French ships, and now the main French guns could not fire on them. They were less than thirty yards astern of Pluton and no more than fifteen yards from the bow of the Ville de Paris.

"Fire as you bear!" was the order shouted down the line of waiting gunners. The crews leapt into action, Seagull shook and rolled, and now she bellowed her own thunder and lashed out in revenge at both Frenchmen. The shots smashed through the woodwork, raking the full length of the enemy decks, cutting a path of carnage and bloody mayhem. This was a hell that could only have been devised by man; no evil devil could orchestrate such pure horror.

Ben waited patiently, his whole body felt to have tightened into a knot. His sweat stained face totally frozen in concentration kept perfectly still as he stared along the barrel of his gun. He tightened the lanyard attached to the trigger, and prayed that the order to fire would come soon.

"Steady lads!" the gun officer called.

Suddenly the bow of the Frenchman loomed large in Ben's sights. He steadied himself, counted to ten then twitched his hand just enough to fire the beast. The heavy cannon kicked hard, but he stayed with it determined to see his shot hit. Everything was lost in the dense cloud of smoke that exploded from the muzzle.

Deafened by the continuous roar and almost blinded by the thick clouds of powder smoke, they worked like demons intent on revenge. There was no time or energy for talk; nor was there time to worry about the dangers, or the flying hell around them. As the damage inflicted on the enemy became apparent, the gun crews cheered almost hysterically, shaking their fists and screaming defiance. They managed to fire another two shots before they were past their target. Further along the decks the guns still roared until they too were out of position.

Ben patched up a deep cut to Fletch's upper arm, while Fletch rubbed the stream of blood making lines through the dirt of battle.

"Keep still!" Ben said. He finished off tying a strip of torn cloth around the wound. "You'll live," he smiled.

The French Captain on board the Formidable was doing his best to turn his ship back towards the battle. He must have felt despair as the rear mast of the Pluton came crashing down, splintering and tearing onto the already severely damaged deck. Neptune and Pegasus had now also crossed her stern, adding to the damage the Seagull had created.

The Ville de Paris was now out of control. A fire raged in her lower deck and she broke formation, just as the Hero tried to cut in front of her and finish off what the others had started. The two hulls crashed together with such violence that the sound could be heard on every ship in the battle. It was like a couple of mountain rams crashing head to head. The French warship was so badly weakened by the punishment the other English ships had given her crumpled with the impact. Hero bobbed like a cork as the heavy weight of the other ship crushed her, knocking her sideways. A blinding flash, a deafening roar, a surge of heat, so hot that it melted the barrels of the guns, consumed both ships as the forward magazine on the French ship exploded in an enormous fireball.

Both lines were now in disarray. Captain Mitchell had managed to even the battle slightly, but now his ship was again into the wind. He turned away from the Formidable and struck at the rear of the French line. Pegasus being lighter and faster had engaged with the Pluton again. The French ship's masts had fallen, her decks were shattered and torn, and yet somewhere a gun still fired from her.

Neptune clung close to Seagull's stern. With skill, bravery and good fortune, some of Seagull's sails had been fixed enough to be of use again. Together they hit the last ship in the French line. Seagull once again took the full force of the broadside, which removed what was left of her foremast.

"Get that mess off the deck! Jump to it!" The mate shouted at the crews buried by the falling timbers and sailcloth. Sawing and hacking the crew cleared the web of ropes that threatened to choke the deck, despite the fact that all the time they were under fire from the French warship.

Ben felt weary, he wanted to lie down and give up, the muscles of his arms and legs hurt so badly. There was no respite, he knew now the hell Fletcher had described at their first meeting.

When he thought it could not get any worse, twenty-eight pounds of red hot iron punched through the timbers in front of him, it lifted his cannon off the deck as if it was made of straw. He fell in an untidy heap, and was instantly buried by more falling debris. Strong hands hauled him out and to his feet.

"Hell, that was close," Ben spluttered. "Where's Fletch?"

Helped by Brendan and Mould, they dug through the smouldering heap of timber in search of Fletch. As they searched, a marine in a bright red uniform fell from the rigging and almost landed on top of them. Ben turned the body over; the man's face was a gory sight, the flesh had been ripped away exposing the bone. He covered him with a length of sailcloth.

Fletch was buried beneath a pile of wreckage and only his left foot was sticking out. They shifted what they could, exposing some of his leg. Their overturned gun was pinning the timbers down onto Fletch. With his huge strength Brendan, helped by Bruce managed to lift the gun just enough for the others to drag him free.

"I'm done for lad!" Fletch croaked.

Ben cradled the man's head with his arm, "shut up for once Fletch. The surgeon will patch you up as good as new." He smiled, his teeth glowing white against his sooty features.

Lifting his shipmate onto his shoulder Ben carried him to where the surgeon was working in the cockpit. As he descended the steps, he made his way into what seemed like a nightmare; bodies lay everywhere, moans and cries could be heard mixed with the thunder of war from outside, the decks ran with a thick slime of congealed blood and flesh. One of the small boys dangled like a limp puppet from the woodwork; he had been hit by a flying splinter that had skewered and pinned him there. On his small round face was a heartbreaking expression of fear and pain. They met Bruce on the steps and were all pleased to see each other alive, so much so that they embraced.

"I thought you were both killed!" Bruce exclaimed.

"I quite possibly am," said Fletcher still dangling from Ben's shoulders.

"Be quiet then, I hate noisy corpses." Bruce laughed.

As Seagull emerged from the cloud of smoke, Captain Mitchell's heart sank. Straight in front of them was the Formidable, as yet hardly bearing a single scar of the battle. Every gun along her three fighting decks roared at them and the heavy shots pounded and splintered the already damaged and fragile woodwork. Mitchell ordered his ship to close with the Frenchman, as he knew he could never win a standoff battle with the heavier armed enemy ship.

Captain Atkins could see the peril Seagull was in. Bravely he turned across the bows of the Formidable, and as luck would have it, hardly received a shot from the Frenchman, who was intent on stopping Seagull. At close range, Atkins fired a full broadside into the towering timbers of the enemy warship. Formidable turned away from Seagull, the sudden shock and violent attack from Neptune seeming to have unnerved the French Captain. Atkins did not intend to let the Frenchman go so easily, he turned to pursue him firing all the time. The French captain was no novice and although he had received a terrific punch on the nose, still had the advantage of the wind behind him and fresh gunners. The Frenchman fired a massive broadside at Neptune as it turned, which shredded her sails but did little structural damage to Atkins's ship.

Seagull was given chance to fire again at Formidable, but could hardly manoeuvre to pursue the enemy, due to the damage to her sails and masts.

There was a sudden lull in the fighting as both sides calculated the damage their fleets had sustained, and like tired boxers hanging on the ropes, they took a breather.

Hero and wreckage of the Ville de Paris were hopelessly locked together by their fallen rigging. Fires raged totally out of control on both vessels. A series of explosions sank the Frenchman sending her on her final voyage. She sank shrouded by a cloud of steam and smoke, dragging Hero with her. Like a playful whale Hero was turned over by her rigging, exposing her badly holed keel and then she was gone.

Chapter Thirteen

———— ·•✣•· ————

Like tired fighting dogs, the two forces separated to lick their wounds, and as the light faded, silent shadows drifted away from the battle area.

"Well gentlemen we live to fight another day." Mitchell raised his glass in salute to the other ship's officers that had gathered in his cabin. He looked and felt tired. "I am well pleased that against difficult odds, our ships acquitted themselves so well and yet I'm disappointed that we did not achieve a conclusive victory. Those Frenchmen are out there and still capable of causing havoc."

Commander Benn gave a short report, "we managed to pick up thirty of the Hero's crew, regrettably Lieutenant Small was not amongst them; we also picked up fourteen of the garrison. Out of the frying pan . . ."

"Yes indeed. Thank you Commander Benn."

"At least we have some useful intelligence for the admiralty, as to the whereabouts of certain Frenchmen."

Barraclough made his report, "unfortunately Captain, we have lost the Master Mr. Carter, and his mate who were both killed in action. Also another five officers, eighteen ratings and seven marines are dead. I would say that three-quarters of the crew are injured."

"A sad roll call Mr. Barraclough. I hope you have not forgotten your navigational skills then because they will be needed now."

"Actually Captain, one of the new ratings has been spending a fair bit of time with the master and seems very knowledgeable, perhaps we could give him a chance and promote him to mate; that is if he can handle the post."

They had dined and there was a general air of satisfaction amongst the officers that evening. They toasted fallen comrades and discussed future plans.

In Seagull's fo'c'sle morale was at a low ebb; the air was filled with the smell of cooking, and the stink of battle. There were also the low moans and sobs of injured or dying men calling out their loved one's names, or cursing God for their luck.

"How do you feel Fletch?" Ben squatted by the side of the wooden pallet his friend lay upon.

"I'll survive, thanks to you."

Fletch put on a brave smile, his chest was covered in battle-soiled bandages, dark brown stains marking where the wounds were.

"You'll be up and about in no time."

"Don't say that, I wanted to stay here until we reached England."

Just at that moment, the boson stuck his head through the hatchway.

"Burrows, the Captain wants a word with you." He was gone without waiting for an answer.

Ben felt a great deal of apprehension as he stood outside the Captain's door. His mind raced as to the reason he had been summoned. A fear at the fore of his thoughts was that somehow the Captain had found out his guilty secret or true identity. He stood like a schoolboy waiting for the cane outside the headmaster's office. The boson had knocked and entered, leaving him alone in the oak panelled companionway. From within he could hear muffled voices. He tried to listen to what was being said but the noise of the ship made it impossible.

Near where he stood was a gaping hole in the ship's side, so as he waited, he peered out at the lead-black night. It gave him chance to take a couple of breaths of fresh air, and he thanked God for his survival. Fidgeting nervously with his torn and dirty shirt, he tried to tuck the ragged ends into his belt. Glancing down he felt proud of his torn and battle stained trousers, he tried to straighten what was left of them. During the battle, he had cut them off at the knee to stop the loose ends catching.

Barraclough suddenly appeared in the doorway and said, "in you come." The voice was friendly.

The captain was sat behind his square table that seemed to dominate the whole cabin. He still looked tired and sported a bruise to the side of his cheek, which had been caused by a piece of flying timber during the battle.

"Mr. Barraclough tells me that you are not the most accomplished of tops'ils-man; but that you acquitted y'self bravely during our little altercation with the French." Mitchell smiled as he spoke. "He also informs me that you have an understanding of charts, signals, and navigational instruments. Is that true?"

"Yes Sir, well about the charts and things Sir," Ben stuttered.

"Unfortunately we lost both Mr. Carter the ship's Master and his mate, who as you will be aware, was my navigator." Mitchell stared at Ben for a moment, assessing him.

"I understand that you spent some time with the Master and his charts."

"Yes Sir, I have a great love of such things."

"If you prove yourself capable, then you will be promoted to Master's Mate. Can you also write?"

"Yes sir, quite a good hand."

"Where did you learn about sea charts?"

Ben was not sure how to answer. He decided on the truth.

"From a Mr. P. Burrows, Sir."

"Burrows, do you mean Hawk's old navigator?" Mitchell said with a wry smile.

"Yes Capt'n."

"Is he a relative of yours?"

"Yes sir my . . . my uncle, Sir."

"Then, Mr. Barraclough we have been most fortunate," the Captain said to his first officer with a satisfied smile, "your uncle had a fine reputation."

Ben was surprised at the speed of things. He moved out of the fo'c'sle immediately, and was put in with the other junior officers. Barraclough took him under his wing. Together they went down to see the purser to rummage through the ship's slops as they were referred to, that is the cast-off clothes which were ready to wear.

"This is the chart room," he said. He held open the narrow door next to the Captain's cabin. "But of course you know that, I've seen you in here a few times."

"Yes sir, Mr. Carter allowed me to look at his charts."

Ben inspected the various instruments. A smile flickered across his lips as he gently traced his fingers over them. He opened several charts and laid out the one he needed on the angled tabletop.

"Keep your nose clean here and you'll be all right." Barraclough said in his broadest West Country accent.

The English ships managed to limp into port on Saint Dominique. It had recently managed to gain independence first from the Spanish, and then from the French, who had tried to colonise it as soon as the Spanish relinquished it. The Island's people, led by an ex-slave, had managed to evict the French forces, and then declared themselves an independent, neutral republic. At any one time, there could be French, Spanish, and English ships in the deep natural harbour, and none would break the peace until they were out of the port's safety.

Seagull dropped anchor in the bay; with her upper masts missing and battered woodwork she looked a sorry sight.

Most of the crew were given a few hours shore leave, and a stern warning not to create any trouble with the locals. As soon as they set foot on the quayside Ben and Fletcher linked arms and swaggered along the jetty singing at the tops of their voices.

"You young officer types'll not mind drinking with us poor tars then." Fletch chided Ben.

"Not as long as you mind your manners," Ben laughed.

"I know a great little place 'ere fer a mug o'grog," Brendan said. "Come on me hearties look lively." His huge legs powered him along the sea wall towards the town. Ben, Bruce and Fletch had to run to keep pace with him, Mould just sauntered behind them puffing on a fresh pipe.

They entered the smoke-filled room, which was absolutely heaving with bodies; the noise was deafening and the heat overpowering. The tables had all been pushed out of the way to make more room, but even so the men still stood squeezed together.

The waterfront taverns here were real melting pots; the crews of the different nationality warships, merchants, slavers and pirates drank together, usually in peace, although it was not unknown for there to be trouble. Anything from a gold pocket watch to a wife could be bought somewhere in the flourishing black markets along the waterfront.

The grog the taverns sold was a devilish concoction distilled by the locals in the hills above the town. It was potentially much more dangerous to the seamen than the harsh life at sea. Some said it kept away the scourge of life at sea, scurvy, as well as yellow fever and malaria.

"Knock it straight back," Bruce yelled over the din at Ben. The fiery liquid hit the back of his throat like a red-hot cannonball. Ben coughed and spluttered, gasping for air.

"Ha! Ha! That'll do you good." Brendan slapped Ben's back almost sending him to the floor.

"I'd rather face the French than drink this." He stared into the brew as if trying to see what it contained. Fletch had already finished his.

"Come on lad sup up."

"Well, well, look who we have here: Master's mate Burrows." Hodges elbowed through the press and gave a mock salute.

"Be off with you Hodges. We want no trouble tonight." Bruce shouted above the din.

"Trouble, who me? Nay Bruce lad, I've just come to congratulate the lad."

"Be off with you man," Brendan said.

"Are you not going to thank me for offering my congratulations then lad?" Hodges moved right in front of Ben their noses almost touched.

"If your wishes are sincere, then I thank you," Ben said, just to keep the peace.

"And if not, what then lad?" Hodges sneered as he spoke. "You're not drinking yer grog, maybe you're not man enough to keep it down. Here let me help you." Hodges tipped Ben's mug spilling the contents down his shirt.

Sudden anger flared up inside Ben. He struck out with his left hand hitting the others shoulder, knocking him backwards.

"So the lad has spirit," Hodges growled.

A crude blade suddenly appeared in his hand. He waved it in a circle. "Come on then lad."

The crowd around them parted forming a rough tight-packed circle. There was a slight knot of anticipation tightening Ben's stomach but he had grown up quickly over the last few months. He moved away from the circling blade, his eyes fixed on it.

Suddenly, Hodges darted forwards lunging out with the blade. Ben sidestepped the attack, and using Hodge's own momentum against him he swung his arm in a wide arc landing his mug hard on the side of his attacker's face. The earthenware vessel shattered on the man's cheekbone, splitting the flesh. Hodges, unable to halt his attack staggered, crashing heavily into a table.

A cheer went up from the onlookers. Hodges turned snarling angrily then lunged forwards again, but the movement was predictable and Ben easily dodged out of his path, like a matador dancing before a bull. Hodges stopped a moment, and mopped at the wound on his cheek, his eyes looked slightly glazed and his breathing was irregular. He lunged again. Ben landed a punch straight into Hodges' nose. He felt a shock of pain shoot right up his arm from his knuckles as bone met bone. Another cheer filled the room as Hodges ploughed face first into the dirt floor.

"What a punch!" Fletch declared. He threw his arm around Ben's shoulder, and then held his arm aloft. "I declare Ben to be the champion!" a great cheer went up. "You should have taken up booth boxing. You could make a right royal living out of the fairs."

"I think I've broken my hand, the man has a skull as thick as a cannonball."

"Come on Ben get this down yer." Bruce gave Ben another mug filled to the brim.

They propped Hodges unconscious frame against a roof support and went back to the serious business in hand. They drank and sang almost until first light, it had the desired effect of driving away the frightening demons that seem to appear after a battle; the relentless 'what ifs' and 'maybes,' that can haunt a man after being surrounded by death.

The next day Ben wished that he was dead. There was very little about the evening he could recall. He vaguely remembered falling from the quayside and landing upside down in the jolly-boat that was taking them back to their ship, but it was all a bit of a blur.

His head ached, buzzing, worse than after the fight with the French. No matter how much water he drank he could not quench his thirst; his knuckles were swollen and he decided that fist fighting was not his style.

"Good God lad, you look like a dead fish," Barraclough said. "That gut-rot they serve ashore is not fit to wash the bilge pumps out with. Smarten y'self up lad, or the Captain will ditch you back into the fo'c'sle, head first."

Heeding the warning, Ben kept out of everyone's way for the rest of the day; that evening he declined an offer to go back into town. Instead he made himself at home in his new quarters and although it was quite cramped he had more space than he had had in his old mess.

Sitting working at his small desk he was pleased with life in general. He had only one personal item; the good luck rabbit's foot that Jenny had given him during the cold winter on the moors. He always kept it around his neck and although it was attached to a different bootlace now after the other broke, it meant just the same to him.

Neptune and Pegasus were repaired much quicker than Seagull, and it was decided that they should make their way back to England. Mitchell sent dispatches with them telling of the engagement with the French and mentioning Captain Atkins's bravery in drawing the fire from the enemy ship, which probably saved Seagull from being sunk.

When Seagull finally put to sea, almost a month after the other ships had left, she was rather sickly looking with her clipped wings. There had not been any suitable timber to replace the upper spars of her three masts, and so she carried only half her normal sails.

"I've checked these figures for you Mr. Burrows. Well done, I only found one slight error." Barraclough, himself an accomplished navigator, had checked Ben's calculations for him before giving them to the Captain.

Feeling quite pleased with himself, he made a couple of entries in his log.

"How's it feel to be a Master's Mate?" asked Barraclough.

"I'm not sure really. I'll get used to it."

"You wouldn't rather be aloft would you?"

"Oh no! Definitely not." Ben felt a little dizzy thinking about the climb up to the yardarms. "The uniform is better too." He smiled.

Each day Barraclough would stop for a short chat in the cramped little chart-room that was Ben's new place of work. A friendship developed between them. They sat together one evening, drinking some of the ship's beer. Ben wore one of the dead navigator's uniforms. The ship's sail-maker had done some basic alterations; even so the jacket and trousers still buried their new owner.

"Will you stay on after we've reached Portsmouth?" Barraclough asked.

"Do I have a choice?"

"Well, most pressed men jump ship at the first opportunity, but not if they've been promoted."

"I don't know yet."

"You're a dark horse Mr. Burrows. You could have a career with the Senior Service if you stay on after Portsmouth."

"I'm not sure what I want to do."

"One day I'll retire, and start a stud farm; I have a lady friend who lives just to the north of Portsmouth, she owns quite a few acres. I visit whenever possible. One day . . ." Barraclough shook his head wistfully as he spoke.

Seagull leant with the wind, her huge sails puffed out as naturally as anything in nature. On the poop deck there was little conversation; everyone watched England come into view. Ben stared at the Captain and Barraclough who were a couple of paces in front of him, and wondered if he'd ever be as good a sailor as they were. He could only admire the way they seemed to know by some sixth sense which sail to order to be brought in or unfurled; the ease with which they could read the tide and use it to position Seagull with almost pin-point accuracy. They came into port as the majority of the fleet was leaving. The year was 1805, Admiral Lord Nelson, after chasing the French fleet across the Atlantic and back, was sailing his fleet south towards Cadiz. He hoped to try to finish off the remains of the combined Spanish and French fleets that had eluded him for months.

Captain Mitchell was in a bad mood, he somehow sensed that the naval struggle with France was at a climax, but he also knew that there was no chance of him being part of it. He sent his regards to the Admiral almost as soon as they docked, with the forlorn hope of being given another commission so as to be part of the forthcoming adventure.

Nelson had sent back a polite reply thanking him for the intelligence he had sent home with the Neptune, who was sailing with the fleet, and wished him well.

Ben had not expected to be so busy after they had reached port, but a full inventory of ships stores had to be carried out before he and the other officers could take leave. Mr. Gill the ship's purser was as fastidious as any accountant and every last item had to be ticked off.

"The first thing we must do, is get you properly dressed, I know a little tailor just off the dock who'll work wonders with those old uniforms," said Barraclough.

At last, Captain Mitchell allowed his officers to take shore leave. Ben and Barraclough went ashore together.

The shop had a curious low front with a door hardly more than five feet high, forcing both men to duck as they entered. A strange pungent, oily smell filled the room; a single lamp flickered nervously, casting dancing shadows along the rows of rolled material along the wall. Suddenly, the blanket that acted as a door at the far end of the room was thrown open. A small tubby figure dressed in shirt, waistcoat, and trousers entered with a flurry. His lapels were covered in chalk dust and were studded by a row of pin-heads.

"Mr. Barraclough, what a pleasure. How many years since I last saw you?" He rubbed his hands together in anticipation, and then studied the oddly dressed young man by the Lieutenant's side.

"And what have we here?"

"This is Mr. Burrows a friend of mine. As I'm sure you can see that the uniform he has inherited does not do him much justice."

The little tailor wandered around Ben; as he pulled and tugged at the over-size uniform he made funny little throat noises. Then with a piece of chalk he began making marks and lines.

"No problem!" he muttered several times.

Ben slipped off the jacket and the tailor disappeared back through the blanket. There was the sound of voices, moments later the man reappeared. He held the jacket for Ben to try again.

"Hmm . . . yes . . . no problem." Away he went again, only to return moments later, with a row of pins gripped firmly between his lips, "no problem." He took a couple of measurements, drew a few quick chalk lines and then away he went again. Within the hour they were back on the street, the jacket, waistcoat and trousers looked brand new and fit perfectly.

Ambling back through the hustle and bustle of the town, they reached the end of a row of shops where they were met by a young midshipman. They all saluted smartly.

"I'm glad I found you Mr. Barraclough. Captain Mitchell sends his regards, and asks that you meet him at the Admiralty Buildings as soon as possible." He saluted again and then ran off on another mission.

Ben was enjoying the feel of his transformed uniform. When he thought his friend was not looking he would sneak a look at himself. Occasionally he would stretch out his arm so that he could see the decorative braiding of the sleeve. He also was aware of the admiring looks the ladies gave him as they passed.

"Good heavens man I didn't realise you had been promoted to Admiral." The Captain joked good humouredly when he caught sight of Ben. He was very relieved to see them both after having spent three fruitless hours with the pompous and arrogant Sea Lords.

"Sorry to interrupt your leave gentlemen before it even gets under way, but I have to travel to London. I would like you both to accompany me," he waited for their nod of agreement. "Good, I'll explain on the way. Your refit looks excellent Mr. Burrows; I hope they do as well with the Seagull."

A carriage awaited them and with no further ado they set off. The countryside changed over and again as they headed towards the capital; the noise of the coach drowned out any conversation and so they travelled almost in silence, buried in their own thoughts and trying to get a little sleep.

Chapter Fourteen

•◦❋◦•

With the evening came a cold, damp mist that penetrated into every corner of the coach. Ben sat by the window trying to watch as the countryside rolled past but little of it could be seen for the mist and high hedgerows. His mind was on the first coach trip he had made with Linton that had taken him north. He wondered how his friends at home on fells were. He shook his head and felt as if his whole life was one long worry.

"Are you alright Mr. Burrows?" the captain asked.

"Oh . . . yes Capt'n, thank you, I'm fine."

The three mariners sat huddled beneath woollen blankets as they made the painfully slow journey towards London. Sometime early the following morning they pulled in at a coaching house to change the horses. It felt good to be able to stretch and leave the confines of the coach. A very welcome hot meal waited for them inside the inn.

"Ha-ha!" Barraclough said as he entered. "Tuck in Mr. Burrows; this will keep out the cold."

Ben did tuck into the meal; a thick meat stew accompanied by fresh crusty bread rolls and mulled ale. It was all served by a buxom maid whose ample delights and bubbly personality brightened everyone's mood.

Barraclough entertained the maid with some amusing tale he whispered in her ear and she went away giggling.

He was obviously amused too and sat back looking very pleased with a huge smile on his lips.

"Gentlemen I think we will make the most of this break to stretch our legs," Mitchell said.

The first signs of daybreak were showing on the horizon, and thankfully the wind had dropped but the mist still swirled in wispy, ghostly clouds through the lights in the inn yard. They stopped near a small paddock and by the diffused lights of the inn, watched a fine-looking stallion being put into his stall by a young handler.

"That's a fine animal," Barraclough said.

"Ever owned your own horse Mr. Burrows?" The Captain asked.

Ben was caught a little off guard by the sudden question. "No Sir, I've looked after my uncle's, and some belonging to a friend," he said. He hoped the captain was not going to pry deeper.

"Mr. Barraclough wants to give up the immense pleasures of serving King and country, to do nothing other than breed horses. What is your opinion of that?"

Ben realised the captain was only teasing him, yet there was something about the tone of the Captain's voice.

"Well speak up man!"

Ben still speechless, stared at the Captain, then turned to Mr. Barraclough for help. The Lieutenant gave him a reassuring wink.

"Perhaps he has good reasons for such a wish sir," Ben said.

The Captain stared at Ben and then smiling said, "we have a diplomat, as well as a navigator in this young fellow." Laughing heartily he patted Ben on the back as they headed back towards the coach. Warmed by the food and comforted by the ale, all three of them slept a little as soon as the coach continued its journey.

The journey took three days; it was mid-afternoon as they entered the outskirts of London. The green of the countryside was replaced by the squalor, filth and stench of the city. Tightly packed houses, their grey weathered walls crumbling from neglect were crammed into narrow streets. The city was a constantly changing kaleidoscope of views; the squalor gave way to prim, neat parks, suitable for their Royal Majesties to take a peaceful drive through; dirt-thick streets changed into wide straight avenues, shaded by trees standing like guardsmen in almost perfect, yet unnatural straight lines. Neat and tidy houses belonging to the middle classes, formed crescents that overlooked parks and heaths, kept tidy for the sake of it. Ben was impressed only by the sheer size of the city; it did not appeal to him and he decided that he would much rather be in the fells around the Linton's farm.

They reached their destination, the home of Sir Walter Cliffe, the minister responsible for affairs in the New World. The broad gravel drive led to a grand building, where eight vast barley sugar columns supported a canopy of white marble stretching along its entire front.

As the coach crunched to a halt, a number of footmen appeared to deal with their luggage. A severe-looking butler met them as they entered the marble-floored vestibule.

"Follow me gentlemen." He said looking down his nose at their slightly travel soiled uniforms.

Sir Walter, was a tall man with a jovial face that looked out of place with the very sombre suit and fine wig he wore. "Greetings Captain, it's some while since we last met. Please gentlemen, take a seat." Shaking hands with the captain whilst he spoke he indicated for them to sit around a solid oak table illuminated from above by a fine lantern window. He spoke with an easy, confident voice.

"I'd better explain. I don't know how much the Admiralty has told you."

"Not much!" Mitchell interjected.

"Yes, well. The new governor of Jamaica is to be married this week; we are holding the reception here," he said with some pride. "And you are to take him and his new bride back to the West Indies; as soon your ship is repaired and made seaworthy again." He smiled at the group sat around him.

"Make yourselves at home for the next few days. I'm sorry, but I have to be here there and everywhere." He stood up and shook Mitchell's hand again. "I'll see you all at dinner tonight."

With that, he left. The mariners stared at each other briefly, it was obvious the Captain was not used to being so lightly or abruptly dismissed; he cleared his throat and wandered to the window to stare out over the elegant gardens. Barraclough and Ben exchanged a brief glance, Ben pulled a face, and Barraclough winked and smiled.

The same severe butler entered to inform them that their rooms were ready.

"Well gentlemen I think we need to make the most of it and get some well earned rest." Mitchell said as they parted.

Ben could not believe the room he was given. A lace trimmed four poster bed stood against one wall, and tall mirrors disguising the wardrobes behind covered another; he explored the small ante-chamber and was staggered by the sight of a huge marble bath on ornate scrolled legs which filled one corner of the room.

"This is the life. I could live like this" Barraclough said.

He and Ben were sitting out on the balcony that extended from their adjoining rooms. Sharing a bottle of chilled champagne, they smoked thick cigars their host had thoughtfully sent them. Ben had not really mastered smoking, and he was not too sure that he wanted to, but he felt obliged to keep his superior officer company.

"You've seen nothing yet. Wait until the guests arrive, then you'll see some finery. The Captain could live like this you know. His family are very well to do, plus he has had more than his share of luck with prize ships in the past too. His only problem is, that he's the third son, not much chance of inheriting the family wealth, but he is determined to build a fortune equal to that of his family."

"He'd rather be with Nelson," Ben observed.

"Aye lad you're right. He's the best Captain I've ever sailed with; granted he has some funny little ways, but he's never a man to put on airs and graces, and he never asks a man to do what he himself could not do." There was a definite affection in the way he spoke.

Captain Mitchell arrived. " Excuse me gentlemen may I join you?"

Ben and Barraclough leapt to their feet. "Of course Sir, our pleasure."

"Thank you, do sit down," he said, and then there was a slight pause. "The new Governor has sent his regards, and asks that we all be present at the reception. I have taken the liberty of sending for a tailor I know to come fit us all with uniforms more suitable to such an occasion; he should be here within the hour."

The tailor duly arrived; he was very different to Barraclough's man in Portsmouth, tall and slim, he moved around them like a professional dancer, and his three assistants who seemed perfectly choreographed bearing cloth samples and design books accompanied him.

After showing off his designs, he made hurried notes and bombarded his assistants with orders and commands; they left with what could only be described as theatrical flourish.

As soon as they left, Ben and Barraclough resumed the serious task of consuming another bottle of champagne.

That evening at dinner they learnt more of their task and destination. Their host was a generous provider and the meal was accompanied by a constant flow of wine. After the meal they all withdrew to a large sitting room for brandy and cigars and of course some rather serious conversation.

The next two days provided an unexpected holiday and there was nothing to do but take advantage of it. Most of the time they sat and relaxed on their balcony overlooking the parklands below. Anywhere else, they seemed to be in the way, with all the preparations that were going on for the wedding reception. They found a room that was obviously an armoury; the walls were full of various weapons in artistic arrangements and magnificent, vast paintings of battles with advancing infantry and booming cannons.

"Come on my boy, time for some fencing practice," Barraclough said.

He tossed a rapier to Ben and armed himself with one too. For over two hours they worked with the foils until they both were ready for a rest.

"It might just save your life sometime to become confident with a blade," Barraclough said, blowing hard.

The uniforms arrived the morning of the reception and created some mirth between Ben and Barraclough, as they dressed together. The Captain had really gone overboard with the trimmings he had ordered for them.

"If the lads in the fo'c'sle could see me now," Ben laughed as he admired himself in front of the mirrors, setting his bicorne hat at a jaunty angle he strutted around the room.

"The ladies will never resist you. Watch out lad, or they'll all be after you."

The weather was perfect; clear blue sky, with just the gentlest of breezes to prevent the day becoming too hot. Gleaming coaches, pulled by perfectly matched silk coated horses with jingling harnesses began to arrive with their guests. The crunch of the gravel beneath the coach wheels, and the growing hum of voices seemed to fill the air with expectancy.

In the garden to the rear of the house, a small string orchestra played Mozart amidst the exquisite scene; the music mixed with the heady scents of lavender and roses, conjuring up a fairy tale atmosphere. It drifted through the topiary hedge avenues that wound like a serpent around the garden. There were occasional arches covered in clematis and ivy which led to secret romantic bowers. These secluded, private corners were cooled by pools filled with cascading crystal water, from the mouths of mythical animals and the urns of nymphs.

It was the social occasion of the year, and everyone was out in their finest; they promenaded like flamingos, strutting and chatting, gathering in small groups to gossip and speculate about the new bride.

Ben was feeling rather conspicuous as he and Barraclough first stepped out of the house in their new uniforms. They stood a moment to survey the scene and get their bearings. Ben's stiff shirt collar was beginning to chafe his neck a little, so he stuck his finger down between the skin and the material to try and ease the pressure. They set off across the lawn to a pavilion that was serving drinks.

As they strolled they took time to admire the ladies, and it was just as Barraclough had promised; beautiful women, in silks and laces giving them long sideways glances from behind their fluttering fans. Ben could not keep his eyes off one or two of the young ladies, and his ego was boosted to find that they in turn were eyeing him from beneath the lacy edges of silk parasols and obviously whispering about him.

"Watch out for some of these fillies lad, they can have a severe sting in their tails," Barraclough warned.

The 'crème de la crème' of the English aristocracy had gathered for the occasion and were now waiting in the drive as His Majesty King George the Third arrived. They vied for places as he stepped from his coach and greeted them. When the news circulated around the grounds that the happy couple's coach had just pulled into the drive, the level of excitement heightened.

Sir Arthur Compton, the new governor, had been a bit of a ladies man in his youth; he was well liked in the right circles, even though he was a bit of a rogue. He liked to be at the races and was a member of most of the clubs and night spots of the city, frequently enjoying late night revelling. At thirty-five he had been written off as an incurable bachelor, and so it was of great interest to quite a number people, especially some of the court wives, as to what the young lady was like who had finally snared him.

A fanfare played by Household Guards, which was the grooms old regiment, heralded their arrival on the lawn, and summoned the guests to gather round. A toast was drunk to the King, and then to the happy couple.

The guests milled about the couple, waiting impatiently to be introduced to the stunning beauty that clung to Compton's arm like a bird of prey.

"My words, you two look like a couple of peacocks strutting about." The Captain said; he sported a broad grin and his face was slightly flushed as he spoke.

"I'll introduce you to the happy couple as soon as it's convenient." He was whisked away, and immediately both arms were taken by ladies; he obviously said something amusing and both his companions giggled girlishly behind their fluttering fans.

"They'll never get the Captain, there's many a broken heart in his wake." Barraclough said with a broad grin.

A little while later the Captain returned looking very content with himself and without his escorts. "Gentlemen please follow me line astern," he said.

Without waiting for them, he changed course, and headed across the manicured lawn. He saluted smartly as he caught the King's eye, but never faltered with his step. Ben and Barraclough set off after him; they managed to offload their glasses on a passing waiter as they dashed past. They bowed and saluted as they too crossed the King's bow, but pressed on after their Captain.

The couple were standing with their backs to the naval contingent, and only after Captain Mitchell made a polite cough did they turn. Ben froze; it was as if his legs were no longer part of him. He struggled for breath, turning a deathly white.

"Steady old chap, I warned you about the drinks." Barraclough extended his arm to help steady him. Fortunately, the Captain did not see.

"May I present my first officer; Lieutenant Barraclough, and my Master's Mate and navigator Mr. Burrows."

The whole company exchanged nods and smiles, apart from Ben, who tried to hide inside his hat.

It had been four years since he had seen her, and he knew she recognised him, their eyes clashed together like flying sabres. She remained cool, showing no outward sign of recognition.

"Will you be sailing with us?" She said grandly to Ben.

"Indeed yes ma'am." Barraclough proudly interjected.

"How wonderful." She gave him a smile that could have melted solid stone.

Another rush of well-wishers broke in, and the three naval men were pushed into the background, much to Ben's relief.

The two ladies, who had earlier been hung on the Captain's arm closed in, and Ben used the diversion to make his escape. A feeling of panic twisted his insides; he began to tremble, his mind racing.

'Had she recognised him?' He wondered, although he knew that there was no doubt about it. 'Why hadn't she given him away? Would she tell her new husband perhaps?' There seemed to be no answer. He found himself alone by a small pool hidden away from the rest of the garden by a high hedge of dark leaved rhododendrons. A feeling of despair and total exhaustion flooded over him. Sitting on the stonework, he blew a heavy sigh and wondered how on earth he'd get out of this predicament.

"Surely thing's cannot be that bad." A soft voice said.

Ben jumped like a startled deer, almost toppling backwards into the pool. It was one of the young ladies he had been admiring earlier.

"You look as if you've seen a ghost." She sat very close to him.

"It's the heat, and these tight collars," he said with a weak smile.

He moved away just a little.

"I've not seen you before, I'm Annabelle." She held out her long slim arm, a pure white lace glove covered her hand and forearm.

"Ben Burrows ma'am," He said, rather formally as he tried to regain his composure.

"You are funny." She giggled, and moved a little closer.

He could feel the heat of her thigh against his leg. He was reluctant to move, but alarm bells began to ring at the back of his mind.

"You two look cosy." The voice cut the air like a whip.

He felt as if his heart had stopped completely. There was no need for him to look up to discover the owner of that voice.

Annabelle jumped to her feet as if she had been scalded by the water of the pool; her eyes blazing. Her hands on hips, she stared at Ruth, but she was no match for the strong will of the Yorkshire woman. She was forced to concede, and look away.

"Do run along dear, I wish to have a private word with this gentleman." She stopped, and pretended to be searching for the name. "Burrows, is that right, did you say it was Burrows?"

Ben gave no answer, trying to contain the sudden rush of emotions.

Annabelle threw her head haughtily in the air. "We will talk about this some other time Ruth," and left with great indignation.

"Oh Ben, I thought you were dead. Why did you not write, let me know?" She stood directly in front of him taking his hands between hers. "How handsome you are and certainly much taller, I barely reach your shoulder now. The uniform suits you."

She spoke like an excited little girl; Ben was more than a little taken aback as it was the last response he had expected from her.

"Ruth . . ." he was lost for words.

"You've kept our secret about that night?" she asked

"Yes of course, were you never questioned?"

"Oh yes of course, I just said that you were fighting and that he fell out of the loft."

"Did you never tell them that it was you that knocked him over?"

"Good God no! Father would have been furious with me."

"But that means they still believe I killed him."

"Well yes, but it doesn't matter now anyway."

"It does to me."

"You have a new identity, a new life, what more could you want. What about me? I'm married to this stupid oaf because Mama thinks it will be good for me and the family of course." She pouted. "I've to travel halfway around the earth to some Godforsaken island full of stupid plantation people with their stupid wives and families, and you just have adventures, it's not fair."

He moved away, unsure of himself; just her presence, smelling her soft alluring fragrance, aroused again buried feelings. Their eyes locked, she smiled, the time and distance rolled away, they were children again in his uncle's barn. Their hands touched, they embraced and kissed a kiss of such intensity that their bodies seemed to float in mid-air. The sounds of the party faded away. Reluctantly they broke apart, but their souls stayed welded together.

"We must rejoin the others, it's not proper for us to be here together," Ben said, regaining his composure.

"It was the best thing that could have happened; my odious brother made my life hell at times," She said with a hard expression.

"I still can't believe you let them think I was the one to kill him."

She followed him, straightening the front of her dress with the flats of her hands.

"It will be so romantic. Together again, after all this time; on the high seas for months on end."

He stared in disbelief at her, his mouth hung open, as he tried to find something to say.

"You're married!" he spluttered. "Romantic! Are you completely mad? It will be a nightmare!"

She came close to him, pressing her body against his.

"Yes, romantic. Not only husbands can have a little lace around the edges of their life." She said with a wicked grin. "Oh Ben, don't punish me. This marriage is not of my making."

Ben stepped back retreating until the stonework of the pool caught the backs of his legs.

"We shouldn't be alone together," he mumbled.

"Oh Ben!" She sounded just as she had done when as children they had played together and she had dared him to do something. "Perhaps you are no longer attracted to me." The words hung in the air for a moment.

"You know that isn't true."

"Are you still in love with me?" she purred, her voice was as soft as silk.

"I don't think that matters somehow," he faced her, "what of your feelings?"

"Ladies aren't allowed them, it seems." It was she who turned away this time. "I was not even consulted as to whether or not I wished to marry this man."

"Would you have married another then?" He said his voice almost a whisper.

"Do you mean you?" She gave a mocking laugh, "ha . . . do you think for one moment that my mother and father would have allowed me to marry you? You, sir, killed their pride and joy, their son and heir; which in my Mother's eyes is only slightly less of a sin than the fact that you are a mere orphan raised by a lowly innkeeper."

"We could have run away together."

"I am not brave enough to give up all this," she ran her hands over her fine dress, "what could you have provided? Oh no, Mr. Burrows, we could never have been happy."

"I think you mean, madam, that you could never have been happy."

"Perhaps I do. Yes perhaps so, but it would have only brought misery for us both."

"Then are you saying that you are happy now?"

"Happiness is all well and good, but it does not bring with it the finer things of life."

"That depends on what you regard as the finer things." He left her with a curt bow, "your servant ma'am"

It was uncomfortable to think of that night again, but there were so many happy memories too. Seeing her again he knew he was still very much in love with her. She had always teased and led him on; he smiled as he thought he had always followed willingly.

A flash of memory came to him, of a similar day to this, warm with bright sunshine in the hills around Bingley. They ran so fast that their legs could hardly keep pace, and inevitably they tumbled. Head over heels they somersaulted down the closely cropped hillside landing in the middle of a prehistoric stone circle. For a moment they lay in the warm sunlight just staring at the drifting clouds.

"Look," she said pointing upward, "that one there, it looks like a dragon." Ruth panted.

"No, it's a horse, with a knight of the '*Round Table*' on its back. See that long strand, that's the knight's lance," Ben said.

Ruth was up again and ran into the circle to sit on a central altar stone. She laid full length on it, arranging herself so that her long hair draped over the end of the stone and with her arms crossed over her chest she announced. "I am Saint Ruth captured by the wicked Wizard of the Mountains." She dutifully closed her eyes and accepted her fate.

Ben remembered how he had only been able to stare at her, stunned by her beauty and almost immobilised by the vision.

"You are the Wizard and must threaten my life," she ordered.

Ben found a dead branch and wielding it like a sword he came and stood over her. He stood with the sword poised above her heart wishing he could steal it forever.

"Stop!" She commanded and then released the buttons down the front of her summer frock exposing her breasts and stomach. "Now strike your wicked blow you foul wizard and history will damn you forever."

He remembered how aroused he had been as he stood above her, and even now the thought of her was unsettling.

There had been an uncertain pause and then suddenly she sat up and wrapping her arms around her body said, "Do you love me?"

"Yes." He replied simply.

"How much? Would you die for me like a Greek Hero?"

"Yes."

"Would you fight off hordes of demons and even the devil himself?" She stared intently up at Ben and he remembered the look in her eyes, wild and passionate. "If there was a flash of fire and the devil came to carry me away, would you save me?"

"Yes of course, you know I would." His reply was just a hoarse whisper.

"Yes I know you would," she whispered. Like a leaf blown by the wind she was up and running again shrieking loudly as she danced around the circle. "I know you would."

Wandering almost in a daze through the confusion of the party, his body tensed almost as if expecting an attack as a hand gripped his upper-arm.

"Where have you been? You look awful" Barraclough said.

"I'm going for a lie down, I'll be alright." He smiled reassuringly.

In his room, he drew the curtains, carefully hanging up his jacket he unbuttoned his shirt and flopped onto the bed.

Suddenly the door flew open, he sat up startled.

"Oh! I am sorry; I thought this part of the house was unoccupied." Annabelle said feigning surprise. Her chest heaved as though she had been running. "I had to get away, that awful son of Sir Walter's, he keeps pestering me for a dance. Do you dance?"

With her heel she kicked the door closed, and then moved to where his jacket hung, the tips of her fingers toyed with the sleeve. Her eyes never left him, as she strolled around the room, working her way closer to him. She moved away with a deliberate manner towards the window and opened the curtains slightly, bathing a moment in the narrow beam of bright sunlight.

"Do you think I'm beautiful?" Her voice was slightly husky. She pouted her lips and stood just a second longer in the spotlight.

"Yes, very," his voice barely carried to her.

Raising her arms she untied the ribbon that held her hair then shook it loose; the long dark curls bounced over her shoulders, resting in the deep open cleavage of the dress. Slowly she removed her gloves, and then advanced on him again.

"You will have to forget Ruth now she is a married Lady." Annabelle said.

Ben wondered if that would ever be possible, especially as he was to accompany her to her new home in the West Indies. Annabelle was very close to him and he could smell the soft fragrance of her perfume and feel the soft material of her dress.

"Do you think I'm as beautiful as The Lady Ruth?" she breathed the words into his ear.

"More so, I'd say," he lied.

"I'll wager you say that to every girl." Her lips were close to his. "This time I don't think we'll be disturbed, do you?" she said letting her gloves float to the floor.

CHAPTER FIFTEEN

Captain Mitchell was in a poor humour. He had just received word that Seagull would not be ready for eight to ten weeks. That would probably mean that he would lose most of his crew, apart from his officers. It also ruled out any chance of him joining Lord Nelson's fleet, which rumour had it was about to engage the enemy off Cadiz.

He had been back on board for almost a week, and there was nothing other than repairs to keep the crew busy. He knew from experience that it was not good for his crew's morale. The decks were covered in timber for the repairs and everything was in a jumble.

Ben knocked at the Captain's door; it had taken awhile for him to build up enough courage to approach his Captain.

"Enter."

Ben rather sheepishly entered the cabin.

"Now then Mr. Burrows, why the glum face?"

"Sir, I would like to request a few weeks leave."

"For what purpose Mr. Burrows?"

"As you well know Capt'n I was pressed into service. My friends, and the people I was staying with, will wonder what has become of me."

"Pressed men very rarely return to sea once they've been home. I have found you a very useful junior officer I would hate to lose you so soon."

"I'm certain that I will return here Captain."

"I hope so, Mr. Barraclough speaks highly of you."

"Thank you sir."

"Very well, be back here for the twenty second of next month. That gives you six weeks."

"Thank you Captain."

Ben had never done a great deal of riding, but decided that it was preferable to taking the coach. He purchased a horse from a dealer recommended by Barraclough. It was a stocky-looking beast with shaggy hair but his friend said it seemed sound of limb and although it would never win any major race, it would serve Ben's needs well enough. Taking some provisions tied up in a saddlebag he was about to leave when Barraclough appeared in the stable doorway. "Thought I'd see you off," he said. "Here you might need these." He handed Ben a couple of pistols, plus powder and shot. "You never know who's out there."

They shook hands. Ben smiled, "I'll be back on time."

Once clear of the city he had the sudden and wonderful feeling of freedom. Yet he was unsure of his emotions; he knew that now he had the chance to escape the harsh naval life, but he was not sure that he wanted to. Barraclough had asked him straight out when they were alone, as to whether or not he intended to return; Ben had answered quite truthfully that he did intend to.

The journey north was a long hard slog. By the end of his first day, he had reached Reading, where he managed to find simple lodgings for the night. Next morning, after a filling breakfast of ham and bread, he was back on the road for seven o'clock, determined to try to make Bingley within the week. Day after day he headed north towards Derby, and then through the ever-expanding industrial hub of Yorkshire; the growing steel city of Sheffield, with its mines and belching black smoke stacks.

He dozed a little as his horse plodded along a road and up onto the moorland of the peak district. Some sense woke him in time to realise that he was not alone. A single horseman was cantering up behind him. Ben cocked one of the pistols and hid it in the folds of his overcoat.

Within a few minutes the rider caught up with him.

"Hello there," the man called. "My name's Gill, Arthur Gill. I was wondering if I might ride with you? There are a number of gangs of highway men along this road."

"Oh . . . I didn't know," Ben said. My name's Ben Burrows."

"Navy man are you?"

"Yes I'm on leave, I'm going to visit friends up north."

"I'm on my way to Huddersfield, so if you don't mind I'll keep you company."

"Yes indeed, I'm glad of someone to talk with; this horse has a very limited conversation."

By nightfall, they were far from anywhere and decided to shelter in an old, broken down barn by the roadside. It had started to rain heavily and they were glad of the shelter. They cleared one corner beneath what remained of the roof and built a small fire. Outside the rain was heavy and the temperature had dropped considerably.

"I think it could snow before morning." Gill said. "I'm not certain, but I'm sure I just saw a figure over there." He peered out into the gloom.

They both watched for a while but there was not another sighting.

"We'd best be on our metal, we're probably in the gangs territory now." Gill said.

They ate a meal and settled down close to their fire. All was quiet, only the crackle of the fire and the hiss of boiling sap as it leaked from damp twigs, disturbed their thoughts. Suddenly the horses, which were tethered inside the building near them, became restless.

Quietly Ben and Gill cocked their pistols. They waited in silence with every nerve tingling, facing the only way in through the broken down wall. Gill fetched a musket from his saddle and cocked that too.

"Hello in the building." The voice was strong and confident.

"May I share your fire? My name is Bellamy, James Bellamy, I'm a travelling preacher."

"Enter Mr Bellamy," Ben called.

"Mr. Bellamy, please extend your arms as you enter, you can't be too careful these days, you know," Gill shouted

A silhouette appeared against the night sky; it was a sizable silhouette wrapped in a heavy woollen cloak, made even bigger by the extended arms.

"Come warm, and dry yourself Mr. Bellamy," Ben said.

Gill stirred the fire to increase the glow allowing him to get a better look at the newcomer. After removing his cloak, the man pulled a sizable rock near to the fire and sat down with confident ease.

"My name's Burrows and this is Mr. Gill, a fellow traveller."

"So gentlemen, what a night, the weather on these moors can be dreadful. I'm very grateful to you, for allowing me the comfort of your fire." He pulled a large hip flask from beneath his jacket and offered it around. "I'm on my way to Harefield, to see some friends and of course spread the *good word.*"

Gill took the flask and sipped at it. "Fine brandy Mr. Bellamy."

"Medicinal of course," he said, and then he laughed throwing his head back. "Actually, I just like the stuff." His laugh was infectious, and broke the slight tension around the fire.

He went back outside to fetch his horse. Gill still had his musket across his knee pointed vaguely towards the entrance. He was not chancing that the stranger coming back in with a couple pistols cocked.

"You are very cautious Mr. Gill," Ben said.

"I've been robbed twice on this road," Gill replied.

Bellamy tethered his horse and unsaddled it, giving it a good pat and rub before he left it. He threw a heavy blanket down near the fire to sit on. From his saddlebags, he pulled some bread and cheese, and a bottle of wine. "I don't have much gentlemen, but I'd be pleased to share with you."

"No need sir, we have already had a meal. Perhaps we could give you some of our salted beef."

The offer was accepted and then Bellamy opened the wine and passed it around.

"Is this medicinal too?" Ben smiled.

"Absolutely, it's also very tasty." He roared with laughter again at his own joke.

They had just settled down again, when there was another shout. "My words, it's as busy as a market," Bellamy said.

There was the metallic clicking of flintlocks being cocked and for a nervous moment, they waited and watched.

A figure appeared in the gap in the wall. A very different figure to the last, this was tall and lean, almost feminine, but the voice was baritone with a strong Yorkshire accent. "May I join you?"

"Why not?" Ben said, just a little sarcastically.

"The rain is freezing." The new comer said. He joined the circle trying to get close to the fire. "I got lost in the mist, and it's so many years since I came this way, that I think I've been going in circles."

Bellamy offered him the wine bottle and some bread, which was gratefully taken.

"Bread and wine, it's like taking communion, you should be a priest." The new arrival said."

"I am," replied Bellamy "well, I'm a preacher."

"May I ask your name?"

Gill sat forward, "it is not good manners to ask a man's name, or his business at the fireside."

"Oh I'm sorry; my name is Sladdin, Jeffery Sladdin."

Everyone seemed to relax a little. There was some small talk before everyone found a comfortable place for the night. Not that there was much comfort, but at least they were dry and warmer than being outside.

Gill still had his musket across his knees and always one eye on the space in the wall.

Ben also slept with one eye open. The peak of his hat pulled down over his face, giving the impression of him being asleep. He catnapped knowing that Gill would only be half-asleep too.

Outside the rain fell even harder, long steely rods that could freeze the soul as well as the body, its sound drowned out everything else. Gill suddenly sat up a little, his head cocked to one side.

"What is it?" Ben whispered.

"Maybe nothing, but I was sure I heard something."

There was another sound; even Ben heard it this time. With a pistol in each hand Gill carefully and silently went to the far corner of the building.

Sladdin was awake too, "Where's he going?" he whispered.

"To the other side of the room," Ben whispered back.

"Why?"

"If there is someone out there, and they decide to come join us with weapons drawn, then they'll not expect someone behind them."

Ben kicked the fire back into life. He threw on more kindling and poked at it with a stout branch.

"They'll be able to see us now." Sladdin said with concern.

"Yes."

"But . . ."

"Shush . . . please Mr. Sladdin, I need to listen." Ben picked up the musket; he tingled with anticipation and enjoyed the feeling.

There was a sound as if someone had stood on some loose stones and sent them tumbling. Then there were even more sounds as more stones tumbled.

"Come out with your hands up," a voice shouted. There was a pause and then an afterthought, "and throw out your weapons." The voice had a hard edge to it.

Bellamy was now awake too he looked at Ben for leadership. Ben just held his finger to his lips.

There was a tense pause as the stalemate played itself out. Ben cocked his musket and handed a pistol to Sladdin.

"We'll come in and drag you out if you don't hurry!"

A gun was fired, but the sound was carried away with the rain and it did not have the desired effect. Another shot, this time into the building. The lead shot ricocheted around the walls like a frantic bee.

Both Bellamy and Sladdin were at their nerves end, but Ben held up his hand for them to be calm. All eyes were on the tumbled down section of the wall.

"Hey in there, you stupid bastards are making me very angry!"

"Go away, come back in the morning, I'm tired," Ben shouted in a bored tone.

"Tired, tired, I said come out, are you stupid?"

"Not as stupid as you are, out there in the wind and rain," Ben answered.

Someone made an exasperated sound and a figure appeared in the gap of the wall.

"Take another step and I'll shoot you dead." Ben said confidently.

Another stalemate, the figure hesitated. Ben fired above his head. There was a curse, and the figure stumbled back the way it had come. A second shot came into the building and zinged off the stonework. Sladdin's grip had been tightening on the pistol, suddenly it went off, and he dropped it as if it was red hot. Ben gave him a quizzical glance.

"Sorry it just went off."

Gill suddenly was on the move; he ran up the stones and was outside in a flash. As he reached the top of the wall, he fired both his pistols.

"They're gone" he shouted, "three of them I think."

The rest of the night, they took turns to keep watch, but Ben hardly slept at all.

The next morning the rain had cleared and the four rode out after a quick breakfast of bread and cheese. As they rode along the track, they were more wary of their surroundings. Gill would suddenly canter out in front for about two or three-hundred yards to try and spring any ambush that was waiting.

"So Mr. Gill, I think you have some military training too, the way you handled the situation last night," Ben said.

"Yes I was a sergeant in the dragoons for over ten years."

"Do you think they'll be back?"

"I doubt it; they are looking for easier targets than four armed men."

That afternoon they reached a crossroad and both Sladdin and Bellamy said they must leave. "Thank you both," Bellamy said. He shook hands with Gill and Ben. "I'm sure that you saved my purse and maybe my life last night."

Another hour later and Gill also took his leave. "Good luck Mr. Burrows, I'd like to wish you a safe journey."

"Thank you Mr. Gill. I wish you the same, and perhaps we shall meet again someday." They shook hands and went their separate ways.

It was five days since leaving Portsmouth, when Ben finally skirted Bradford, set in its smoke capped basin, with only the tops of the mill chimneys and an odd church steeple poking through the smog.

He waited on the outskirts of Bingley at Cottingley Bridge until it was almost dark. His poor horse looked all in from the journey and was glad of the breather. He was confident no one would recognise him so he decided to walk his mount down the main street to the street where his Uncle's inn stood.

Leading his horse along the road, he felt slightly guilty for not contacting them for such a long while. He stopped, almost afraid to face them again. He took a deep breath as he went under the familiar arches into the rear-yard of the inn. He led his horse into the familiar stable and was drawn to the spot Bart had laid on that fateful day. After removing his horse's saddle and making sure it had feed and water, he threw his dark blue naval overcoat around himself, covering part of his face.

There was a single light burning in one of the upstairs rooms; he knew it to be their bedroom. He gave a confident knock at the door; the sound echoed around the yard and along the hallway behind the door. He saw the curtain twitch in the light, as someone peeped out. He knocked again.

"I'm coming . . ."

Ben recognised the voice of his Uncle. A small square bob hole opened.

"Yes?"

"I was wondering if you could put me up for the night Landlord?" Ben said. He had tried to disguise his voice by imitating Barraclough's West Country accent.

"Indeed Sir come in. Mek thee'sen comfortable in't snug, fire's still glowing; I'll give it a stir." The door was thrown open for him. Ben took off his cap and coat, and then sat in the comfort of home. He soaked it in a moment; remembering the smell, the low dark beams the wide-open fireplace and the carved wooden benches.

"Not often we are honoured by the presence of the na . . ." the voice trailed away, and he stood frozen in his tracks.

"BEN! Ben it's you lad, it is. Lord help us. Stay there till I fetch your Aunt Dot."

She flew in like a whirlwind, and despite the fact that he towered over her; she dragged him to her bosom. "Oh my little lamb where have you been?" Her face ran with tears of joy. She clung to him not daring to let go. Ben tried to answer, but gave up under the bombardment of questions that the couple fired at him.

"For pity's sake, let the lad speak," his Uncle said.

"I would like some supper and something to drink," Ben said.

"Of course lad, what are we thinking of." His Aunt bustled away.

When she returned they let him eat awhile before asking anymore questions. Eventually they got round to why he had run away.

"I was a bit confused and Ruth said it was best that I escape before her father had me hanged!"

"Did you knock him out of the loft deliberately?" Aunt Dot asked.

"No of course not, in fact . . . oh never mind. No, it was just an accident."

Aunt Dot made him a hot drink, and brought out what used to be his favourite treat, oat cakes.

"Are you going to give yourself up; Sir Geoffrey's a fair man?" Aunt Dot asked. She sat next to Ben and held his hand as if he were a small boy again.

"I've only five weeks leave. If I give myself up now, my Captain will think I've deserted." He knew it was a very lame excuse.

"What good would it do? It won't bring back Hutton-Beaumont's lad. He's serving King, and country now; that's more use than him being in jail." John said. She clutched Ben's hand even tighter.

"Your friend Reverend Linton called some weeks ago." She said to change the subject. "They wondered if we had heard anything. They said they had checked with the navy, but no one with your name was known. They are worried sick about what happened to you."

"There's a good reason for that, I used the name of my friend in Barrow, Burrows instead of my own. In a way it helped me to get promotion. Mr. Burrows, was such a well respected and well known navigator, that as soon as they knew he had schooled me, they were glad to let me do the job."

"I'll make your bed up," she said.

"It's proper champion to see thee again lad," John said. He disappeared for a moment behind the bar, he winked at Ben as he fetched a bottle of his best malt. "Let's have a proper drink to celebrate."

As the first rays of dawn came sleepily through the neat little windows of the snug the three were still by the fire.

"I'll see t'horse, you get some sleep lad," John said.

"I've already done it," Ben said.

In his room it was as if he had never been away, it was so familiar. After his Aunt had kissed his forehead and left, he sat awhile and studied his old room. The memories flooded back. Silly things: the pleasures and joys of youth, the excitement of Christmas mornings, the misery of childhood illnesses. He found the marks he had made on the side of the doorframe that plotted his growth. His finger traced across the grooves. It was mid-afternoon when he finally awoke. He washed in the enormous ceramic bowl on the table under the window; he fingered the familiar cracks around its brim, and smiled.

"How's life here?" He was helping his Uncle in the cellar to shift the empty barrels.

"Times are very hard lad. Most o'lads is out o' work. Most mills 'as taken on them new machines. Bairns are starving to death, we've had riots, and all sorts. If parliament don't get us out of this war with France, there'll be no England. The Luddites are preaching revolution, and a lot are listening. Enoch'll be smashing more than just looms, you mark my words. Not even owners 'as any brass left, it's all been spent on what they call progress. If you want my opinion, progress is a poor substitute for a full belly."

"I'm truly sorry to hear that." Ben thought a moment. "Would it help you if I stayed on here a while?"

"Not really lad. Much as we'd both love your company again. Things can never be as they were."

"I'm very sorry Uncle."

"Nay lad these things happen. Only t' good Lord knows why. We'll get by. Anyway I'm proud of you being in't navy, especially as you're an officer now."

"I'm only a master's mate."

"Same thing. Best thing you can do lad, is be away to see your friend Linton, and then get back to sea. Both your Aunt and I are satisfied now we know you're safe."

The following morning, he reluctantly left with no one in the town the wiser about who the naval gentleman was that had been staying at the Inn.

High on Rombald's moor he stopped, and absorbed the scene. Far below, he could see Keighley, capped by a dark cloud of smog that belched from its forest of chimneys. He followed the route he had taken once before, via Silsden. He thought of Jenny, the young girl in Mace's gang who had befriended him and he wondered what had happened to her. A chilling thought ran through his mind as he wondered if perhaps she was still alive.

It was market day in Skipton and the road to the castle was packed solid with traders and their wares. Dozens of animals seemed to be wandering at will, their owners trying in vain to control and pen them, but it was utter chaos.

The dusty air was heavy with the smell of the market. He did not stop, as somehow the scene spurred him on, and he found himself impatient to reach Cartmel. His saddlebags were filled with an assortment of food, so he ate as he travelled. His aunt had packed them to bursting with food before she had tearfully wished him goodbye. He had been tempted to call and see the Baxter's, but he knew that would only delay him even longer. When finally he reached Levens Bridge, he had to take a break, despite being so close to his destination. He spent an uncomfortable night in the chair of an inn, because they had no spare beds. However, the next morning they served him a hot breakfast and he felt refreshed. His mount too looked sprightlier; he had pushed it hard over the past few days.

It was almost noon as he reached the top of the fell road. He was forced by the beauty of the fells to stop awhile, and try to take in the view that surrounded him. There was the slightest hint of a breeze which carried with it the soft smell of the woodlands down in the valley. He felt intoxicated by it all, and spurred his mount on again.

He felt his breath catch, his stomach churn, as he caught the first sight of the gate to the cottage. Impatiently he tugged at the chain that held the gate, his emotions bubbled up and he swore angrily until it finally fell away from the woodwork. A thin spiral of smoke swirled calmly out of the chimney, and in the downstairs rooms pale lights welcomed him. He threw himself from his mount right outside the kitchen door.

"Ben!" Emily screamed. They embraced, he was quite a bit taller than she was now and he lifted her with ease; she in turn threw her arms around his neck.

"What's all the commotion? Ben! God be praised." Linton said. He looked a very old man. He and Ben embraced. "It's so good to see you lad. How we missed you." His eyes filled with tears that freely spilled down his cheeks. "Oh my boy, how we have missed you."

Emily kissed them both, as she joined in the huddle.

"You always were good at arriving when a meal was on the table," she joked. She ruffled his hair with her hand as she had done when he was teenager.

They all sat around the kitchen table and Emily brought food. He ate hungrily, enjoying every morsel. Between each mouthful, he tried to answer their bombardment of questions.

"Your friend Mr. Burrows has been a constant visitor here, seeking news of you. He was so upset. He contacted everyone he knew in the navy to see if you had been pressed. You must call see him tomorrow," She said.

They talked late into the night; Ben went through the story he had told his Aunt and Uncle. They both looked disappointed when he told them how little time he had to spend with them.

He went to his old bed, above the now empty dormitory. Through the grimy window in the roof he watched the stars slowly circle over him; already he was missing Seagull. He tried to understand his emotions: he had pushed himself so hard to reach here, and now he could not stop thinking about his ship. He slept badly, chased by nightmares, shimmering images of Mace, Ruth, the sound of the angry cannons, and screams of the dying and injured crewmen, but always ending with Ruth. He was up early. When the sun came over the hills across the wide valley, he was out washing in the trough outside the barn. He stretched, and stood a moment arms outstretched naked from the waist up. Suddenly aware that he was not alone, he turned towards the house. Emily stood by the little garden-gate in front of the kitchen, and tucked a stray length of hair behind her ear as she caught his glance.

"Morning," She said in a hoarse whisper. "I thought you would have slept late after your long journey."

She carried a bundle of washing to hang out. Ben took it and carried it for her; slowly they worked their way down the clothes line, stopping every few paces to hang up the next piece of washing, just as they had done so often in the past.

"I'm glad you stopped off in Bingley your family were beside themselves with worry when Linton called to see them."

They reached the end of the line, and he had to make an effort to try to concentrate on her words. He remembered from when he was here with the children that they had all declared her the most beautiful woman in the world, and in her simple working clothes, he had to admit that she was more than a match for any of the ladies he had seen in their finery in London.

She was aware of his stare, and flattered by it, "put your shirt on," she smiled, "you always were too handsome for your own good."

She playfully hit him with a tea towel.

"I thought I might go see Mr. Burrows this morning."

"Oh, I want some material from Dalton, I was going to ask Finlay to take me, but perhaps we could go together in the gig."

Linton saw them off, holding the gate for them to pass through. Emily had put on her best bonnet and cloak and she looked a picture sat on the little seat of the gig. Ben stared a moment before he climbed in beside her. They were squeezed together by the side irons of the seat.

They chatted all the way and it was not long before they arrived at the milliner's shop in Dalton. Emily proudly showed him off in his best uniform to the ladies of the shop. They fussed and cooed around; one of the young girls was sent into the back room for her blatant staring at the strikingly handsome young man.

"How you have blossomed, young man," the matriarch said. It was in her usual stern manner.

"Yes, he's changed so. He's quite a young man now." There was pride in Emily's tone. The Matriarch gave Emily a curious sideways glance along the length of her beak-like nose.

When the girls of the shop learnt that he had met the King and been to London they all wanted news of fashions and gossip.

"Alice," the matriarch snapped. "Don't stare girl."

"But he's beautiful ma'am"

"Men are never beautiful, especially young men in uniform. They are dangerous to young ladies and not so young ladies, if they permit their defences to be lowered." She looked directly at Emily.

"No ma'am, but he really is." The girl's eyes never left Ben's face.

Ben smiled; he had coloured up slightly, but he held out his hand to the girl. She advanced slowly as if hypnotised and the other girls drew and held their breath. Ben took her hand and slowly raised it to his lips and gently brushed her knuckles. For a moment she looked as if she might swoon, there was a sigh as the other girls breathed out at last. Even the matriarch looked a little light headed. She clapped her hands "Back to work girls."

Emily linked arms with Ben, "I'd best take him away."

Ben blew a sigh of relief when they finally left the shop.

"Do you have that effect on all the young ladies you meet?" Emily teased.

"It varies to be honest," he said with a broad grin.

They sat back in the gig. There was a pause as Emily stared at Ben for a moment.

"You *are* beautiful you know," Emily said.

Ben turned to face her, "And so are you Madam," he said.

They laughed and Ben sent the pony on its way towards Barrow. It was like old times except Ben had so much more to tell; about the ship, his new mess mates, his friend Barraclough and of course Captain Mitchell.

They were soon in Barrow, which had grown considerably since his last visit. He was forced to stop a minute to get his bearings. A broad smile crossed Ben's face when at last they reached Mr. Burrows' shop. Emily went into the shop first. She stood quietly by the counter, until Mr. Burrows appeared from the backroom.

"What an honour ma'am I do hope I did not keep you waiting?"

"I have a surprise for you," she said. Something in her eyes gave away the secret, and he instinctively knew what the surprise was.

"Oh my words! Oh did you ever." He clapped his hands together his face aglow with happiness.

Ben held out his hands, and the old man took them, suddenly speechless. Mr. Burrows pulled away and wiped his nose with a spotted cloth he took from his pocket. "I have a cold coming on I think," he said. The old salt turned away to hide his tears of joy. They talked for a couple of hours.

"I don't think the Captain was sure whether or not I'd return."

"And will you?" Emily suddenly asked. She had sat quietly in the corner whilst the two friends had talked. Ben looked up he had almost forgotten she was there.

"Yes of course. I promised that I would."

"Come on Ben. I'm sorry Mr. Burrows, but we must be going."

"Certainly ma'am, I understand. Give my regards to The Reverend."

"I'll be back in a couple of days," Ben said with a broad smile.

He had almost expected Mr. Burrows to be angry with him for what had happened, and so it came as a great relief when they had instantly recaptured the bond between them.

Emily took the opportunity of doing some shopping whilst they were in town. By the time they headed for home, the gig was overflowing with parcels and bags. That evening they sat out in the warm evening air drinking homemade lemonade and eating fresh baked bread.

"Do you remember little Tim?" Linton said.

"Yes, what happened to him?"

"Well, when he left here he went to work as helper to a stockman on Jagger's farm near Coniston. He did very well there, but they had to lay him off, so I've set him on here and he starts next month."

"Doing what?" Ben asked

"Well we always have jobs around here to do and I thought we might put a few beasts in the lower pasture this year."

"Sounds like a good idea, you will have to write and tell me how you fare."

They chatted by the fire like old times and Ben realised just how much he loved them both. He knew that it was going to be hard to leave again.

The following morning Ben was up with the sun. Whilst the rest of the house slept, he was riding down off the fells towards Barrow. Mr. Burrows had eagerly awaited his arrival. As soon as Ben was through the door, he was ushered into the back room.

"I have something for you. Sit down." He placed the heavy object on Ben's knee. "It brought me luck." Ben turned the heavy sextant over in his hands, speechless at the generosity of the gift. The ornamental scrollwork along the sight tube had almost been polished away, but the name down the side was still clearly legible. 'Ship's Master P.A. Burrows R.N.'

"It's magnificent! I can't accept it."

"It will do you more good than me. I have no use for it. It would make me very proud to know that it was again serving King and country."

"Thank you. I don't deserve it."

"Nonsense lad. You did me the honour of choosing my name to give to the navy. Whenever you use this fine instrument, I hope that you will think kindly of me."

"How could I ever think any other?" Ben could not get over the generosity of the gift, for he knew the instrument meant a great deal to his friend.

"I can't stay too long; I've promised the Lintons that I'll be home for the evening meal."

"You're a good lad."

"I wanted so much to see everyone, and now . . . all I can think of is getting back to sea. Is that not awful?"

"I think not lad. I was just the same; and I think every Jack-tar's the same: it get's hold of yer guts and yer soul, sailing does."

"Jamaica. That's where we're bound this next time. Captain Mitchell's put out over the whole affair; he'd rather we'd been given orders to sail for Cadiz to join Lord Nelson."

"I remember your Capt'n as a Commander. He's a mighty fine sailor lad. If he'd played his cards right, he'd be an admiral today. His family has all the right connections. Refused point-blank to marry he did. Their Lordships like their Captains to be married, and it's essential for Admirals."

From amongst the rolls of charts, Burrows produced a tightly rolled length of fine canvas. With loving care, he unrolled it. "I started this chart, back in eighty-five; perhaps you could finish it for me, bring it up to date like."

The chart, which was a work of art, was of the Caribbean Sea. Each island's coastline was plotted and accompanied by precise measurements; these were in italic script with beautiful swirling lines. Around the edge, the whole thing was decorated with a horde of mythical sea-monsters; each corner was adorned with a well-endowed mermaid perched precariously on a rock. They spent several hours over it, Mr. Burrows pointing out the many dangerous reefs and sandbars that had been the end of many ships. He also gave Ben the best approaches to each of the main islands, in particular Jamaica.

"Kingstown," he said his finger lightly touching the map. His mind was suddenly dragged back through time and across the sea, "that's a town that will open your eyes my lad." He shook his head, and gave an expressive short whistle.

Ben left with his mind full of the West Indies and the voyage. As he rode back up the steep fell road, he thought of Ruth. He was confused about his feelings for her. He wanted to hate her, and yet when he had last seen her, when they had kissed, it was as if time had stood still.

Back at the cottage, everything else was forgotten and they sat and chatted endless hours; they picnicked by the river and walked through the woods collecting firewood to burn outside on an evening. It made him sad to see Linton looking so tired and old, but Emily said that it was a terrific tonic for Linton to have him back again.

Although Ben wanted to be back with his ship, the days still passed much quicker than he had expected, and all too soon he had to make his farewells. His horse was well rested and looked fit and ready to go. With panniers bulging with food and gifts, he set off back towards Portsmouth. The weather was unusually mild and dry for mid-September. Ben kept on the move for ten or eleven hours every day, only stopping to allow his horse some rest. He had spent almost all his pay buying gifts for the Lintons and Mr. Burrows before he left Barrow, and so he took advantage of the fine weather, sleeping out a couple of nights rather than taking lodgings.

Portsmouth was its usual hectic self; every busy street seemed to be packed with people. He made his way following a hand drawn map to the lodgings where Mr. Barraclough said he would be staying.

"Mr Burrows, himself. Am I glad to see you? Least of all because Mr. Harvey the ship's surgeon and myself had a wager of three guineas as to whether or not you would return: I of course had every faith in you."

"You seem in high spirits Mr. Barraclough."

"Sit here my friend. Indeed I am in wonderful spirits."

"I trust your stay with your lady friend was agreeable," Ben said with a smile.

"What a woman Ben; all that any man could desire."

"I presume then that you will not be sailing with us to the Indies."

"Not so hasty my lad. My first duty is with my Captain. Much as she has plenty to offer a man, I cannot let my personal comforts cloud my judgement regarding where my first loyalties must lie." For a moment, Barraclough held his face in a stern expression. He could feel Ben's eyes on him and slowly he cracked.

"By jingo lad you're a keen'un," he laughed. "To be honest, a man gets used to being his own counsel. She was very demanding, in many ways. I'll be glad of the rest. Here take a drink of this." He poured them both a drink from a black bottle. They sipped in silence a moment.

"How was your leave? I hope you set the record right with those we dragged you from."

"Indeed yes, they were just glad to know that I was safe."

"Well there is no time for lounging here; the captain said we were to report for duty as soon as you returned."

Outside the streets were as busy as ever and together they made their way back to the dockyard. One of the ship's boats waited for them to ferry them out to the Seagull. Ben had managed to sell his horse and tack for quite a good profit. He was well pleased with the deal and jingled the coins in his pocket as they approached their ship.

"Glad you could spare the time Gentlemen." Mitchell said.

There was more than a hint of sarcasm in his voice, as they came aboard. The two men came to attention in front of the Captain. They had both been smiling up to that point. Captain Mitchell looked black as thunder.

"We will be able to set sail with the tide first thing on Sunday. Just three days. I want everything ready, and all hands on board, as soon as possible." Mitchell barked at them. They were on the poop deck, and Ben's attention was drawn to a second-class ship of the line as she limped in; she was one of the first to get back from Nelson's first engagement with the French off Cadiz.

"Are you listening, or would you prefer to return to the fo'c'sle."

"Begging your pardon Captain, I meant no offence."

"Well look lively then, you must both have something to do, other than stand gawping out to sea." The Captain marched away mumbling to himself, hands clasped firmly behind his back with his shoulders hunched up, his head down.

"Take no notice Mr. Burrows, that broadside was not really fired at us."

"I thought it would be weeks until the ship was ready."

"Aye, well I think he's chased the carpenters, he'll not settle until we put to sea."

The next three days were one long hectic rush, as Seagull took on stores from the never-ending convoy of boats and barges that came alongside. The Captain's humour did not improve until he finally gave Barraclough the order to weigh anchor and set sail. In his small cabin, Ben heard the shanty begin and listened to the tramping of feet above him as the hands began to force round the capstans dragging the heavy anchors out of the river mud. It was long hard work, but by the time the tide had reached its highest, Seagull was ready. A flurry of orders filled the air; Ben could imagine the activity amongst the intricate web of rigging. The topsail men climbed high above the decks to unfurl the sails, and as soon as the sailcloth fluttered open the ship began to come to life. There was a change in the ship's movement, and he knew they were out of the sheltered waters of the harbour and cutting through the open sea. He sorted out the order of his charts and placed his fine new chart from Mr. Burrows alongside the ship's chart of the same area.

CHAPTER SIXTEEN

———————————•◦❁◦•———————————

It was a great day to be sailing even on a rather cumbersome vessel such as Seagull, which nevertheless made a majestic sight, as her broad clean sails puffed out proudly in the wind.

Ben was busying himself in the chart room. His promotion to Master's Mate was now official, but because the Captain had not taken on a new Master, he was now acting Master and feeling very pleased with himself.

He laid out the necessary charts, fingering them lightly, straightening their edges and admiring their precise artwork. Selecting a pair of dividers from the top of the desk, he stepped them across the chart, rechecking his original calculations. The work was helping to keep his mind off who they were to pick up when they reached London. In his best hand, he slowly made the first entry in the ship's log.

Captain Mitchell had also buried himself away in his cabin. He was angry with himself for allowing the situation back in Portsmouth to get to him and for sounding off at Barraclough; who was after all his most loyal friend.

On deck, it was business as usual. Barraclough stood like a statue, filled with pride as Seagull bulldozed her way through the slightly choppy water. He stood silently on the quarterdeck a while, then closed his eyes to better absorb the smell and feel of the sea. The wind as it tugged at him made him glad that he was at sea again.

The Thames was as busy as any high street; merchant ships and naval vessels crowded the wharf and dockyards. Every shape and size of ship was to be seen. Fleets of broad-beamed Thames barges choked the waterways, carrying every imaginable commodity; coal, iron, silk and spices.

A naval barge met Seagull at Woolwich where the passengers and their considerable personal effects were loaded aboard. Officers and men were on deck to welcome aboard their passengers. The ship's marines provided a guard of honour for Sir Arthur, whose father had served a very distinguished career as a Captain of Marines. Ruth looked to be dressed for the races; she wore a deep purple, broad-brimmed hat, decorated with an enormous ostrich feather, which was constantly in need of holding down in the strong breeze. Her long, flowing cape and billowing dress matched the hat perfectly. As she was lifted rather regally onto the deck, she gave the whole ship a cursory glance, like a Monarch surveying her lands.

"Captain Mitchell!" she said pushing past her husband, and holding out her arm. "How wonderful to see you again, and what a magnificent ship."

There were rumours that she had already put a very tight rein on her husband, and despite his reputation, she was very much the head of the house. She acknowledged Barraclough, with a broad, almost sensuous smile, but ignored Ben, walking straight past him, much to his relief.

As soon as they were dismissed, Ben retreated to the safe womb of his little office. He knew that in the close confines of the ship he would be bound to bump into Ruth at some stage. The new Governor availed himself of the Captain's drinks cabinet at frequent intervals, and by the time they reached the open sea, he was quite inebriated. Barraclough had to assist him to his cabin.

"Just a spot of seasickness chaps." He giggled as the ship's surgeon and Barraclough manhandled him into his bunk. Ruth made herself at home. She appeared several times on deck, standing beside the Captain or whoever else was on the poop or quarterdeck. There was tremendous interest in her from the ship's company and she smiled benevolently at even the lowest rating.

"Perhaps you would like to take the wheel ma'am?" Barraclough was escorting her around the ship; he had fallen, like most others, under her spell. He explained how the ship was steered and the use of the various sails. She of course listened intently, flattering him constantly about his knowledge of such things.

"But how do you know which way to point it?" she asked simply.

"We have a young fellow called a navigator, who plots our course, with the use of various instruments; he keeps us on the straight and narrow, if you get my drift." He checked to see if his little quip had registered with his companion and was delighted when she smiled and said how amusing he was.

"We use the compass here to show us our direction."

"Is that the other young gentleman I met at the wedding reception?"

"Yes indeed ma'am. Would you like to take a look at the charts?"

"How perceptive of you Mr. Barraclough, I would be thrilled to see our progress."

"I'm certain Mr Burrows would be only too pleased to have you call each day to check our passage across the Atlantic."

Ben was a little taken by surprise, when Barraclough suddenly pushed his way in. He gave Ben a broad smile and a sly wink.

"Her Ladyship was interested to know how we know which way to point the ship," he said with an odd grin. "I informed her Ladyship, that you were the man to ask."

She stared at Ben, with her head cocked slightly to one side. Her presence seemed to completely fill the cabin. A sudden rush of mixed emotions choked any reply deep in Ben's throat. He stood his ground determined not to let her get the upper hand; there was very little room to move in the crowded cabin.

"Have you been avoiding me? I must declare that I have not seen you since I came aboard two days ago," She said.

It was obvious she was enjoying his embarrassment. Her fingers toyed along the edge of the table tracing towards Ben's hand.

"No ma'am, but I have been busy," came his curt reply.

Barraclough gave them both a sideways glance, he studied their eyes, locked together; he had a nose for scandal, and sensed the electric in the air. It made him more than just a little curious. He had expected his young friend to be pleased at their appearance. Was something going on between them he wondered?

"Perhaps you could show her Ladyship some of your charts," Barraclough said, still studying their faces.

She stood tantalisingly close to Ben; her soft fragrance in the confines of the cabin was intoxicating.

"These are the charts I shall be using on this journey," he said. He was trying to sound relaxed.

She moved even closer, until they were almost touching. His explanation tailed away and he could not hide his agitation.

Barraclough saw his friend's discomfort and guided Ruth out to see something else. As she left she said, "I'll be back to see where we are each day."

Ben was angry with himself as soon as she was gone. He knew she was only teasing him, playing one of her games. She had him by the heart strings and could play whatever melody she liked on them and they both knew it.

Later that day they met in the close confines of the companionway leading to the galley; this time Ben could find no route of escape.

"You are avoiding me. You naughty boy," she teased. Her fingers trailed across the front of his uniform.

"Ruth please don't tease, we are not children now and there's much more at stake here."

"Oh dear, is Benjamin cross with little me for teasing him?"

"Leave it!" He snapped with sudden strength. She stepped back, her face was flushed, her eyes blazed angrily.

"Be careful how you speak to me *Mr. Burrows*," she stressed the name. "I have your life in my hand, and I can crush it like a dead flower anytime I please." There was venom in her voice and she held her hand high squeezing her fingers as if crushing something.

"I think you have forgotten the truth of what happened to your brother."

"It would be your word against mine; do you think for one moment that they would believe you?" She prodded his chest and bustled away.

Later that day Ben sensed he was in for trouble when the Captain suddenly sent for him.

"Good afternoon Capt'n. You sent for me?" He stood to attention, his head slightly bowed beneath the low timbers of the cabin.

"Indeed it is not! I do not know what has been going on. But I have had a complaint from Lady Ruth that you have been most discourteous to her."

Ben tried to stutter an explanation, but the Captain held up his hand to silence him.

"I have apologised for you. Keep out of the way. We should reach Jamaica within the next three days, and then I want a full explanation."

Ben went back on deck feeling totally dejected. He cursed his bad luck and decided he would never understand the workings of the female mind. The fresh breeze made him feel better, and he watched as the gun crews went through their daily practice.

"Don't look so forlorn. You want to be glad you missed the broadside she gave the Capt'n. It's a wonder he didn't have her clapped in irons the way she raved." Barraclough said. He came and leant on the rail beside Ben. "What's between you two? I said you were a dark'un," he whispered.

They stood together a while, watching the dark storm clouds slowly intercept their course. It suddenly turned cold. The first wind of the storm flapped the canvass above them.

Seagull shook and shuddered as she rolled and pitched in the storm. The wind had increased and the sea was rising and falling almost twenty feet. Below deck, the noise of the sea violently thrashing the hull was deafening. The crew worked in the wind and rain to try to lash everything down. One of the forward carronades broke loose and skidded dangerously across the deck, it came to a halt as it hit the fo'c'sle bulkhead. As the ship pitched the other way, the loose gun set off again. Two crewmen made a vain attempt to catch the rope attached to the gun carriage. When they finally had hold of it, the sheer weight of the gun dragged them across the deck. More men joined in the chase laughing loudly at the predicament of their mates; finally, it was lashed down without doing too much damage.

Barraclough and Ben had watched the chase from the poop deck.

"There you are Mr. Burrows, never a dull moment in the King's navy. Even in the midst of a storm we lay on entertainment." He was trying to cheer up his friend, but it had little effect.

After his watch Ben retreated to his chartroom, but gave up trying to keep it in order. Each time he replaced the charts and equipment, they would just fly onto the floor again as the next wave struck. He went into the corridor to go on deck to see if he could be of any help. Ruth was leant against the opposite doorway, and was obviously ill.

It took him three attempts to get to her across the wildly bucking companionway. It was pointless trying to make himself heard over the din of the storm, and so he pulled her by the arm into her cabin. Sir Arthur lay flat on his back in the narrow bunk looking almost green. His face, chin and clothes were splattered with vomit.

"How on earth do you endure this?" She croaked trying to hold down the few remaining contents of her stomach.

He put her on the bunk beside her still unconscious husband. The ship trembled violently and they were thrown together. He landed on top of her in an untidy heap.

"So! You would attack me now." Despite how bad she felt, she still managed a wicked giggle.

He tried to untangle himself, but each time he tried to stand, the motion of the ship laid him out again. Angry and frustrated he struggled to his feet. She tried to pull him tightly to her, but he somehow managed to slip out of her grasp and crawled across the deck towards the door.

"I'm sorry," her voice was soft and gentle.

He turned to look at her, he so wanted to believe her.

"I didn't mean to get you into trouble: you know what a wicked, selfish temper I have. Can we still be friends?"

"How can we, when you hold the past above me like an executioner's axe?"

"You said you loved me once. Do you still?" She chipped at his defences.

Ben was bewildered by her sudden change, and made no reply. For a long moment he studied her face, was this just another tease? Waiting until the ship angled him towards the door, he let it roll him across the cabin.

Still he made no answer, determined not to give her ego the satisfaction it demanded. He fought his feelings, somehow managing to hold down the words that wanted to burst out. With a shake of his head, he left the cabin, but she followed; before he knew it she was in his arms in his chart room.

There was a sudden unbelievable explosion of passion more violent than the storm as their lips met. They fell to his bunk and in the height of the storm made love with a fury to match the heaving tempest that battered the ship.

Almost as quickly as it had begun, the storm blew over. Ruth returned to her husband and Ben tried to sort out his tangled emotions.

Above the deck, one of the huge yardarms hung drunkenly from the mast, with a tangle of rigging wrapped around it. The call of 'Land Ahoy' drew everyone's gaze to the lookout in the tops'ls.

"Where away!" cried the Boson. "Three points off the larb'd bow." Came the reply.

Ben scanned the horizon with his telescope. A dark purple-blue line appeared. It gradually thickened, until it was visible with the naked eye. He took quick readings from the compass, ship's clock and sextant, and new immediately that they had reached the West Indies.

"Well Mr. Burrows?"

"Aye Capt'n, the storm has taken us a little further south than I had anticipated, but I expect the islands there to be the Caicos Islands."

It was an effort to keep his mind on the work to be done; he could now make out that what had seemed like one land mass was in fact a chain of small islands. Ben knew that the West Indies archipelago was made up of over seven hundred islands that stretched from South America, forming a barrier around the Caribbean Sea up to North America. He felt a thrill, as he thought of the famous men whose names had become synonymous with this tropical paradise. Men like Columbus, Kidd, Captain Henry Morgan, and the most feared pirate of them all, Blackbeard. To reach Jamaica they had to sail close to a number of French and Spanish owned islands; only Hispaniola to the south was a free state. Scanning the horizon Ben compared the layout of mountains and islands with Mr. Burrow's charts. He was sure that they were on course for a channel known as the Windward Passage, which would take them directly to Jamaica. A second call from the masthead caught everyone's attention.

The call had brought most of the crew on deck as well as Ruth and her still rather green husband.

"Sail Ahoy!"

Seagull was caught in a funnel, with a tiny island to one side, a dangerous reef to the other and a stiff following wind. Two Spanish ships, with the advantage of the wind blocked off the channel.

"Clear for action Mr. Barraclough," the captain said in a cool voice.

"Excuse me Governor, but I must ask you and your Lady wife to retire to the safety of my cabin."

"Do you mean you intend to engage them in battle?"

"If necessary Sir. I can see no alternative." The Captain said without taking his eyes off the distant sails.

"What about our . . . er, my wife's safety?"

Orders were bellowed around them, and the Captain was paying the Governor little attention.

The fifes and drums of the marine band could be heard over the hullabaloo of preparing the ship for battle. The men were in good spirits and they readily took their positions steeling themselves for the next few moments.

"Captain! I demand that you think of our safety before your own glory."

The Captain closed his scope with a loud snap, he studied the Governor's face, then handed him the scope.

"Perhaps Sir, you could tell me what other option I have. I suggest that you go with Mr. Burrows to the safety of my cabin." His voice was cold, his speech precise leaving no room for any argument.

"Mr. Burrows I shall expect you back here before we engage the enemy."

The tattoo of the marine's drummer boys suddenly stopped, and a heavy silence drifted across the deck. The clamour of preparing the ship for battle was over, now each man waited, his own thoughts his worst enemy. Only the sound of the ship as it battered its way through the surf could be heard. Then from somewhere a voice began to sing a lively shanty and soon all the gun crews and topsail men joined in and the mood on board lifted.

The Spanish warships were veterans, circa seventeen-hundred. One was a 'first rate' class ship with a hundred guns plus, the other was of the same class as Seagull, with seventy-four guns. White cotton-balls of smoke suddenly fluffed out from the triple-decker, as her captain fired his ranging shots; it showed a little inexperience or anxiety on his part. Great plumes of water lifted well short of Seagull's larboard bow. Despite the fact that she carried more guns than Seagull, the total weight of shot she fired in a broadside was less than that of the English ship. Her top deck was only armed with long barrelled twelve pounders, as opposed to the twenty-four pound cannons on Seagull's top deck.

"Trim yer tops'ls!" Suddenly the ant like figures high above the decks were scurrying to obey the commands. Three holes appeared in the foremast's main sail, at the same time the sound of the shots carried to the officers standing on the poop deck of Seagull.

"I think he's a might nervous." Mitchell said, his telescope fixed firmly to his eye.

"Hard a-larboard, we'll cross her bows, and keep away from her escort." The helmsman spun the huge wheel; Seagull swung hard over.

In the rigging, the sail trimmers worked to correct the sheets to the new tack, and marksmen climbed into the tops to wait for the action to come.

The Spaniard could not bring a single gun to bear on Seagull, as the old cumbersome ship tried to respond to the new situation. The broadside was deafening; Seagull rocked as her guns bellowed their challenge at the Spaniard. Immediately the smoking barrels were swabbed out, and reloaded. The next two volleys followed like clockwork, bringing down the foresails and part of the Spaniard's foremast in an untidy heap. Licking at his lips, Ben realised suddenly that his mouth had gone very dry and that he was clutching the handle of his cutlass. When he had been in a gun crew, there was no time to think about what was happening, but now he had to stand, and just wait.

The thick cloud of acrid smoke cleared slightly. For the first time the other ship was in view, her Captain having been forced to take a long route round to bring her into the battle. The bright red coats of the marines stood out against the white of the sails as they climbed to their positions. The crackle of musket fire filled the air, as Seagull and the triple-decker closed. The English guns fired a fierce broadside of canister shot, which splintered the woodwork, raking across the exposed decks of the Spaniard, cutting her crew to bloody shreds. Ben drew his cutlass, and held it at the ready. Barraclough gave him a reassuring smile, and then was lost in the black cloud that drifted everywhere across the decks. Seagull's fire rate was almost double that of the Spaniard, and as the ships came together with a load groan, there was little left of the upper woodwork of the older ship. The ships themselves seemed to snarl at each other as they grated together like a couple of old bears.

All along the rails, hand to hand fighting had broken out. Men swung like angry apes from the rigging onto the opposite decks. Suddenly in front of Ben a sailor dressed only in ragged trousers dropped to the deck; his face was black with soot, and in his hand he carried an ancient sword with a dark stained blade. The man was nimble as a cat. He dodged to the side as he attacked, cutting through the cloth of Ben's sleeve. The sharp pain in his upper arm speeded the flow of adrenaline. Every nerve, every sense was alert. Ben skipped lightly to his left avoiding the next attack. With a great sweeping motion, he lashed out with his own blade. He and Barraclough had spent many hours in swordplay, and he felt confident. His opponent was no stranger to this type of fight. He easily parried the blow with his own blade. He hissed through brown teeth, and then threw himself forward. Their blades locked together. Ben could smell the man's foul breath. He pushed hard, forcing the man back. They were only separated by a single arm's length, out of his belt the Spaniard pulled a short dagger, and stabbed at Ben with it. The blade never reached its target. A sweeping glint of steel cut the hand from its wrist in mid-air. The severed limb still holding the blade landed at Ben's feet.

"Finish him! By George or he'll do for you," Barraclough's voice cut through the deafening din of battle. With a backhanded sweep, Ben slashed the Spaniard across the throat with his cutlass. Instantly a gushing, pumping wound yawned open. Gurgling and gasping the Spaniard tried to hold the wound closed with his handless arm. Barraclough nodded at Ben and then disappeared back into the fight. The English marines had formed a square on the Spaniard's quarterdeck. They were gunning down the opposition with mechanical precision.

Barraclough had kept his eye on the other Spanish ship and to make sure there were no nasty surprises he had kept back enough of the gun crews to be able to defend the Seagull from attack. Like a ghostly spirit, the second Spanish ship appeared through the dense fog of smoke that now surrounded the battle. There was a tremendous crash as she collided with Seagull. The three ships locked together, with the English vessel sandwiched between the two Spanish ships. The carnage raged across all three decks. The officers of Seagull were now hard pressed to protect the poop, and it seemed at one point as if they would be driven off. Only the timely appearance of a small number of marines saved the day. There was a stunning explosion. It rocked all three ships. Deep in the bowels of the triple-decker her main magazine suddenly erupted. A fire on her lower deck had finally managed to consume the ancient timbers, engulfing the store of black powder. A series of other explosions tore the ship apart, as more powder exploded along the decks. Her foremast had already fallen, and her main and mizzen mast fell like axed trees. The blazing sailcloth hissed as it hit the water, adding great clouds of steam to the dense cloud of smoke that was billowing out of the mortally wounded vessel. The event changed the whole battle, for now Captain Mitchell's priority was to cut free his ship from the blazing, sinking Spaniard that clung with deadly tendrils to the side of his ship.

"Mr. Barraclough take a party and cut us loose, before she drags us all to the bottom." Ben followed Barraclough down to the quarterdeck, almost losing his footing on the slime of the blood-soaked deck. He came to an abrupt halt bumping into the back of someone; he suddenly recognised the face beside him.

"Fletch! My God, how goes it." He said his spirits suddenly lifted.

"Fine, glad to see yer still with us."

"Come on," Ben rallied his old messmates to him, "we need to free the ship." He was confident and the men followed him without question.

The party hacked and chopped at the tangle of rigging whilst the marines gave them covering fire. The two—and three-inch thick ropes took a great deal of effort to cut. Brendan had joined the work party and was adding his considerable strength to clearing away the tangled rigging.

Another explosion threw them to the deck and Ben felt the hair on the back of his neck singe as flames licked over the ship's side. What was left of the triple decked Spaniard was finally cut loose, and slowly the crippled ship floated away from the battle to die alone, her guns silenced forever.

As they returned to the poop deck, Ben caught sight of the Captain. He stood proudly erect leaning on his sword, an inspiration to his men, but as if in slow motion Ben watched in horror, as the Captain sank to the deck clutching his upper chest. Bright crimson blood covered the clutching hand. Barraclough was first to reach the Captain, but as he bent over him, he too slumped sideways. Ben rushed towards them. He felt a flood of relief as

Barraclough staggered to his knees. He managed to drag the Captain under the shelter of a fallen spar.

"Sniper!" Barraclough pointed up to the first yardarm of the Spaniard's foremast.

Cutlass in one hand, exhilarated, Ben climbed the mizzenmast rigging faster than he had ever done before. He spotted the sniper, perched high above them with a perfect view of their decks. Fearlessly, with cold determination, he balanced on the end of the yard and ran the length of the spar. Trusting to luck that the frayed, damaged rigging would hold, he worked his way through the tangle of battle towards the Spanish marksman. Grasping a loose rope he kicked out leaping into midair, the rope swung him in a wide arc so that he landed on the very end of the Spaniard's lower yardarm.

Occasional stray bullets whistled and sang around him as they cut the air and chipped the woodwork; a musket ball zinged past him from below but he paused only long enough to get his bearings. Ben climbed up through the tangle of ropes and sailcloth to the level where the sniper was sitting reloading his musket. Working his way along the spar, he prayed that the sniper was too busy to see him.

There was a look of shock on the man's face when he finally caught sight of Ben standing almost above him. Instinctively he turned his part loaded musket and fired. The ramrod was still down the barrel and it shot out like a steel harpoon.

It was Ben's turn to be surprised; the flying rod caught him a stinging blow that cut a deep line across his cheek knocking him sideways. By some miracle he managed to keep hold of the rigging with one hand. For an instant he spun perilously above the deck far below. Hooking his ankle around the woodwork, he managed to heave himself back onto the yardarm, just in time to protect himself from the oncoming attack.

With sword in hand the sniper lunged wildly at Ben. Ben spun back out into space and the sniper, carried by his momentum shot past him to the end of the spar. By the time Ben had regained his footing the man was charging again. This time Ben swung out in a more controlled arc and caught his opponent with a single blow from the hilt of his sword as he flew past. Luck was with the sniper this time, because somehow he managed to catch a loose rope and swing to the next spar. Ben followed swinging with great agility between the spars. He caught up with the sniper and finished him off with a slashing cut across his back. The sniper screamed and with flaying arms and legs fell to his death on the deck below.

Ben glanced down and could see Mr. Barraclough dragging the Captain to safety across the deck. His own face and shirt were covered in blood from the cut along his cheek; tearing a strip from his shirt he tied it around the wound. Instead of returning to his ship, Ben swung his way through the nightmare web of ropes and splintered timber until he was above the Spaniard's quarterdeck and then like a veteran he whizzed down a rope to land safely on the deck.

The Spanish Captain, a man in his late forties was surprised to see the young Englishman land within a few feet of him. The Captain smiled confidently drawing his rapier from his belt; he was certain that he could deal with the situation. His officers were in front of him watching the decks, and were unaware of his predicament.

Ben circled the Spaniard, who made soft cooing noises, his sword almost at arm's length and the tip of his blade scribing little circles in the air, daring Ben to try an attack. The clang of their sword steel alerted the other Spanish officers, but due to the fight in front of them, they were unable to assist their Captain. He might have been a much better swordsman than Ben, but he was physically out of condition. He was blowing hard after only a couple of attacks. Very soon, he was resting the tip of his sword on the deck to take a breather. Ben felt a wave of confidence flood through him, he felt calm and collected, more so than at any other time in his life. It was a strange unexpected sensation. He realised that he could beat his opponent. The Captain made an all-out attack, but his strength had gone. Ben flicked the sword from the man's hand, as if he was the master, and the other the student. He held the tip of his blade to the Captain's throat.

"It would be prudent of you, Captain, to order your men to down their arms." The two men stared into each other's eyes for a moment. The Captain could see the determination and commitment of the young Englishman. He understood very little English but the meaning of the words was obvious. The order was given and all along the deck they threw down their weapons as they saw their Captain paraded with the tip of a sword at his throat.

When Ben arrived back on board Seagull, her crew gave him a huge cheer.

"Bravely done Mr. Burrows," Barraclough called from the quarterdeck. They exchanged salutes.

"What of the Captain?" Ben called.

"He'll live thank God. You get to the surgeon and let him see to that cheek."

Seagull's crew were in a jubilant mood, and cleared the decks and secured the Spanish ship to the sound of loud singing, the thought of prize money lifting everyone's spirit.

Ben went below to check on Ruth's well being. He knocked and entered the cabin. Immediately Ruth threw herself around his neck.

"Oh," she wailed "it was so frightening."

Ben looked over her shoulder to see that a cannon shot had blown a hole through the cabin porthole leaving a yawning gap three feet in diameter; the shot had exited through the bulkhead leaving another jagged hole. The Governor lay flat on the bunk, snoring away; totally oblivious to what had gone on.

"Are you hurt at all?" Ben asked

"No, but it was very frightening. You've been wounded."

"It's just a graze. I'll get the ship's carpenter to fix that hole, and at least he will be able to stop the wind blowing in here."

"Wait." She said and after dipping a small hand towel in some water she washed the blood from his cheek. "There you are my brave sailor; you must get some iodine for that wound."

"I must get back on deck," Ben said.

She kissed him full on the lips, a lingering kiss of old love.

CHAPTER SEVENTEEN

---⚬❀⚬---

Whilst the Captain was recouping his strength, Mr. Barraclough temporarily took charge of Seagull. From the ship's quarterdeck, he surveyed the battle damage, patiently watching the crew as they worked to make repairs and clear up the debris from the decks.

Usually he was meticulous about his uniform when on deck, but the bandage around his temple made his hat sit at rather a comical angle and he was very self-conscious of it. Each time he tried to straighten it, it just slipped back again and he was losing patience with the thing.

Ben was with a number of the other junior officers on the poop deck waiting for Mr. Barraclough to issue them their orders for the day. They watched, rather amused, but trying not to laugh at the First Lieutenant's attempts to adjust his uniform.

In line behind Seagull was the captured Spanish ship. Second Lieutenant Myers was in charge with ten hands, plus the Spanish crew to sail the ship and a small detachment of marines to guard the prisoners. Despite the damage it had received in the battle it would still make them all some extra 'prize money' when they reached port.

"How's the Capt'n now?" Ben finally asked Barraclough.

"He'll live; he's sat up, but he looks a bit pale. The sniper's bullet went in just under his collarbone; fortunately, his heavy coat and jacket took the power out of the shot. Mr. Harvey the ship's surgeon, after a little bit of prodding about has been able to get it out again. How's your face?"

"I'm fine thank you," Ben said. He patted at the long cut along his cheek. "I must say, the excitement of battle really makes you feel a little drunk. I don't remember feeling a thing when I received this."

"It was a good job you were not drunk when you skipped across those yards up there." Barraclough smiled. "You'll really attract the ladies with that scar; they'll imagine it was received in a duel, perhaps for another lady's honour." He laughed.

"You're an old romantic; they'll be frightened to death of me."

They stood together a little while just watching the sea and the distant islands as they took shape. There was hardly a cloud in the sky and the steady breeze made sailing a real pleasure.

From the deck-rail, Ben saw his old messmates and asked permission of Barraclough if he could go speak with them.

"Watch yer'sens, Admiral on board," Fletch joked.

"How are you all?" Ben asked smiling broadly at everyone.

"We're fine lad," Brendan boomed. "We were mighty proud of our old messmate when you paraded the Spanish Skipper at the tip of your blade."

They all nodded agreement and raised imaginary glasses to him.

"I'll say," Fletch said, "it was a brave deed, the way you went after that sniper; there's many a sail trimmer be proud to hop across yardarms the way you did." He patted Ben on the back and continued, "I taught him all he knows you know."

"All in a day's work you know." Ben said tongue in cheek.

There was some guffawing and general merriment, but Ben had been watching their approach to the island and knew it was time to get back to his duties. Shaking all his old mate's hands, he ran back to the quarterdeck leaping the steps three at a time.

Barraclough greeted him back with a smile. "Keep in with your old mates; you never know when they might save your life." he said sagely. "Go check on our visitors please Mr. Burrows, and make sure they are ready to go ashore as soon as we land, I don't want them in the way, and we've enough work on our hands."

Ben went below and knocked politely on the guest's cabin door. There was a sound from within and then a muffled call, which Ben assumed to be his cue to enter.

Inside the cramped cabin there was not much light; the damage had been made weatherproof with some stretched canvas, but now there was no window.

"Oh Ben it's you, I'm so glad. My husband," she pointed to the prone figure in the bunk who was obviously still fast asleep and snoring loudly. "He's taken a little too much brandy I fear, and I can't wake him."

She touched Ben's face running her finger along the cut, as their eyes met they embraced and kissed, a long passionate lovers kiss.

"I wish I could stay with you Ben."

"I wish I could believe you, but I think you would not be very happy hidden away in a little house in Portsmouth whilst I was at sea. My meagre wage would hardly keep you in handkerchiefs for the year, let alone the rest of your needs."

"So will we ever meet again after you sail away and leave me to my fate?" she pouted.

"I can only read the stars for directions, not to predict the future. To be truthful I hope so, but I can't imagine how."

"I'll never betray you Ben; it was my fault that you ran away, I made you do it." Her voice was uncharacteristically humble and soft, almost a whisper.

"We were much younger then, I should have known better. Your marriage is off to an odd start, not many brides are unfaithful on their honeymoon."

"My husband," she pointed at the prone body "I think was unfaithful to me on our wedding day, so why should I worry. I am going to allow myself dalliances too."

"Is that what it was, a mere dalliance?"

"No, sorry Ben, I didn't mean that."

"I must go; Mr. Barraclough will be expecting me to report back."

"Just one more kiss then, and that shall be our last until we meet again." She said with a tender smile.

They kissed again this time it was less passionate, more a parting gesture resigning them to their fate; they embraced a moment longer.

They righted the new governor, slapping his face and shaking him vigorously, and slowly he regained consciousness. He blinked at them with a puzzled look on his face, obviously not sure where he was.

"I'll leave you to get ready to go ashore." He left with a quick salute.

It was a busy time on board as they finally dropped anchor in the safety of the harbour. The ship's launch was made ready to take the governor and his belongings ashore, a task Mr. Barraclough oversaw himself just to make sure that they were out of the way as quickly as possible.

On the pier waited a very grand carriage with a cavalry escort of twenty Dragoons.

"Thank you, Captain, for your hospitality and speedy delivery," Sir Arthur called from the prow of the launch. He had made a remarkable recovery and stood as if he was the returning conquering hero.

Captain Mitchell was on deck for the first time since being wounded; he supported himself on the deck rail, and saluted graciously to the departing launch. He blew an audible sigh of relief as soon as the launch reached the harbour wall and said, "Call the officers to my cabin Mr. Barraclough, I want an assessment of our damage."

The meeting was short and to the point; it was obvious that the captain was still not feeling too good and glad to be able to take to his bed again. Barraclough again took command and the repairs were organised, and a team was sent ashore to find timber and extra carpenters for the repairs. Ben and Barraclough went ashore to find a chart maker to update the ship's charts and maybe find new ones.

"We might look for something of the American coast, the colonies are erupting and we may find ourselves there before too much longer."

Ben smiled as they entered the little shop, it reminded him of Mr. Burrows and he felt instantly at home in it. Barraclough busied himself looking at various tools and instruments in the shop whilst Ben busied himself with the charts. He was really surprised and pleased to see one of Mr. Burrows charts amongst the shop's stock.

"I learnt my navigation with the gentleman who made this chart," Ben said

"So did I young sir," the man smiled, "Burrows and I sailed together twenty years or so ago. Perhaps if you see him again you'll remember me to him. The name's John Blackburn."

"I think he has spoken of you to me Mr. Blackburn."

"Well, we were good mates, and in one or two near scrapes too."

As Ben continued his inspection of the charts, they chatted like old friends, mostly about Burrows but also about the charts. Satisfied Ben took what he needed and he and Barraclough headed back to Seagull.

"You never did just tell me about what was going on between the Lady Ruth and yourself," Barraclough pried.

"Yes you're right." Ben replied as the climbed back aboard the ship's barge.

"Well?"

"You would not expect me to be indiscreet for the Lady's sake."

"Well no of course not, but . . ." he left the sentence hanging in the air.

Ben just seated himself and then said nothing, Barraclough mumbled under his breath, and was still mumbling as they climbed aboard Seagull.

On their third day in harbour, word was sent from the Governor and his wife, inviting the Captain and his officers to a banquet being held at the Governor's palace in two days time.

"Damn and blast, do these people have nothing on their minds but amusement; don't they know we have other things to do?" Mitchell said. The Captain sat at his desk, he was angry about the delay in harbour and still feeling under the weather from his wound.

"What else do we have to do?" Barraclough said with a smile.

"We're missing the real action; Nelson will have already come to blows with the French!" The Captain dropped his head into his hands in a sulk.

"The men are due some shore leave, and it would not hurt to sample some fine food and wines." Barraclough held the smile, he knew his Captain well.

"Oh blast; as usual you're right, send word that we will be delighted to attend, tell the men that as long as the repairs are finished they can take a turn ashore."

There was a new urgency to the work, all hands put in maximum effort spurred on by the chance to go ashore and the damage was soon repaired.

On the night of the banquet, the Captain of Dragoons and an escort appeared again on the harbour with three carriages to transport the officers from Seagull to the Palace. In their best uniforms, Captain Mitchell, three of his lieutenants, the ship's purser, the ship's doctor, two senior midshipmen and Ben all took their places in the carriages and were delivered to the Governor's Palace.

The route from the gate to the house was lined by footmen smartly attired in matching uniforms each holding aloft a blazing torch to light the way. A procession of coaches crunched their way along the gravel drive to deposit various dignitaries and wealthy inhabitants of the island before the brightly lit open doorway of the palace.

Seagull's party stood to attention on the driveway as Captain Mitchell gave them a cursory inspection. Once he was satisfied they were all up to standard he led them up the steps and through the open door. They entered into the foyer where they were met by music and the dazzling lights of brightly lit crystal chandeliers.

The Governor and his wife stood together greeting the guests as they arrived, shaking hands and smiling graciously as a stream of guests entered the ballroom. Ruth held out her hand to each of the Seagull's crew, never giving Ben a second glance as he passed by.

The ballroom was an amazing spectacle of swirling colour as ladies in all their finery danced and flowed to the music. Gaudily dressed footmen and waiters moved effortlessly through the throng transporting drinks on silver trays to the guests.

From behind fluttering fans women, young and some a little more mature, regarded the handsome looking sailors with great interest; they giggled and exchanged glances, eyeing the men up as though they were trinkets in a bazaar.

This had not escaped the notice of Captain Mitchell, who as always had an eye for the ladies. Without any hesitation, he steered a very definite course in their direction and was soon out on the dance floor with a very attractive young woman in a stunning cobalt blue dress.

Following their captain's example, his officers were not slow in finding a dancing partner and joined in the dance. Ben's partner was a dark haired beauty in a crimson ball gown who smiled constantly up into his eyes. They swirled around the dance floor a couple of times before the dance ended and everyone took a breather retiring to their seats or standing on the sidelines. Ben had lost sight of his colleagues and wandered out into the garden for a breath of air; it was a stifling evening with hardly any breeze.

Leaning on the balustrade surrounding the veranda he watched the lights of the port far below. He could just make out Seagull in the moonlight and wondered what his old messmates were doing. He reflected on the journey from England and was so engrossed in his thoughts that he never heard the soft footsteps behind him.

"Penny for your thoughts."

He knew the voice and did not turn around, "I think you will be happy here, this is far better than the smog of London or the chill of a Yorkshire winter."

She stood beside him for a moment and then placed a small gold locket and chain on the stonework beside him; without another word she slipped back to the glamour of the ball. He still did not look over his shoulder, just stood motionless keeping his attention on Seagull. He eventually picked up the locket and after feeling it a moment he slipped it into his waistcoat pocket.

The banquet itself was a sumptuous combination of fish, fowl, and game, all decorated and flavoured with exotic fruits and spices. As if by magic, the wine glasses were never actually empty, as soon as they were down to a quarter full they were topped up again by the hovering flock of attendants. It seemed as if there were endless courses, which appeared with mechanical precision one after another, until even the most enthusiastic gourmets were forced to concede defeat and sit back completely sated.

Barraclough was accompanied by a giggling young woman whom he was obviously teasing mercilessly about the seemingly bottomless crevice of her cleavage between her very ample bosoms. Ben could overhear the banter and laughed at the boldness of his friend whilst trying to hold a conversation with his own partner, who also giggled at the conversation going on next to them.

Soon the ladies retired and cigars were distributed to the gentlemen along with a sizable portion of brandy. The conversations were varied and generally slightly boisterous: the colonial Gentlemen did not adhere to the refinements and behaviour of London society. The main topic was the war with France and the likelihood of war with the American Colonies; there was great unrest and it would be a good time for them to strike whilst the British navy was tied up with Napoleon's bid to conquer Europe. They were interested to hear Captain Mitchell's opinion of the current situation.

"Of course I am not privy to their Lordship's plans, but I think you can rest assured that whatever happens His Majesty's Royal Navy can deal with the situation."

"We hear that Lord Nelson has chased down the combined fleets of French and Spanish ships."

"I have no news on that situation, I'm afraid gentlemen; you know as much as I on the outcome of that meeting."

That seemed to satisfy them that their fortunes and property in the Indies were safe for the time being at least.

A fanfare brought both ladies and gentlemen out into the gardens to witness the finale for the evening: a spectacular firework display. The orchestra had also moved onto the lawn and accompanied the whole thing with stirring music that was occasionally lost to the huge explosions taking place.

As Ben watched he found himself searching out Ruth in the crowd; she was dutifully beside her husband gleefully clapping at the display. He watched her a moment, before he turned his attention back to the fireworks. There were a couple of loud bangs that took his mind back to the horror and excitement of battle.

Finally, the party made its way back indoors and the guests began to return home duly impressed with the new Governor and his Lady. The carriages filled one by one and rolled away into the night.

Seagull's officers returned to find that the crew's night in the town had been a little bit too lively and that a couple of them had landed in the local gaol for the night. Captain Brand, the marine's commander had everything under control and the crew were all back on board.

The sun was just rising as Ben climbed on deck. He nodded to the men on watch and rather than retire he went to the quarterdeck to watch the sun climb above the horizon.

"A glorious sight Mr. Burrows." Captain Mitchell and Barraclough came and stood beside him to watch.

"Indeed yes Capt'n."

A call from the masthead lookout broke the mood, "sail on the larboard bow!"

Everyone's attention turned to the distant horizon where it was just possible to see the shape of sails silhouetted against the pink sky. They watched a moment and then a second ship came into view.

"Call the men to battle stations Mr. Barraclough, in these uncertain times we cannot be too careful."

The usual pandemonium ensued as drummers beat the call and men dashed to their places. Within minutes, however, an expectant silence fell over the ship; only the creaking of timber and the breeze in the rigging dared to make a sound.

"British frigates Captain." The lookout called to everyone's relief.

CHAPTER EIGHTEEN

"Gentlemen," Captain Mitchell addressed the assembled crew from the quarterdeck rail, "we are pleased to welcome back Captain Atkins of His Majesty's ship Neptune; he has brought news of extraordinary interest to us all. Admiral Lord Nelson has engaged the combined enemy fleets off Cadiz near Cape Trafalgar and has won a memorable victory against Napoleon's forces." A huge cheer roared across the deck.

"This wonderful news, will I am sure go down in the annals of British history, as a testament to the bravery and endurance of all British sailors. Its main significance is of course that the terrible threat of invasion that our Islands have been under for the last few years is at an end." More cheers. "Once again gentlemen, Britannia rules the waves!" Cheers and hats filled the air as the men danced jigs and slapped each other's backs.

"However, gentlemen." Silence slowly fell over the assembled crew, "there is some devastating news; Admiral Lord Nelson has fallen to a marksmen's bullet and is dead."

Now there was total silence, a look of disbelief crossed most faces; Nelson was the invincible hero of every British sailor. All heads were bowed as the captain said a prayer for Nelson and all fallen comrades. Men shook their heads in disbelief, a few even wiped away a tear from their weathered and battle hardened faces.

After dismissing the crew, Ben was ordered to fetch certain charts and meet with the ship's officers in the Captain's cabin as quickly as possible.

In the seclusion of his little chartroom Ben gathered the charts as requested and was about to set off when for the first time he remembered the locket he had tucked away in his waistcoat pocket. He stopped and pulled it out carefully flicking it open. Inside there was a finely painted miniature of Ruth and a lock of her hair. He touched it briefly, before he snapped it shut and returned it to his pocket. Grabbing the charts and with them bundled under his arm he dashed to the Captain's cabin. When he arrived, the officers were seated around the Captain's table but the Captain stood at the head of the table looking very angry. He nodded to Ben to take a seat.

"It would appear gentlemen that we would have been far more use to our Admiral off the coast of Spain rather than acting as nursemaid to His Majesty's Governor. With so many of our ships of the line damaged we are to return to duties in home waters, whilst Captain Atkins and Captain Prowse of the Sirius who both were in attendance at the great battle will remain here," Mitchell said.

He sat down looking slightly less stressed than before. The tramp of feet on the decks above as men worked the huge capstans to raise the anchor and the main sails for a moment filled the cabin.

"However, we have orders to return via the Canaries to investigate rumours that there still may be some Spanish ships at anchor there. Without frigates as escorts we will have to be very careful how we approach; there shouldn't be any ships liable to give us any trouble but we cannot be certain. So gentlemen let's be about our business and get underway."

The decks looked a little like a market, with crates of fresh fruit and chickens piled up everywhere. Neptune had brought stores and munitions for Seagull, and these were still being stored away as Seagull unfurled her great mainsails and caught the wind.

Ben was watching the hilltop above the harbour from the quarterdeck as they pulled out. He noticed Barraclough almost sneaking up alongside of him but said nothing.

Barraclough whispered in Ben's ear, "I'll get the story from you yet."

"Perhaps, but it is one that you may not thoroughly enjoy."

This snippet was almost more than Barraclough could bear and it pushed him to the limit of his endurance. "Mr. Burrows would you be happy to see a First Lieutenant in his Majesty's navy beg?"

"Indeed I would not Sir; I expect First Lieutenants to be as sturdy as the oaks of this ship Sir, and nothing less," Ben said. He spoke trying to imitate the Captain's voice, "begging is way below someone of that prodigious and lofty rank."

"Then put me out of my misery!"

At that moment, the Captain appeared and looked quizzically at them.

"Just a little fun between us Sir, nothing else," Barraclough said.

The Captain stood silently a moment but it was obvious that he wanted to talk. "I feel slighted again by their Lordships. We should have been there with Nelson; it's our right to be in the thick of things." Mitchell was still very angry as he spoke. "Anyway, our orders advocate a little piracy if possible as we return, and by thunder I intend to be well compensated for our misfortune of circumstance."

Ben and Barraclough both smiled at the prospect of a chance to increase their prize haul. They stood in silence for almost an hour until the bell rang and they were able to retire for a meal.

They were less than two days out of harbour when they spotted two ships on the horizon. The ships were much smaller and faster sloops and Seagull had very little chance of catching them, but even so they set sail to follow as best as they could. They lost them in the dark and by next morning, there was nothing near them other than a number of dolphins playing in and riding their bow wave.

"Mr. Burrows I would like you to prepare a course to take us to the north of Tenerife, but we must avoid the massive defences around the city of Santa Cruz where we may find a few prizes waiting for us."

"Aye aye Sir," Ben saluted and was about to leave.

"We need a safe place to anchor. We cannot attack the harbour with Seagull, it is far too well defended, but I think we may be able to go in with the ship's boats and strike before they even know we are there."

"Begging your pardon Sir, I have already studied the coast to the north, and found that there may be a suitable bay which seems to be almost inaccessible from the land side, and could possibly afford us cover and a safe anchorage."

"Very well Mr. Burrows, well done. Show me." Mitchell exchanged a pleased glance with Barraclough.

Ben laid out the chart, placing a compass on one corner to stop it rolling back up.

"Here capt'n, there is a small town named San Andrés," pointing with his finger, "according to this chart there may also be a watchtower, perhaps with some artillery. Here is a headland and the bay I suggest is here, sheltered by a small peninsula and another headland."

"Hmm yes, well done Mr. Burrows." The Captain said, studying the map and rubbing his chin at the same time.

"The problem Gentlemen is that we cannot afford to be spotted before we attack. The battery to the north is very impressive with the guns in dugouts along the cliffs." The Captain pointed on the chart to the battery. "We need to make sure that there is something in the harbour before we attack."

"Excuse me Captain, perhaps once we reach Mr. Burrow's bay I could take a detachment of my marines overland and take a look." Captain Brand of the marines offered.

"Capt'n, no disrespect to Captain Brand, but the bright red of his men will stand out for miles against the dark pumice of the island." Ben said, "I would like to volunteer to go ashore, and climb what I believe to be a small mountain range here," he pointed to the map, "from where I should be able to get a good view of the harbour."

The Captain looked at Barraclough, before he spoke. "Bravely said Mr. Burrows but it will be a risky business, you will need someone with you."

"I would be delighted to also volunteer," Barraclough said.

There was a pause as all considered the options.

"The capital, La Laguna, is to the south west of Santa Cruz. I can't see that there will be any sort of military presence further north than San Andrés," Ben said.

"Looking at your chart, Mr. Burrows, I suggest that it may take a couple of days for you both to get into position," the Captain said.

"Probably, I have no firsthand knowledge of the island and it would seem that the best idea would be to allow perhaps five days for us to get into position and back." Ben replied.

"Very well, we shall put you ashore and head back out to sea to wait, rather than risk being seen, or worse still, being trapped in that bay."

"The main citadel also has a large battery and garrison. Even Admiral Nelson himself, God rest his soul, came to grief there," Barraclough said.

"Aye, to the cost of his men and his arm," Mitchell said.

The meeting broke up and Ben went back to his charts to check the ship's current position and the best course to set. Sitting on the edge of his bunk, he went over the map trying to memorise every feature on it. Ben had the locket open on his table; he was surprised at the gift, and for a while, he toyed with it as he studied the map. Later he closed it and hung it around his neck, tucking it beneath his shirt with the rabbit's foot.

"Our Mr. Burrows is indeed a promising young man," the Captain said to Barraclough as they shared a bottle of port.

"Yes, I like the young man, he certainly shows potential" Barraclough replied.

Captain Mitchell nodded, "I don't want either of you taking unnecessary risks; if you are in danger then retreat."

CHAPTER NINETEEN

———•◦❀◦•———

Ten days later the towering volcano in the centre of Tenerife was on the horizon. Seagull beat a course to the north before she turned back to come around the eastern tip of the island. It was incredibly hot with not a cloud, but fortunately, a strong enough breeze to power Seagull's huge sails and keep the crew cool.

"Come to quarters as quietly as you can Mr. Barraclough, I would rather not announce our presence, and I don't want any nasty surprises when we are in that bay," said Mitchell.

As silently as a shadow, they slipped into the bay and into the shelter of the surrounding high cliffs. There was a short curved beach of black sand closely hemmed in by sheer cliffs of veined volcanic rock. The sea was crystal clear and very inviting on such a hot day; with hardly a ripple it shimmered in the bright sunlight.

"It seems your reading and interpretation of your charts is accurate enough Mr. Burrows." Captain Mitchell said. "This is indeed a good place for such a clandestine operation to begin."

Armed with pistols and cutlasses, like intrepid explorers off to seek out the unknown, Ben and Barraclough clambered down into one of the ship's boats both carrying rucksacks with water and some rations. Two rows of oarsmen waited with their oars high in the air, amongst them was Fletch and Brendan. Captain Mitchell saluted them from the quarterdeck as they took their seats amidst the red coats of the marines who were escorting them as far as the beach.

"Good luck to you both," Fletch said touching his forelock towards Mr. Barraclough.

"Thank you Fletch," Ben replied.

Barraclough nodded, his mind was on the task ahead, and it was not going to be easy he thought as they neared the beach with its curtain of towering cliffs.

With hardly a sound, the boat beached and instantly Ben and Barraclough were over the side and onto the sand. As the boat pulled away, they were up and into the shelter of the rocks.

"My word, Mr. Burrows it is mighty warm here." Barraclough said.

"I'll say that sand was as hot as a fire hearth." Ben replied.

They had climbed about fifteen feet up the cliff when they heard the flap of sailcloth as Seagull unfurled her main sails and turned into the breeze to head back out to sea.

"Well, we're on our own now my lad." Barraclough whispered.

They decided that they were far too hot in their uniform coats and buried them beneath a pile of rocks on a sheltered ledge. Now in just their waistcoats they felt a little cooler and proceeded to climb. It was not an easy climb; the volcanic rock was sharp and crumbled under their feet making the climb quite dangerous.

The next time they caught sight of Seagull she was in full sail and almost over the horizon. They had stopped for a breather and Ben was taking compass bearings to decide which way they should be heading. Suddenly they were over the top and into a small sandy gully that made their journey much easier. Ben bent to pick up some of the alien earth they stood on.

"It's like the cinders of hell," he said.

"Aye, it reminds me of the stuff from the smelt mills, the clinkers they clean out of the iron furnaces."

By the time it was getting dark they were both ready for a break. Slinging their packs down they almost collapsed to the ground.

"That was some climb; could you not have found a more accessible beach?"

"You know what you say to me, look on it as another of life's little challenges," Ben quipped.

Barraclough mumbled something and then unpacked some food from his rucksack. Splitting some biscuits and a little rather stale cheese they tried to make themselves comfortable for the night.

"I doubt if we'll find much freshwater here, we need to take care of this." Barraclough said. He handing a water flask to Ben.

When the light had totally faded, the temperature dropped a little, but it was still warm enough for both men to sleep in just their shirtsleeves. For awhile, they did a little star spotting; the pitch black night being ideal for identifying the various constellations.

"Do you never want your own command?" Ben asked.

"Not really. I was once ambitious, but I prefer being first officer for Captain Mitchell. We've served together for so long now I feel secure where I am."

"Secure! Ever since I've joined the ship it seems we've had someone wanting to blow us to pieces."

"Ha-ha you're right there my lad, but at least you know your enemy here," Barraclough chuckled.

"Is that your idea of security?" Ben said.

"Could be worse."

"I suppose so, I just can't think how."

After their exertions it was not long before they both fell soundly asleep.

At first light they were both woken by what sounded like a scream.

"What on earth was that?" Barraclough said.

They crawled to the top of a nearby rock; about fifty yards from them was a dust track, where an old man and a young woman were being pushed about by a couple of untidy-looking Spanish soldiers. One soldier grabbed the girl by the hair and flung her to the ground. As she fell the other soldier caught her blouse and tore it from her exposing her naked flesh. The old man tried to intervene but one of the soldiers punched him to the ground and then kicked him several times, all the while laughing loudly.

"Well Mr Burrows what shall we do?"

Ben blew a sigh. "As gentlemen we cannot tolerate such behaviour."

"And if there are more soldiers?"

"We are in deep trouble." Ben smiled with a glint in his eye.

They exchanged a quick glance, and a smile that said 'what the hell.' A pistol in one hand and a cutlass in the other they were down onto the track in seconds. The Spanish soldiers looked totally flabbergasted as they suddenly realized that they had company.

Ben and Barraclough charged headlong at the soldiers, who quickly recovered their wits and grabbed their muskets. With a clash of steel, Ben crashed his cutlass against the barrel of one of the guns; its owner swung the butt like a club at him. He parried it with his pistol and with a flash of his blade he opened the man's neck from ear to ear.

Barraclough was also in control of the situation with the other soldier and was returning his cutlass to its scabbard with a slightly theatrical flourish.

Ben picked up the old man whilst Barraclough handed the girl her blouse, the couple were extremely grateful to be delivered from the hands of their assailants. Ben was in for another shock when Barraclough began to converse with the girl in fluent Spanish.

"Come on old chap, it seems we are in time for breakfast."

"I had no idea you were so fluent in Spanish."

"We all have our secrets Mr. Burrows." Barraclough marched swiftly on.

The shepherd showed them back to a small whitewashed brick house nestled in a secluded valley. There were a few chickens scratching about in the dusty soil and some goats gathered around a drinking trough that was fed sparkling water from a spring.

The girl offered them a couple of rustic looking chairs and brought food and stone goblets. They ate a hearty meal of goat's cheese, fresh bread and tomatoes washed down with a local wine. The girl then brought them fruit, oranges and bananas.

"What on earth is this?" Ben showed the banana to Barraclough.

"Banana, very tasty. Try one."

Ben did indeed like the taste, although he liked it even more after the girl had removed the skin for him. Barraclough laughed at his companion's embarrassment.

After a short rest, they followed the old man who said he could show them a goat trail that would safely deliver them to a vantage point overlooking the main harbour. Before they left the girl gave them each a scarf to keep the sun off their heads.

It was a hard slog. The paths were steep and quite treacherous; even goats would find some of them difficult, and the heat was overpowering. After climbing in and out of a number of steep valleys and clambering over several almost sheer cliffs they reached where they wanted to be.

It was an excellent vantage point high above the harbour and although they were some way inland, using their telescopes they had the view they wanted. They found an overhang that gave them some shelter and settled down to take notes.

The old man returned with a cloth bag filled with cactus fruits, which he showed them how to peel and eat. He soon left them to their business saying he would return later.

"It looks like a French frigate and two trading ships." Ben said still with his eye to the glass.

"Yes, I'll wager those are the two we saw mid-Atlantic." replied Barraclough, also peering down his scope.

"Do you recognise the frigate?" Ben asked

"No, but I'll bet it's a refugee from Trafalgar."

"I think you are right Mr. Barraclough, look at her gun ports, they've suffered a great deal of damage." Ben strained to try and get a better view. "I don't even think she's seaworthy, there's a gaping hole in her weather-deck."

"I wonder if her guns are working, it would be a very nasty surprise for us if she suddenly began firing whilst we are trying to take those traders. It looks as if they are working on her," Barraclough said.

For the rest of the day they watched, there was plenty to make note of around the harbour. The trading ships had been busily unloading something, but it looked as if there were a number of wagons waiting to refill them. As the light faded it was interesting to see where watchtowers and lights were operating.

"It looks as if they are making ready for some sort of festival in the town." said Ben.

When the old man returned to the outcrop he was met by two loaded and cocked pistols.

Barraclough greeted him and they exchanged a short conversation, "it seems there is a fiesta here all next week."

"That could certainly help; we might be able to sneak a couple of boats in without being spotted."

"Good thinking. If we can take the boats in along the coast with Seagull standing off we might be able to sneak away with a good prize." Barraclough was pleased with the idea of sneaking the trading ships away without the guard knowing a thing about it.

Ben had been keeping a close eye on the time for their return. They had just two days to get back to the bay and wait for Seagull to pick them up. After packing away his notes and scope he suggested that they make a move at first light.

"So you never did really give me much of an answer regarding the Lady Ruth."

"No I don't suppose I did." Ben said pushing on in front. "I suppose we all have our secrets Mr. Barraclough."

There was a sigh from his friend as he realised that once again he was not going to have his curiosity satisfied.

They were making good time when there was a commotion ahead and the old man who had been some way ahead of them ran to them. In an obviously alarmed voice he warned them that there was another patrol camped right in their path.

"Now is the time for one of your bright ideas Mr. Burrows!" Barraclough said.

They gingerly climbed to the crest of the rocks, below them were fifteen troopers sitting eating, whilst their mounts nuzzled around the poor stubble between the rocks.

"We have no choice for it, but to find a way round. Ask your shepherd friend if that is possible," Ben said with authority.

Mr. Barraclough whispered to the man who pointed out another path that squeezed through a crevice in the rocks. "He says that there is a way but it is very dangerous, and he would not dare attempt it."

"I don't see that we have much option, there are far too many for us to try and take on, and if we wait they may stay there all day. The clock is ticking and we must make haste or miss meeting up with Seagull."

They waited a short while to see if the soldiers would move off, but when one began to light a fire it was obvious that they were there for the night at least.

"Mr. Burrows, I fear we are going to have to take the more hazardous route back."

Without a sound they headed off, the shepherd wishing them luck but still refusing to go with them. It was soon obvious why, because as soon as they were through the crevice and along the track, they reached a sheer climb up the sharp jagged rocks. By the time they reached the first summit their hands were cut and bleeding; using cloths torn from their shirts they wrapped their hands and pushed on again. Blowing hard and sweating in the heat they inched along a narrow ledge, to one side the heat of the rocks, to the other, a drop of five hundred feet or more.

"A little bit higher than the topsails Mr. Burrows." Barraclough said. He tried not to look down.

Ben decided not to answer. His fingers strained and trembled as they sought out the merest of finger holds along the rock face; he shuffled along testing the ledge before stepping out. From below them were sounds of rocks falling, clattering and ringing as they bounced down the rock face and ricocheted off outcrops before hitting the ground.

It seemed an eternity but at last the path widened and they were able to relax. It was already mid-afternoon and this path was too difficult to risk travelling in the dark, so they took a short breather and then once again they were off following the precarious path.

They rounded a corner and were delighted to find that they were almost at the coast. However, between them and the sea was a deep valley with almost sheer cliffs to climb. Slowly they descended the cliff trying to find safe footholds to use; it was slow work. Ben recognised the path below as the one where they had first encountered the girl and her father. Fifteen feet from the bottom Barraclough let out a wail as the rocks beneath him crumbled away, in a spray of dust he bounced to the valley floor.

Ben was deeply concerned he called out, "my dear friend, are you hurt?" He leapt down beside Barraclough.

"I've twisted my ankle; I just hope that it's not broken."

Ben helped free Barraclough's foot from his boot; it was badly swollen and once out of the boot it was obvious that it was not going to be much use for a while.

They discussed the situation. It was almost dark and there was now only a few hours before Seagull would come to pick them up. It was far too dangerous for the ship to wait for them even in such a secluded bay.

"You must go Mr. Burrows and make contact with the ship. I'll be safe here if you can help me into the shade."

It was the most sensible idea. "Very well, I'll bring back help as soon as I can. Here you keep the rest of the water and no dancing or you might bring that patrol down here," Ben said.

Taking only his telescope, he set off up the steep climb. The strange coloured rocks fascinated him and he made a mental note to come back some time when he had more time and investigate them further.

It was a tough climb, taking all his strength to both cling on to the rocks as well as climb. By the time he reached the summit, it was far too dark for him to go any further. He wedged himself into a crevice in the rocks and waited, probably only sleeping for an hour or so. At first light he was on the move again, but it was another two hours before he reached the cliffs overlooking the bay. When he finally reached them he was careful to keep low in case there were enemy forces about. Rounding a jagged outcrop, he was shocked to see Seagull heading back out to sea. Using the glass of his telescope, he tried to signal the ship, but she just kept sailing away. He cursed a while and then realised that it was not achieving anything and decided to head back to make sure Barraclough was alright.

He was tired and thirsty but his first concern was for Mr. Barraclough. Before retracing his steps he found their hidden jackets and carried them back with him. When he eventually made it back he could tell Barraclough was happy to see him so soon.

"All I had was a view of her stern, I tried to signal them, but to no avail."

Ben looked at the injured ankle, it was a deep purple in colour and twice its normal size. Barraclough was obviously in great pain with it.

"Seagull will be back in the morning, don't think our Captain will desert us, he'll be back every day until he either picks us up or is certain we are indisposed in some way."

"In the meantime we need water and food, I wonder if our shepherd friend could help again," Ben said.

"It's a hell of a climb back that way for you Ben, and that patrol could still be hanging about."

"Well I'm already as parched as a salted herring and starving, these rocks are none too appetising," Ben said, "your ankle needs attention too. I can get back before sundown. Plus to take a look at that girl again would make the effort well worthwhile."

He rolled up the two jackets and made a backrest for Barraclough to lean against.

"I can remember the route we took from here back to their home, I'll not be long."

So, off he went again, muttering and cursing at every slip and loose stone. He soon reached the place where they had first met the old man and girl and from there he was able to find his way to their little farm. He bounded from rock to rock until finally he was back in the sheltered valley where the shepherd and his daughter lived. She was busily milking a few goats, sitting in the shade of an old barn, and looked shocked to see him suddenly appear. As best he could, he tried to explain his problem in a mixture of words and signs.

In the meantime, the shepherd had returned and was obviously concerned for his new friends. The girl bundled together food and bottles of wine wrapping them all in a shawl. She was pleased to see that Ben was still wearing the scarf on his head she had given him earlier to keep the sun off. She signed to him that she thought it looked well. Smiling she made some comment to her father, who laughed at her comment.

After taking a bite of food and a quick drink Ben, signalled that he was ready to go. Warily they followed the path back to where Barraclough lay. He looked quite ill when they arrived, but after a drink and some food he soon chirped up again.

"I'm pleased to see you Mr. Burrows; it was rather an ignominious end I was facing here had you not returned."

"Oh ye of little faith." Ben quoted, "I'd have had a devil of a job to explain to the Captain how I'd misplaced you, had I not come back."

The girl was busy putting a tight bandage around Barraclough's ankle; Ben took a well earned snooze in the shade of the rocks. The old man lashed together a number of spindly looking branches to make a crutch for Mr Barraclough to use. Happy with her bandage the girl went to fetch more food and water to last them through the night.

When the sun had set there was a very eerie feel to the arid gorge. Above was a clear star-studded sky and apart from an occasional birdcall it was silent. The small group huddled together and spoke in muted whispers, not sleeping until late into the night.

At first light they began the difficult climb. The swelling in Barraclough's ankle had gone down a little, and he was able to put a little weight on it, which meant he could climb with help. It was a tough climb for someone fit but despite the pain Barraclough hardly slowed them at all.

When they reached the cliff top there was a beautiful sunrise that sent a shimmering beam of light from the horizon to the beach below them. For a moment they all stood to appreciate the golden orange waves glistening and dancing in the new morning light. A silhouette in the sun which Ben knew was that of Seagull made the vision even better.

They shook hands with the old man thanking him for his help; the girl hugged them both, kissing their cheeks. She gave Ben an extra squeeze and stroked his cheek before slipping away with a slightly flushed face.

An hour later they had descended the dry pumice rocks and waited on the black sandy beach for their ship to arrive.

CHAPTER TWENTY

───•◦❀◦•───

Ben sat facing Fletch in the ship's cutter as they headed back to Seagull.

"Nice to see you safe and sound Mr. Burrows," Fletch said. "We were all concerned about you yesterday when there was no sight of you."

"Thank you for your concern Fletch. We were only moments late, and *I* was a little concerned as I watched you sail away."

The cutter bumped against Seagull's towering hull, allowing Ben and Barraclough to climb back on board. Mr. Barraclough had to be helped by two crew members because of his damaged ankle.

Captain Mitchell stood waiting for them. "Welcome back; from the looks of you both I can see you have plenty to report." He noticed Barraclough's obvious discomfort. "Get the doctor to look at your wound and then both of you report to me in my cabin."

An hour later Seagull was well out to sea again and in the Captain's cabin all the ship's officers were assembled to hear Mr. Barraclough's report on the mission.

"Well done the both of you," Mitchell said. "If there are three prizes to be taken we will perhaps not feel so aggrieved at missing the action of Trafalgar."

The meeting took quite some time until every last detail was decided. The plan was simple: Seagull would stand off the island under the command of Mr. Barraclough who due to his ankle injury was hardly capable of leaping on board enemy ships. Three separate boarding parties would simultaneously attack the enemy ships; if the French frigate could not be sailed she was to be sunk, whilst the other two would be sailed out to join Seagull.

"I shall take the ship's launch and board one trading ship; Lieutenant Carnes will take a cutter and take the other; Lieutenant Myers will take the last cutter and try to secure the frigate." The captain looked over toward Ben. "Mr. Burrows if you are too tired after your exploration, you may stay on board Seagull."

"I'll be fine after some sleep thank you Captain."

"Very well; you may accompany Mr. Myers attacking the frigate."

Ben was relieved to take to his bunk for a few hours sleep. It was the commotion from above on deck that aroused him. The ship's crew was being mustered and divided into three groups for the attack; her boats were already in the water and being towed along.

"You watch yourself Mr. Burrows," Barraclough said. He had hobbled over to the ship's side rail as Ben clambered down to join his boat crew.

Seagull was two miles off the coast when her boats were silently released. Nerves jangled as muscles strained to row the heavy boats towards the shore. Marines, in the prows of the boats with their muskets cocked, watched in anticipation the nearing battlements of the harbour defences. The whole scene was deceptively peaceful; the town's lights flickered on the waves, somewhere in the distance a few bars of music wafted towards them, and there was the gentle lapping of the waves against their boat's sides.

Tension in the little boats was already high, and when a rocket scorched into the sky bursting into a brilliant shower above the fortress, there were several gasps. Suddenly the sky lit up again as more rockets were launched.

"Lord I thought we'd had it there."

"Shut up Fletcher!" Myers snapped.

Music and the sound of the carnival reached the flotilla. Captain Mitchell signalled the boats to split up as they reached the harbour entrance. He knew how risky this approach was; Nelson had lost his arm here doing this very same manoeuvre.

Ben nervously fingered the hilt of his cutlass; he had two loaded pistols and the sword tucked into his belt. As they approached the frigate he could see that a lot of the damage he had seen before was almost repaired.

As they gently bumped against the frigate's side he could see that the other two boats were also in position. Like temple monkeys they silently scaled the ship's side and crept on deck. Ben was closely behind Myers with Fletch and his other old mess mates even closer behind.

The fireworks and music were covering any sounds they made as they spread out over the deck keeping to the shadows.

"Mr. Myers, I think she will sail," Ben whispered.

"Aye Mr. Burrows, but we need to cut her off the wharf."

Ben with Bruce, Fletch and big Brendan began to hack at the heavy ropes that held the ship fast against the stonework. Amazed that there were no guards to be seen, the attackers relaxed a little, and soon moved to the second rope. Their luck was short-lived. Out of the hold sprang a number of Frenchmen armed with cutlass and knives. A pistol shot rang out as Seagull's marines charged with fixed bayonets to deal with the enemy sailors. The shot had been heard across the wharf and the alarm was being raised.

"Mr. Burrows see if you can find shot and powder," Myers ordered.

With his old mess mates they were quickly below decks and searching out the magazine. "Here!" Bruce called and emerged with bags of powder.

"Canister shot," Ben said. He handing the heavy bags to Fletch and Mould, and together they charged back on deck.

The marines were already firing across the wharf at a number of soldiers who in return were peppering the ship with musket fire. Suddenly the Spanish guards charged as an officer appeared sword in hand and yelling orders. They closed fast on the ship, which had barely moved despite the crew's efforts.

"Get that bloody gun loaded," Myers bellowed.

It was the last thing the young officer ever said; his head was thrown backwards as a musket ball hit him full in the face. Immediately he was surrounded by his crew.

"Dead." The marine sergeant announced.

"Good God! Mr. Burrows, you're the senior officer now," Fletch said.

Ben was more worried about the fast approaching Spaniards. "Come on we need to sight that gun," Peering along the sights of the twelve-pounder, he tried to keep his nerve despite the sound of the soldier's boots clattering on the cobbles of the wharf.

"Steady . . ." His heart was racing faster than the boots. With careful concentration he tugged on the gun's lanyard, it reared up and backwards, barking a cloud of fire, smoke and deadly shot at the fast approaching enemy.

The wharf suddenly looked like a butchers table, after the frightening hail of shot had chopped and dismembered all in its path. The rear ranks were splattered and covered by the remains of their comrades; it was more than their nerves could stand. Within seconds they were in full retreat.

It bought some time, and as they moved slowly further from the harbour wall. Seagull's crew were already aloft unfurling the sails.

"She's only half rigged," came a shout from above.

"Never mind, get as much sail out as possible," Ben said "Mould, take the wheel, Fletch, we need some powder and shot."

He took time to make sure the other ships were also on the move and did not need any assistance. Neither of the other parties had found much opposition and were quickly underway. A hail of musket fire from the harbour wall had them all ducking for cover. The marine sergeant had his men return fire, but the enemy fire was so heavy that as soon as the marines stood or knelt to fire they were shot down.

There was a deafening roar from the fortress guns and the air filled with a sound like blankets flapping in the wind. Another roar and then several loud thumps told Ben that they had been hit. Splinters and sail cloth spun and fluttered through the air as a number of shots hit the masts.

Unseen from the decks, two ship's boats laden with French sailors had caught up with them and they were now smashing their way into the rear cabins. They poured out onto the decks screaming at the tops of their voices.

Ben was on the quarterdeck, cutlass in one hand, pistol in the other; he fired, and then drew his second pistol and led a counter charge. Firing almost point blank into the nearest sailor he slashed and fought his way across the deck. Brendan, Bruce and Fletch were beside him and together they cut a wide path through the attackers. Brendan using his huge strength threw the enemy about as if they were rag dolls and protected Ben's left flank. Fired by adrenalin they cleared the deck until they had reached the marines who had also been fighting bravely.

Ben had time to look for the other ships and realised that all three ships had now cleared the harbour entrance. He ducked behind some debris as another volley of shots howled from the fortress guns. Most of the shot did little damage, just lifting great plumes of water around the ships.

"Hell Ben, oh sorry, Mr. Burrows, from pressed man to frigate's Captain in no time at all."

"Don't remind me Fletch, we need to inform the Captain of our predicament here," Ben replied.

"Never you fear laddie, we can sail this wee frigate all the way home if needs be," Bruce announced.

"Well, when we have the best navigator in the whole navy 'Acting Captain Burrows,' how can we fail?" Brendan bellowed.

They all laughed loudly and then ducked for cover as another salvo screeched towards them. Fortunately, it fell short and it was obvious that they were out of range of even the biggest of the harbour guns.

Seagull appeared out of the dark and fired a salute as the three ships neared. Ben stood alone at the frigate's wheel and tried to imagine the pride and pleasure of captaining such a vessel. He enjoyed the moment, and as the wind tugged at his tunic he let out a contented sigh. He was delighted with his capture, of that there was no doubt, but yet he felt a certain emptiness. For some while his conscience had been bothering him. He had made good friends, and his mates trusted him, but he felt to be deceiving them all over his true identity.

Ben and Jonathan Mould went below decks; it was an eerie place in the light of their lanterns. It had an odd look to it, many of the guns were missing and there was all the paraphernalia left by the carpenters who were still working to repair the ship. Each wave as it broke on the bow echoed as the ship shuddered to it. The ship's magazine was well equipped and there were some basic stores but other than that it was very much a ghost ship.

The Captain's cabin had neither doors nor windows, but a large oak table stood sentinel in its centre, waiting patiently for its next master. Ben saw a few charts scattered about and gathering them up, he decided that they might be of some use. There was a leather satchel filled with what appeared to be letters and personal papers, he decided to take those too.

Mould suddenly caught Ben's arm and signalled him to be quiet and cautious. There was a sound; it was like a small sob. They strained to find where it was coming from, slowly worked their way across the deck. A heap of sailcloth against the bulkhead wall moved slightly. Dagger in one hand Mould yanked the cloth to one side. There was an ear-piercing scream and a diminutive figure made a dash for cover. Ben caught the scrawny arm of a young lad, who squealed and wriggled. When Ben finally let him go, the lad picked up a discarded chisel and held it out at arm's length pointed directly at Ben.

Ben held out his hand to the lad and smiled reassuringly.

"Careful Mr. Burrows, he means business," Mould warned.

Still with his hand extended Ben moved closer to the lad who still made short stabbing movements towards him. He gave another reassuring smile and again offered his hand, but consumed by fear the boy made a lunge with the chisel stabbing Ben in the forearm. Mould made a single slash with his dagger and the boy fell like a stone.

They both stood a moment. "What a waste," Ben said.

"Look what we have here," Mould said. He had moved the rest of the sail cloth.

They pulled open a casket to reveal a line of perfect gold bars. They both let out a low whistle.

"So, that's what the lad was guarding," Ben said.

Neither dared move, they just stared at the gold as it caught the light of their lamp.

"There's a King's ransom here Ben!" Mould exclaimed, protocol forgotten.

They realised that there were eight other identical boxes. Ben threw the cloth back over them.

"You tell no one until we are back on board Seagull, understood." Ben gave Mould a menacing look. "I don't want a mutiny on my first command, however temporary. There's enough gold here to make the most honest of men think about it."

"We could slip away in the night and live the high life for the rest of our lives," Mould winked.

"Mould, the high life you'll get talking like that, is at the end of a rope."

"Aye, aye Capt'n you're right, as you say."

They went back on deck and watched as they fast approached Seagull; Ben kept his eye on Mould, although he felt he knew him well enough to trust him.

Lieutenant Myers, three marines and two ratings had all been killed in the capture of the frigate; their bodies along with fifteen enemy sailors had been respectfully wrapped in sailcloth and were transferred to Seagull for a burial service to be held for all those killed in the action. Captain Mitchell with his officers behind stood on the quarter deck and read out the names of the deceased as their remains were slid into their watery grave. When all were buried he read from the bible and then added some words of his own as to the men's bravery and sacrifice.

Captain Mitchell was delighted with the night's work and even more so when Ben took him to see the gold.

"My words Mr. Burrows you could have become a very wealthy man had you kept this to yourself."

"Only Mould knows about it Capt'n, I was afraid some of the others might try make a run for it with the frigate and the gold."

"Not very trusting of you, young man."

"No Sir, but it is a very tempting sight."

"Oh yes, you were very wise to take that course, and your share of this prize will make you a pretty wealthy young man anyway."

Seagull with her new flotilla headed for England, and everyman was excited by the prospect of prize money when they reached home.

Ben had already been given permission and given encouragement to take his lieutenant's certificate and Barraclough had loaned him all the books he needed to sit the test. It was more usual to first become a midshipman, and then a lieutenant, but as Ship's Master's Mate he qualified to be able to miss that step. Every opportunity he had he studied the well thumbed manuals, and tried to memorize them. The Captain had smiled encouragingly when Ben had asked permission to take the certificate, saying that he felt sure he was up to it. Now, though Ben had misgivings about everything, he knew he had to clear his conscience before he could feel worthy of the trust and friendship of his crew mates.

Outside the captain's cabin he straightened his uniform before knocking.

"A-ha there you are Mr. Burrows." The Captain said. "Mr. Barraclough informs me that you are well advanced with your studies for your lieutenant's certificate and I wish to tell you that you are promoted to 'acting Lieutenant' for your recent actions."

Ben looked a little bewildered; he was so deep in his concerns over the deeds of his past that he was completely caught off guard.

"Your bravery and fortitude will be mentioned when we reach Plymouth, and if you are still intent on taking your lieutenant's certificate I'm sure it will throw some great weight behind your cause." He suddenly realised Ben's sombre mood. "You look somewhat troubled Mr. Burrows."

"Capt'n, I would like to make a confession to you. I have sailed with you for four years and you have always been very fair with me. I'm extremely grateful for the chance of promotion, but perhaps what I have to say may prejudice that decision."

Mr. Barraclough stood up. "Shall I leave?"

The Captain looked at Ben for his opinion.

"No Mr. Barraclough, I would like you to hear this also," Ben said.

The Captain offered Ben a chair "Please make yourself comfortable, I can see this is a grave matter."

Ben told them the whole story, head down not daring to look at either of the other officers. When he had finished there was a short silence.

"Mr. Burrows, I'll wager most men serving in today's navy have at least one skeleton in their lockers; many are convicts given a choice of jail or the navy, even more are here because they have a secret they would rather not confront. Few of them have the courage to inform their Captain of their deeds."

The Captain looked over towards Barraclough who had sat unobtrusively through Ben's confession. He rubbed his chin and then in a quiet voice said, "I can see that you've had deep feelings of guilt over this affair. It's obviously gnawed at you, but it is water under the bridge now."

The Captain nodded in agreement. "It doesn't alter my opinion of you at all, or of the fact that I think you would make a good lieutenant some day. Your developing skill as a navigator and your bravery under fire bode well for your future."

"Thank you Sir, but can you advise me what I should do when we return to England?"

"You've made a new life for yourself here, I'm certain that your involvement in the lad's death should not trouble you so. You say his sister was as much to do with it as you had. Let the matter end there."

It was obvious that Ben was not totally satisfied with that answer.

"Sleep on it," Barraclough suggested.

With that Ben thanked them and went back to the security of his little chart room. He could not believe how little they thought of the matter which had been such a weight on his conscience. He realised that they were both navy men through and through and what went on ashore was of very little consequence to them. It did not help him much and he almost wished he had not gone to the trouble of telling them.

He busied himself clearing up his charts and came across a small wooden box where he kept a few bits and bobs he had picked up along the way. He took from it the small rabbit's foot Jenny had given him when they wintered together. He wondered why he had kept it, and smiled fondly as he thought of her, 'what on earth will have become of her.' The locket from Ruth he opened and placed it carefully on the table. He remembered her words from the barn one time, when she had prophetically announced that 'he belonged to her'. How true that was, and he realised that he needed some way of exorcising the ghosts and guilt of the past. His conscience was clear regarding what had happened in the stable on that fateful night. He had so wanted to make sure that Ruth did not get the blame; that he had carried the guilt for her. It seemed highly unlikely that Ruth would admit now that she was to blame for the loss of her brother, so he would have to confront the issue without implicating her. One thing which did worry him from time to time was that: he knew how much she had hated her brother, which raised the uneasy question; did she deliberately push him out of the loft?

CHAPTER TWENTY ONE

Standing on the quarterdeck Ben was feeling quite pleased. His calculations and setting of the sails had brought them exactly to where he had planned. As Lizard Point came into view there was a sigh of relief from the ship's company as they realised that they were almost home.

Standing alongside the other ship's officers there was a definite air of pride about them all. Seagull was a big ship with a broad beam, but under full sail and with a following breeze she seemed almost to sprint along.

"Well done Mr. Burrows, I was confident that you would get us here," Captain Mitchell said. He stood proudly on the poop deck, aware that most eyes were on him, waiting to obey his every command.

"Well Mr. Burrows, what now, have you decided on your future?" Barraclough said.

"I shall take my certificate as soon as possible and wait to see if the Captain will have me back on board," Ben replied.

He was using the ship's large telescope to watch the Point slip past. He stood back to allow Barraclough to use the scope.

"I have good lodgings in Plymouth, with a certain aptly named Mrs. Baker who makes the finest of home cooking and provides a snug and warm mooring. I am sure she would have a spare room for you if you would care to join me."

"Why yes, thank you. I was not sure what I was going to do; it would be nice to be ashore awhile."

It was raining quite hard as they dropped anchor, but the crew's spirits were not dampened. With several months' pay due and the prize money from three more ships, they were all feeling quite wealthy. Old hands knew that the Admiralty were not quick at honouring their debts, but they were confident of something.

There was a great deal to do for all the officers. The purser had enlisted Ben's help with his final stocktaking and was panicking because there seemed to be some stores missing. He was responsible to the Victualling Board and could be personally charged for any stores unaccounted for. It took two hours of painstaking bookwork to make everything balance out correctly. As Master's mate and with no ship's Master Ben also had the responsibility of checking various other details; the ship's log had to be brought up to date, and the daily weather conditions and the ship's general status had to be added.

It was six hours before they finally were allowed to go ashore. The ship's boats were busy ferrying stores and men to the quayside, and as Ben hung over the side checking a delivery of timber he was approached by Fletcher.

"Beggin' your pardon Mr. Burrows, I was wondering what your plans were now? Not being nosey or anything, but if you were staying with the ship yer old mess mates thought that we might enlist again with you."

"Thank you for asking Fletch, I hope to take my Lieutenant's certificate and then serve under Captain Mitchell again."

The Captain and Barraclough heard the conversation, "It seems Mr. Burrows has not just impressed the officers of this ship." The Captain said.

"Aye Captain he's a popular lad alright."

Still it rained and it was dark before Ben and Barraclough were able to head for Mrs. Baker's lodging house. The streets were busy as always and made worse by great puddles that made walking difficult. At last they reached the house and were welcomed by a woman dressed in a prim dress protected by a floral apron.

"Welcome back Mr. Barraclough. I hope you will be staying a little longer with me than last time?"

"I hope so too dear lady, ship's rations do not agree with me at all, and I have dreamt of your puddings and cakes the entire voyage"

"I think you tease me as always Mr. Barraclough," she said. It was obvious, that she was flattered by his attention. "And who do we have here?"

"This is a friend and shipmate of mine. I hope you will also be able to accommodate him, Mrs. B." Barraclough said in his broadest of accents.

"Oh indeed, I have just the rooms for you both; my daughter will turn the beds down for you."

The rooms were very comfortable and after the sparse accommodation on board ship seemed luxurious. Crashing down on the bed Ben let out a deep breath blowing hard through his lips.

"My words, I thought a whale had breached there!" Barraclough said. "Is it alright if I come in?"

Ben sat up and offered an armchair to his friend.

"I suppose it's just a reaction to everything; it's nice to find a comfortable bed after so long."

"You're right, the trouble is when I'm at sea I want to be somewhere more comfortable, but as soon as I land I want to be back out to sea again."

Mrs. Baker appeared with a tray, china cups tinkling as she climbed the stairs.

"Now, Gentlemen, I've taken the liberty of making some tea and there's cold roast beef and some of my homemade bread for you."

"Mrs. B, you spoil us, we may stay here indefinitely with such treatment."

They tucked in to the heap of beef and bread she had brought, enjoying every morsel. Ben kicked off his boots and rested against the bed head, whilst Barraclough sprawled out in the chair, his long legs stretching almost right across the room to relax and enjoy the tea.

"The Captain has dispatched your request to sit your examination for the lieutenant's certificate. I'll wager you will be called before the board this week."

"I hope I'm ready. I'll never be at ease with sailing as you are, but I am satisfied with my navigation and these last few months I have felt more confident."

"My advice is don't try and give any elaborate answers, stick to what you know and you will be fine."

"I think we need a visit to your tailor friend again, my jacket has suffered and every one of my shirts is torn to shreds, I don't think I have one with both sleeves intact."

They had a carefree few days; Mrs. Baker fed them until they had to ask her to lighten the meals a little.

"If I eat anything else, I shall need to replace my uniform entirely." Ben said tugging at his waistcoat which suddenly seemed very tight.

A letter came to say that he was to attend the examination board the next Monday. Ben nervously went through the books, Barraclough helping out by asking questions and generally testing him over naval procedure and different aspects of gunnery, navigation and sailing. The lieutenant's exam was very important, because unlike the army where commissions could be bought and officers were expected to be Gentlemen, the navy insisted that its officers knew their job. It was still an advantage to have money, and to advance to captain a man needed a patron: someone with money who could pull a few strings and help him to further promotion.

Whilst the ship was in dock there were many jobs to be done; repairs carried out at sea were checked and damaged timbers replaced, her rigging and sails all had to be checked and repaired or replaced. The ship's gunner had to make sure all the weapons were in sound condition and working, as well as checking that the ship's powder magazines were fully stocked and dry.

Ben and Barraclough went for their own refit to the tailors to replace their battle worn jackets and trousers. As usual the little tailor fussed around with pins and chalk in his mouth, muttering to himself and then disappearing behind the curtain door. Two hours later the job was done and their uniforms looked brand new.

The Admiralty buildings on the morning of Ben's examination could only be described as chaotic. All ranks milled together and went about their business with not a care for their surroundings, but Ben was somewhat overawed by the place. He had had a nervous start to the morning with Barraclough having to help straighten his cravat and uniform. Mrs. Baker, knowing the importance of the day, had made a special breakfast and although Ben had declared that he was not hungry she had cajoled him into at least eating some of her best scones. She had also pressed and brushed his jacket and shirt, and as he left the house she stood on the house step like a proud mother waving him off.

Eventually he found the correct office. Mr. Barraclough shook his hand wished him luck and said he would wait in the mess two floors down. There were about twenty other candidates and Ben had to sit on a windowsill. He could not help studying the others. Most looked very nervous; all of them fidgeted and glanced uneasily at the door every few minutes. He tried to keep Barraclough's advice foremost in his thoughts but after waiting an hour his patience was wearing thin.

Finally, a clerk appeared and he was called in. When he entered, he was confronted by three senior officers all of whom he recognised. One of them was Captain, now Commodore Atkins who greeted him with a knowing nod of his head. Rear Admiral Hunter and Admiral Benn made up the committee, all very well respected seamen.

"So, Mr. Burrows we meet again." Atkins said.

"Indeed yes Sir."

"I have read your Captain's account of your brave action on that day; you are to be congratulated for such a deed."

"Thank you sir. If I may be so bold, it was due to your brave intervention at a very crucial moment that saved our bacon on that occasion." Ben replied hoping that his flattery was not too obvious.

Atkins smiled: he was delighted the young officer had also highlighted his bravery before his peers.

The rest of the examination went well too, and after two hours Ben was confident that he had done his best. He was tired and his collar felt too tight and perspiration was flowing freely down his face.

"Thank you Mr. Burrows, we will forward your results within the week."

Once outside the room Ben blew a sigh of relief. It had been harder than fighting the French. He mopped his brow and began to descend the wide marble staircase when a shout from above caught his attention. He turned and to his dismay, it was the girl who had come to his room at Ruth's wedding reception: Annabel Hunter.

"Well, well, Mr. Burrows, how are you?" Her voice trembled as she purred the words.

"Very well thank you, madam," he said.

She was on the step above him, and looked straight into his eyes. She thought he looked even more handsome than the last time they had met.

"Shall we take tea together?" she asked.

"I regret madam that I have a prior engagement, perhaps some other time." He really was not in the mood for this encounter.

After the passion of their last encounter, she had expected him to be far more pleased to see her. She was not used to being refused.

"Very well Mr. Burrows, tomorrow then." She said obviously piqued, "There is a small tearoom further along the street from where the famous author Charles Dickens was born, I will meet you there at ten-thirty."

"I'm not sure."

"No buts Mr. Burrows or is it Stone?" There was a change in her tone, her voice was slightly more aggressive.

She skipped back up the stairs obviously very pleased with herself, then turned and added, "I have news of our mutual friend, something you will definitely be interested in."

Leaning against the banister Ben felt quite sick. This was a disastrous end to what had already been a very stressful day.

"Well my friend how did you get on, you look mightily worried?" Barraclough asked.

"Oh sorry Mr. Barraclough, yes all went very well. I think so at any rate."

"Something's troubling you?" Barraclough knew Ben too well not to notice.

"I've just bumped into one of Lady Ruth's old friends. She wants to meet me tomorrow."

"No harm in that."

"I didn't tell you, she came to my room the day of Ruth's wedding reception, and . . . well you can guess the rest. She also just called me Stone, she pretended it was a mistake, but her tone was quite menacing."

"Your good looks will be the death of you one day." Barraclough laughed.

They had a full and satisfying meal at their lodgings and then spent the evening at a local inn. It was noisy and busy, filled with men of all ranks spending their pay. It helped to take Ben's mind off the following day, and after a couple of ales he and Barraclough were joining in the singing and having a great time.

Next day, Ben stood outside the door to the little tearoom and adjusted his best uniform for the umpteenth time. He had recently followed fashion and started wearing his hair in a ponytail; his black curls were pulled tight and tied back and protruded from underneath the back of his hat. He decided that this was much more difficult than waiting to take a broadside from a French warship.

To his surprise she was not there. He took a table in the far corner and ordered tea. The place was quite busy, and he attracted quite a bit of attention especially from the younger ladies in the room. He had not long to wait before she breezed in with her usual confidence, knowing that every head in the room was turned to watch her arrival.

"Ah there you are, Mr. Burrows, I was not sure that you would come."

Ben stood to attention and offered her a seat, when he was sure she was comfortable he resumed his seat. There was an awkward silence for a few moments.

She removed her shawl exposing an exquisite dress. Quite a few heads turned to admire the handsome couple as Annabelle took her seat. She noted the smiling, admiring glances of the room's occupants.

"You said you had news of Ruth," Ben whispered.

"Have you ordered already?"

"Yes, I'm sorry, would you like some refreshment?"

It was like a fencing lesson. Annabel parried every attempt Ben made to steer the conversation back to Ruth. Eventually he gave up and she sat staring at him with a look of triumph on her face.

"I'm very jealous," she said over the rim of her teacup. "Whenever we are together your thoughts seem to be with Ruth. Although I do seem to remember grabbing your attention for some considerable time on a particular evening in London."

Ben had forgotten how attractive she was; her hair in fine ringlets framed her pretty features and she had flashing blue eyes that sparkled with the joy of living. The low cut, square-shaped neck to her dress seemed to offer her perfect round breasts like tantalising, plump fruits in a shop window. Ben had to admit to himself that she was indeed a very beautiful young woman, and that there would be few men who would not be delighted to be sitting opposite her in the intimate setting of the tearoom.

"Indeed, Madam, you had my full undivided attention," Ben said. He was trying to appease her, and not at all sure why he was being so hostile, except she now knew his real name.

Her face flushed ever so slightly, as her tongue traced the edge of the cup, "and yet Mr. Burrows I come a very poor second place in your thoughts, despite my offerings that day." Her voice was a hoarse whisper.

"I'm truly sorry about that, I cannot help what my heart feels. I don't mean any offence."

"Nor can I. You have hurt and offended me, Mr. Burrows."

Ben studied her for a moment. He guessed it was her pride rather than her heart that he had hurt. He realised he needed to tread more carefully, dealing with her was like walking through a pit of vipers.

She looked angrier as she continued. "If I were a man, I would call you out for a duel, but as I do not have that luxury then I may have to find satisfaction another way."

Ben was unsure what she meant, "If you were a man, then the question would never arise." Ben quipped trying to lighten the mood.

"So now you make light of me too. I understand you were before my father yesterday." She said changing tack to confuse him.

"Yes I was."

In another mood change, she said "Your style has changed greatly since we last met. You seemed a bit of a boyish bumpkin, although you certainly proved your manhood." She smiled wickedly at him. "I like the change to your hair and the scar across your cheek is very fashionable. Gentlemen are paying a fortune to have one."

"Annabelle, I have no idea what you want. I apologise for any insult, but I cannot change my feelings. I came here because you said you had news for me." He was losing his patience and ready to leave.

"Back to Ruth again, I had hoped that you had come because you wanted to see me again," she said.

"Annabelle . . ." he whispered, "our last meeting was very special to me, but there were no promises."

She sat a moment studying him. The mood was broken by the arrival of the girl bringing more tea. She asked if they wanted anything else and then left.

In an almost surreal moment, Annabel poured them both tea. Fussing with the saucers, and handing Ben a napkin, she transformed into a mother hen.

"Ruth has had a baby," she announced. "A girl."

Ben flushed as a mixture of emotions washed across him; suddenly he realised that she knew more than she was saying.

"Ruth and I were at school together." She poured tea as she spoke. "We met just after a very sad incident when her brother had been killed in a fight of sorts. She always did make up stories about things."

She sipped her tea watching him, but Ben showed no emotion.

"Since then we have been best friends, and we share all our little and not so little secrets. We have even devised a secret code when we write, like spies use, so that no one else can read our letters." She almost giggled as she spoke.

"Did you mention our encounter that particular day in London?" he said.

"Perhaps, although it is nice to think that one has a little edge on one's friends and rivals, something tucked away for a rainy afternoon to add spice to a meeting."

"Are they both well?"

"Oh yes indeed, Sir Arthur is delighted with his offspring too. He was very proud as everyone congratulated him on his prowess and marvelled that the child was born just nine months almost to the day after their arrival in Jamaica."

Ben sat back, "I am sorry, but I have to be off, I am to report to my Captain today."

She ignored him and carried on, "Ruth says that Sir Arthur was drunk and totally incapable the whole journey. Fortunately he is too dim to think very deeply about things." She placed her cup on its saucer and gave Ben a very meaningful look. "It seems odd then that she should have had a child, although she did let me into a couple of secrets regarding the long passage at sea."

"Forgive me ma'am I do not mean any offence, I must be away." He wanted to be on his own to think. Was she inferring that he was the child's father? "I have really enjoyed our afternoon, and I hope that we will perhaps get together before I set sail again."

"Don't lie to me Mr. Burrows, it is bad enough that you so obviously prefer another. You could have had the good grace to pretend otherwise at least. I feel slighted Mr. Burrows. I am not the forgiving type and I have a rather vengeful soul."

"You must do as you see fit ma'am, I cannot change anything."

Ben stood up and left the table with a courteous bow. When he reached the door he paid the girl and left without a backward glance. He realised he had not handled it at all well and that he had probably made himself a vicious enemy.

It was much cooler outside and Ben blew a sigh of relief as he reached the road overlooking the docks. He could see the bustle that surrounded the ships as barges came and went. He smiled remembering his friend Barraclough's words about wanting to get home and then immediately wanting to be back to sea. Most of all he thought of Ruth and her child, and his heart ached to see her again.

CHAPTER TWENTY TWO

Two days later Ben and Barraclough sat in Mrs. Baker's living room like a couple of country gentlemen. Ben, feeling rather affluent, had purchased a new set of civilian clothes and boots. They were making plans to journey to Barraclough's home town of Taunton for a week or so, if the Captain would allow it.

A knock at the door interrupted their thoughts, Mrs. Baker entered followed closely behind by their Captain. Immediately they jumped to their feet.

"Gentlemen," the captain said.

Ben offered him a seat, he was curious about the sudden visit; usually the captain sent a runner with messages. It must be important. He took his chair again after the captain made himself comfortable in one of the armchairs. "You two look at home and relaxed here." He smiled and took a moment to compose himself. "I do apologise for this interruption," he said.

Predictably Mrs. Baker was back, "I just thought I'd bring you all a nice cup of tea."

"How thoughtful ma'am, I see why my officers are always in a hurry to reach your establishment." The Captain smiled graciously as he held the door for her retreat.

He resumed his seat, "To the point gentlemen, I have rather a mixed bag of news." He stood up and paced slowly in front of the hearth, raising the level of tension in the room.

"Firstly: congratulations Mr. Burrows you have been promoted to Lieutenant and secondly: I have accepted a new commission to Captain a new frigate, The Adventurer."

There were smiles all round, but Ben sensed there was more. He knew from the way the Captain cleared his throat and clasped his hands firmly behind him that there was bad news too.

"However, I also have some rather bad news: it would appear Mr. Burrows that your past has finally caught up with you. I have here a letter for you to attend a court martial regarding the death of Master Bartholomew Hutton-Beaumont of the North Riding of Yorkshire next Friday."

Ben took the letter and he let out a groan as he read it. He handed it to Barraclough to read.

"Tell them the truth just as you told me, and remember now is not the time for chivalry. If, as you told me it was the Lady Ruth who actually pushed the lad over the top, then you must say so."

Captain Mitchell looked uncomfortable, "I shall stand by you, and speak on your behalf. You are too important a member of my crew to lose over this issue."

"And I shall also give you my fullest support" Barraclough said.

"I can't betray her trust!" Ben exclaimed.

"Don't be a fool man, she had every opportunity to clear the matter when she first recognised you; it's just a game to her, can't you see." Barraclough said.

"But . . ."

Captain Mitchell stood directly in front of Ben, "Listen, no one will think any the worse of you for telling the truth, but the consequences of protecting her could be catastrophic for yourself." He placed his hand on Ben's shoulder, "Good God man you could end up on the gallows."

The inner turmoil Ben felt was overwhelming. He realised he was going to have to admit to himself that Ruth would always toy with him and that his friend was right it was just a game to her.

It was going to be along week, and so Barraclough insisted that Ben should go have his new lieutenant's uniform made. "it will impress the court favourably to see you have been recently promoted." Barraclough ended the argument.

Friday arrived all too soon. It was a grey miserable day; Ben walked through the crowded streets in a daze, hardly noticing the rain or anything of what was going on around him. Barraclough steered him safely around the worst puddles in the road and safely to their destination. By the time they reached the Admiralty Building they were soaked to the skin.

A young lieutenant greeted them and offered a bench for them to sit and wait. The time seemed to drag, a clock in a tall wooden case ticked away the minutes. Eventually they were called into the room where the court was to be held. Ben was pale and he felt that he might be sick. It took a great deal of effort to stand still and not fidget as he stood next to Barraclough waiting for the senior officers to take their places.

By chance, it was the same officers who a week before had examined him for his Lieutenant's certificate. He glanced at each one trying to find a friendly face, wondering what each had in mind.

One by one, they sat down along the slightly curved table across one end of the cavernous hall. The court clerk stood, and cleared his throat and then after a nod from the senior member of the board, he read out the charge in a thin almost squeaky voice. He then introduced Captain J.P. Todd as the officer to act as investigator for the court. Todd was a small wiry man in his late forties. Due to a severe and recurring bronchial infection, he had been forced to retire from active service. He wheezed slightly with each breath as he made his way to the centre of the room. He was obviously nervous, and he stood a moment to prepare himself, the papers in his hand visibly shaking.

"I have been appointed Investigator for His Royal Majesty's Navy." He stopped to catch his breath, and then patted his lips with a crisp white handkerchief. "We are to determine whether or not Lieutenant Burrows, formally known as Benjamin Stone of Bingley in the West Riding of Yorkshire, is guilty of murder. If so he is to be handed over to the civil authorities for trial by the Crown." He stopped again obviously out of breath after the long speech. "I am now required to charge the same with the offence of murder and ask for his plea." He turned, looking directly at Ben, who was a little to his left. There was a long silence Barraclough gave Ben a quick nudge.

"The court is waiting sir" Todd said.

"Not guilty of murder Sir," the words were spoken quietly but confidently.

"You must speak up Sir." Todd barked again.

"Not guilty of murder Sir," Ben said a little too loudly. The words echoed around the room. He felt uncomfortably hot, and wished that he could control his nerves; he tried to keep as still as possible.

"Lieutenant Barraclough, you and lieutenant Burrows may be seated."

Ben felt behind him for the straight-backed chair. He gratefully sank onto its hard seat. The Captain returned to his desk and consulted more papers. The click of his heels echoed loudly as once again he returned to the centre.

"We do not have any witnesses for the prosecution. However, a warrant for the arrest of Master's Mate Burrows alias Benjamin Stone was sent to us by the father of the victim, Sir Geoffrey Hutton-Beaumont of the North Riding of Yorkshire, Kings Magistrate in that county. It has been established by investigation of this office, that Benjamin Stone, and Lieutenant Burrows, are indeed the same." He turned again to Ben. "Do you deny that you are indeed Benjamin Stone, and that you are the person mentioned in that warrant?"

"No I do not deny it Sir, my name was Benjamin Stone." Ben replied, his voice now under control.

"Would you kindly tell us then the events of that day?" He consulted his notes. "The twenty-second of November in the year of our Lord Seventeen Hundred and Ninety-Eight." Captain Todd returned to his desk, and then sat down.

Ben stood up. He steadied himself, before speaking.

"I was working in the stable at the rear of Uncle John's inn, when Ruth came in to see if our bitch Bess had had her pups." He knew the lie about why she was there did not matter.

"Excuse me who is Ruth?" One of the officers asked.

"Ruth is the daughter of Sir Geoffrey Hutton-Beaumont Sir."

Captain Todd came to his feet, a surprised look on his face. "Do you mean the wife of the Governor of Jamaica?"

"Yes Sir." There was a slight pause, as Captain Todd once again searched through his notes.

"Continue." The Rear Admiral commanded from the centre of the table.

"As we looked at them, the pups that is, Batty, I mean, Bartholomew, rushed at me from where he had been hiding in the hay loft."

"Why should he be hiding? And why should he attack you?"

"He was very jealous of my friendship with his sister. We had fallen out on several occasions. He often spied on us."

"Had you ever fought before?"

"Yes sir, but only as boys. He was two years older than I was Sir, but he only occasionally came to my Uncle's with Ruth. I kept away from him if I could. He was a bit of a bully; he hurt me quite badly once in a fight, I think I was about eleven." He stopped a moment. "On this particular day, Ruth and I had climbed into the hay loft to see Bess. As I said, he suddenly leapt at me. We rolled through the hay, towards the unprotected edge of the loft. He grabbed Ruth, but she wriggled away and pushed at him with a broom, then suddenly he lost his balance and fell over the edge; a drop of about two fathoms." He stopped as his mind filled with that horrible moment.

"If that was the case . . . why run?" there was suspicion in every syllable.

"I panicked, Sir."

"Why?"

"He was the son of the Magistrate, I thought no one would believe me, and well . . . I just panicked Sir. Ruth said her father was bound to hang me."

"Is that all you have to say?"

"Yes Sir, there is nothing else to say, that is the honest truth of the events. If I had had the power to prevent his fall then I would have done so."

Captain Todd came more slowly to the centre of the room again.

"Unfortunately apart from the deceased, the only other witness to this incident is in the West Indies. However I have here the warrant issued on that day, by Constable John Fowles, the constable of Bingley." He held up the document. "There is also a statement by him. He was the first to be called to the scene, by John Stone, the owner of the Inn, and Uncle of the accused." Todd wiped his lips, and then took a sip of water. "He states that the Lady Ruth said—here I am quoting from the constable's notes—'That there had been a terrible fight, and that Benjamin Stone had killed her brother'. He also noted that some time later she said that he had just fallen out of the loft." He placed the document before the Rear-Admiral. "However, I also have here a statement by Doctor C. Cartwright of Bingley who examined the body. His report states that there were no marks on the body to indicate a fight as suggested by the Lady Ruth. The young man's neck had been broken, and that it was his opinion, that this was caused by the fall." He returned to his desk, again mopping at his mouth. "There is no other evidence My Lords."

In fact, Ruth had changed her story several times. When she told her friends, she described how she and Ben had been embracing as lovers when her brother attacked them, and described in detail a fictitious battle which became more horrific with each new version. When her father had questioned her, she had told him several different versions of the events. Captain Todd was overcome by a bout of coughing that doubled him over and he was forced to sit until the spasm had passed.

"Because of the lack of any evidence in this case, and because of the defendant's service record, I consulted the deceased's father for his opinion regarding this matter. He has agreed to uphold the decision of this court." He sat down again, trying to hold back another fit of coughing. Rear Admiral Hunter, chairman of the court, stood. He surveyed the court a moment then in a loud yet tired sounding voice asked if anyone else had anything to add. He directed his gaze to where Captain Mitchell sat. There was a slight pause as Captain Mitchell came to the centre of the table. He saluted smartly.

"Obviously I can make no comment regarding the incident, but I can vouch for the character of the defendant. I regard him as a very trustworthy junior officer, who has served bravely under my command. I recommended promotion for him, and stand by that decision. He bravely removed the sniper that wounded myself and Mr. Barraclough, my First Officer. Not only that, he then went on to capture the Spanish Captain of the ship we were locked in battle with, a very brave and gallant act."

"Thank you Captain. If that is all then I propose that we adjourn to discuss this matter." The officers of the bench filed into an ante-room. The atmosphere in the courtroom relaxed a little. Ben blew a long sigh.

"Don't worry lad, I can't imagine for a single moment that they could convict you of murder. Not on such confusing evidence." He patted Ben on the shoulder.

For the first time Ben glanced around the room; he was surprised to see three figures sat at the back of it. He recognised Sir Geoffrey Hutton-Beaumont immediately, but had no idea who the other two where. Captain Mitchell went across to where Captain Todd sat. They had known each other for a great many years. When Todd was a Lieutenant, he had served for a short period under Captain Mitchell.

"Hello Todd, old chap, the chest sounds bad."

"Aye damn thing. I'm tied to a blessed desk all day now. I hate it, damn glorified clerk that's all I am now. My arse's square as a box with sitting all day like someone's granny."

"We had some good times," Mitchell said to change the subject.

"Those were the days by thunder! This is a rum affair. I can't honestly say I know what to believe. With those three watching from the back I feel damned awkward," He cocked his head towards the figures at the back of the room. "Anything can happen, Hutton-Beaumont's a fair chap, but he has a lot of clout with Whitehall, and I think he could overthrow any verdict we reach here if he had the mind to. Your lad had better have the luck of the devil."

Mitchell smiled, "if that's the case, he'll be fine."

The door of the anteroom opened. All eyes were drawn to it. The clerk appeared he came over to Captain Todd. They exchanged whispers, and the Captain nodded grave faced, as he listened. He stood, and then gave Captain Mitchell a wave to follow him; they disappeared behind the door.

Ben grew more nervous as the time slowly dragged on. He trusted his Captain to do the best that he could for him, but even so, he wondered if it would be enough. It was a full half hour before the clerk re-emerged again. He went to the back of the room, and led Hutton-Beaumont, with his two companions back into the anteroom. The door remained firmly closed for another hour. The long wait was very wearing on everyone's nerves. Ben was relieved to see the reappearance of Sir Geoffrey, followed by the Rear Admiral. The rest of the court trooped back in. It took another few minutes for everyone to regain their seats; once again, Captain Todd came to the centre of the room.

"We have not yet reached a satisfactory verdict; the lack of evidence, other than that given by the defendant makes any decision difficult. However certain questions have arisen that we would like answering." He came and stood in front of Ben. "The first question: Have you seen the Lady Ruth since the incident?"

"Yes Sir."

Captain Todd closed his eyes a moment composing his next question. "Could you tell the court where and when?"

"In London after her wedding and on the passage to the West Indies aboard H.M.S. Seagull."

"Did you speak with her?"

"Yes Sir."

"And do you think she recognised you?"

"Yes Sir."

"Did you speak about the incident?"

"Yes sir we did."

"Can you tell me why, if she recognised you, she did not tell your Captain, or her new husband who you were?"

"No Sir."

"Did you think she would do?"

"I was not sure Sir."

"Did you threaten her so that she did not dare?"

"No never! No Sir, I did not."

"If she accused you of murdering her brother to the constable in Yorkshire, was she telling lies that day?" Ben felt cornered. He could not tell the court the real reason they were together, nor could he explain Ruth's accusation, it had been she who had told him to run, saying that she would explain what had happened.

"Well, are you accusing her of lying?"

"She was upset Sir, perhaps . . ." His voice trailed away he could not think of any more to say. A thin line of sweat ran down his face. The droplet hung on the end of his chin before dropping to the floor.

"Lieutenant Burrows, your life is at stake here. You must give us the truth, and answer my questions. Now at the bride and groom's reception did you approach her or she you?"

"I was introduced to Ruth, begging your pardon Sir, the Lady Ruth, and her husband by Captain Mitchell."

"Was that the only time you spoke to her that day?"

"No Sir. There were many secluded paths and bowers in the garden, I was speaking with another lady, when she joined us."

"Did the other lady stay?"

"No Sir, The Lady Ruth asked her to leave"

"Why?"

"I'm not sure Sir."

"And what did you discuss?"

"The passage to the Indies. She said how nice it would be for us to be travelling together." Captain Todd turned back to his peers he straightened his jacket, obviously lost for words. He made an appealing gesture to the Rear Admiral. The Sea Lord rose from his seat. He glanced a moment towards Ben then addressed himself to the room in general.

"I must admit to being a little confused by this case. We certainly do not have any evidence to convict the defendant of murder. It is obvious that the Lady Ruth could on several occasions have revealed his true identity. We can only guess her reasons for not doing so." The Rear Admiral stopped a moment. "Lieutenant Burrows, I do not know what really happened on that day, only you have the answers. But because of your service record, and the fact that Captain Mitchell speaks so highly of you; I do not see any point in continuing this court martial. This court is absolved."

The final words seemed to hang in the air, echoing around the room. The presiding officers stood and then returned to the anti-room. Ben could hardly contain his relief. It was as if the sun had come out from behind the clouds. Barraclough and Captain Mitchell shook Ben's hand but he was speechless, unable to respond, he smiled, a little dazed, with a foolish grin on his face.

"Excuse me Mr Stone; Sir Geoffrey requests a private word with you." It was one of the men who had been sat with Hutton-Beaumont. "If you will kindly follow me Sir."

Ben followed in the wake of the man, out of the courtroom, across a marble-floored hall into a small dimly lit room. The walls of the room were lined with bookshelves eight foot high, laden with scores of heavy leather bound volumes. Down the centre of the room was a long narrow table of polished walnut, Sir Geoffrey sat in one of the high-backed chairs that stood like sentinels around it. He was almost afraid to look at the tired figure at the table. There was a gentle click of the door behind him as his escort left the two of them together.

"It's been a long day lad, pull yourself a seat." The voice was soft, it sounded as tired as the figure looked. "I am sorry that we meet again in these circumstances. I have great respect for your family, and I have always thought kindly of you."

They both sat down, Ben was filled with dread at what Sir Geoffrey would say. He knew that his fate was in the others hands.

"Bartholomew was my only son. I know that he was far from being an angel; but he was my son." There was a long silence. Sir Geoffrey thought about the boy he had overindulged, and knew that he was as much to blame as anyone for the way the boy had turned out. One scandal after another had followed the boy through his adolescence. Only weeks before his death he had been forced to pay compensation to a family from Eldwick, whose daughter they alleged had been beaten and raped by him. There were many other incidents, including another two alleged rapes and assaults.

"You and I know there was much more going on than was revealed in there today. I have to thank you, for not saying anything, and for your discretion." There was another long pause. "It would do no good to take the matter any further. I intend to let the case drop, if you will say here and now in private to me that it was just an accident . . ." Another pause, "You see, my biggest fear is that you are covering for Ruth." This had always troubled him; had Ruth in fact been the one who had deliberately pushed his son to his death. She had never made a secret of how much she hated her brother.

"It was just as I said Sir. He charged at me, we wrestled and he lost his footing. There was no safety rail Sir. I bitterly regret it. I would have saved him if I could."

"Yes I believe you would have. I just hope that this does not spoil a very promising career for you. You have obviously done well, and your captain speaks very highly of you."

"Yes Sir. Thank you Sir." Ben stood. He hesitated a moment as there was a question burning his lips.

"It was not Ruth who gave you away; in fact I am not sure who it was that discovered your identity. I am a very good friend of Admiral Hunter; our girls were inseparable at school. He just informed me that he thought he had found the person responsible for my son's death."

The thought dawned on Ben that this was Annabelle's revenge; he guessed that she had told her father.

"Very well Lieutenant Burrows," he smiled, "let that be an end to it, you may go a free man."

"Thank you Sir, it has troubled me all these years and at last I can put it behind me."

As Ben reached the door he waited for Sir Geoffrey to join him, and then they shook hands. "I shall inform your Uncle that I have seen you and that the matter is put to rest. I know he has been deeply worried about the situation."

"Thank you Sir Geoffrey."

Ben immediately went to find Barraclough.

"Come on my friend, Mrs. Baker will have a spread waiting for us" Barraclough said.

Ben stepped out of the building and took a deep breath. At long last his conscience was clear. Standing on the entrance steps Ben took a moment to savour the sensation of freedom. There was a warm glow inside as the feeling slowly seeped into every corner of his being.

CHAPTER TWENTY THREE

Ben stayed in for the next few days, juggling with his thoughts and emotions. He had been allowed to keep his promotion, and allowed to return to duty if he wished. It was coincidence that on the third day just as he had decided to quit the service he watched Captain Mitchell from his bedroom window alight from a cab outside Mrs. Baker's front door.

"Sorry to interrupt you gentlemen again." The Captain placed a number of newspapers on the table. He stood, his back to the drawing room fire, he waited until Mrs. Baker had left. He placed a long parcel onto the table, and then cleared his throat for a speech.

"Have you seen your name in print Mr. Burrows?"

"No Capt'n."

Ben picked up the papers and read the page where it had been folded back. There was an account of the trial and Ben was referred to as 'one of the services bravest young Lieutenants'. There was an account of his capture of the Spanish ship, and how he had swung through the rigging to fight hand to hand with the Spanish Captain. It went on and on, so much so that Ben was not really sure who it was talking about.

"It seems you are a hero Mr. Burrows."

"Here here," Barraclough chipped in.

Ben studied the long parcel; he was fascinated to see what it could be.

"I have to say Mr. Burrows, that I would welcome you back into service upon any ship of mine. I have no doubt that you may perhaps be thinking of quitting the service." The Captain decided to take a seat. "Gentlemen, as you may have heard the abolition of slavery is having a pronounced effect on our world. There is trouble brewing everywhere, especially in the West Indies where countless fortunes including my own family's could be in severe jeopardy." He knew how to gain interest from his audience and the theatrical pause heightened the moment.

"I have been commissioned to go hunt pirates no less, in the Caribbean. Apparently they are again rife as the American States refuse to ban the use of slaves; illegal shipments of slaves are being made. Two rather ancient ships, the frigate The Solebay and a sloop have been sent to patrol the West African coast but I doubt if they will be very effective." He fidgeted for a moment, "we are to work independently of the two regular fleets in the Caribbean, with a range covering the whole of the Atlantic too; in other words as far south as Brazil, and as far to the east as the Cape Verde islands."

Ben saw the surprise on Barraclough's face, who let out a low whistle, "pardon me Captain, but do you not think we are a little long in the tooth for pirate hunting?"

"Speak for yourself man, I'm in my prime," Mitchell said. There was abroad grin on his face, "anyway with Burrows here to look after us we can't fail." They all laughed heartily, and relaxed to take tea.

"Will you not miss the Seagull Captain?" Ben asked.

"She was getting a little like my First Lieutenant here, a bit long in the tooth. The Admiralty in their wisdom has decided to decommission part of the fleet now that the threat of naval action from Bonaparte has subsided. But mark my words they will regret it. Our new ship The Adventurer is brand spanking new and as fast and manoeuvrable as a sloop I'm told."

The Captain brought the tea ceremony to an end as he placed his cup firmly down into its saucer.

"It is my pleasure to inform you that your promotion will stand, and that you are now Lieutenant Burrows or Stone whichever you choose."

"Thank you Sir." A feeling of pride accompanied by a slight pang of emotion made Ben feel rather self conscious.

"Also that you have been granted your share of the prize money, for your part in the capture of the Spanish treasure ship. That day's work has made us all rich men." Mitchell said. "Aye yes. Will you both stand?"

Ben and Barraclough stood together.

"This is a token of my appreciation for your service Lieutenant Burrows, and a reward for your valour against the Spanish warships."

Ben gratefully took the parcel. It felt heavy and solid; he wasn't sure what to expect. Carefully unwrapping the soft cloth Ben was excited to reveal a long sword in a black scabbard. He shook with excited emotion as he carefully drew the gleaming blue steel blade from its sheath. The handle fitted snugly into his hand, it was guarded by a broad crosspiece that swirled in a loop to a pommel at the end of the handle. The hand-guard was decorated with etched scrolls and a cut-out in the form of a rose. The long blade glinted in the firelight. Near the hilt, along the length of one side was an inscription. 'For Valour. Lieutenant B. Burrows RN. H.M.S. Seagull 19th November 1806'. Ben proudly showed it to Barraclough, who read the inscription with a broad smile across his face.

"You deserve it lad. Well done."

"If you will forgive me, Gentlemen, I must again take my leave in a hurry." He refastened his cloak, and then turned back to Ben. "Oh! I nearly forgot—these letters were waiting for you at the Admiralty."

Ben took the letters; he recognised the precise and neat hand of Emily on the first one, but the other was in a much more flowing, yet irregular hand. Despite Barraclough's inquisitive glance, he stuffed them in his jacket pocket. The Captain shook both men's hands before he left.

"I need your decision tomorrow, or I will have to find myself a new crew." With that he left.

Ben drew the sword again, and re-read the inscription. Feeling slightly choked with emotion, he caressed the fine workmanship of the cool blade. Barraclough excused himself, realising that his friend needed a little time to himself.

Carefully Ben opened the letter with the unfamiliar hand. It was scented, written on a fine quality paper, the joint of the paper made secure by a heavy blob of sealing wax. It was dated two days before they had sailed for Jamaica.

Dear Ben

Although we were never formally introduced, I have no doubts that you will remember me from the wedding reception of Sir Arthur and Lady Ruth. I was very surprised that you and she were acquainted. I hope we can meet again before you sail for the Indies. I told papa about you. He was livid, he said that I should not consort with lower ranks, you know how pompous Admirals can be. Please, please call and see me, or at least write. Fond farewells. Annabel Hunter.

He was about to open the second letter when his friend returned, he folded them together and replaced them back in his pocket.

"Good news I hope?"

"Yes thank you, although I have not yet read them both."

Barraclough looked a little put out; he sat down near the fire and with a taper, lit the lamp at his side.

"When we were at Ruth's reception, did you know many of the guests?" Ben asked.

"I knew a few. Why?"

"Does the name Hunter mean anything?"

"It certainly does, that was the buxom creature that was making eyes at you all afternoon. It was lucky for you her father was not there. He guards her like a temple virgin. You've met her father, Hunter, Admiral Hunter, he was chairman of your Court Martial. Surely you knew who he was?"

Ben nodded and realised that it was probably Annabelle who had given his identity away.

"I hope that if you did any wild seed-sowing that day after you disappeared from the party that it did not fall on any fertile ground."

"No, nothing like that. I was curious, as to how the Admiralty found out about my identity."

"Perhaps . . . Ruth?" Barraclough said.

Ben shook his head. "No, she wouldn't have done it. No, I'm sure it was not her. Annabelle Hunter is a much more likely candidate."

Sitting alone in his room later that night Ben opened the other letter which felt to have been pressing hard against his chest all evening. He had been hard-pushed to resist opening it, inquisitive to know its contents.

Dearest Ben,

I hope you are well, and had a safe journey back to your ship. I doubt if you will see this before you sail, but I hope that it finds you on your return. I have some very bad news. Your friend Mr. Burrows in Barrow has passed away. It was very sudden, and he felt no pain. The doctor said it was a heart problem. I spoke to him just the day before he died; he knew that he was ill, and sent you his kindest regards. He gave me word that you are to contact the solicitors McHenry and Watchman on your return. He had an old friend with him, a Dutchman called Van Heild, I believe he mentioned him to you. Mr. Van Heild has kindly been looking after the affairs of the business since Mr. Burrow's death.

We miss you very much, and hope that you will soon come home. Linton has been very ill since you left. He talks non-stop about you, and sends you his love.

I look forward to seeing you soon; take care and come home safely.

Kindest regards Emily Linton.

Ben was shattered by the news. It seemed to throw his whole world upside down. He had not realised just how much he missed his old friends. With the letter in his hand he went and knocked on Barraclough's door.

He entered and apologised for the interruption then handed the letter to his friend. He waited a moment then said, "What can I do?"

"Well the thing, is what do you want to do?"

"I would dearly like to accompany you to the Caribbean again."

"Would that be the lure of a certain lady?"

Ben took a seat on the end of the bed and studied his friend's face.

"I feel I need to go back to my friends in the north, but if the Captain wants our answer tomorrow . . ."

"Hmm I see your dilemma. Maybe it will take a couple of weeks for us to take over the commission of the frigate and maybe you will have time to make a brief visit home."

Ben felt a certain relief at that suggestion.

"I'm really pleased you are going to join our little excursion, I'm sure that knowing our Captain as I do, that it will be at the very least an interesting expedition."

The following day they went to meet the Captain on his new ship. There was of course the usual chaos and in the midst of it all was the Captain, with his sleeves rolled up, heaving and tugging on ropes.

"Well what do you think?" he asked as he saw them arrive on deck.

There was a smell of newness about the ship, the smell of fresh sawn timber, of ship's tar and new rigging. Her design was very different from Seagull's, a much narrower beam and no poop deck, only a small quarter deck.

"She looks good," Barraclough said.

Ben had climbed up to the quarter deck and was surveying the scene. He liked it and knew that he wanted more than anything to sail on her. Just as he descended onto the main deck Fletch and his old mess mates came over the side with heavy boxes of stores.

"Mr. Burrows, good to see you." Fletch touched his forelock in salute, "congratulations on your promotion, and I'm glad everything turned out alright with the other thing too."

"Aye thank you Fletch you old scallywag." They shook hands.

"Captain Mitchell said you might come back so all yer old mess mates signed-on."

"I can't believe it; pressed men never willingly sign on again." Ben said. He felt pleased that they should be loyal to him.

Walking behind Barraclough, Ben followed into the Captain's new cabin. "Sir I have a request."

The captain looked a little suspiciously firstly at Ben and then at Barraclough.

"I very much wish to sail with you, but I have some affairs that need my urgent attention back home."

The Captain sat on a crate and pondered the situation a moment.

"Very well, it will take another two to three weeks at least before the ship will be ready. You can take a post ship from Bristol north and then I will send one of our escort sloops to pick you up and we can rendezvous somewhere out at sea."

"Thank you Captain, that is most generous, I'm lost for words."

"Then don't bother, make sure you are on the dock in Barrow in three weeks time and don't be late."

With that Ben headed back to his digs. There was a coach for Bristol at regular intervals and he needed to be on the first one he could.

"You're a lucky man. The Captain thinks highly of you to arrange all that; because it's highly irregular you know."

Ben packed his clothes, paid Mrs. Baker said his goodbyes and went to catch the coach. Barraclough had gone to see Ben off on the coach.

"I'll get your sea trunk on board and sort you out a chart room."

"Thank you. Don't look so worried, I'll make sure I'm in time for the sloop to pick me up."

The coach pulled away and Ben waved from the window before settling down for the bumpy journey to Bristol.

CHAPTER TWENTY FOUR

After hunting around the port in Bristol, he eventually and with only minutes to spare caught the post-ship north. Ben found himself a seat on top of a few crates on the deck, and for once not being involved in the sailing of the ship, he sat back to enjoy the journey. At last, he was heading north. The harbour had been chaotic but once out into the open sea there was a steady breeze that sped them along the coast. He took time to pen a letter to his Uncle John, and tell him the news of the Court Martial and his promotion and of course to apologise for not being able to call to see them on his way north.

He had the letter from Emily, and wondered why he had to attend the solicitors. It would be good to see the Lintons and he just hoped that he would have time to share a meal or too with them, remembering just how good Emily's cooking was.

Unfortunately the ship had to make several stops; Milford Haven, Fishguard, Liverpool and finally Barrow. By the time they docked Ben was quite out of patience. However, the sight of Barrow's harbour walls and the familiar hills in the distance put him in good humour.

What to do first was his dilemma, he was so impatient to see the Lintons and yet he wanted to visit the old shop of his late friend. His decision was almost made for him, as where the post ship moored was only a few hundred yards from the shop.

With trembling hands he pushed open the door. He wanted so much for his old friend to be there to greet him, but instead he was met by that unforgettable unique smell of the shop. The shop counter looked just the same as when he had left, piled high with an assortment of things. It all did look a little tidier however.

"Hello" Ben called.

There was a shuffling from behind the curtain that hung in the doorway behind the counter. A smiling character with bushy sideburns and rather gaudy smoking jacket appeared.

"Yes sir what can I do for you." The man spoke with an obvious Dutch accent.

"I am Benjamin Stone."

"My word, goodness, I'm lost for words, it is so good to see you."

They shook hands like old friends reuniting after a long absence.

"I feel as if I already know you Mr. Stone. I am Petrus Van Heild"

"Please call me Ben and I feel as I know you too, Mr. Burrows so often spoke of you."

"And of you also to me."

They disappeared into the back room; it was again almost as Ben had last seen it.

Petrus made a cup of tea and they sat and chatted for an hour or so.

"Forgive me Petrus, but I also must go see my friends the Lintons. I will be back tomorrow and then I will go see the solicitors.

"I have a horse you may take; he is a strong animal and will make light of the journey into the fells."

The big chestnut was indeed just the animal Ben needed and he pushed it hard and made good time home to the Linton's. It was good to see the hills again, smell the fields, and listen to the birds singing. He could not help but stop a minute before he reached the farm, just to compose himself.

The reunion was a tearful event with Emily weeping joyfully as she hugged Ben who was now several inches taller than she was. Linton too could not hide his emotions and mopped his face as he sat in his old chair by the fire. Ben took his old seat opposite him near the fire and the years of separation just faded away.

"I will stay overnight if I may, but tomorrow I need to return to Barrow and visit this solicitor." Ben produced Emily's letter as he spoke.

"He was so proud of you," Emily said.

She smiled lovingly at him; how he had grown and although he had always been a good looking boy she was amazed just how handsome he was now. They sat around the table to eat and after Linton's prayer of thanks for bringing them all together again, they tucked in.

"I must say the thought of your cooking if nothing else has always drawn me back," Ben said.

"It is far too long since there was such chatter and laughter in this kitchen." Linton said.

Ben proudly showed them his sword from his captain, and went through what had happened at the Court Martial. He also related some of his adventures but deliberately made them seem less dangerous so the Lintons would not worry. They talked late into the night before Ben retired to his old room in the barn loft.

The following morning after a hearty breakfast Ben saddled his horse and told Emily that he would visit the solicitor as she had advised in her letter. They stood a moment in the yard. He gently touched her cheek; she smiled and squeezed his hand.

"You've been sadly missed here," she said.

"Yes and I have missed you both. You have had such an impact on my life, far more than I could ever have guessed. I have had such adventures, seen amazing places, all because of your kindness."

"Tim has being a doing a fine job for us; he lives in the old cottage down by the stream. Perhaps you can see him before you go, he would love that."

Feeling slightly weary, Ben headed back to town again. He called by Tim's cottage on the way but there was no one home. Back in Barrow, he left his mount at the shop and following Van Heild's directions set off to find the solicitors' office. Ben was amazed how much the rest of the town had expanded during his absence. He found his way to the address in Walney Road after asking directions several times. At least this time, dressed in his uniform there was no chance of him being caught by the 'press-gangs'.

A well-polished brass plate by the side of the door read 'McHenry & Watchman Solicitors.' He pulled the bell chain, and waited. It was some time before anyone answered. He was about to ring again just as the door slowly opened.

"Yes?" A dusty old character stood in the doorway. He stared at Ben with grey emotionless eyes.

Ben explained the reason for his call. The man just nodded, and then waved a slightly bent hand for Ben to follow him. It was a slow journey. Eventually he was shown into an office at the very far end of the building. The office smelt of the coal-fire that smouldered at one end of it. Ben was left alone, surrounded by great mountains of precariously balanced paperwork and folders. The ancient shelves sagged beneath their weight and he hardly dare move in case the whole lot came down. Unsure what to do next; he tentatively sat in a rather worn high backed leather chair, that creaked ominously beneath him. An aspidistra lounged beside him; its dark green fronds were bent in a relaxed manner and looked totally out of place.

"Hello there my friend." The voice had a soft Edinburgh accent, but its owner was still out of sight.

The man emerged from behind another insecure heap of papers. He wore a tweed suit which made him look more like a gamekeeper than a solicitor.

"No need for introductions I'm sure. I know just who you are. I have all the papers ready for you," he smiled.

"I'll miss the old sea-dog; we were friends for many years. I used to look after his Aunt's affairs when she ran the business, God rest her soul." He cleared a space on the desk and then laid out a folder containing a thick wad of sheets.

Ben recognised the artistic writing of his friend on several of the papers, but he was not given chance to read them. Two documents were laid out before him, one was a Will, and the other a letter.

My dear Ben,

It appears that God has decided that we do not meet again in this life, but I am not too down-hearted as I know that we shall meet again someday and exchange yarns. I hope that you have kept in good spirits and that you have received further promotion, and added to my old charts.

As you are aware, I have no family. I therefore thank God that I have two good friends, yourself, and my old ship-mate Petrus. You can trust him with your life; I have on several occasions. I have asked him to move into the shop to look after things until you wish to sort them out.

He has no family, and if you could find a place for him it would make me very happy; he'll keep you shipshape.

Kindest regards
Philip A. Burrows.

Ben felt a swell of emotion as he gently fingered the letter. He smiled at the curious way Mr. Burrows put little tails on the end of certain letters of some words.

"In essence our departed friend left everything to you, except for the shop which he left to be split between yourself and Mr. Van Heild."

He handed another document to Ben. "Despite his appearance he was quite wealthy. There is money to the value of six thousand pounds, and property, three houses to the value of another six hundred pounds, and then of course the shop and all its contents. Here is a letter of introduction to the bank." He handed Ben another document. "They have been in charge of Mr. Burrow's capital. There is also a steady rent from three houses. Congratulations, you are a wealthy young man."

Perched on the very edge of the chair, Ben was having difficulty believing what had happened to him.

"Are you all right, would you like a wee dram?"

"Oh! No thank you sir. It has all come as a bit of a shock."

"Aye, aye well, it's an ill wind, so they say."

"And what of your fee sir?" Ben asked. He was trying to be practical, and to shake his thoughts into order.

"My fee? Nay laddie I thought you knew your friend. He saw to all that afore he departed."

The solicitor rang a small hand bell, "Roberts will show you out, thank you, and if I can be of service in the future don't hesitate to call."

Back out in the street, Ben was still trying to gather his thoughts as he wandered back to the shop.

"Hello! Petrus." He called as he entered.

The Dutchman's smiling face appeared and greeted him.

"You have seen the solicitor, what do you want to do with the shop?"

"Well it is not just up to me, you part own it too."

"I was thinking that if you are staying in the navy you would want to sell it."

"Only if you do. If you want to stay on and live here until I return again I have no objection to that."

"I don't have any plans. I have no family and nowhere that I could really call home."

"Then that settles it, you must stay here for as long as you want. Our friend would have wanted that too."

There was a great deal to sort out regarding the running of the shop. Van Heild thought he could manage to keep it going and Ben was very pleased to think that it would carry on trading. Ben returned to the fells for a few days and managed to do a few jobs around the farm for the Lintons.

His old friend Tim turned up and joined them for a meal. "We had some fun around this table Mrs. Linton."

"We certainly did Tim. At least I don't have so many mouths to fill these days."

"I work here full time now, don't I Missus?"

"Yes indeed Tim we would be lost without you."

"I'm head stockman for the farm now," he said proudly.

"You always were good with the animals. I'm very pleased you help out here."

"Do you need anything?" Ben asked.

"What do you mean?" Emily asked.

"Well, it seems that I am quite a wealthy chap now, and I wondered if I could help you out."

"It's a kind thought Ben, but the farm is making a small profit and both Linton and I have all we need." She hugged and kissed him on the cheek. "You may need your money some day."

Ben left and rode back to Barrow, his conscience was clear and he felt he was on top of the world. The days went far too quickly and on Ben's final day in Barrow Van Heild tugged a heavy looking leather bound trunk out and presented it to Ben.

"Our friend said that this was for you." Van Heild said handing over an intricate looking key.

Ben looked questioningly at the trunk, but Van Heild just smiled and nodded at it. Inside were a number of parcels wrapped in oilskins. One by one Ben opened them; revealing a number of nautical instruments, then a set of pens and bottles of coloured ink for the charts, and finally at the bottom was the inlaid casket that contained the fine pair of pistols Burrows had been so proud to show Ben just after they had first met.

Speechless he studied the treasure trove laid out on the floor. Van Heild placed a friendly hand on his shoulder. "He made me promise to give you these."

"Yes, I always admired them." His voice was full of emotion. "I'll leave the pistols with you if I may; I would hate to lose them."

"When shall you return again?"

"I don't honestly know. I shall do though, and that's a promise. In the meantime, I would ask you to keep an eye on the Lintons and make sure that they are well and safe."

All too soon, Ben had word that a navy sloop was in the harbour and he had to pack and make ready to leave. To his delight the Lintons had arrived and after many tears and hugs, Ben set off again aboard the sloop that was to take him to the West Indies to meet up with Captain Mitchell's ship.

CHAPTER TWENTY FIVE

---•◦❀◦•---

"Good morning Lieutenant Burrows." Lieutenant Rhodes, Captain of the Orion greeted Ben. "Welcome aboard," he said.

"Thank you, I'm sorry if I have caused you any inconvenience," Ben replied.

He came to attention to salute his temporary Captain. They were both about the same age, although Rhodes had by far the longer service history, being in the navy since he was eight years old.

"Not at all, but it is fortunate that we do not have to collect all our crew from their homes or we would not get very far."

Ben ignored the sarcasm and supervised his luggage as it swung aboard from the barge that had brought him out to the Orion. As soon as that was done he organised his quarters, which were really just a corner of the officer's mess. He was not expecting to be on board for more than a couple of weeks, so he was not too worried.

Two hours later, they were out to sea, and standing on the quarterdeck, Ben was enjoying the feeling of the waves and the wind. He positioned himself to the right hand side of Rhodes, alongside another young lieutenant below the flapping ensign.

Once the sails were set, on a fair day like this, then there was little to do but keep an eye on the crew and enjoy the journey. Lieutenant Rhodes had been studying Ben for some while, jealously wishing that the newspapers had things to write about his own career.

"Perhaps you would be kind enough to command the starboard watch during your stay with us," Rhodes said.

"Yes indeed Mr. Rhodes thank you."

"I've heard a lot about you Mr. Burrows. They say you are a very fine navigator and swordsman. The newspapers have had plenty to say about your daring deeds."

"I had an excellent tutor for both skills Mr. Rhodes, and I'm sure that you know not to believe all you read in the papers."

"You must be highly thought of by Captain Mitchell for him to arrange our detour to collect you."

Ben decided not to pass comment instead he made himself busy with the ship's compass.

"Perhaps you could give my mid-shipmen some advice regarding the art of navigation."

"Of course I'd be delighted to Mr. Rhodes." He was not sure if the other was being a little sarcastic again.

As usual at noon readings were taken for the ship's log; this was the official start of the day. The rest of the day was broken into four and two hour watches so that all the men had rest time during the day to allow them to stand the watches through the night. Ben ran an impromptu class with three mid-shipmen and Mr. Rhodes's first officer acting Lieutenant Hill.

"I trust you will join me in my quarters for supper this evening Mr. Burrows."

"Thank you, Mr Rhodes."

The small cabin was fairly cramped that evening as Orion's small band of six officers sat down for supper. There was plenty of good-humoured banter but Ben noticed that Lieutenant Rhodes stayed slightly aloof from it.

"I understand you were at Trafalgar Mr. Rhodes," Ben said.

"Yes I was I was second Lieutenant to Captain John Conn of the Dreadnought." Rhodes said. His manner was rather stiff and formal.

"And what about you Mr. Hill?" Ben turned his attention to the rather more amiable young officer.

"I was a midshipman on the Ajax. We were in Nelson's weather column, but sadly we had very little to do."

"It must have been a glorious day I think," Ben said.

"You I believe were in the Caribbean on HMS Seagull, Mr. Burrows."

"Yes, our Captain was in a very poor humour when we were given the assignment. He very much wanted to sail with Nelson on that day." Ben just smiled back.

"It certainly was a far more profitable excursion I think. Three prize ships, one a frigate and filled with gold," Rhodes said.

"It came at a price sir; we lost a number of good officers and men." Ben said. He felt a little put out and became rather defensive.

"Do you think we will find many pirates Mr. Burrows?" Hill asked sensing the sudden tension.

"I'd say there is a very good chance of it. Have you been to the Indies before Mr Hill?"

"No, apart from the journey to Cadiz, I have hardly left home waters. I long to see action."

"Well Mr. Hill, I think you may have that longing well satisfied, if my recent experience of service with Captain Mitchell is any sort of yard stick."

For about an hour, the little dinner party went on, Ben noted that Rhodes had relaxed a little, but he was glad that he would soon be joining his old crew. As usual his thoughts were with Ruth and he hoped that she was settling into her new life.

Two days later Ben was standing morning watch. It was still dark, but the sun was just beginning to lighten the far-off horizon, when one of the crewmen approached him.

"Excuse me Mr. Burrows, but can you smell something a bit stale like?"

The sudden question caught Ben off guard a little. He sampled the air sniffing it, and realised that there was an odd, rather sour smell.

"Begging your pardon Sir, but I can tell you what that is." A figure said stepping from the shadows. "That's the stink of a slaver."

"Do you have experience of such a vessel; sorry I don't know your name?"

"John Jones," the man touched his forehead in salute. "I have indeed Mr. Burrows. One such ship transported me away from my family and my country when I was only ten years old."

Ben scanned the horizon but there was no sight of it. "Well, John Jones, I think we need to wake the captain."

Rhodes came on deck looking a little bedraggled; he had not combed his hair or fastened his shirt and he was still trying to stamp his foot into his left boot.

"This had better be damned important Mr. Burrows," he snapped.

"I think so Mr. Rhodes. John Jones, a man with experience of slave-ships, says that the strange smell spoiling the fresh morning air is indeed a slaver."

Rhodes looked blank at Ben obviously not understanding the significance of the words. He sniffed the air a few times, but still showed little understanding of the situation.

"Our mission, Mr. Rhodes, is to disrupt and prevent the slavers," Ben said

"I know our mission Mr. Burrows. My first priority is to get you to your ship," Rhodes snapped back.

"With respect Mr. Rhodes, Captain Mitchell will not be happy unless we have at least investigated this ship."

There was a pause; Rhodes was obviously trying to decide what the best course of action was, to gain time he fiddled with his shirt and jacket buttons.

"Very well Mr. Burrows, seeing as you are more familiar with the ways of Captain Mitchell, we will investigate."

Those gathered around waited for the next order, but Rhodes still looked out of his depth, there was a very long pause.

"May I make a suggestion Mr. Rhodes?" Ben finally broke the silence.

"Yes, what do you think Mr. Burrows?"

"As yet she is not in sight, which I assume means she is behind us somewhere as the wind is very much behind us. If we tack to starboard and come round in a large arc then we may well end up behind her giving us the advantage of the wind."

"Yes . . . yes well, very well, you see to it then Mr. Burrows, I need to get dressed and have some breakfast before I do anything else." He headed for the steps down to the main deck. "Do you think we should call the men to quarters?"

"Not yet, let them get the most sleep they can, it will be dawn before we are in position," Ben replied.

With Rhodes out of the way Ben took charge and after a few quick calculations set the new course. The sloop responded well and swung away turning sideways on to the fresh breeze that had been pushing them along before.

There was a noticeable tension amongst the men of the watch as they peered into the gloom to try and spot the slaver.

Ben had been busy with his calculations when he was suddenly struck by a terrifying thought. "Jones," he called "have you seen action before, been in battle I mean?"

"No Sir, only with my missus," He said with a flashing grin.

That had been Ben's sudden thought, he had no idea how experienced a crew he had, and he also realised that they had not even had any gun practice since he had joined the ship. Ben wished he had his old messmates with him.

Acting Lieutenant Hill appeared, "what's going on, why have we changed course?"

"Well done, Mr. Hill, at least you noticed," Ben said.

Ben explained the situation and what he intended to do. He also found out that Hill's battle experience was limited to his time on the Dreadnought.

The younger man came and stood next to Ben and asked, "Has Mr. Rhodes said for us to confront this slaver?"

Ben smiled at him, "I think we need to see what we are up against first of all,"

There was a call from the masthead that had everyone scanning the horizon. Silhouetted against a brightening orange sky, were the masts of a ship; it was difficult due to the distance to identify it.

"She may see us," Hill said. He was obviously slightly agitated.

"No don't worry, the reason I put us on a westerly tack was so that we would be on the dark side of her. We'll be behind her before she sees us."

Rhodes appeared back on deck looking more the part of Ship's Captain than he had done earlier. "Any news Mr. Burrows?"

"We have spotted a sail on our starboard bow," he handed his telescope to Rhodes. "Another hour and we can change tack again and come behind her."

"What do you plan then Mr. Burrows?" Rhodes was obviously annoyed that Ben was taking charge.

"I thought I would wait for your orders Mr. Rhodes."

It took a little longer than Ben had estimated but they were soon in the wake of the slave ship and even though they were up wind the smell was appalling. As they closed with the slaver they could now see her better, and what they saw was not good.

"My God Burrows she's at least a forty gunner."

"Yes, I guess she's an old Spanish war ship." Ben replied, "They must have made the lower decks into a hold for the slaves."

"A private word please Mr. Burrows." Rhodes stepped to the rear rail of the quarterdeck away from the other officers assembled there.

"You have put me in an awkward spot Mr. Burrows. My orders were to get you to St. Kitts and onto Captain Mitchell's frigate, not start our own war out here." He hissed the words facing away from the other officers.

"I apologise, but I know Captain Mitchell, and he would expect nothing else of us but to deal with this matter."

"Deal with it!" Rhodes exploded. "How the devil do we deal with it, as you put it? That's a forty gunner and it may have escaped your notice Mister but this is not HMS Seagull with seventy four guns, but a sloop with twenty guns and a crew of one hundred and twenty men that have never been in action!"

Ben was trying to hide his amusement at the others outburst, not that the situation was funny, on the contrary, but he found the man's obvious confusion rather amusing. He waited a moment before speaking to allow the other time to calm down a little.

"I doubt if she will have all her guns or be fully crewed. We have the advantage of the wind and position to give her a severe worrying."

"Mr. Burrows, I don't intent to lose my first commission trying to give a slave ship a *worrying*." His voice had gone up in tone and volume. "She is not flying any colours. How do you know she is not an ally?"

"If she is a British ship and involved in slaving then she is breaking the law and we have a duty to stop her. If she's French then we are at war; as for the rest of Europe at the moment, I'm not sure who is friend and who is foe," Ben said with a polite smile

"Are you making fun of me Mr. Burrows?"

"No, Mr. Rhodes and I apologise if you thought that."

There was a long pause, and Ben knew that if they did not act quickly they would lose the advantage they had. The decision was made for them; the slaver fired her two stern cannons at them. The shot went wildly wide but the gauntlet was laid down.

"Mr. Burrows, I have a confession, although I was indeed at Trafalgar, our ship had very little involvement and other than that I have never been in an exchange with another ship."

Ben suddenly understood Rhodes's reluctance to engage with the slaver. He realised that the crew were quite raw but never considered that the officers were the same.

"Perhaps Mr. Burrows, you would take temporary command, it is preferable to losing the ship." Rhodes looked very uncomfortable. "It seems, that now we have little alternative but to take action."

Ben realised how difficult and brave a decision that was on Rhodes's part, but realised it put him very much on the spot.

"Very well Mr. Rhodes, I am honoured that you place such confidence in my abilities."

"As I said Mr. Burrows we have all heard of your daring exploits and abilities. Be careful, it's my career on the line here."

"Mr. Hill, kindly get your drummer boys to beat to quarters." Ben said in a calm voice.

Back amongst the other officers Ben sized up the situation. They were closer now than he would have liked, but there was still time. Giving orders for the guns to be loaded with chain shot rather than ball, Ben took command and tried to sound as confident as he could. His intention was to get much closer before he fired his first shots.

"Mr. Hill, please take the starboard guns, I'm going to bring her hard about, and when we heel over I want you to bring down that slaver's sails."

"Aye aye Mr. Burrows!"

The sloop responded well, changing direction almost immediately. Hill waited and watched for Ben's signal. The broadside of nine guns filled the air with spinning chains that made the strangest of sounds as they flew at the slaver. For a moment, the ship was lost in a great cloud of smoke. As it cleared a little, a great cheer went up from Orion's crew as they saw the result of their handiwork. Two of the slaver's sails fluttered like kites in the wind and a yardarm from the rear mast was swinging precariously above the deck.

"Come about!" Ben shouted. "Mr. Hill, load with shot if you please."

Once again the agile sloop changed tack and again she slewed over and obligingly raised her larboard guns. Rhodes was in charge of them and waited for Ben's signal, watching the other officer like a hawk. 'Fire' he yelled when Ben signalled him, and the guns barked another salvo, not quite as well timed as the first, but it had the desired effect.

The slaver's stern guns fired again and all on the deck of Orion ducked as the shot caught their sail, punching two holes through it. Ben had seen the slaver's gun ports along its side open and knew it would try to manoeuvre to bring more of its guns to bear. He knew that they were reasonably safe keeping to her stern.

The slaver's sails were in complete disarray and obviously hampering her crew's attempts to bring her into a better position. Ben could imagine the scene on her decks.

They were now close and the slaver's stern towered over Orion.

"When we come about this time Mr. Hill, wait for my command, we don't want to send our shot into the ship's hull."

Ben looked reassuringly at Rhodes who was looking a little pale despite the soot stains on his face.

"As soon as we fire our next volley Mr. Rhodes, please order the marines and crew up and over," Ben said.

It was a devastating broadside. They were so close that as their shot hit the slaver the splinters showered Orion's deck. The iron balls smashed through the stern timbers at such an angle that they hit the slaver's crew on deck from below.

Grappling irons flew across the water locking the two ships together. There was the rattle of small arms fire from above, and a couple of Orion's crew fell. The small marine contingent on board returned musket fire and the slaver's muskets disappeared.

"Come on!" Ben shouted above the din.

Ben leapt for one of the ropes, climbing hand over hand he walked up the ship's side. His blood was fizzing with adrenalin giving him almost superhuman strength. As he went over the rear rail he realised someone was by his side. Jones was beside him wielding a broad bladed axe. Ben drew a pistol and heavy cutlass from his belt and together they advanced across the treacherous surface of the damaged deck.

Out of the smoke emerged a huge character who growled as he swung his broad blade at Ben. Just in time Ben saw it coming and managed to parry it with his own sword, but the strength of the blow sent him reeling backwards. He stumbled over a piece of broken planking and crashed painfully to the deck.

More of Orion's crew and her marines were now on board, distracting his attacker. Right across the deck now, men were fighting for their lives. Rhodes had arrived over the ship's side almost at Ben's side with a rather dainty sword in his hand. The huge slaver now turned his attention to Rhodes and slashed in a wide arc with his cutlass. Rhodes's sword shattered and he too was sent staggering across the deck.

Ben was up; he yelled trying to distract the slaver from following Rhodes, who was looking severely traumatised by the whole event. Despite his size, the man was agile enough to turn and face Ben as soon as he heard the shout. Their swords locked together a moment before they pushed each other away to give themselves room to swing their blades. Twice more their blades clashed.

Rhodes bravely rejoined the fight armed with a wooden club. Like dogs baiting a bear, the lieutenants circled the monstrous man. Rhodes moved in, but badly timed his attack. With a swift upward slash of his sword, the slaver disarmed him, and then followed through smashing the hand guard of his sword into his face. Rhodes went down in a pool of blood.

Ben was angry now and caught the slaver off guard. With a mighty backhanded swing he chopped the slaver in the ribs. There was the sickening sound of breaking bones and a gush of blood that should have finished the fight, but the man let out a fearsome growl and turned on Ben. Surprised at the slaver's strength, Ben had to dance out of reach across the broken decking; he drew his second pistol and aimed right between the slaver's eyes. The single shot kicked back the man's head, and blood oozed from the wound, instantly he dropped.

Ben knelt to check on Rhodes's condition and was relieved to see him open his bloodshot eyes.

"You'll be fine Mr Rhodes," He said reassuringly.

Rhodes just nodded and then passed out. Ben grabbed a couple of his crewmen.

"Get Mr. Rhodes back on board The Orion," he ordered.

Somehow, he managed to find himself next to Jones who was looking weary and blood-spattered.

"Well Mr. Jones I think we have dropped into a bit of a hornet's nest here,"

Working together, they fought their way along the deck. It was tough work, the damaged deck made staying upright difficult, and they were attacked from all sides. At last, they found the slave ship's Captain and together they cornered him. The man at first thought about fighting on, but he suddenly lost the will to fight and dropped to one knee offering Ben his sword. When what was left of his crew saw him, they also threw down their weapons.

Orion's crew cheered loudly as Ben took the offered sword. Everyone took a breather; suddenly the stench of the ship and the heat of the day seemed very oppressive. Ben was about to lift the main hatch cover when he spotted Jones.

"Mr. Jones perhaps you would like the honour of setting those below deck free."

Jones studied Ben a moment and then smiled his gratitude he threw off the hatch cover but was forced to stand back for a moment. He called into the gloom and one by one frightened individuals shading their eyes from the light appeared on deck. They looked thin and weak; they were dirty and bewildered, huddling together for protection.

CHAPTER TWENTY SIX

Captain Mitchell took up his usual place on deck to watch the arrival of the Orion. A wry smile crossed his lips when he saw the second ship. It was obvious by their ripped sails and damaged timbers that they had been in some sort of conflict. He hoped that Ben was uninjured; he knew he was going to need all his reliable officers on this mission. He turned to speak to Barraclough.

"Either Young Mr. Rhodes is of the same ilk as our Mr. Burrows, bringing home a prize on his first venture, or I'll wager that Mr. Burrows has had more than a little to do with there being an unexpected ship arriving with Orion."

"Yes, he has a strange knack of finding excitement doesn't he?" Barraclough said.

"He has a strange knack of improving his fortune too. That ship will fetch five thousand guineas."

Eventually a barge came over from Orion. Ben was quite impatient to meet up with his old crew and tell his friend Barraclough of his adventure. When the barge reached Adventurer's side, he had to wait his turn to climb on board behind Mr. Rhodes and Hill.

Lieutenant Rhodes came and stood to attention in front of Captain Mitchell, who tried not to look too astounded at the young officer's appearance. Rhodes's face was still badly bruised and he looked a little bit like a panda, with two black eyes and a crooked nose. The Captain tried not to stare too intently at him.

"Well Mr. Rhodes it would appear that there is quite a story behind the ship you brought home with you."

"Yes indeed Captain," Rhodes replied. He sounded as if he had a severe cold. The young officer was not enjoying the scrutiny his face was receiving. He tried to stand as straight as possible, but to be truthful he was still a little groggy. He straightened his collar, and fidgeted from one foot to the other. "May I introduce Acting Lieutenant Hill, a veteran of Trafalgar, serving with Capt'n Conn on board the Dreadnought," Rhodes said. He was trying to divert the attention away from his face.

Hill snapped to attention and gave a perfect salute. Ben had told him all about the Captain and he wanted to impress him if he could.

"I am sure that I have no need to introduce the other officer in my party Captain."

"No, indeed you do not Mr. Rhodes." Mitchell smiled at Ben. "So Mr. Burrows, I'm glad to finally have you on board. What have you been up to this time? It would seem that poor Mr. Rhodes has suffered from his first encounter with you." The Captain moved his shoulder awkwardly remembering just how close he had been to death, and how due to Ben's bravery he had been saved.

"It is a bit of a long story Capt'n," Ben said. They shook hands.

"Well I'm delighted to have you back with us; it's been rather quiet without you."

Mr. Barraclough called for the surgeon to look at Rhodes's face, and to see if anything could be done to at least straighten the nose a little.

In Ben's small chart room Barraclough sat on a stool and chatted with him as he unpacked his clothes and personal effects. Knowing Barraclough's love of sweet things, Ben had brought him a fruit cake and a stone jar of honey from the Lintons.

"We shall eat the cake on Sunday with the Captain," Barraclough said. "We are to meet his family. I knew they had land out here, but I didn't know that they resided here full time. His father has plantations in the Windward Islands as well as here on St Kitts. Although with the abolition of slavery I think things have been more than a bit tough for him and all the growers."

That evening Captain Mitchell sat at the head of the table with his officers. He liked entertaining and he particularly liked his junior officers to be there. He had a notion that he could learn as much about a man's ability when relaxed and off guard as in the heat of battle.

"So Mr. Rhodes, I've had a glance at your report on the capturing of the slaver, but perhaps you can tell me more."

"To be perfectly honest Captain, I was knocked unconscious during the hand-to-hand fight. I am sure Mr. Burrows could be of more help."

"It was indeed a brave decision to go after a much larger ship Mr. Rhodes," Barraclough said.

"I assumed that was what you expected of us," Rhodes replied.

"Oh yes Mr. Rhodes, I expect all my junior officers to be able to make such decisions, but it was something of a risk," Mitchell said.

Rhodes looked uncomfortable, not sure as to whether the decision was being questioned.

Ben saw Rhodes's discomfort and decided to come to his aid. "If I might say Captain, Mr. Rhodes led bravely and we were all inspired and confident that the mission would be successful."

"And what about after Mr. Rhodes was knocked senseless?"

"I assumed command, being the most experienced officer in the boarding party."

Captain Mitchell allowed himself a smile. "Why is it, Mr. Rhodes that I have a feeling you might have been encouraged into this enterprise by another?"

Ben and Rhodes exchanged guilty glances across the table.

"Not that it matters; you did a good service to our cause, one less slave trade ship, and Captain for us to deal with in the future. So I would like to propose a toast to our future success as the scourge of all ships involved in that vile trade."

There was some small talk and then the Captain made another announcement.

"Three days from now, we shall be attending a dinner at my father's house. It may seem strange in this heat, but of course it will be Christmas day the following day, so I am sure it will be something of a treat for us all." He paused a moment to take a drink. "I am not happy with the readiness of our crews, so we shall put to sea for two days for gunnery and handling practice. How much real experience do you have Mr. Rhodes?"

"As you know, Captain, I was at Trafalgar and we were under heavy fire for quite some time, but we never actually engaged with the French. So attacking the slave ship is really the limit of my experience."

"Perhaps then I will put Mr. Barraclough with you as he knows what I expect and will add his experience to training your men." Mitchell said. "Mr. Burrows, I would like you and your charts in here first thing."

At first light the two warships were already far out to sea. The second sloop had not yet arrived at the island and Mitchell was getting a little concerned over its absence. He had not realised that he would be getting such inexperienced officers and crews for his ships. Adventurer's crew were mostly battle-hardened veterans from his last ship, but it was obvious that Orion's officers and crew were very green.

Ben had his charts out on the Captain's table; he had unrolled a particular chart of the islands around St Kitts. His old friend back in Barrow had spent a great deal of time on this one, decorating the borders with spectacular watercolour paintings.

"We need to know every channel and island of the whole archipelago if we are to be of any use. Unless that other sloop gets here I think we have little chance of anything other than chasing shadows." Mitchell said. "In confidence, Mr. Burrows, what of Mr. Rhodes?"

"Just lacks experience Captain. He was brave enough when we boarded the slaver, but I think that perhaps he lacks confidence in himself."

"Was it his idea to chase the slaver?"

Ben took a moment, not that he was afraid to say that he was responsible, but he didn't want to claim the glory. "I suggested to him that it was a good idea. He was more concerned initially about getting me on board Adventurer, but I convinced him we should at least investigate."

"Mr. Burrows I need to know if I can rely on the other Captains in my fleet and how they will react under pressure. I was not filled with confidence as to Mr. Rhodes's abilities after our soirée last night."

"Captain, I think Mr. Rhodes will be a very good officer given time. I think that he needs to perhaps serve under a more experienced officer before he captains his own ship."

"Thank you for your candid comments Mr. Burrows. I think I shall leave Mr. Barraclough there for a little while; he has the ability to bring Mr. Rhodes along without him feeling as if he is being undermined."

They pondered over the charts for some while, and the enormity of their task became even more evident.

"A hundred ships couldn't police these waters properly!" Mitchell declared.

"No sir, there are sandbanks and reefs everywhere just waiting for the innocent sailor."

The ships began their gunnery practice and Ben could not resist a smile to his old messmate Fletch as they both remembered their combined effort of firing the ramrod across the waves.

Ben made his way along the gun-deck through the deafening noise; he finally stood beside Fletch and his other old mates.

Fletch, his face blackened with soot and shirt soaked with sweat said. "You'll not miss this work Mr. Burrows."

"I can certainly live without it Fletch."

Just then a series of signal flags run up by the Orion caught Ben's attention. He checked to see if the Captain had also seen them. He went back to the quarterdeck at a brisk trot.

"Sail to the east Captain."

"Yes; rest the guns Mr. Burrows, I hope it's our missing ship."

The crews stayed in position although they took a welcome rest and tried to find somewhere cool in the heat of the day. Some hurried aloft and the ships turned to meet the possible threat.

Orion being the slightly faster ship and having a three mile advantage on Adventurer was relaying messages back. Ben, with his eye to his telescope was reading them for the Captain.

"I think your hopes are realised Captain, it seems as if it is a British sloop."

"Good. At least we have some chance of being effective here now, although I still doubt that we can be very effective."

The new arrival signalled a greeting to Adventurer as she neared.

"Return the greeting and invite her Captain on board immediately," Mitchell said.

Ben passed the message on and a string of flags fluttered their way up the mast to convey the message to the ship's captain. In his telescope, he caught his first glimpse of him. The man stood proudly erect on the quarterdeck obviously leaving the menial task of reading the signals to his first lieutenant. Their ship's barge was already being swung out and her crew stood ready to man it.

Ten minutes later the shrill sounds of the boson's pipes welcomed aboard the newly arrived captain in the traditional naval style. Salutes were exchanged, each officer in turn touching the neb of his hat.

"Lieutenant Dean of H.M. Sloop Unicorn reporting for duty, Sir." He was very much taller than Mitchell.

"I had expected you here before now Mr. Dean."

"Yes Sir, my apologies. Have you come out to look for us?"

"No Mr. Dean, but I find myself with an escort ship with very little experience amongst the crew. Which does not answer why you are so late arriving?"

"Excuse me Captain, but as we were about to leave to join you, I received despatches which had to be taken to the West African fleet, that is to say the Solway and her escorts."

The new man impressed Mitchell, the questions had not flustered him at all, and he had not shifted once. He guessed he would be a good man in the heat of battle.

"Did you find the Solway?"

"Yes Captain, her captain, and crew are not in good humour Sir. They have suffered from a number of illnesses and are being attacked constantly by Arab pirates."

Mitchell looked thoughtful for a moment. "How much experience does your crew have?"

"None would be a fair answer Sir. They are all newly pressed men barring my officers and two bosons. I have a marine officer who has a tendency to be seasick in any sort of weather and a cook who is intent on poisoning us all." Dean said with a good-humoured nod.

"I'm pleased that at least you can see the funny side of your predicament. What of yourself Mr. Dean?"

"I was a midshipman on board Vanguard, with Rear-Admiral Sir Horatio Nelson at the battle of the Nile. I was wounded in the back by a stray musket ball, but thank the Lord that it was only a minor wound. Our Captain, William Faddy, God rest his soul was not so lucky and died from his wounds." He allowed himself a moment.

"I then served on the Majestic with Captain Gould who had recently moved from the Audacious. It was under his command that I was commissioned as lieutenant."

"Very good Mr. Dean, I will look forward to you joining us for dinner this evening. In the meantime I suggest that you run out your guns and get your men ready for action."

With that, Dean went back to Unicorn and Mitchell asked Ben to accompany him to his cabin. The two sloops were already firing disjointed salvoes as they reached the cabin.

"What do you think of Mr. Dean then Mr. Burrows?"

"Very impressed Sir, he is confident and sounds to have an excellent pedigree."

"Yes Mr. Burrows I agree, and I think we need captains like that for this venture."

Ben worked all the afternoon with his charts trying to learn as many of the dangerous reefs as he could. They seemed endless and he realised that neither the navy's or his friend's charts were complete.

That evening after the ship had returned to the deep water port of Basseterre on St. Kitts their officers met for dinner in a wharf side tavern. Suckling pigs, fresh bread and endless bottles of wine made the party a very jolly occasion.

"Gentlemen, a toast to his Majesty the King," all stood although some were a little bit unsteady.

Dean had sat himself opposite Ben; they acknowledged each other across the table.

"So you are the famous Lieutenant Burrows who set alight the Portsmouth press."

"I'm afraid so Mr. Dean. You were at the Battle of the Nile on Nelson's ship; I'd be interested to hear that story."

"Nothing much to tell really."

"Do I hear correctly," the Captain called down the table "do we have a story? Stories are always welcome at my table Mr. Dean. Please speak up; I'm sure everyone would be interested."

There was a general mumbling of agreement which crushed any objection Dean was thinking of.

"Well, my friends, I was fourteen years old and I had been a midshipman for four years, when we were picked by Lord Nelson to be his flagship for the forthcoming chase of the French fleet across the Med to Egypt." He paused for a drink and was amazed how quietly his audience waited for his next words. "Although there were only a few hours left until nightfall and Brueys' ships were in a strong defensive position, being anchored in line in a sandy bay, flanked on one side by a shore battery on Abu Qir Island, Nelson ordered an immediate attack. Several of the British warships, led by Captain Thomas Foley in Goliath, were able to manoeuvre around the head of the French line of battle, and behind their position, although the Culloden ran aground. The Audacious sailed between the Guerrier and Conquerant. Our ships anchored as they came alongside the French. With the wind behind them they could pick their positions, and the French ships at the rear of the line could do nothing to help." He paused and was pleased to see that everyone around the table was hanging on every word. "The French frigate Serieuse made the mistake of firing at the Goliath, but a broadside from the Orion left her shattered and sinking. Captain Miller of the Theseus took advantage of the French gunners firing high and moved his ship closer, rightly guessing that in the heat of the battle they would fail to lower the elevations of their guns. On the seaward side of the French line, Nelson on board the Vanguard, took us in and anchored alongside Spartiate, a seventy-four gun fortress of a ship. Her timbers looked so solid that the devil himself would never break them down. The five leading French ships were between the fires of five British ships to larboard and three to starboard."

The story took two hours to relate and when Dean finished there was silence for just a moment, and then three cheers were called for and there was a deafening burst of applause.

"Well Mr. Dean that was a truly epic account of the events. It makes me proud to be a Captain in the mightiest navy that the world has ever seen, Rule Britannia." He held his goblet high above his head.

CHAPTER TWENTY SEVEN

The harbour was bustling, a number of trading ships had arrived, and a few smaller ships bringing guests to the Christmas Eve Ball.

Ben was examining Rhodes's face, around his eyes were still discoloured and he was suffering from pains in his cheeks where the bruising and swelling was still quite bad. "Perhaps Captain Mitchell will give us a few moments ashore to look for an apothecary. You need something for this," he said.

What at first had been a matter of perhaps just slipping ashore, turned into a full-scale invasion. Mr. Dean and Barraclough said they should go too, because of the town's unruly reputation, and they decided that they should take a couple of ratings with them. Of course, Fletch and Brendan were first in the queue to be picked; Ben also picked John Jones the ex-slave to accompany them.

The harbour had been chaotic, but the town's streets were even worse. They were pushed and jostled making their progress very slow. They carefully watched each other, after they had been warned about a gang of pickpockets. At last, they found the apothecary, a double fronted shop with very dingy, dark glass in its windows.

Inside a pungent, heady mix of various oils, spices and herbs filled the air, creating a calmness that contrasted starkly with the turmoil outside. They looked at each other, unsure of what to expect.

A woman, as round as she was tall, in a vivid green and orange dress appeared through a net curtain. All manner of small objects were plaited into her hair and her eyes seemed far too big for her face, which disappeared behind a huge smile.

"Oh my words" she giggled. "I'm invaded by the navy, and not for the first time I might add." She roared with laughter.

"We were wondering . . . ?" Ben began.

"You was wondering, if I could fix this young man's face." She came from behind the counter, her bare feet slapping on the stone floor. It was very cramped in the shop and everyone else had to squeeze out of the way. Carefully she prodded and investigated the bruises. "This ain't good, your cheek bone is broke, you could end up losin' all them fine white teeth."

She ploughed her way back through the squash and disappeared into the back room. They waited, not daring to speak only daring to exchange quizzical glances. Fascinated by the shelves of strange looking bottles and even stranger looking dried roots and herbs, Ben poked about on a shelf examining objects with wonder.

"Fletch you and the others stand outside, it's getting too hot in here. Keep out of trouble and don't wander off." Barraclough whispered his order.

Suddenly she was back; she held a stone jar above her head. "Now then young sir this will do the trick." Pulling Rhodes into a wicker chair, she re-examined him. Carefully, as tender as any mother she applied the ointment, and then wrapped a bandage around his face. "He needs this applying three times a day," she said. She prodded Barraclough in the chest "You his bossman?" Barraclough nodded as if he didn't dare speak. "Well then, you must make sure he does it."

She turned towards Ben, "there are ghosts hunting you, you think you have put them to rest, but an old dark shadow will break your neck given chance," she whispered.

"What do you mean?"

"From your past, something nears. I can feel it, but I can't tell you more."

Ben felt a bit uneasy, he did not take much notice of witchcraft, but this was somehow different.

Suddenly there was a commotion outside. "Come on lads." Dean said and was out of the door.

There was an almighty free-for-all going on; Fletch had blood streaming from his nose and Brendan was busy crashing some poor soul into the wall.

"They've grabbed Jones sir."

"Who did?" Ben shouted.

Then he saw Jones being frog marched by three big brutes, "after them" Ben cried.

He ran and in a single leap was up on top of a low wall, running along it he was clear of the melee. At full stretch, he dived and landed on top of the kidnappers. They were all bowled over, and Jones managed to wriggle free of them. There was no time for talk; Dean and Barraclough arrived and they chased the attackers off.

"I trust you're no worse for wear Mr. Jones.?"

"I'm all right thank you Mr Burrows."

"God where's Rhodes?" Ben said

What had started as a brawl now involved the entire street; people were throwing punches and stones, and some were wrestling. Street vendors tried in vain to stop their wares from being looted, lashing out at anyone who came near.

Reaching the shop they were relieved to see Rhodes had had the sense to keep out of the fight this time. They all took shelter inside again.

"Glad you remembered to come back for me." Rhodes said.

"Mr. Rhodes you already look much improved, the swelling seems to be down." Ben said.

Outside whistles were blowing and it was soon obvious that the local militia had turned up to calm the situation.

"Them folks out there certainly likes to party, they are just high spirited you know," the shopkeeper said, "you boys owe me three shillings for this medicine."

"Expensive herbs," Dean said.

"It ain't the herbs that's expensive, it's my knowledge that comes at a price." She gave him a broad smile.

The militia armed with muskets and bayonets were lining the street and had the situation back to normal. They had made a number of arrests and were herding a small crowd towards the town gaol.

"I think we had best get back." Barraclough said "and for goodness sake get yourselves tidied up."

They tried cleaning themselves up as they returned to the ship, but it was still rather obvious by the dirt smudges on their uniforms that something had transpired. Unfortunately, Captain Mitchell was there to greet them. "Well gentlemen what have you been up to now?"

The lieutenants stood before him like naughty schoolboys for a moment.

"Get cleaned up, I'll remind you gentlemen that we are to dine with my family tonight, and I don't want them to think that my crew is made up entirely of street urchins."

A little humbled they were about to dismiss when the captain passed another comment.

"I admire your bravery Mr. Rhodes, going on another adventure with Mr. Burrows," he smiled, "Mr. Barraclough and I have got quite used to the chaos that seems to surround him, because wherever Mr. Burrows is, something quite unexpected is bound to turn up."

Barraclough winked at Ben, who took the jibe in good spirit. They retreated to the wardroom to clean up.

The two acting captains, Rhodes and Dean, volunteered to stay on watch and in charge of the flotilla whilst Captain Mitchell, his lieutenants, his ship's surgeon, and purser went to the Christmas Ball.

The Mitchell's family residence on the island had been a Spanish fortress at one time, and still retained its battlements and drawbridge. It had been strategically very well placed with a commanding view over the harbour and bay. Inside, however, was a very different thing; the old mess hall and barracks had been converted into a ballroom and banqueting rooms with fine chandeliers and luxurious wall hangings. On an elevated platform, where a cannon had once stood, a small orchestra now played light music as the guests gathered.

As Adventurer's officers entered through the gatehouse, Captain Mitchell gave them all the once over. He was pleased with their well-pressed, smart turnout, only the surgeon Mr. Harvey seemed to let them down. He was always an untidy looking man, with a grey rather moth eaten wig, which was not really his size and seemed to be constantly slipping to one side or the other.

Inside the party was already underway. The Captain presented his officers to his father who smiled graciously at them one by one.

"Enjoy yourselves gentlemen please, and do join in the dancing later. We have an abundance of ladies chomping at the bit ready to dance, but unfortunately we only have a collection of gout ridden old men for them."

Ben studied the captain's family for a moment; the two older brothers had little of their father's likeness, but his captain was from the exact same mould as Mitchell senior. The older brothers barely acknowledged their siblings presence, but it was obvious that there was true affection between father and youngest son.

Ben was suddenly taken by the hand and whisked onto the dance floor by a tall young woman in a flowing ball gown. He was trying his best not to injure the delicate feet of his partner when someone collided with the middle of his back. At first, he thought it was just his poor navigation on the dance floor and took no notice of the person behind him, and then he was bumped again. He turned and his head went into a spin.

"Why Lieutenant Burrows, what a wonderful surprise." Ruth said.

"Lady Ruth," Ben bowed in acknowledgement.

"Do you mind if we change partners," Ruth said

The other woman looked rather bewildered, as they exchanged partners, but she had no time to argue as her new partner twirled her away and the matter was forgotten.

They danced together for some while not speaking, but occasionally their eyes would meet and exchange a knowing glance. Even when the music changed, they didn't let go, they just followed the timing into a much slower waltz.

When dinner was announced and they were forced apart, Ben rejoined Barraclough who had just been released from the clutches of another of the island's belles.

"You two are like the needle of a compass and the North Pole; you just seem to find each other by magic," Barraclough said.

The table was set out on the lawn, lit by hundreds of candles and lanterns. Ben could just see where Ruth was sitting and occasionally their eyes would meet. Twenty-three courses were served, a lavish display of the family's wealth. The small orchestra had also moved outside, and as the meal ended, the dancing began again. Small clusters of gentlemen discussing various issues puffed on cigars and consumed great quantities of port. The ladies who were not dancing stood in small gaggles gossiping behind their quivering fans.

Ben and Barraclough had taken up a position on the edge of the lawn where a cool breeze came around the side of the main building. Mitchell senior approached them. "Please gentlemen remain seated." He offered them cigars. "You have a difficult task before you. You've been a good officer and friend to my son in the past Mr. Barraclough."

"He's a fine captain and all his men are true and loyal to him Sir."

"I'm afraid I can't see you having much effect on the situation here."

"We can but do our best Sir," Barraclough replied.

"Yes, but if the government were so serious about this slave issue, then they should have sent more ships." He looked at Ben, "you're Burrows?"

"Yes Mr. Mitchell I am."

"Read about your exploits in the Times, well done. What do you think of this slavery issue?"

"Parliament has said it is illegal; what I think is of no consequence sir."

"Aha, a budding politician. My son speaks highly of you Mr. Burrows, I see why."

Off he wandered like an old steam train leaving a thick trail of smoke in his wake.

Barraclough's dancing partner approached and away they went, leaving Ben to watch the festivities. He was not alone long; Ruth came and sat demurely beside him. For a moment they sat like strangers but it did not last long.

"I'm so pleased to see you Ben; you can't imagine how dreary life is out here."

"You have a little girl now I hear."

"Yes she's beautiful, just like her mother, except for the jet black hair." She twisted her auburn ringlets as she spoke.

"May I ask you to dance?" Ben said.

Together they looked the perfect couple and they danced in almost perfect harmony, so much so that some of the other dancers stood aside to watch. Ben wished that, their audience and the other dancers would simply disappear and leave them to float away. Her eyes never left his face and her moist-lips seemed to be begging for a kiss. When the music finished, they, for a brief moment were unaware of it and danced a few more steps.

There was obviously some gossiping going on behind those wing-like fans, which seemed to be beating ever faster now. Curious glances were exchanged as the handsome young naval lieutenant bowed to his partner and kissed her hand.

Ruth retreated to her husband's side. What the curious did not know was that as the hand was kissed a message to meet back in the house in ten minutes was agreed. Ben was dragged into another dance by a young woman with pure white skin topped by a mop of ginger hair. Afterwards, he slipped away from the merriment.

With all the guests out in the gardens, the house was deserted apart from a few servants cleaning up. Ben entered the dining hall and waited. He was nervous, not just about meeting Ruth, but the fact that there would be hell to pay should anyone see them here alone together.

She appeared, and like a tornado took his hand and towed him into the library. Behind high stacked shelves, they kissed so passionately that they both had to draw apart to gain their breath.

"Ben, I've missed you so much."

He had been determined that it would not be like this, he had been determined that they would just talk like old friends and then go their own way. As usual, his common sense went out of the window as soon as she was near, and what could have been a simple exchange was now a dangerous assignation.

"We must go back; your reputation is at stake."

"Hang reputations; take me back to England with you. Your name is cleared now and we could find somewhere to live."

"I doubt that I could ever afford you. It's not possible and you know it."

Ruth studied him a moment, "my poor Ben, always I have made trouble for you. Can you not trust me?"

"It's me I don't trust. Once before you gave me advice and I was stupid enough to take it." He moved away from her. "Believe me Ruth, if I thought there was a chance in a million of us being together, I would move heaven and hell to make it happen."

There were voices outside the room and they knew that they had not long before they would be discovered.

There were tears on her cheeks, "then we must leave it to fate to keep washing us up on the same shore."

"Yes, well put," he said, "our meetings usually are a little like a shipwreck."

Ruth went to the door, "she's yours," she said, "the little girl. I called her Dorothy after your aunt Dot."

Before Ben could answer, she was gone.

TWENTY EIGHT

———•◦❀◦•———

For the whole of January, Captain Mitchell's little fleet chased shadows around the islands. It was hot and occasional high winds made sailing hard and dangerous work. There had been a number of sightings of suspicious looking ships, but never out in open water where the faster sloops could hunt them down. Luck seemed against them; either the light or winds were wrong, or sandbanks and narrow channels were in the way of a successful chase.

Ben was scanning the horizon from the quarterdeck; he could sense the captain's frustration as yet another ship escaped them. He wondered how much longer it would be before they had some success with the mission. The morale of the men was down, and although they were being kept busy, they were beginning to grumble.

"We shall retire to my cabin Mr. Burrows please."

Ben left one of the midshipmen in charge of the watch and followed the captain below. Since Mr. Barraclough had been away on the Orion, Ben had temporarily been promoted to first lieutenant and he was relishing the extra responsibility.

"Well Mr. Burrows, what is your opinion?"

They bent over the captain's table studying the charts. The size of their task was obvious to see. Over the last few weeks, Ben had worked hard on the charts making many new additions and improvements, but there was still a lot of detail missing.

"Perhaps we should return to St. Kitts and pick up fresh victuals, and work the northern islands for awhile. Perhaps work towards the Keys, the Americans are still trading slaves openly, and we could be lucky there."

"Yes, well done Mr. Burrows, the weather's getting worse and the purser has already been complaining about the lack of fresh food."

"We've better charts for the area north too. I'm sorry Captain I can't add much more. Perhaps to anchor in a bay somewhere and try surprising a slaver, but the men will soon become restless in this heat."

"Perhaps I should put you in charge, as you are the only one to find a slaver." Mitchell laughed.

"It was only chance Sir, and a piece of luck. I've not been much help to you recently."

"Don't worry Mr. Burrows I'd not wish command of this venture on any one."

The ships were caught in a ferocious gale as they headed back to St Kitts, and had to stand out to sea for two days for fear of being driven onto the rocks. The two sloops positioned themselves to the lee of the bigger Adventurer, but they were still getting a pounding from the wind. As fast as the storm had arrived, it went and the sea was calm once more.

As they entered port, Captain Mitchell was very surprised to see his father and elder brother waiting on the quayside. Sensing something was amiss he immediately dispatched the ship's launch to fetch them.

Mitchell senior was still out of breath as he began to speak.

"Sir Arthur and his very attractive wife have been kidnapped." He threw a large piece of parchment onto the table. "A ransom note was delivered by a local Indian chap two weeks since."

They were in the Captain's cabin seated around the table. Ben passed the note to the captain, his hand trembled a little giving away his anxiety. He had glanced at the note, which was written in a tidy hand, except for the signature at the bottom, which was just a scrawled 'M'.

"Twenty thousand guineas, to be left on some God forsaken rock." Mitchell senior threw his hands up in despair. "How could we possibly raise that sort of money out here?"

"Do you know who this 'M' is father?"

"No, never heard of him."

Later that afternoon, the ship's officers were all gathered together to discuss the situation. As usual, Ben spoke out first; the fear of what might have happened to Ruth had made any logical thought difficult.

"We need to find out who this 'M' is, and where he sails out of. Perhaps it might be worth asking some discreet questions in the taverns here."

"Any excuse to get into the taverns."

They all laughed at Barraclough's jibe. Barraclough knew his friend would be deeply troubled by the event, and he was just doing his best to cheer him up.

"You're right Mr. Burrows, someone may know their whereabouts."

Lieutenant Rhodes volunteered his services, wishing that it had been his idea, and once again he was slightly jealous of Ben. The potion had cleared the bruising from around his eyes and his nose was back in line, but his pride was still in pieces.

"Mr. Rhodes, I have the more important task for you of making sure all three ships are restocked and ready to sail as soon as possible. Mr. Dean you will sail for Jamaica and see if you can find out anything from that end."

Ben, Barraclough, Fletch, Brendan and Bruce looked a motley crew, dressed in clothes from the stores. The captain smiled when he saw them, "my God Mr. Barraclough you've let yourself slip."

"Aye Capt'n it's the company I keep these days."

"No unnecessary risks." He gave them all a warning glance, "is that understood . . . Mr. Burrows?"

Ben smiled, "aye aye Capt'n.

As they slipped ashore the light was fading and they mingled with the locals. There were a number of taverns to choose from, so they decided on the seediest looking one to start with.

Inside was surprisingly quiet; all the wall seats were occupied by locals, leaving a table right in the middle of the room empty. They sat a little self consciously at the table and ordered ale. Three old tars sat in a window seat opposite; they all puffed on long clay pipes. One of them put down his pipe a moment as if to speak and then thought better of it and carried on smoking.

A serving girl came over to them, she looked like a gypsy with long flowing hair and tight blouse. "You're new." She said.

"Why don't you join us?" Barraclough said.

She threw a long tanned leg over the stool next to him and gazed into his eyes.

"So what is it you require?" her voice purred.

His companions laughed as Barraclough tried to compose himself.

"We're looking for an old shipmate of ours, signs himself 'M' sometimes." He jingled a few coins together, "I can make it worth your while."

"Sorry I don't know any M's, I have to go." She flipped her skirt so that she could uncurl her long leg from the stool.

"Well what do you think?" Barraclough said.

"I think we'll get some sort of answer very soon." Ben stared at a bald headed character that came over from behind the bar, where the gypsy girl had vanished.

"Let me give you fellows some advice, don't ask questions in here. We don't like snoops."

"We're just seeking and old shipmate. Maybe you can help?" Once again, he jingled the purse.

The bald man looked over his shoulder, "Meet me out back in ten minutes, and I'll see what I can do." He slinked back behind the bar.

"I think it might be a good idea to get out of here now." Barraclough said.

Nobody really felt like arguing and they were relieved to be out of the confines of the inn. Fletch headed towards the entrance to the back yard, but Ben grabbed his collar and pulled him back.

"Where are you going?"

"I thought . . . ."

"Aye well don't think Fletch, you don't do it too well. We'd not last a minute in there, I'm surprised at you." Ben said.

They headed back along the street and onto the wharf as quickly as they could, watching over their shoulders the whole time.

The serving girl stepped into their path, surprising them all. "You want an island called St Augustine, maybe two hundred miles south of here," she said. "Hand it over."

Barraclough gave her a wry smile, for a moment he looked as if he might not give her the purse. Her eyes never left his, but there was a smile as she felt the soft leather of the purse sit in her palm. It changed to fear as Barraclough grabbed her wrist.

"Who is this character that signs himself 'M'"

"Let go, I don't know him. He's been about for a couple o'years or so. Englishman, very unpleasant from what I remember of him." She freed her wrist and was gone.

"Come on, let's get out of here," Barraclough said.

With both Bruce and Brendan behind him Ben felt safe from attack, but even so, they were all nervous as they headed back to their boat to take them back to Adventurer.

Ben swung a compass in a wide arc across the chart on the Captain's table. Everyone peered at a number of small islands it enclosed.

"There it is," Mr. Mitchell senior, exclaimed, "I remember now, it's part of the Saint's islands in the Antilles. It's been deserted for about a decade; there were some small plantations, but yellow fever and some very unfriendly natives wiped everyone out."

"It's nearer than the girl said, if it is there," Ben said, "probably only about one hundred and thirty miles."

"Right under our blasted noses, we've been trawling empty waters for weeks; damn we've just gone in circles." Captain Mitchell was obviously displeased.

Four days later, they spotted the islands marked on Ben's chart as St. Augustine's Island. In Captain Mitchell's cabin the officers were seated around the table, waiting for their orders.

"Very well gentlemen, Mr. Burrows will join Mr. Rhodes on Orion and go take a closer look at the island. I want you to find somewhere that we could safely execute a night landing. According to the charts there are a couple of sandy bays on the opposite side of the island to the town, I want you to investigate them. You need to be in and out quick as you can, I don't want to lose the element of surprise. I don't want to see these pirates just fleeing in all directions; we've had enough chasing about."

Adventurer was stationed over the horizon well out of view, as Orion made all haste in towards the island. Ben was under strict orders not to do anything other than take a look at the beaches and check them as a possible landing place.

"I've placed a couple of lookouts to watch for reefs," Rhodes said.

Ben was studying the bay through his telescope, "Take us in a little closer please Mr. Rhodes."

The sloop changed tack and sped in towards the sand. Rhodes was nervous; his last experience with Ben on board made him extra cautious. He also scanned the island but he was making sure that they were not being observed.

"Perfect, Mr. Rhodes let's take our leave of here for the moment."

Orion headed back to join Adventurer as fast as she could. Rhodes was satisfied that they had not been seen, and Ben was sure that the beaches were just right for them to land.

As soon as the sun set, the ship's boats were lowered; when they were clear of Adventurer, all commands were passed in a whisper. They glided, almost silently through a pewter sea. The crews were nervous; with pounding hearts they rowed towards the sound of the breaking surf. There was hardly any light at all, but just occasionally an oar blade would glint in the light from the moon, that hung red on the distant horizon. Somewhere a bird called, as it circled like a ghost above the distant shore.

Ben clung to the tiller in the rear of one of the boats; he peered into the blackness to spot the telltale white foam that marked the shoreline. At last, he spotted it and almost without warning they grounded on the soft sand; instantly men were into the water heaving the boats ashore.

There was no time to lose they ran across the beach, up steep dunes and into the undergrowth. Panting with the effort Ben threw himself down with his back against a rock. Everywhere around him, puffing and blowing bodies hit the sand. After they had all regained their breath, Barraclough, who was in charge of the expedition, gathered everyone together. "Captain Brand, you take your marines onto that ridge and dig in. We might stir up a real hornet's nest here. Mr. Burrows are you ready?"

Ben nodded; he had picked Fletch and Brendan to go with them into the town, confident he could trust them to stick together. Dressed in an assortment of clothes from the ship's slops the four of them headed into the cover of a swaying forest of sugar canes. It was impossible to be quiet, the dried cane leaves crunched with every step, but as they neared the town they realised there was no need for stealth.

"It sounds as if it's more fun being a pirate than a tar," Fletch said.

Torches burned bright on every corner and there was the sound of singing and music coming from several different areas. They reached the first building, which had once been a fine house, but all that was left was a burnt out shell. Sneaking in through what had been the kitchen door, they took shelter behind what remained of the walls. Keeping low they peered out at the town. They had a good view of the quayside. One tavern in particular seemed to be the centre of attraction; there was a constant stream of drunken bodies swaying in and out of its door.

There was a sudden crash as Fletch knocked over an old charred table.

"For goodness sake man, watch it!" Barraclough hissed.

"That place over there, seems to be the place we might find something out," Ben said.

"Right, try and look natural. No weapons on view and try to watch where you are going," Barraclough said.

They walked nonchalantly along the street trying to act naturally, Brendan threw his great arm around Ben's shoulder and they headed for the tavern.

"Once inside, find a table and keep your eyes and ears open," Barraclough said.

The din was incredible; there was a swirling cloud of tobacco smoke and the smell of sweaty bodies. Somewhere in the haze a lone voice sang to no one in particular.

Barraclough found a free table in one corner; and they slid into its seats without anyone taking any notice at all. A pretty serving girl with a bright smile approached them; she skipped around a pair of flailing arms that tried to grab her, and then stopped dead in her tracks. She made a funny sidestep to her left.

"Ben," she whispered, "Ben is it you?"

Ben stared at the girl, he had not really noticed her before, but suddenly it dawned on him who it was. He was about to get up to greet, her but she hissed at him to keep still.

"Behind me, to the left take a look, but be careful." She looked afraid and there was real fear in her tone.

Leaning out inch-by-inch Ben looked past Jenny. Barraclough leant out the other way to take a look.

Ben's heart sank when he recognised the face in the corner. "Mace," he said. Seeing that face again was like a nightmare.

"Get out Ben, Mace runs this lot; he'll kill you for sure." Jenny was petrified. She managed a weak smile, "meet me in the churchyard, near the stone cross, at two."

They left as unnoticed as they had entered. Outside they slipped into the shadows and back into the old part of the town where the church dominated the main square.

"I don't know what the devil that was all about," Fletch said, "but it sure scared the living daylights out of me."

"Shut up Fletch," Barraclough said. "Come on in here."

They ducked down an alley and then in and out of another burnt out house, until they reached the churchyard.

"Trust you to have a fancy piece in every port," Brendan said.

"So who is this Mace?" Barraclough said. "He certainly looked a nasty piece of work."

"Oh he is and if he has his scrawny fingers in this den of thieves then we are certain to have our hands full." Ben said. "Jenny might be able to help us though, she has before."

"I'll bet she has." Fletch interjected.

"Is this the same ruffian that got you shot?" Barraclough said.

"Yes, I have a few scores to settle with him, not least the hurt he did to my friends."

They settled down and waited in silence. The old church clock was stuck at quarter past five, which seemed to make the time drag even slower. As usual, it was hot and sticky but resting against the stones of the church kept them a little cooler. Barraclough kept flicking open his pocket watch and straining in the poor light to see the hands. From where they were sat, they had a clear view of the stone cross and the churchyard gate.

"One forty-five," he said as snapped his watch closed for the umpteenth time.

A figure appeared in the gateway and after looking carefully around entered the churchyard. It seemed almost to dance the distance to the stone cross and then disappeared in its shadow.

Ben was only a few yards away; he ran almost doubled, his right hand was behind his back with his fingers tightly wrapped around the handle of a knife. He had come into town armed with a dirk down each boot and another slightly longer blade in the back of his waist sash.

"Ben I can't believe it," Jenny squealed. She threw her arms around him and showered kisses all over his face. "I've thought about you so many times. I bet you forgot all about your little Jenny."

Ben pulled the rabbit's foot from out of his collar. "I'd never forget you," he said.

They kissed again, more passionately this time. He led her back towards the church where the others were hidden and made a few quick introductions.

"We are looking for Sir Arthur Crompton and his wife from Jamaica," Ben said. "Have you seen them?"

"Is that the Governor fella?" Jenny said

"Yes, have you seen them?"

"Mace has them locked up in the old barracks. You'd never get to them there's always a guard."

"We need to get word back to the Captain and tell them that they are here," Barraclough said. "We can always bring the frigate into the bay."

"No you mustn't, they know you are in the area and have set a trap. They have guns all along the jetty and harbour wall under covers. I heard them planning it. Mace said to let the navy into the bay and then pound them from all sides."

"Thank you Jenny. We must get back; I'll meet you here tomorrow night if you can get away again."

"Yes of course I can. About the same time?"

"Yes and be careful, I seem to remember we were always in trouble where Mace was concerned," Ben said.

The others set off back; Ben stayed just a moment longer and embraced Jenny again, they kissed and then she pecked his cheek before skipping away without a backwards glance.

"Not a word Fletch." Ben warned as he caught up with the others.

An hour later and they were back onboard Adventurer, and in Captain Mitchell's cabin.

Ben explained the need for caution dealing with Mace. Jenny he did not explain about, although Barraclough remembered Ben's story of his flight across North Yorkshire and his winter in a cave with the gang.

"Well at least we know a little of our enemy for once Gentlemen. What we don't know is how much of a fight they'll put up. Finding them is a real stroke of luck; I was doubtful that in amongst all these islands we would," Captain Mitchell said.

"I'd guess they'll be as tough as anything we've come across, none of them will fancy the gallows and they are all seasoned fighters," Barraclough said.

Their meal arrived and they put off any decisions until after they had eaten. Ben was certainly glad of the food and a chance to think a moment. He watched the Captain, who was obviously studying the problem right through the meal, doodling with his fork on the table between eating.

"Very well," the Captain said at last. "Our escort will begin a bombardment just after daybreak, and attack the harbour wall from outside the harbour. We shall put our heads into the lion's mouth, and sail straight into the harbour. However, we shall rake the jetty and harbour wall with ball and grape shot as we enter. At that time in the morning I think most will be the worse for drink and in the dark I doubt if they'll get organised."

There was a general consensus to the scheme. Ben looked a little troubled and not as enthusiastic as his fellows.

"Out with it, Mr. Burrows, what's your problem?"

"I think Sir, that we need to get the hostages out of their prison and into the safety of the fields before we attack. Or at least use the attack as cover to free them."

"Mr. Barraclough could it be done?" the Captain asked.

"I think so, but we would need to be in place before the ships begin their attack. I suppose we could be in and out in no time."

"This 'we' you speak of, I suppose is yourself and would it be Mr. Burrows you include?" he said with a smile.

"Well now you mention it Captain, Mr. Burrows would indeed be a likely candidate. Plus he has a tryst with a certain lady."

"Well I trust that your tryst will not get you into the same trouble as before." The Captain smiled and winked at Ben.

"I suggest Captain that we take a couple of hands with us again," Barraclough said.

Before dawn the ships disappeared over the horizon and hoped that no one had seen them come or go. It was a long day. Ben was not relishing another meeting with Mace, but at least now he was not as green as he had been before. For quite a while he held the little rabbit's foot and was amazed to find Jenny after all this time, especially when it seemed as if Ruth was also on the same island.

CHAPTER TWENTY NINE

There was a nervous tension on board Adventurer's launch as she headed back to the island. On its prow Ben was ready, every nerve tingling as he anticipated the boat grounding. As soon as it did he was over the side and onto the beach, he ran doubled over until he reached some cover; there he waited for the others. This time, only four figures jumped ashore and scuttled across the sand into the undergrowth beyond.

"Ahoy, who goes there?" a voice split the night.

Without answering, the four disappeared into the sugar cane which crunched and snapped under foot.

"Stop or I'll fire."

Ben signalled the others to follow and they tumbled into a dried stream bed. It sounded as if a platoon of Dragoons was cutting its way through the dried stalks of cane towards them.

They lay low; Ben wriggled along the stream bed until he had a good view of the sandy ridge above them. Three figures came into view; they were obviously making as much noise as they could to give themselves reassurance.

"There are only three, but we need to shut them up," Ben whispered. He gathered the others close. "Fletch, stand up as if you're giving yourself up, but be surprised that they don't know who you are, tell them you work for Mace. I'll be behind you."

Fletch was not too certain as to how good a plan this was, but with only a moment's hesitation he was staggering to his feet. Barraclough went to the left and Brendan to the right, whilst Ben stayed in the shadow close behind Fletch.

"It's me lads, it's me Fletch."

"Who?"

"Fletch, I'm one of Mace's men."

One of the men approached, he carried a short-barrelled blunderbuss, not accurate over distance, but it could shred a man into small pieces close up.

"What you doing out here? You know we're supposed to be taking turns on watch." The man said. His companions were now beside him.

"Bit too much to drink lads, you know how it is." Fletch laughed loudly.

Ben shouted 'now' and Barraclough appeared out of the dark swinging his sword and chopped down one of the men, Brendan took another, Ben quick as a flash was at the third with the blunderbuss. Grabbing the gun barrel with one hand, he slit the man's throat wide open with a single slash of his blade.

"I need to keep my eye on you," Fletch said. "You're getting too good with this throat slitting lark."

They hid the bodies in the ditch covering them with dead leaves.

"Right lads we need to be extra cautious. Ben you take the rear, and we had best all be quiet." Barraclough stared at Fletch as he said it.

When they reached the first of the houses the town was very different from the night before; torches and lamps lit the streets and there were hardly any shadows to hide in. Although music drifted from the inn, it was obvious that there was no drunken revelry going on as before.

Barraclough signalled them to retreat back into the cane again. Treading carefully they made a wide arc towards the churchyard. They slipped through a gap in the broken-down wall and managed to find a place to wait.

"I hope we can trust this girl Mr. Burrows," Barraclough whispered.

"I know we can, Jenny would never betray us."

All that they could do now was wait. Fletch pulled a strip of dried beef from his jacket, took a bite and passed it around. It gave them something to do and they all sat content taking it in turns to doze a little.

This time they were better armed; each had a cutlass, dirk and heavy pistol that could be used as a very effective club after firing. It was not much if they were discovered but it gave them a fighting chance to get away.

A figure suddenly flitted between two of the ornate gravestones and then disappeared. Again it moved, silently zigzagged towards them.

There was a metallic click as Fletch cocked his pistol; Ben placed his hand on it to warn him to be patient. Out of the darkness Jenny sprinted until she reached the church, where she ran straight into Ben's arms.

"Are you alright?" Ben asked.

She was panting hard and it took a few minutes for her to regain her composure. "I wasn't sure you would come," she panted. "Mace has everyone on alert. He's threatened to hang anyone caught drunk."

"Does he know we are here?"

"Someone spotted a ship yesterday, and warned Mace."

"We need to wait until first light, and then our ships will appear. Do you think you could lead us to where they are holding the governor when they arrive?" Ben said.

"I think so. But you must be careful there is an armed guard in the dungeon where they are being held and sometimes three or four in the barracks above."

They settled down against the church wall and waited once more. Jenny cuddled close to Ben.

"Do you remember when we cuddled to keep warm on the moors?"

"Yes I do," Ben smiled.

"I've been a good girl since then." She tried to see him in the gloom. "I saw you in Barrow one time; Mace had already seen you. I tried to tell him it wasn't you, but whatever else he is, he is not a fool. I was so frightened for you. It was only after he came back all covered in blood and cursing your name that I found out what had happened. I feared he had killed you." She paused long enough to take breath. "Are you married?"

"Good heavens no!" Ben said. He was rather surprised at the sudden question.

"Mace found me a family in Barrow to work for. I looked after two brats and I had to clean the house. He wanted me there, because the owner was in some sort of business and I had to tell Mace who came and went and what they talked about. I prayed that you were alright."

"When did you come out here?" Ben asked.

"Three years ago. Mace made a huge amount of money from the information I was getting him, not that I saw a penny of it. He said there were vast fortunes waiting to be made out here." She cuddled closer still. "I don't have a man. Mace has never made me go with the sailors like he does with the other girls, he just leaves me alone. All I do is serve in the tavern."

"How did you get here?"

"Oh simple, Mace made so much money he bought a ship, the crew was easy to find. He hired every scallywag and low life he could find and came out here. The Dutch had already deserted the town, yellow fever killed most of them, and no one lives on the rest of the island. He made this his base and with his crew they went into pirating."

"Let's get some rest," Ben said.

The thought of Mace chilled him to the bone. He remembered the night Mace came to the Linton's, the journey north with his gang and the havoc caused to the Reverend Baxter.

Everywhere was silent, the nightly chorus of frogs and insects faded as the first glimmers of light showed, somewhere a cock crowed.

"Right lads make ready," Barraclough whispered.

Barraclough led them close to the outer wall of the church. They followed it to a portion that was tumbled down and as quickly as they could they were through and into a shell of a house.

Their timing was perfect, unseen by them the ships were getting into position. Orion with her guns at the ready was stationed on the outside of the harbour wall.

Captain Mitchell gave the order and a single bright red flare shot high into the sky and burst with a loud bang. It was the signal for Orion to open fire. The flash and roar of her guns woke anyone unaware that she was there. Adventurer was heading right into the harbour mouth with all but her topsails furled.

As Orion's shot hit the already dilapidated harbour wall mayhem seemed to break loose all around the wharf. Chunks of masonry, timber, and injured bodies were scattered in all directions.

The pirates had expected the navy ships to try enter the harbour first and so all their guns faced that direction. They knew how quickly the next broadside would hit and that they had not enough time to reposition their guns. Some did make the effort to redirect them, but the majority just scattered trying to find safety.

Part of the harbour wall collapsed and Orion now had an almost clear shot at the town. Her next volley screamed through the air bringing down waterfront buildings as well as most of the rest of the wall. Orion's crew let out a cheer as a beacon tower at the end of the wall tumbled into the water.

Jenny led them to the wharf and pointed out the old barracks building. Ben broke cover and with the others following he ran towards it. Another broadside, and Ben could hear the shot pass over him and batter into the brickwork behind. He spotted Adventurer as she entered the harbour and knew that any time now the whole town was going to be reduced to rubble.

Somewhere in this mad dash, Jenny was separated from them but there was no time to go back for her. As they reached the door to the old barracks, Brendan pushed past Ben and charged it with his shoulder. The hinges burst as the huge Irishman charged through. Ben and Barraclough went through the doorway almost together; they exchanged reassuring nods. In the dim light it was difficult at first to see where the guards were. Jenny had been right, there were four of them, and although they normally slept or played cards the excitement outside had them at the ready.

Fletch stood in the doorway a moment too long, with the light behind him he made a perfect target. A shot rang out and down he went like a stone. Instantly they were all caught up in the hand-to-hand fight.

Barraclough had just one thought on his mind, and that was to find the hostages. Jenny had said that they were being kept through a door to the left. He skewered one of the guards with his sword, and then kicked open the door into what he hoped was the dungeon. Foolishly, he went straight through and too late saw the flash of a musket muzzle. The shot caught his thigh and he tumbled head over heels down the steps.

Outside there was an almighty explosion and it was obvious that Adventurer was now in position and bombarding the waterfront. Some of the shot hit the barracks building, shaking its stonework.

Ben followed Barraclough; he had dispatched the guard he had been fighting and seen his friend go down after the shot. He was through the doorway and down the steps in an instant, fearlessly going to the aid of his friend. Fortunately, the guard had not had time to reload.

"Are you all right?" Ben asked Barraclough as soon as he reached him.

"Yes. Look out!" Barraclough yelled.

The guard swung his musket like a huge club hitting Ben hard on the shoulder with the butt knocking him over and sending him rolling across the straw covered floor. He had lost his sword and pistol in the fight, but he still had one of his dirks down his boot. As he rolled back to his feet, he drew it and held it out like a sword.

"Ben!" A female voice suddenly cried.

Ben turned and realised Ruth and her husband were both chained to the wall; in the gloom of the single torch and commotion, he had not noticed them. There was no time to help them, the guard charged him swinging the musket around his head. Ben ducked out of the way and just managed to nick the man's arm with his knife. Bellowing like a bull the wounded man threw himself at Ben. They rolled over once and then the guard was still, Ben had turned his blade and the guard had jumped straight onto it.

"Ben, I knew you would come," Ruth cried.

"Come on man get us out of here," Sir Arthur shouted. "Who the hell is Ben?" He looked curiously at Ben wondering how his wife knew this ruffian, but there were far too many other concerns at that moment to worry about that.

There were a number of other heavy thuds and some of the roof beams crashed down showering roof tiles and debris everywhere. Brendan had just finished with the fourth guard when a flying beam toppled him, pinning him to the wall. Cascades of dust showered down from the roof as another shot shook the building.

An enormous padlock locked the hefty iron chains. Ben tried to force it with his knife but it was too tough.

"The guard has a key!" Ruth exclaimed.

The dungeon door burst open again and through the swirling dust, a figure appeared on the stairs.

Ben almost snarled the word, "Mace!"

"So, it's you again," Mace called "you're like a damned curse. But this time I'll deal with you properly."

"You are only good at dealing with defenceless women and children, Mace."

"We'll see shall we?" He flicked the tip of his sword left and right and then leapt from the steps towards Ben. He soon realised that Ben did not have a sword and so he went straight for him. With slow deliberate steps he stalked his prey, slashing and thrusting left and right driving Ben back against the wall.

"Come on boy let me rid the world of you."

He made a straight-arm stab that caught Ben in the shoulder and drew blood. Mace laughed and circled around again looking for the chance to strike. He made another couple of short stabs that Ben could parry with his much shorter blade, all the time he was trying to get to Barraclough's sword.

Just in time, Mace realised what he was doing and skipped sideways a couple of steps and using the tip of his sword, he flicked the other weapon across the dungeon and out of Ben's way.

"Oh no my boy, I like the odds as they are," Mace teased.

"Daren't you face me in a fair fight?"

Mace laughed, "I'd never have got this far if I'd given people even half a chance. Fair fight . . . there is no such thing boy. No, but I shall enjoy watching you squirm after I've run this blade through you."

Mace attacked again, but this time Ben parried the sword and grasped Mace's arm. Flinging his shoulder into Mace's chest, Ben gave himself more room. Losing his balance a little Mace staggered back a few paces. He realised that Ben had grown a lot since their last encounter. Ben leapt at him. They rolled over locked together in an embrace of death, but somehow, Mace kept hold of his sword and repeatedly hit the bleeding wound on Ben's shoulder with its hilt.

The pain was terrible and forced Ben to let go his grip; he tried to roll away to get to his feet, but Mace, as agile as a cat and beat him to it. He was up and kicked viciously into Ben's ribs knocking the wind from him. Each time Ben moved, Mace gave him another bruising kick, until Ben lay still.

"Now boy you know not to mess with Mace." he stamped the heel of his boot into Ben's back with each word. Kicking

Ben over onto his back he straddled him standing above him a look of contempt on his face. The tip of the blade was inches from Ben's throat.

"Mace, no!" Jenny cried.

She threw herself from halfway down the steps and landed next to Ben. It distracted Mace just enough; Ben kicked hard into the man's groin. As Mace doubled over clutching his groin, Ben rolled over and away. He grabbed Barraclough's sword from the straw and managed to regain his balance clutching his aching ribs. Mace still managed to keep hold of his sword and rushed headlong at Ben. Still in pain, and aching from the kicks in his ribs, Ben was just in time to parry the thrust. He had learnt some tricks since their last encounter, and he still had the shorter blade in his left hand. As their swords clashed together he plunged the blade into Mace's upper arm. With a squeal Mace staggered away clasping his arm to stop the blood flow.

"That's for my friend Linton," Ben growled.

Mace went wild, as if throwing some sort of mad fit. He lashed out trying to regain the upper hand. His whole face was contorted with an angry snarl.

Despite the noise Mace was making Ben heard another sound, one he knew well. It was like someone trying to say 'f' and 'v' together repeatedly and really fast.

To Mace's amazement, Ben leapt sideward to cover Jenny. Seconds later the building shook; part of the masonry disintegrated into dust, and a number of iron cannonballs burst in through the walls. Like a tornado, they passed through the air embedding themselves into the far wall. The ceiling crashed down followed by roof beams, an enormous amount of dust and several bodies from the room above.

Ben checked that Jenny was all right; he had to move some debris to find Ruth and her husband, but it was difficult to see anything in the dense cloud of dust. Luckily, the small cell they were in had survived and they were safe. Ben struggled from beneath the rubble and debris with one thought on his mind, to find Mace.

Climbing the tumbled down walls Ben found himself outside and with a good view of the harbour and town. The barracks building was reduced to rubble, but perched on what had been the roof Mace stood looking much shaken. The sight of Ben brought him to his senses.

They both picked their way across the rubble to get at each other. Hopping as nimbly as a mountain goat from one pile of rubble to the next, Mace rushed forward. Ben managed to sidestep him but on the loose stones he had difficulty striking back. Mace hesitated a moment. This was not his battlefield of choice, he was far more at home in the shadows of a dark alley and despite his hatred of Ben his instincts sent him for cover. He retreated along the roof beams towards the town.

Ben had other ideas. "Stand and fight me Mace," he bellowed.

He went after him leaping and scrambling across the rubble as the rest of the building began to fall about him. He was so angry and frustrated at Mace's sudden reluctance to fight that in a mad fit of temper he petulantly threw his sword after him. It bounced and clattered on the stonework.

Mace turned with a sneer; he was not going to miss this opportunity. "Now that, my boy was *stupid,* wasn't it?" Mace edged along a fallen roof beam, he balanced with one arm out to his side like a tightrope walker and his sword arm extended.

Ben stood his ground, realising just how foolish he had been to disarm himself. He shook his head and smiled ironically, he almost wanted to laugh at his own stupidity. He fixed his eyes on Mace's, "I've waited for a long time to settle my score with you. I don't need a sword to bring an animal like you down."

"That uniform can't save you, *boy.*" Mace skipped near across a couple of beams. "I'm going to slice you into little pieces, and then I'm going to do the same to that little whore of yours."

Most of the other fighting was over, and eyes everywhere were watching the two of them on top of what had been the barracks building. Ben slowly backed away along another beam that projected out over the water. Mace was close, after he had stepped lightly across from one beam to the next. Ben stepped over onto another beam which rocked under his feet and moved slightly. Mace followed and the whole thing slid violently sideward.

Ben took his chance and with one great leap caught Mace's arms. They tumbled over the stonework both of them landing heavily knocking the wind from them. Mace wriggled across the rubble and had Ben pinned down by the throat forcing his head backwards over the edge of the wall. The pressure was almost breaking his neck and he was starting to lose consciousness. Ben clutched at Mace's arm trying to release the grip but his strength was failing, in a final effort he managed to get hold of Mace's cheek. Mace turned his head and bit the fingers so hard it drew blood and managed to force Ben's head back even further.

Ben was barely conscious when he felt Mace's grip slacken and then go limp. Suddenly, Mace coughed and blood spluttered from his lips. Behind him, Jenny held a dagger with blood dripping from its blade.

Mace gurgled something, and more blood dribbled out over his chin. For a moment, there was a look of complete disbelief on his face, then a sneer and then nothing. He fell forward onto Ben.

She tugged Mace's limp body out of the way and then threw her arms around Ben. His neck felt broken and his arm throbbed, but he still managed a smile of gratitude to her. Covered in dust and splattered with blood he managed to sit up.

There are times when you have the feeling that someone is watching you and Ben felt it at that moment. He turned to see Adventurer's jib right behind him with Captain Mitchell hanging from it.

"Time for that later Mr. Burrows. Where is Sir Arthur?"

It was like descending a shale hillside getting back into the building; everything beneath his feet seemed to be on the move. It really was a shambles, but he spotted his friend Barraclough and Brendan digging through the rubble. "Sit down" he ordered, "I'll find them."

He found the guard's body and took the keys from his belt.

"Oh Ben, thank you," Ruth said.

Ben helped Sir Arthur to his feet. "Can you walk Sir?"

"I can bloody well run to get clear of here young man."

Ruth was about to embrace Ben but she was beaten to it by Jenny. There were many people who would have loved to see that moment when Ruth was struck dumb. For a few moments, she stuttered and spluttered, "Who is this little strumpet?"

Ben stared at Ruth a moment almost in disbelief, why he wondered, was he so devoted to her. "This, brave young lady is the one who saved your life."

The two women exchanged glares and Ruth was devastated to discover that her famous scowl was having no effect at all. Jenny had no idea who the other was or her connection to Ben, but her instincts told her she had to be on her guard.

It took two days to round up all the pirates. In the meantime, Orion headed back to St. Kitts to bring reinforcements. Sir Arthur had decided that the island should now become part of the British Empire and be renamed after himself.

Back on board Adventurer, Ben and Barraclough were being seen to by the ship's surgeon. He had spent over an hour prodding and poking about in Barraclough's leg wound and finally announced that there was no need to remove the injured limb. The musket-ball had passed right through the soft flesh of his inner thigh and after being cauterised with a hot iron should recover fully.

Barraclough looked a little the worse for wear he adjusted his bandages as he spoke to Ben, "I thought I was going to lose my blasted leg there."

"That would have ended your dancing career."

Satisfied that his friend was going to be all right, Ben went to see his old messmates to check on them. Fletch was bandaged up, the shot had probably broken a rib, but had then been deflected away. Brendan had a couple of bruises on his face, but he was his usual cheery self when Ben arrived.

"Mr. Burrows" Brendan said, "how are you now?"

"Oh fine thank you. What about you two?"

Ben pulled up a stool and they chatted for a short while until a young midshipman appeared and asked him to attend the Captain. He thanked them for their help and left.

"Mr. Burrows I hope you are feeling fit and well?" Mitchell asked.

"Fine thank you Captain."

Ben squeezed into the cramped cabin. Squashed around the table, were the Captain, Sir Arthur, and Lady Ruth.

"Mr. Burrows, I must thank you for your bravery." Sir Arthur said. They exchanged nods. "I have put together a small token of my gratitude for you and your team of rescuers. Fifty acres each of fine farm land for you and Lieutenant Barraclough, and a further twenty acres each for the two ratings here on this island."

Ben was taken aback and totally lost for words. He was trying not to let his eyes wander towards Ruth, but it was not easy. Eventually they exchanged the faintest of smiles.

"Thank you Sir Arthur, I never expected that I would own land in such a place as this."

"Well Lieutenant, you may not wish to be a farmer right now, but the land will certainly have a good value once this island is put back to production again. There will be many back in England willing to pay a good amount for it."

"Well done Mr. Burrows. Now there are other matters to attend to." Mitchell said. "Lieutenant Rhodes has taken Orion back to St. Kitts to fetch reinforcements. I am hoping that he is bringing one of the new West Indian regiments back with him to police the island for a while."

After the meeting, Ben asked the Captain "would it be alright if I went and had a look at this land that I now own?"

"Yes indeed Ben," it was not often that he used an officer's Christian name. "You deserve it. You've come a long way since we first met."

Ben had stepped out at quite a pace despite the heat; following a dusty track into the foothills behind the taown. As he reached a steep incline he looked back to see a figure waving and chasing after him. He rightly guessed it was Jenny.

"Ben, I've been looking for you," she panted.

"I had no idea where you were," he said.

"Can I walk with you?"

"Yes indeed, twice now you have saved my life, I am beginning to think that you are perhaps some sort of guardian angel."

"Oh Ben, don't make me laugh, I'll never be awarded wings, I'm afraid."

She linked arms with him and together they climbed to a place overlooking the town. Ben decided that at that moment if there was such a place as heaven, then he had probably found it. They sat on a boulder in the shade of a palm.

For a short while, they said nothing just watched the work going on below them. The captured pirates had been put to work clearing the town and rebuilding the harbour wall and jetty.

"Jenny, I have been thinking. I would like you to go stay with my friends the Lintons." He had thought about this for the last few days.

"I'aint going as no maid again."

"No I didn't mean that. I meant as a companion, for although you and Emily are very different in many ways, I'm sure you would be excellent company for each other."

"And I suppose you will stay here with your Lady Ruth."

"I'm still in the navy and do my duty, I will go just where I am bid, but there is one place I will go back to as soon as I'm able, and that is to my friends in Cumbria."

"When?"

"I really can't say, but some day."

"Why can't we stay here together? You own land here, we could be really happy."

"I have commitments in England; I have the shop and Mr. Van Heild to look after, the Lintons will expect me back some time. No I'm sorry Jenny, it is a tempting thought, and it's not that I don't want to stay with you but . . ." he shrugged his shoulders.

"I know," she said, "it was just a dream of mine that is all."

"Don't be sad Jenny, you will love the fells, and I promise I will see you there some time soon."

He leant back against the tree and fell into a deep sleep. When he awoke, the light was fading and Jenny was snuggled tightly up against him. "Come on or the Captain will have me up for desertion, and I'm starving." They ran back to the harbour hand in hand like any young lovers.

Ben helped Jenny with what few belongings she had aboard the trader bound for England. He had written a letter of introduction for her and a private letter to Emily to ask her to take care of Jenny until he came home. He also sent a letter to Petra at the shop in Barrow and one to his Uncle John. Further along the quay, Ruth and her husband were joining a ship to take them back to Jamaica. As the ships cast off and made ready to sail, Ben sprinted through the town and out onto the headland. He scrambled to the highest place and watched as the two ships left harbour.

For a moment he was overcome with emotion, but as the ships neared he waved his arms frantically at them. He could see Jenny waving a brightly coloured shawl, but on the other ship only the crew acknowledged him.

The end

ABOUT THE AUTHOR

Tony Mead visited H.M.S. Victory as a small boy and became fascinated with Nelson's navy. He works as an artist and writer from his home in Brighouse West Yorkshire. His book combines his passion for the sea and his native Yorkshire landscape.